By Robin Hobb

ROBIN HOBB

BLOOD of DRAGONS

Volume Four of the *Rain Wilds Chronicles*

HARPER Voyager

An Imprint of HarperCollinsPublishers

This is a work of fiction. Names, characters, places, and incidents are products of the author's imagination or are used fictitiously and are not to be construed as real. Any resemblance to actual events, locales, organizations, or persons, living or dead, is entirely coincidental.

HARPER Voyager

An Imprint of HarperCollins*Publishers*
195 Broadway
New York, New York 10007

Copyright © 2013 by Robin Hobb
Cover art by Jackie Morris
ISBN 978-0-06-211691-8
www.harpervoyagerbooks.com

First Harper Voyager mass market printing: November 2014
First Harper Voyager hardcover printing: April 2013

Harper Voyager and) is a trademark of HCP LLC.

Printed in the U.S.A.

10 9

I miss you, Ralph.

CONTENTS

CONTENTS

CAST OF CHARACTERS

THE RAIN WILDS CHRONICLES

THE KEEPERS AND THEIR DRAGONS

ALUM: A pale-skinned keeper with silvery gray eyes, very small ears, and an almost flattened nose. Enamored of Skelly. His dragon is Arbuc, a silver-green drake.

BOXTER: This short, copper-eyed, stoutly built keeper is cousin to Kase. The orange drake SKRIM is his to tend.

HARRIKIN: Tall and slim, at twenty he is older than the other keepers. Lecter is his foster brother, and they are very close. He is a protector of Sylve, and their bond is a strong one. His dragon is Ranculos, a scarlet drake with silver eyes.

ICEFYRE: This ancient black drake was entrapped in ice and still bears the signs of that long encasement. Freed from the ice by human intervention (Fool's Fate), he has become Tintaglia's default mate. He bears no love for humanity.

JERD: This blond female keeper is heavily marked by the Rain Wilds. She is as aggressive and assertive in getting what she wants as her dragon, Veras, a dark green queen with gold stippling.

KASE: Boxter's cousin has copper eyes and, like him, is short, stout, and heavily muscled. His dragon is the orange drake Dortean.

LECTER: Orphaned at seven, he was raised by Harrikin's family, and the two remain close. His dragon is Sestican, a large blue drake with orange scaling and small spikes on his neck. He has an uneasy partnership with Davvie.

NORTEL: This competent and ambitious keeper has clashed in the past with Tats over Thymara. His dragon is the lavender drake Tinder.

RAPSKAL: Heavily marked by the Rain Wilds since birth, he seems as changed in his mind as his body. His peculiarities are offset by his sincere, boyish charm and handsome features. He is absolutely certain that Thymara will be his. His dragon is the small red queen Heeby, who may be slow-witted but was the first of the dragons to take flight.

SYLVE: Youngest of the keepers, but more mature and thoughtful than many of the male keepers. She is slight, blond with pink and gold scaling. Harrikin is her protector and partner. Her dragon is golden MERCOR. He is not the largest of the drakes but is the most thoughtful and often asserts a quiet leadership.

THYMARA: Sixteen years old, Thymara was born with black claws instead of nails and was exposed at birth. Rescued by her father and resented by her mother, she has grown up with a deep awareness of the restrictive rules imposed on those changed by the Rain Wilds. A competent hunter, she struggles to determine what her role will be in the new society in Kelsingra. She has an uneasy bond with azure Sintara, the largest and most dominant of the queens.

TATS: He is the only keeper not born in the Rain Wilds. Son of a slave, he still bears the facial tattoos of that status. His attraction to Thymara threatens his friendship with Rapskal. Small and feisty green Fente is his queen.

TINTAGLIA: The sole dragon to hatch from the ancient wizardwood cases, she emerged a true queen capable of flight immediately. Initially she assisted the serpents to migrate up the Rain Wild River in the hopes of seeing a new generation of dragons emerge (the Liveship Traders trilogy), but has apparently since abandoned the crippled creatures. She created the Elderlings Malta and Reyn and took young Selden Vestrit as her poet.

WARKEN: This tall, long-limbed keeper lost his life on the journey to Kelsingra. Baliper, his scarlet drake, has refused to accept a new keeper.

THE BINGTOWNERS

ALISE KINCARRON FINBOK: Descended from a poor but respectable Bingtown Trader family, Alise entered into a loveless marriage arrangement with Hest Finbok. The gray-eyed, freckled redhead has repented at leisure and has now become involved with Captain Leftrin. She has been rebuilding her childhood friendship with Sedric.

HEST FINBOK: A handsome, well-established, and wealthy Bingtown Trader's son, perhaps the only action he has ever been forced to perform was marrying Alise. He is ruthless in the pursuit of his own pleasures and has concealed from Alise and his family the true nature of his relationship with Sedric Meldar.

REDDING: Hest's current paramour, he is very pleased to have replaced Sedric in Hest's life. He hopes to enjoy Hest's extravagant lifestyle with him while building his own fortune through Hest's connections.

SEDRIC MELDAR: Secretary and former lover to Hest Finbok, and friends with Alise since childhood. He has accidentally bonded with the copper queen Relpda. Now partnered with Carson Lupskip, he is struggling to adapt to his new life in Kelsingra.

TRADER FINBOK: Hest's father is a successful Bingtown Trader who is growing weary of his son's self-indulgence and his failure to produce an heir. Married to Sealia Finbok, Hest's doting mother.

THE CREW OF THE TARMAN

BELLIN: Deckhand. Married to Swarge, she is a quiet,

powerful woman and a stabilizing influence on the crew.

BIG EIDER: Deckhand. A large and powerful man of simple thoughts and a good heart.

CARSON LUPSKIP: Hired by the Trehaug Rain Wild Council as a hunter for the expedition, Captain Leftrin's old friend has now become a dragon keeper as well. Spit is a small, temperamental, and potentially dangerous silver dragon. Tall, powerfully built Carson is partnered with Sedric.

DAVVIE: Apprentice hunter to Carson Lupskip and the son of his old friend, Davvie is like a nephew to Carson. The fifteen-year-old is bonded to Kalo, the largest of the drakes. The blue-black dragon's previous keeper, Greft, proved a traitor to the expedition. Davvie is partnered with Lecter.

GRIGSBY: Ship's cat. Orange and insouciant.

HENNESEY: First mate on the Tarman and something of a ladies' man. Competent and loyal to his shipmates.

JESS: This hired hunter had a secret agenda of his own. He lost his life on the upriver journey.

LEFTRIN: Captain of the liveship Tarman, he has lived and served aboard the ship since he was a boy. Heir to his family, he is now bonded to Tarman for life. He has gray eyes, brown hair, and a robust build. He has fallen in love with Alise.

SKELLY: Leftrin's niece and presumed heir currently serves as a deckhand so that she will know every position on the liveship she expects to inherit. She is infatuated with the keeper Alum, but has an arranged marriage and a fiancé awaiting her in Trehaug.

SWARGE: The tillerman for Tarman. Quiet and knowledgeable of the river and its ways, he has served aboard the ship for more than fifteen years. Married to Bellin.

TARMAN: The oldest existing liveship is a river barge, long and low, with many secrets of his own as to why he is able to attain such speeds and go where few ships can follow. He has painted eyes on his bow, but no figurehead.

MISCELLANEOUS CHARACTERS

ALTHEA VESTRIT: First mate on the liveship Paragon out of Bingtown (the Liveship Traders trilogy). Aunt to Malta Khuprus and Selden Vestrit, she is married to Brashen Trell.

BEGASTI CORED: Chalcedean merchant, this bald, rich trading partner of Hest Finbok's has been forcibly recruited by the Duke of Chalced to obtain dragon parts by any means.

BRASHEN TRELL: Captain of the liveship Paragon out of Bingtown. Married to Althea Vestrit.

CHANCELLOR ELLIK: Adviser and "sword arm" to the aging Duke of Chalced. Once they rode to war together and were comrades. Now he is reduced to serving the Duke. He is dismayed to see the Duke's health and power unraveling and anxious to seize power before the Duke's death plunges Chalced into civil disorder.

CHASSIM: Eldest daughter of the Duke of Chalced. Widowed several times, she has once more become a part of the Duke's household.

DETOZI: Keeper of the messenger birds at Trehaug, she is engaged to Erek, a bird keeper from Bingtown.

DUKE OF CHALCED: Chalced's aging despot is ruthlessly desperate for the dragon parts he believes will restore his health and vitality. He is capable of any cruelty to get what he wants.

EREK: Bird Keeper of Bingtown, and engaged to Detozi, he is a knowledgeable bird handler who takes his duties very seriously.

JANI KHUPRUS: Matriarch of the Rain Wild Trader family, she is a powerful and determined woman. At one time, the Khuprus family controlled the lion's share of the trade in wizardwood and built many of the surviving liveships. Mother to Reyn Khuprus, her family fostered Selden Vestrit.

KIM: Keeper of the Birds, Cassarick. A Tattooed, this former slave came to the Rain Wilds seeking a better life and is endeavoring to build a fortune.

MALTA KHUPRUS: Born a Vestrit of Bingtown, the Elderling "queen" now resides in Trehaug with her husband, Reyn. Malta and Reyn were tormented and then claimed by the dragon Tintaglia, and their bond has never been an easy one (Liveship Traders trilogy).

PARAGON: Once called the Pariah, the mad liveship has entered a more stable time in his life, but remains a challenging vessel. He helped escort the serpents up the Rain Wild River on their journey to becoming dragons. Fiercely attached to his humans.

REYALL: Acting Keeper of the Birds at Bingtown; nephew of Detozi.

REYN KHUPRUS: Younger son of the powerful Rain Wild Trader family, he married Malta Vestrit and was claimed by the dragon Tintaglia (the Liveship Traders trilogy).

SELDEN VESTRIT: Youngest son of the Vestrit family, he was claimed by the dragon Tintaglia when he was still a boy and changed by her to an Elderling. He has been missing for some time after setting out on an errand for Tintaglia to collect news of any other surviving dragons (the Liveship Traders trilogy).

SINAD ARICH: A Chalcedean merchant who strikes a deal with Captain Leftrin via blackmail of the captain. The Duke of Chalced holds his family hostage.

THE CHALCEDEAN: Hest's nemesis is a Chalcedean nobleman. Under duress from the Duke to obtain dragon parts, he has become a tormented and ruthless man who will do whatever he must to ransom his family. Proper name Lord Dargen.

TILLAMON: Older sister to Reyn Khuprus, she is heavily changed by the Rain Wilds and has begun to live the life of an outcast within her own society. Unwed and isolated, she seizes the opportunity to build a new life for herself.

PROLOGUE

CHANGES

Tintaglia awoke feeling chilled and old. She had made a good kill and eaten heavily, but she had not rested well. The festering wound under her left wing made it hard to find a comfortable position. If she stretched out, the hot swollen place pulled, and if she curled up, she felt the jabbing of the buried arrow. The pain spread out in her wing now when she opened it, as if some thistly plant were sending out runners inside her, prickling her with thorns as it spread. The weather had become colder as she flew toward the Rain Wilds. There were no deserts, no warm sands in this region of the world. Heat seemed to well up from the earth's heart in the Chalcedean deserts, making it nearly as warm as the southern lands were at this time of year. But now she had left the dry lands and warm sands behind, and winter's stranglehold on spring had claimed its due. The cold stiffened the flesh around her wound, making each morning a torment.

Icefyre had not come with her. She had expected the old black dragon to accompany her, although she could not recall why. Dragons preferred to be solitary rather than social. To eat well, each needed a large hunting territory. It had only been when she had left his side and he had not followed that the humiliating realization had drenched her: she had been following him, all that time. She could not recall that he had ever requested her to stay; neither had he asked her to leave.

He had all he needed from her. In the early excitement of discovering each other, they had mated. When she grew to full maturity, she would visit the nesting island, and there lay the eggs that he had already fertilized. But once he had impregnated her there was no reason for him to stay with her. When her eggs hatched into serpents that would slither into the sea and renew the endless cycle of dragon-egg-serpent-cocoon-dragon, the memories of his lineage would continue. Eventually, there would be other dragons for him to encounter, when he chose to seek their company. She felt puzzled that she had lingered with him as long as she had. Having hatched so alone and isolated, had she learned undragonlike behavior from humans?

She uncoiled slowly and then, even more gingerly, spread her wings to the overcast day. She stretched, already missing the warmth of the sands, and tried not to wonder if the journey back to Trehaug were beyond her strength. Had she waited too long, hoping she would heal on her own?

It hurt to crane her neck to inspect the wound. It smelled foul, and when she moved, pus oozed from it. She hissed in anger that such a thing had befallen her, and then she used the strength of that anger to tighten the muscles there. The movement forced more liquid from the wound. It hurt and stank terribly, but when she had finished, her skin felt less tight. She could fly. Not without pain, and not swiftly, but she could fly. Tonight she would take more care in selecting her resting place. Taking flight from the

riverbank where she presently found herself was going to
be difficult.

She wanted to fly directly to Trehaug in the hope of lo-
cating Malta and Reyn quickly and having one of her Elderling servants remove the arrowhead from her flesh. A direct
route would have been best, but the thick forests of the
region made that impossible. For a dragon to land in such
a thickly treed area was difficult at the best of times; with
a bad wing, she would certainly go crashing down through
the canopy. So she had followed first the coast and then the
Rain Wild River. The marshy banks and mud bars offered
easy hunting as river mammals emerged on the shores to
root and roll and as the forest creatures sought water. If she
was fortunate, as she had been last night, she could combine
a stoop on a large meal with a safe landing on a marshy
riverfront strip.

If she was unfortunate, she could always land in the river
shallows and crawl out onto whatever bank the river offered.
That, she feared, might be her best option this evening. And
while she did not doubt that she could survive such an un-
pleasantly cold and wet landing, she dreaded the thought of
attempting to take flight from such a place. As she had to
do now.

Wings half extended, she walked down to the water's
edge and drank, wrinkling her nostrils at the bitter taste
of the water. Once she had sated her thirst, she opened her
wings and sprang into the sky.

With a wild flapping of her wings, she crashed back to
earth again. It was not a long fall, but it jarred her, breaking
her pain into sharp-edged fragments that stabbed every interior space of her body. The shock jabbed the air from her
lungs and crushed a hoarse squawk of pain from her throat.
She hit the ground badly, her wings still half open. Her
tender side struck the earth. Stunned, she sprawled, waiting
for the agony to pass. It did not, but gradually it faded to a
bearable level.

Tintaglia lowered her head to her chest, gathered her legs
under her, and slowly folded her wings. She badly wanted to
rest. But if she did, she would awaken hungrier and stiffer

than she was now and with the daylight fading. No. She had
to fly and now. The longer she waited, the more her physical
abilities would wane. She needed to fly while she still could.

She steeled herself to the pain, not allowing her body to
compensate for it in any way. She simply had to endure it
and fly as if it did not hurt. She burned that thought into
her brain and then, without pausing, opened her wings,
crouched, and launched herself upward.

Every beat of her wings was like being stabbed with a
fiery spear. She roared, giving voice to her fury at the pain,
but did not vary the rhythm of her wing beats. Rising slowly
into the air, she flew over the shallows of the river until
finally she lifted clear of the trees that shaded the river's
face. The wan sunlight touched her, and the wilder winds
of the open air buffeted her. The breezes were heavy with
the threat of chilling rain to come. Well, let it come, then.
Tintaglia was flying home.

Day the 15th of the Fish Moon

Year the 7th of the Independent Alliance of Traders
**From Reyall, Acting Keeper of the Birds,
Bingtown
To Erek Dunwarrow**

Enclosed in a standard message cylinder.

My dear uncle,

My delayed response to your offer is due to my utter surprise at receiving it. Over and over, I have read it, wondering if I am ready and more: if I am worthy of what you propose. To vouch for my promotion not only to a master within the Guild but also to select me to take over your personal birds and cote . . . what can I say to such an honor? I know what these pigeons mean to you, and I have faithfully studied your breeding journals and your documentation of how you have improved the birds for both speed and vitality. I have been in awe of your knowledge. And now you propose to put your birds and your careful breeding plan into my hands?

I shudder to think you will take this amiss, but I must ask you, are you certain you wish to do this?

If, after consideration, you still wish to offer me this extraordinary opportunity, then yes, I will accept it and endeavor for all the rest of my life to prove worthy of it! But be assured, if you have reconsidered, there will be no ill will between us. To know that you even considered me worthy of such an honor and responsibility makes me resolved to strive to be the keeper that you believe I can be.

With humble thanks, your nephew,
Reyall

*And please assure my aunt Detozi of my good wishes
and utter delight in her good fortune in wedding you!*

CHAPTER ONE

ENDING A LIFE

She opened her eyes to a morning she didn't want. With great reluctance, she lifted her head and looked around the single room. The cabin was cold. The fire had been out for hours, and the cold and damp of the unseasonably cold spring had crept relentlessly in while she huddled under her worn blankets waiting for her life to go away. It hadn't. Life had lingered to ambush her again with cold and damp, disappointment and loneliness. She clutched her thin covers to her chest as her eyes wandered to the stacked and sorted papers and parchment that had occupied her for the last week. There it was. Alise Finbok's life work, all in one stack. Translations of ancient papers, speculations of her own, careful copies of old documents rendered in black ink with her best guess at the missing words inked in red. Deprived of any significant purpose in her own life, she had retreated to ancient days and taken pride in her scholarly knowledge of them. She knew how Elderlings had once lived and interacted with dragons. She knew the names of Elderlings and dragons of old; she knew their habits; she knew so much about a past that no longer had any relevance.

Elderlings and dragons had returned to the world. She had witnessed that miracle. And they would reclaim the ancient city of Kelsingra and take up their lives there. All the secrets she had tried to tease out of old scrolls and moldering tapestries meant nothing now. Once the new Elderlings gained their city, they would need only to touch the memory stone there to discover all their history for themselves. All the secrets she had dreamed of discovering, all the puzzles she had longed to solve were finished now, and not by her. She was irrelevant.

She surprised herself when she flung the blankets suddenly to one side and stood up. Cold wrapped her instantaneously. She stepped to her clothing trunks, the grand traveling trunks that she had packed so hopefully in the days before she left Bingtown. They had been stuffed when she began her journey, full of sensible clothes fit for a lady adventurer. Stoutly woven cotton blouses with a minimum of lace, split skirts for hiking, hats with veils to ward off insects and sun, sturdy leather boots . . . little but memories remained of them now. The hardships of travel had softened the fabrics. Her boots were scuffed and leaked, the ties now a series of knots. Laundering clothes in the acidic waters of the river had been her only choice, but seams had weakened and hems had frayed. She drew on a set of her worn clothes with no thought as to what they would look like. No one was going to look at her anyway. She was finished forever with worrying about what she looked like or what people thought of her.

An Elderling gown, Leftrin's gift to her, hung on a hook. Of all the clothing she owned, this alone retained its bright colors and supple softness. She longed for its warmth but could not bring herself to put it on. Rapskal had said it and said it clearly. She was not an Elderling. She had no right to the city of Kelsingra, no right to anything pertaining to Elderlings.

Bitterness, hurt, and resignation to the reality Rapskal had voiced formed a tight, hard knot in her throat. She stared at the Elderling gown until the brilliant colors shimmered from her unshed tears. Her sorrow only deepened as she thought of the man who had given it to her. Her liveship captain. Leftrin. Despite the differences in their stations in life, they had fallen in love with each other during the arduous journey up the river. For the first time in her life, a man had admired her mind, respected her work, and desired her body. He had kindled a like passion in her and awakened her to all that could exist between a man and a woman. He had created desires in her such as she had never known before.

And then he had left her, here. Alone in a primitive cabin . . .

Stop it. Stop whining. She stared at the Elderling gown and forced herself to remember the wonderful moment when Leftrin had offered it to her, a priceless artifact, a family possession; he had shared it with her, with never a qualm. And she had worn it as armor against cold and wind and even loneliness. Worn it without a thought about its historical significance. How had she ever dared to rebuke the keepers for wanting something as warm and impervious as the "priceless artifact" she had enjoyed so often? And Leftrin? Was she faulting him for her loneliness? *Hypocrite!* she rebuked herself.

Leftrin had had no choice but to return to Cassarick to fetch supplies for them. He had not abandoned her; she had chosen to stay here, because she had believed that recording all that she saw in the untouched Elderling city was more important than being beside him. That choice had been hers. Leftrin had respected it. And now she was faulting him for that? He loved her. Shouldn't that be enough for her?

For a moment, she teetered on accepting that. A man who loved her: What more did a woman need from life? Then she gritted her teeth as if she were going to tear a bandage from a partially healed wound.

No. It wasn't enough. Not for her.

It was time to put an end to all pretenses. Time to be done with that life. Time to stop telling herself that if and when Leftrin returned and said he loved her, all would be well. What of her could he love? When all was stripped away, what part of her was real and worthy of his love? What sort of person would cling to the hope that someone else would return to give meaning to her life? What sort of quivering parasite needed someone else to validate her existence?

Scrolls and sketches, paper and vellum in tidy stacks rested where she had left them. All her research and writing waited by the fireplace. The impulse to burn it all was gone. That had been last night's pit of despair, a tarry darkness so deep that she had not even had the energy to feed the papers to the flames.

Cold daylight revealed that as a foolish vanity, the childish tantrum of "look what you made me do!" What had Rapskal and the other keepers done to her? Nothing except make her look at the truth of her life. Setting fire to her work would not have proved anything except that she wished to make them feel bad. Her mouth trembled for a moment and then set in a very strange smile. Ah, that temptation lingered; make them all hurt as she did! But they wouldn't. They wouldn't understand what she had destroyed. Besides, it was not worth the effort to go knock on a door and borrow coals from one of the keepers. No. Leave them there. Let them find this monument to what she had been, a woman made of paper and ink and pretense.

Bundled in her old clothes, she pushed open the door of the cottage and stepped out into a wet, chill day. The wind slapped her face. Her disgust and hatred for all she had been rose like a tide in her. The meadow vista before her ended in the river, cold, gray, and relentless. She had been caught in it once and nearly drowned. She let the thought form in her mind. It would be quick. Cold and unpleasant but quick. She spoke aloud the words that had rattled through her dreams all night. "Time to end this life." She lifted her face. The wind was pushing heavy clouds across a distant blue sky.

You would kill yourself? Over that? Because Rapskal told you what you already knew? Sintara's touch on her mind was coldly amused. The dragon's consideration was distant and impartial. *I recall that my ancestors witnessed humans doing this, deliberately choosing to terminate a life span that is already so brief as to be insignificant. Like gnats flying into flames. They flung themselves into rivers, or hanged themselves from bridges. So. The river? Is that how you will do this?*

Sintara had not touched minds with her for weeks. For her to return now and to be so coldly curious fired anger in Alise. She scanned the sky. A tiny wink of sapphire against the distant clouds.

She spoke aloud, giving vent to her outrage, as in a single heartbeat despair became defiance. "End *this* life, I said. Not end MY life." She watched the dragon tip her wings and slide down the sky toward the hills. Change took root in her, grew. "Kill myself? In despair over all the days I've wasted, all the ways I've deceived myself? What would that do except prove that in the end I still could not escape my own foolishness? No. I'm not ending my life, dragon. I'm taking it. I'm making it mine."

For a long moment she felt nothing from Sintara. Probably the dragon had spotted some prey and lost all interest in the gnat-lifed woman who could not even kill a rabbit for her. Then, without warning, the dragon's thoughts boomed through her mind again.

The shape of your thoughts has changed. I think you are finally becoming yourself.

As she stared, the dragon suddenly clapped her wings tight to her body and dived on her prey. The immediate absence of the dragon's touch on her mind was like a gust of wind boxing her ears. She was left stunned and alone.

Becoming herself? The shape of her thoughts had changed? She decided abruptly that it was just Sintara trying to manipulate her again with her riddling, puzzling way of talk. Well, that was something else she had finished with! Never again would she willingly plunge herself into a dragon's glamour. Time to be done with that, time to be done with all of it. She turned on her heel and went back into the little cabin. It was also time to be done with childish

demonstrations of hurt feelings. Moving with a purposeful
ferocity that she had thought vanished with her youth, she
tidied her papers into her trunk and shut the lid on them
relentlessly. There. She looked around the rest of the cabin
and shook her head. Pathetic that she had huddled so long
in this small space and done nothing to make it more liv-
able. Was she waiting for Leftrin to come back and bring the
comforts of his ship's cabin with him? Pitiful. She would
not spend another hour sequestered here.

She layered herself into every worn garment she owned.
Outside again, she lifted her eyes to the forested hills
behind the patchwork village. This was the world she lived
in now and perhaps always would. Time to master it. Ignoring the sleety rain, she headed uphill and followed a trail
the keepers had trodden, winding past a few of the other
rehabilitated cottages before reaching the eaves of the dor-
mant forest. Her resolution grew as she left the settlement
behind. She could change. She wasn't chained to her past.
She could become someone who wasn't merely a product of
what others had done to her. It wasn't too late.

When trails intersected, she chose to go up and to her
right, reasoning that on her return, trails that went down
and to her left would take her home. Ignoring the pull in
her calves and buttocks and back, she punished muscles that
had idled for weeks. The work of walking warmed her, and
she actually loosened her cloak and scarf. She looked about
the forest as she had once studied Kelsingra, mentally log-
ging the plants she knew and the ones she did not. A bare-
thorned bramble patch might be thimbleberries, a good
thing to remember come summer.

She came to a small stream and knelt by it to drink from
cupped hands before crossing it and moving on. In a sheltered hollow, she found a small patch of wintergreen bushes,
their scarlet berries still clinging. She felt as if she had discovered a cache of jewels. Making a bag of her scarf, she
gathered as many as she could find. The sharp flavor of the
berries would be a welcome addition to her menu, as well
as efficacious against sore throats and coughs. The ever-
green leaves she stripped, too, relishing their scent and al-

ready imagining the tea she would brew from them. She was surprised none of the keepers had found them and brought them back, and then she realized how foreign these bushes would be to the canopy-bred hunters.

Tying the scarf closed, she looped it through her belt before moving on. She left the deciduous trees behind and moved into evergreens. Their needled branches touched fingertips over her head, dimming the day's light and hushing the wind. The deep bed of fragrant needles and the quiet of the woods after the constant wind made her feel as if she had cupped her hands over her ears. It was a relief.

She moved on through the forest. Hunger found her. She put a few of the wintergreen berries in her mouth and crushed them in her teeth, flooding her senses with the sharp taste and scent. Hunger passed.

Alise came to a small clearing where a storm-blasted giant had fallen and taken a rank of its fellow trees down with it. A vine similar to ivy had cloaked the fallen tree. She studied it for a time, then seized one of the tough stems and pulled it free, though it did not come willingly. She stripped the leaves off it and tested her strength against it. Unable to break it with her bare hands, she nodded to herself. She could come back with a knife, cut lengths of the stuff, take it back to her cabin, and weave with it. Baskets. Fish nets? Perhaps. She looked at it more closely. The leaf buds on it were starting to swell. Maybe winter was starting to loosen its grip on the land. Overhead, a distant hawk gave cry. She looked up through the gap in the forest roof. Only with that glimpse of sky did she realize how much of the day had passed. It was time she turned back. She had meant to gather green alder twigs for smoking fish and had not, but she would not be empty-handed. The wintergreen berries would be welcomed by all.

The downhill hike quickly woke pangs in different muscles of her legs. She gritted her teeth against them and went on. *Serves me right for spending so much time sitting inside,* she told herself grimly.

It was in that stratum of forest where evergreens gave way to deciduous trees that she caught an odd scent. The wind blew more freely here and she halted where she stood, trying to puzzle it out. It smelled rank and yet strangely familiar. It was only when the creature stepped into view on the path in front of her that her mind made the connection. *Cat,* she thought to herself. He was not immediately aware of her. His head was low, and he sniffed at the ground with his mouth open. Long yellow fangs extended past his lower jaw. His coat was an uneven black, darker dapples against blackness. His ears were tufted, and the muscles under his smooth fur bunched and slid as he moved. She was caught in disbelief, filled with wonder at the sight of an animal that no one had seen in ages. And then, almost immediately, her translation of an Elderling word popped into her mind. "Pard," she breathed aloud. "A black pard."

At her whisper, he lifted his head and looked directly at her with yellow eyes. Fear flooded her. Her own scent on the trail. That was what he snuffed at.

Her heart leaped and then began hammering. The animal stared at her, perhaps as startled to see a human as she was to see a pard. Surely their kind had not met for generations. He opened his mouth, taking in her scent. She wanted to shriek but did not. She flung her panicky thought wide. *Sintara! Sintara, a great cat stalks me, a pard! Help me!*

I cannot help you. Solve it yourself.

The dragon's thought was not uninterested, merely factual. Alise could feel, in that moment of connection, that the dragon had fed heavily and was sinking into a satiated stupor. Even if she had wished to rouse herself, by the time she took flight and crossed the river and located Alise . . .

Useless thought. Focus on now. The cat was watching her, and its wariness had become interest. The longer Alise stood there, frozen like a rabbit, the more his boldness would grow. Do something.

"Not prey!" she shouted at the animal. She seized the lapels of her cloak and tore it open wide, holding it out to make herself twice her natural size. "Not prey!" she shouted at it again, deepening her voice. She flapped the sides of her cloak at the animal and forced her shaking body to jolt a step closer to it. If she ran, it would have her; if she stood still, it would have her. The thought galvanized her, and with a wordless roar of angry despair, she charged at the beast, flapping the sides of her cloak as she ran.

It crouched and she knew then it would kill her. Her deep roar became a shriek of fury, and the cat suddenly snarled back. Alise ran out of breath. For a moment, silence held between the crouched cat and the flapping woman. Then the animal wheeled and raced off into the forest. It had left the path clear, and Alise did not pause but continued her fear-charged dash. She ran in bounds, ran as she had never known that anyone could run. The forest became a blur around her. Low branches ripped at her hair and clothing, but she did not slow down. She gasped in cold air that burned her throat and dried her mouth and still she ran. She fled until darkness threatened the edges of her vision, and then she stumbled on, catching at tree trunks as she passed them to keep herself upright and moving. When finally her terror could no longer sustain her, she sank down, her back to a tree, and looked back the way she had come.

Nothing moved in the forest, and when she forced her mouth to close and held her shuddering breath, she heard nothing save the pounding of her own heart. She felt as if hours passed before her breath moved easily in her dry mouth and her heart slowed to where she could hear the normal sounds of the forest. She listened, straining her ears, but heard only the wind in the bared branches. Clutching at the tree trunk, she dragged herself to her feet, wondering if her trembling legs could still hold her.

Then, as she started down the path toward home, a ridiculous grin blossomed on her face. She had done it. She had faced down a pard, and saved herself, and was coming home triumphant, with wintergreen leaves for tea and berries, too. "Not prey," she whispered hoarsely to herself, and her grin grew wider.

Resettling her clothing as she strode, Alise pushed her wild hair out of her face. The rain was finding her now. Time to get home before she was completely soaked. She still had things to do tonight. Firewood and kindling to gather, coals to borrow to rekindle her fire, and water to haul for cooking. And she should tell Carson about the pard so he could caution the others. Then she could make her tea.

A well-earned cup of wintergreen tea. Part of having her own life, now.

✧ ✧ ✧

Day the 20th of the Fish Moon

Year the 7th of the Independent Alliance of Traders
From the Bird Keepers' Guild, Bingtown
To All Guild Members

To be posted prominently in all halls.

It is essential that all members of the Guild remember that our profession is a time-honored trade with rules, professional standards, and secrets of bird handling, training, and breeding that are confined to Guild members. Guild birds remain the property of the Guild, and the offspring of Guild birds remain the property of the Guild. Our reputation and the custom we have built up depend on our birds being the swiftest, the best trained, and the healthiest. Our clients use Guild birds and bird keepers because they know they can rely on us and our birds for message transport that is quick and confidential.

Of late, there has been a spate of complaints and queries about possible tampering with messages. At the same time, we have noticed more citizens turning to private flocks for the transport of messages. To make matters worse, the recent plague of red lice led to many of our customers being frustrated at the lack of available Guild birds to bear their messages.

We must all remember that not only our reputations but our livelihoods are at stake. Our honor demands that members report any suspicions of message tampering.

Likewise, any members stealing eggs or fledglings for personal use or profit must be reported.

It is only by all of us adhering to our Guild rules that we can maintain the quality of service that our patrons expect. Maintaining our standards will ensure that we all prosper together.

CHAPTER TWO

FLIGHT

The dragons looped in wide circles over the river like swallows. Their flight looked effortless. The scarlet one was Heeby, and high above her, flying in an ever-widening gyre was Sintara, a blue gem against the blue sky. Tats's heart soared as he finally spotted a set of emerald wings. Fente. His very own Fente. She had been flying for three days now, and every time Tats glimpsed her aloft his heart swelled with fondness and pride. Tinged, of course, with anxiety.

Foolish one. I am a dragon. To me the skies belong. I know this is hard for an earthbound creature to grasp, but this is where I have always belonged.

He could only smile at her condescension. *You fly like thistledown, beauty on wings.*

Thistledown with talons! I go to the hunt!

May you find red meat!

Tats watched her tip her wings and peel away from the others, heading toward the foothills on the far side of the river. He felt a pang of disappointment. He probably would not see her again today. She would hunt, kill, gorge, sleep, and in the evening she would return not to him but to Kelsingra, to soak in the baths there, or to sleep in one of the awakened dragon sanctuaries in the city. He knew it was for the best. It was what she needed if she was to grow and improve her flying. And he was so glad that his dragon was one of the first to achieve flight. But . . . but he missed her. Her success had left him more alone than ever.

On the shoreline before him several other dragons were attempting what she had mastered. Carson was standing beside silver Spit, holding the tip of the dragon's extended wing as he inspected it for parasites. Spit already gleamed like a polished sword. Tats could tell that Carson was forcing the dragon to stretch his wing in the pretense of further grooming. Spit was rumbling in a way that was both unhappy and threatening. Carson was ignoring it. Not all the dragons were enthusiastic participants in their exercises and practice. Spit was among the most recalcitrant. Ranculos was reckless one day and sullen the next. Midnight-blue Kalo simmered with dignified resentment that mere humans dared to supervise his efforts to fly, while Baliper was openly fearful of the moving river and would not attempt flight near it. *Most of the others,* he thought to himself, *were simply lazy.* Training to fly was demanding and painful work.

Some, however, were intent on achieving flight regardless of the cost. Dortean was still recovering from crashing to the earth through some trees. Sestican had torn a rent in the membrane of one wing. His keeper, Lecter, had held the injured wing opened and wept as Carson had stitched up the tear.

Mercor stood erect, his golden wings spread wide to the thin sunlight. Harrikin and Sylve were watching him, and Sylve's face was pinched with anxiety. Harrikin's dragon, Ranculos, watched jealously. The gold drake lifted his wings high and then gave them a short, sharp snap as it to assure himself all was working. He gathered himself, setting his weight back onto his hindquarters. As Tats watched, Mercor leaped, wings spread and beating frantically. But he could not gain enough altitude for a full beat of his wings, and the best he could manage was a long glide in parallel to the river before landing clumsily on the sandy shore. Tats let out a long sigh of disappointment and saw Sylve briefly cover her face with her hands. The golden dragon was growing thinner as he grew larger, and he did not gleam as he once had. Learning to fly and to hunt for himself was now a matter of survival. For the others as much as himself. Where he led, the other dragons would follow.

Mercor held an odd sway over the others, one Tats did not completely understand. In their serpent incarnations, he had led their "tangle." It surprised Tats that a loyalty from a previous life prevailed still. But when Mercor had proclaimed that the flighted dragons must hunt only on the far side of the river, and leave the game on the village side alone so that the keepers might better provide for the grounded dragons, no one, dragon or keeper, had protested. Now the other dragons watched him limbering his wings, and Tats hoped that if Mercor made a successful flight, they would all become more willing in their efforts.

Once the dragons could fly and hunt, life would become easier for all of them. The keepers would also be able to transfer their lives to Kelsingra. Tats thought of warm beds and hot water and sighed. He lifted his eyes again to watch Fente in flight.

"It's hard to let go of her, isn't it?"

He turned reluctantly at Alise's question. For a moment he was stricken, thinking she had seen to his core and knew how he pined for Thymara. Then he realized she spoke of his dragon, and he tried to smile at her. The Bingtown woman had been quiet and grave of late, and distant. It was almost as if she had returned to being the stranger among them, the fine lady from Bingtown who had startled all the Rain Wild keepers when they had first discovered she was a member of their expedition. Initially, she had competed with Thymara for Sintara's attention, but Thymara's competence as a hunter had soon won Sintara's belly if not her heart. Nevertheless, Alise had created her own place in the expedition company. She did not hunt, but she had helped groom and tend dragon injuries as best she could. And she had known things, information about dragons and Elderlings that had helped them along the way. For a time, it had seemed she was one of them.

But Alise had not been chosen as keeper by any of the dragons, and Rapskal's declaration that the city belonged to the keepers had thrust her to one side. Tats still winced when he thought of that stark confrontation. When they had first reached Kelsingra, Alise had asserted her authority and decreed that nothing must be touched or changed until she had had a chance to thoroughly document the dead city. Tats had simply accepted her rule, as had the other keepers. It surprised him now to realize how much authority he had ceded to her simply because she was an adult and a scholar.

But then had come the confrontation between her and Rapskal. Rapskal had been the only one of the keepers with free access to the city. His dragon, Heeby, had been the first to take flight, and unlike the other dragons, she had not minded carrying a passenger on her back. Heeby had provided passage to the city for Alise many times. But when Rapskal and Thymara had ventured to the city to explore and had returned the next day with a trove of warm Elderling garments to share with the other ragged keepers, Alise had been incensed. He had never seen the genteel Bingtown woman so angry. She had cried out to them that they must put the garments down "this instant and stop tugging at them."

And that was when Rapskal had defied her. He had told her, in his direct way, that the city was alive and belonged to the Elderlings, not to her. He had pointed out that he and his fellow keepers were Elderlings while she was and would remain a human. Despite his own heartbreak that day, despite seeing Thymara beside Rapskal, Tats had felt a flash of deep pity for Alise. And a stripe of shame and regret to see her so quickly retreat and withdraw from their company. When he thought about it now, he felt a bit guilty that he had not at least knocked at her door to ask if she was all right. He had been nursing his own heartbreak, but still, he should have gone to ask after her. The truth was, he hadn't even noticed she had been missing until she reappeared.

Did her effort at conversation mean she had recovered from Rapskal's rebuke? He hoped so.

He smiled at her as he replied, "Fente has changed. She doesn't need me as she once did."

"Before long, none of them will." She was not looking at him. Her gaze tracked his dragon across the sky. "You will all have to start thinking of yourselves in a different way. Your own lives will come to have more significance to you. The dragons will take command of their own fates. And probably ours as well."

"What do you mean?"

Now she looked at him, a direct look with her brows raised as if startled that he did not immediately grasp what she had told him. "I mean that dragons will rule the world again. As they used to."

"As they used to?" Tats echoed her words as he followed her toward the riverbank. It had become a new habit for all of them; the keepers and the flightless dragons gathered in the morning on the riverbank to discuss the day's tasks. He glanced around and for a moment was seized by the beauty of the scene. The keepers were gleaming figures in the fleeting morning mist, for all wore their Elderling garments daily now. Their dragons were scattered across the hillside and along the bank. They were limbering their wings, beating them hard against the meadow grass, or stretching out necks and legs. They, too, gleamed brilliantly against the dew-heavy grasses of the wet meadow. At the bottom of the hill, Carson had given over his efforts with Spit and waited for them, Sedric at his side.

The leadership had evolved, Tats realized. For all Rapskal's charismatic speech when he had returned from Kelsingra, he had not assumed the command as Tats had thought he might. Probably because he was not interested in being a leader. He was handsome and cheerful, beloved by his fellows, but most of them spoke of him with a fond smile rather than deep respect. Rapskal remained as odd as he had always been, introspective one moment and bizarrely social the next. And happy with who he was. The ambition that would have burned inside Tats was not even a spark to him.

Carson was by years the oldest of those who had taken on a dragon. It seemed natural to cede authority to him, and the hunter did not shirk from it. For the most part, Carson assigned the daily tasks to the keepers, a few to groom and otherwise tend to the remaining dragons, and the rest of them to hunt or fish. If a keeper protested that he had a different task in mind that day, Carson did not let it become an issue. He recognized the keepers' individuality and did not attempt to impose his authority on them. As a result, all seemed to accept it.

Alise had quietly claimed some of the menial but necessary tasks of daily living. She tended the smoking racks that preserved fish and meat for them, gathered edible greens, and helped groom the dragons. Sylve, never the most successful hunter, had turned her energies to the preparation of meals. At Carson's suggestion, the keepers had returned to large shared meals. It was strange but nice to return to the communal meals and talk they had shared when they were moving the dragons upriver.

It made him feel a bit less lonely.

"As they used to, and will again," Alise continued. She glanced over at him. "Seeing them in flight, watching all of you change . . . it puts a different light on all that I discovered in the course of my early studies. Dragons were the center of the Elderling civilizations, with humans a separate population that lived apart from them, in settlements like the ones we found here. Humans raised crops and cattle that they traded to Elderlings in exchange for their wondrous goods. Look at the city across the river, Tats, and ask yourself, how did they feed themselves?"

"Well, there were herds on the outskirts of the cities. Probably places to grow crops . . ."

"Probably. But humans were the ones to do that. Elderlings gave themselves and their lives over to their magic, and to tending the dragons. All they did and built and created were not for themselves, but for the dragons who over-shadowed them."

"Ruled them? The dragons ruled them?" He wasn't enjoying the images in his mind.

"Ruled isn't quite the right word. Does Fente rule you?"

"Of course not!"

"And yet you gave your days over to hunting for her, and grooming her and otherwise caring for her."

"But I wanted to do those things."

Alise smiled. "And that is why *ruled* is the wrong word. Charmed? Englamoured? I'm not sure quite how to express it, but you do already know what I mean. If these dragons breed and bring more of their kind into the world, then inevitably they will end up running the world for their own benefit."

"That sounds so selfish!"

"Does it? Isn't it what humans have done for generations? We claim the land as ours and turn it to our purposes. We change the channels of rivers and the face of the land so that we can travel by boat or grow a crop or graze cattle. And we think it only natural that we should shape the whole world to be comfortable and yielding for humankind. Why should dragons be any different in how they perceive the world?"

Tats was quiet for a time.

"It may not be a bad thing at all," Alise observed into his silence. "Maybe humans will lose some of their pettiness if they have dragons to contend with. Ah, look! Is that Ranculos? I would not have believed it possible!"

The huge scarlet dragon was in the air. He was not graceful. His tail was still too skinny, and his hindquarters flimsy for his size. Tats was about to observe that he was only gliding after a launch from a higher point, but at that point the dragon's wings began to beat heavily. And what had been a glide turned into labored flight as he gained altitude.

Tats became aware of Harrikin. The tall slender keeper was racing down the hillside, almost in his dragon's shadow. As Ranculos beat his wings and gained altitude, Harrikin cried out, "Ware your course! Bank, bank your wings left! Not over the river, Ranculos! Not over the river!"

His cry was thin and breathless, and Tats doubted that the huge dragon heard him at all. If he did, he paid him no mind. Perhaps he was full of exhilaration; or perhaps he had decided to fly or die trying.

The red dragon lumbered into the sky, his hind legs dangling and twitching as he tried to pull them up into alignment with the rest of his body. Some of the other keepers were adding their voices to Harrikin's now. "Too soon, Ranculos, too soon!"

"Come back! Circle back!"

The red dragon ignored them. His labored efforts carried him farther and farther from the shore. The steady beat of his wings became an uneven flapping.

"What is he doing? What is he thinking?"

"Silence!" A trumpeted blast of sound and thought from Mercor quenched them all. "Watch!" he commanded both humans and dragons.

Ranculos hung suspended, wings wide now. His uncertainty was plain. He tipped and teetered as he began a wide circle, losing altitude as he did so. Then, as if realizing that he was closer to Kelsingra than the village, he resumed his course. But his weariness was evident now. His body drooped between his wings. The intersection of dragon and river became both obvious and inevitable.

"No-o-o-o!" Harrikin's low cry was a sound of agony. He stood stiffly, hands clutching at his face, his nails sinking into his cheeks as he stared. Ranculos's glide carried him farther and farther from the village. Below him, the gray river's greedy current raced relentlessly. Sylve gave Mercor a cautious glance, and then ran to stand beside Harrikin. Lecter plodded down the hillside toward his foster brother, his broad shoulders slumped as if he shared Harrikin's desperation and already knew the outcome.

Ranculos began to beat his wings, not steadily but in frantic desperation. Their uneven rhythm tipped and tilted him. He fluttered like a fledgling fallen too soon from the nest. His destination was the far side of the river, but despite his battle with the air, all knew he could not attain it. Once, twice, thrice his wingtips scored white on the river's face and then his drooping hind legs snagged in the current and the waters snatched him from the sky, pinwheeling him wide-winged into the grayness. He slapped his wings uselessly against the water. Then he sank. The river smoothed over the spot where he had fallen as if he had never been.

"Ranculos. Ranculos!" Harrikin's voice went shrill and childish as he fell slowly to his knees. All eyes watched the river, hoping for what could not be. Nothing disturbed the rushing waters. Harrikin stared, straining toward the water. His hands went into fists as he shouted, "Swim! Kick! Fight it, Ranculos! Don't give in. Don't give up!"

He lurched to his feet and took a dozen steps toward the water. Sylve, clutching at him, was dragged along. He halted and looked wildly about. Then a shudder passed over him, and "PLEASE! Please, Sa, not my dragon! Not my dragon!" The blowing wind swept his heartbroken prayer to one side. He fell to his knees again, and this time his head bent and he did not rise.

A terrible silence flowed in as all stared at the empty river. Sylve glanced back at the other keepers, useless horror on her face. Lecter moved forward. He set one heavily scaled hand upon Harrikin's lean shoulder and bowed his head. His shoulders heaved.

Tats stared silently, sharing his agony. Guiltily, he stole a glance at the sky. It took him a moment to locate Fente, a winking green gem in the distance. As he watched, she dived on something, probably a deer. *Unaware or uncaring?* he wondered. He looked in vain for either of the other two dragons. If they realized that Ranculos was drowning, they gave no indication of it. Was it because they knew there was nothing anyone could do? He did not understand the seeming heartlessness of dragons toward one another.

And sometimes, toward their keepers, he thought as the blue beauty that was Sintara abruptly swept across his field of vision. She, too, was on the hunt, skimming the distant hills on the other side of the water, unmindful of either Thymara standing alone on the shore or Ranculos perishing in the river's icy grip.

"Ranculos!" Sestican bellowed suddenly.

Tats saw Lecter's head come up. He spun and then stared in horror as his blue dragon began a lumbering gallop down the hillside. Sestican opened his wings as he ran, baring the bright orange tracery on his blue wings. Lecter left his collapsed brother and began his own run on a path that would intercept his dragon, bellowing his pleas for him to stop. Davvie ran after him. The big blue dragon had been practicing flight assiduously, but even so, Tats was astonished when he suddenly leaped into the air, snapping his body into arrow-straight alignment and gaining air with every beat of his wings. Although he cleared his keeper's head, he was barely a wing span above the river's surface as he began his attempt to cross. Lecter dissolved in hoarse screams of "No! No! You're not ready yet! Not you, too! No!"

Davvie came to a halt beside him, both hands crossed over his mouth in horror.

"Let him go," Mercor said wearily. There was no force behind his words, but they carried to every ear. "He takes the risk that each of us must chance, sooner or later. To stay here is to die slowly. Perhaps a swift drowning in cold water is a better choice." The gold dragon's black eyes swirled as he watched Sestican's ponderous flight.

The wind whispered across the meadow, scattering rain as it came. Tats squinted, grateful for the wetness on his cheeks.

"But perhaps not!" Mercor trumpeted abruptly. He reared onto his hind legs as he turned his gaze far downriver to stare at the opposite shore. Several of the other dragons mimicked him. Harrikin shot suddenly to his feet as Spit exclaimed, "He's out! Ranculos crossed the river!"

Tats strained his eyes but could see nothing. The rain had become a gray haze, and the area the dragons observed was a warren of Elderling buildings crumbling into the water. But then Harrikin exclaimed, "He is! He's out of the river. Bruised and battered, but he's alive. Ranculos is alive in Kelsingra!"

Harrikin suddenly seemed to notice Sylve. He swept her into his arms and spun with her in a giddy circle, crying, "He's safe! He's safe! He's safe!" Sylve joined her laughter to his joyous cries. Then, abruptly, they stopped. "Sesti-can?" Harrikin cried. "Lecter! Lecter!" He and Sylve set off at a run toward Lecter.

Lecter's blue dragon had neared the far shore. He arched his body, bending his head and shorter front legs down toward his suddenly dangling back feet, touched the ground with all four feet, wings wide, and for one instant, his landing was graceful. Then his speed betrayed him, and he tumbled in a somersault, wings still open. A mixed chorus of cheers, groans, and a few hoots of laughter met his clumsy landing. But Lecter gave a wild shout of joy and jumped into the air. He spun, froggy grin wide, to confront those who had laughed, demanding, "And can your dragons do better?" He spotted Davvie and caught his lover in a crushing hug.

A moment later, his foster brother and Sylve had engulfed them both in a wild embrace. Then, to Tats's astonishment, Harrikin plucked Sylve free, spun her once, and then, as he landed her, kissed her deeply. The gathering keepers were shouting joyously as they converged on them.

"It all changes," Alise murmured quietly. She watched them embrace, saw them caught up in the mob of their friends, and then turned back to Tats. "That's five now. Five dragons in Kelsingra."

"Ten left here," Tats agreed. Then he added, as he saw that Harrikin and Sylve still held each other, oblivious to the whooping crowd around them, "It *has* changed. What do you think of it?"

"Do you believe what I think matters to them?" Alise asked him. The words could have sounded sour, but her question was sincere.

Tats was silent for a moment. "I think it does," he said at last. "I think it matters to all of us. You know so much of the past. Sometimes, I think you can see more clearly what may become of us . . ." He faltered as he realized his words might seem unkind.

"Because I am not one of you. Because I only observe." She spoke the words for him. As he nodded dumbly, embarrassed, she laughed aloud. "It does give me a perspective that perhaps you lack."

She gestured at Sylve and Harrikin. Hand in hand, they stood beside Lecter. The other keepers surrounded them, laughing and rejoicing. Davvie was with Lecter, and they, too, held hands. "In Trehaug or Bingtown, that would be scandal. There, they would already be outcasts. Here, when you look aside when they kiss, it is not in disgust but to grant them privacy."

Tats's attention drifted. He noticed Rapskal moving through the clustered keepers to stand by Thymara. He said something to her, and she laughed. Then he set his hand to her back, his fingers light on the mounded fabric of the Elderling garb that concealed her wings. Thymara gave a wriggle like a shiver and twitched out of his reach, but no offense showed on her face.

Tats looked away from them and back to Alise. "Or perhaps we look aside in envy," he said, surprising himself with his honesty.

"It is hard for loneliness to gaze on happiness," Alise admitted, and Tats realized that she thought his remark had been directed at her.

"At least, you know your loneliness will end soon," he pointed out.

She rewarded him with a smile. "It will. And eventually, so will yours."

He could not find a smile to answer hers. "How can you seem so sure of that?"

She cocked her head and looked at him. "It is as you said. I have a different perspective. But if I tell you what I foresee, you may not like the answer."

"I'm ready to hear it," he assured her, wondering if he was.

Tats gazed over the gathered keepers and across the river. On the far side, he could just make out both dragons through the falling rain and mist. Ranculos had emerged far downstream of Sestican but was working his way along the riverbank. Sestican was a small blue figure making his slow way up one of the city's main streets. To the dragon baths, Tats suspected. Soaking in hot water was almost all the earthbound dragons spoke of anymore. He let his gaze wander

to the dragons on the near shore. They stared with longing.
Mercor's neck was stretched toward Kelsingra as if sheer
will could lift him there. Silver Spit and squat Relpda stood
to one side, heads cocked like puzzled children. The other
dragons were arrayed in a fan behind Mercor. Blue-black
Kalo towered large over Jerd's small queen, Veras. Baliper
and Arbuc stayed a safe distance from the short-tempered
black drake as they gazed longingly at the far shore. Tinder,
the sole lavender dragon now developing tracery of royal
blue on his wings, stood beside the two oranges, Dortean
and Skrim. The last two dragons reminded Tats very much
of their owners, Kase and Boxter. They always seemed to be
in proximity to each other. Alise's measured words broke
into his thoughts.

"You are young, even by Rain Wild standards. By Elderling count, my studies tell me your life has barely begun.
You have not decades, but lifetimes before you. And I suspect that as Kelsingra comes back to life and its population
grows, you will have many young women to choose from.
You will find someone, eventually. Or possibly several
someones, over the course of your many years."

He stared at her, shocked into silence by such a prospect.

"Elderlings are not humans," she asserted quietly. "Of
old, they were not bound by the conventions of humans."
She looked away from him, across the river to Kelsingra, as
if she could see the future in the misty city. "And I expect
it will be so again. That you will live apart from us, and by
your own rules." She inclined her head toward the rejoicing. "Now is not a time for you to stand here with me. You
should go join them."

ALISE WATCHED TATS hesitate. She thought him brave
when he gave a tight nod and then started down the hill
toward his own kind. He was the only one of them who had
begun this journey as the Tattooed son of a slave rather than
a born Rain Wilder. Sometimes he still believed he was
an outsider. But she could see the truth. He was as much
an Elderling as any of them now, and he would be to the
end of his days. She pondered that as she hiked back to her

cabin and sighed as she opened the door and entered her
tidy domain. They were Elderlings, bonded to dragons, and
she was not. She was the lone human on the landscape for
days in all directions. The only one not bonded to a dragon.
Her loneliness welled up to strangle her again. She shook it
off, turned her thoughts away from the rejoicing and longing on the riverbank, and chose her tasks for the day. Green
alder branches were needed for the fish-smoking racks. And
there was always a need for dry kindling for the cook fire.
Both were becoming harder to find as the village exhausted
the easy supply within an hour's walk. Both remained important gathering tasks and well within her capability. Not
grand or sophisticated work, but it was hers. The vines she
had discovered had proven to be excellent for weaving light-
weight baskets for carrying twigs or kindling. She picked
up one and shouldered it. She had her own life and purpose.
She took up the stout stave Carson had brought to her that
doubled as a walking stick. If she intended to stay in this
part of the world and live alongside the Elderlings and their
dragons, then she had to adapt to her new station.

The only alternative was unthinkable. Return to Bingtown and her loveless sham of a marriage? Return to Hest's
brutal mockery and her shadow life as his wife? No. Better
a bare hut on a riverbank, with or even without Leftrin, than
a return to that life. She squared her shoulders and firmed
her will. It was so hard not to retreat to her supposed use-
fulness as a scholar of Elderlings and dragons. But she was
learning. The work she did now was humble but essential
and satisfying in a very different way from what she was
accustomed to.

Sylve had asked to be shown the way to the wintergreen
berries. They would go together this afternoon to gather
more berries and leaves and scout for other patches in the
area. And they would go armed with staves, lest the pard
returned. She smiled to herself as she thought of how astonished Carson had been at her tale of how she had frightened
the big cat. He had made her promise to be at their shared
meal that evening, to tell everyone what she had seen and
where, and how she had evaded death. Made her promise

also not to venture on such an extended exploration without a partner and without informing someone first.

That night, standing before them and recounting all she knew about the legendary pards from the Elderling manuscripts of old, and then revealing how she had pretended to be a much larger creature to panic the animal had been rewarding. Their laughter at her tale had not been mocking but admiring of her courage.

She had a place now and a life, and it was one of her own making.

✧ ✧ ✧

Day the 22nd of the Fish Moon

Year the 7th of the Independent Alliance of Traders
From Kim, Keeper of the Birds, Cassarick
To Winshaw, General Registrar of Birds,
Bingtown

I think it is ridiculous that a simple accounting error is leading to suspicions and accusations against me. I have told the Council numerous times that I am the victim of prejudice simply because I came to this post as a Tattooed rather than as one Rain Wilds born. The current journeymen feel a loyalty to their own kind that leads to this sort of suspicion and tattling. As they seem to have nothing better to do than spread evil rumors, I have doubled their duty hours.

Yes, there is a discrepancy between the number of birds in our cotes now and the number that existed before the red lice plague completely subsided. It is for a simple reason: birds died.

In the crisis of the moment, I did not pay as much attention to paperwork as I did to attempting to keep birds alive. For this reason, yes, I burned dead birds before other keepers had witnessed that they were indeed dead. It was to stop the spread of contagion. And that is all it was.

I cannot give you evidence of their deaths, unless you wish me to ship a package of ashes from the incineration site. I do not think that is a task worthy of my time.

Do you?

Kim, Keeper of the Birds, Cassarick

Postscript: If any keeper sites are in need of journeymen,

I have a surplus, and will gladly release any of them for service. The sooner my own apprentices can replace those disloyal to me, the sooner the operation of the Cassarick station will become more efficient and professional.

CHAPTER THREE

HUNTERS AND PREY

Sintara waded out of the river, cold water sheeting
from her gleaming blue scales. When she reached the shore,
she opened her wings, rocked back on her hind legs, and
shook them, showering the sandy bank with droplets. As she
folded them sleekly back to her sides, she feigned oblivion
to how every dragon eye was fixed on her. She let her gaze
rove over all of them, staring dragons and frozen keepers.

Mercor broke the silence. "You look well, Sintara."

She knew it. It had not taken long. The long baths in simmering water, flights to muscle her, and plenty of meat to
put flesh on her bones. She finally felt like a dragon. She
stood a moment longer to allow them all to notice how she
had grown before dropping to all fours again. She regarded
Mercor in silence for a few long moments before observing,
"And you do not. Still not flying, Mercor?"

He did not look aside from her disdain. "Not yet. But soon, I hope."

Sintara had spoken true. The golden drake had outgrown his flesh, as if the meat of his body were stretched too thinly over his bones. He was clean, meticulously groomed as ever, but he did not gleam as he once had.

"He will fly."

The words were confident. Sintara turned her head. Her focus on Mercor had been such that she had forgotten there were other dragons present, let alone a mere human. Several of the Elderling youths had paused at their tasks to watch their encounter, but not Alise. She was working on Baliper, and as her hands moved over a long gash on his face, she kept her eyes on her task. The gash was fresh; she was blotting blood and dirt from it, rinsing the rag in a bucket at her feet. Baliper's eyes were closed.

Sintara did not reply to Alise's assertion. Instead, she said, "So you are Baliper's keeper now. Do you hope he will make you an Elderling? To give you a better life?"

The woman's eyes flickered to Sintara and then back to her work. "No," she replied shortly.

"My keeper is dead. I do not desire another one." Baliper spoke in a profoundly emotionless voice.

Alise stilled. She set one hand on the scarlet dragon's muscular neck. Then she stooped, rinsed her rag, and went on cleaning the gash.

"I understand that," she said quietly. When she spoke to Sintara, her voice echoed Mercor's exactly. "Why did you come here?"

It was an irritating question, not just because they both dared to ask her but because she was not, herself, certain of the answer. Why *had* she come? It was undragonlike to seek companionship with either other dragons or humans. She looked for a moment at Kelsingra, recalling why the Elderlings had created it: to lure dragons. To offer them the indulgences that only a city built by humans could provide.

Something that Mercor had said long ago pushed into her thoughts. They had been discussing Elderlings and how dragons changed humans. She tried to recall his exact words and could not. Only that he had claimed humans changed dragons just as much as dragons changed humans.

The thought was humiliating. Almost infuriating. Had her long exposure to humans changed her, given her a need for their company? Her blood coursed more strongly through her veins, and her body answered her question. Not just company. She felt the wash of color go through her scales, betraying her.

"Sintara. Was there a reason for this visit?"

Mercor had moved closer still. His voice was almost amused.

"I go where I please. Today, it pleased me to come here. Today, it pleased me to look on what might have been drakes."

He opened his wings, stretched them wide. They were larger than she recalled. He flexed them, testing them, and the breeze of them, heavy with his male scent, washed over her. "It pleases me that you have come here as well," he observed.

A sound. Had Alise laughed? Sintara snapped her gaze back to the woman, but her head was bent over her bucket as she wrung out her rag. She looked back at Mercor. He was folding his wings carefully. Kalo was watching both of them with interest. As was Spit. As she looked at him, the silver male reared back onto his hind legs and spread his wings as wide as they would go. Carson stood between them, looking very apprehensive. "It needn't be Mercor!" the nasty little silver trumpeted suddenly. "It could be me."

She stared at him and felt her poison sacs swelling in her throat. He flapped his wings at her, releasing musk in a rank wind. She shook her head and bent her neck, snorting out the stench. "It will never be you," she spat at him.

"It might," he countered and danced a step toward her. Kalo's eyes suddenly spun with anger.

"Spit!" Carson warned him, but the silver pranced another step closer.

Kalo lifted a clawed foot, set it deliberately on his tail. Spit squalled angrily and turned on the much larger dragon, opening his mouth wide to show his poison glands, scarlet and distended. Kalo trumpeted his challenge as he snapped his wing open, bowling the smaller dragon to one side as Carson, with a roar of dismay, leaped back to avoid being crushed.

Kalo ignored the chaos behind him.

"I will fly the challenge!" the cobalt drake announced. He lifted his gaze to Sintara. She heard a distant cry and became aware that far overhead, Fente was circling. The small green queen watched it all with interest. The heat of Kalo's stare swept through her, and suddenly all she felt was anger, anger for all of them, all the stupid flightless, useless males. A rippling of color again washed through her skin and echoed in her scales.

"Fly the challenge?" she roared back at all the staring drakes. "You fly nothing; none of you fly! I came to see it again, for myself. A field of drakes, as earthbound as cows. As useless to a queen as the old bones of a kill."

"Ranculos flies. Sestican flies," Alise pointed out relentlessly. "Two drakes at least have achieved flight. If they were the drakes you wanted . . ."

The insult was too great. This time Sintara spat acid. A controlled ball of it hit the earth a body's length from Alise. Baliper surged to his feet, eyes spinning sparks of rage. As he charged, Alise shrieked and ran. A spike on one knob of his outflung wings narrowly missed her. Sintara braced herself, flinging her own wings wide, but cobalt Kalo intercepted Baliper. As the two males slammed into each other, feinting with open mouths and slashing with clawed wings, the air was filled with the shouts and screams of Elderlings. Some fled; others raced toward the combatants.

Sintara had only a moment to take in the spectacle before Mercor knocked her down. Gaunt as he was, he was still larger than she was. As she sprawled on the turf, he reared up over her and she expected him to spray her with venom. Instead he came down almost gently, his heavy forefeet pinning her wings to the earth and pressing painfully on the flexible bones.

She opened her jaws to spew acid at him. He darted his head down, his mouth open wide to show her his swollen acid glands. "Don't," he hissed at her, and the finest mist of golden acid rode his word. The stinging kiss of it enveloped her head and she flung her face aside from it.

He rumbled out his words so that the others heard, but he pressed them strong into her mind at the same time. *"You are impatient, queen. Understandably so. A little time more, and I will fly. And I will mate you."* He reared onto his hind legs again, lifting his forefeet off her wings as he did so. She stood up awkwardly, muddied, her wings bruised and aching as she folded them back to her body and scrabbled away.

The battle between Baliper and Kalo had been brief; both males stood at a distance from each other, snorting and posturing. Spit cavorted mockingly, a safe distance from the much larger drakes, randomly spitting acid as scampering keepers cried out warnings to one another. Sintara saw Alise watching her; the woman's eyes were large and anxious. When she stared at the woman, she backed up, lifting her hands to shield her face. It only made Sintara angrier. She fixed her fury on Mercor.

"Don't threaten me, drake."

He turned his head slightly sideways. His wings were still half open, ready to deal a stunning slap if she sprang at him. He spoke quietly, only into her mind. *Not a threat, Sintara. A promise.*

As he closed his wings, his musk wafted toward her again. She knew her scales flushed with colors in response, the reflexive biological response of a queen in oestrus. His black eyes whirled with interest.

She lifted onto her hind legs and turned away from him. As she sprang into the sky, she trumpeted, "I hunt where I will, drake. I owe you nothing." She beat her wings in hard, measured strokes, rising above them all.

In the distance, green Fente trumpeted, shrill and mocking.

"THYMARA!"

She turned slowly at the sound of Tats's greeting. Tension knotted in her belly. She had been avoiding this conversation. She'd seen in Tats's eyes when she first returned from

Kelsingra that he knew what had happened between her and
Rapskal. She hadn't needed or wanted to discuss it with
him. On the days since then she had not avoided him completely, but she had thwarted his efforts to find her alone.
She had found it almost as difficult as avoiding being alone
with Rapskal. Tats had been subtle about trying to corner
her. Rapskal had shown up on her doorstep the evening they
had returned from Kelsingra, smiling far too knowingly
when he asked her if she'd care to go for an evening walk.

He had come to the door of the small cottage she shared
with Sylve and ostensibly with Jerd as well. The three had
moved in together almost as soon as the keepers had settled
in the village. Thymara could not recall that it had been a
much-discussed decision; it had just seemed logical that the
only three female keepers would share lodgings.

Harrikin had helped them select which of the dilapidated
structures they would claim as their own, and he had spent
more than a few afternoons helping them make it habit-
able. Thanks to Harrikin, the chimney now drew the smoke
out of the house, the roof leaked only when the wind was
extremely strong, and there were shutters for the window
openings. Furnishings were sparse and rough, but that
was true of all the keepers' homes. From Carson, they had
crudely tanned deer hides stretched over pole frames as a
basis for their beds, and carved wooden utensils for eating
with. Thymara was one of the best hunters so they always
had meat, both to eat and to trade to other keepers. Thymara
had enjoyed her evenings with Sylve, and she enjoyed them
even more when some of the other keepers came by to share
the fireside and talk. At first, Tats had been a frequent guest
there, as had Rapskal.

Jerd spent few nights there, returning sporadically to
shuffle through her possessions for some particular item,
or to share a meal with them while she complained about
whichever of the males she was currently keeping company
with. Despite her dislike for Jerd, Thymara could not deny
a perverse fascination with her diatribes against her lovers.
She was appalled at Jerd's casual sexuality and her tempers, her spewing of intimate details and how frequently

she discarded one male keeper to take up with another. She had cycled through several of the keepers more than once. It was no secret in their small group that Boxter was hopelessly infatuated with her. He alone she seemed to spurn. Nortel had been her lover for at least three turns of her heart, and copper-eyed Kase had the distinction of having literally put her out of his cottage as well as his bed. She had seemed as astonished as angered that he had been the one to put an end to their liaisons. Thymara suspected that Kase was loyal to his cousin, Boxter, and wanted no part of breaking his heart.

But that first evening after her time with Rapskal in Kelsingra, of course, Jerd had been home, and full of small and cutting comments. She took care to remind Thymara that Rapskal had once been her lover, however briefly, and that Tats, too, had shared her bed. Her presence had not made it any easier to tell Rapskal gently that she did not want to walk out with him that evening. It had been no easier to refuse him the next day, nor to put him off on the next. When finally she had told him that she doubted the wisdom of what she had done, and that her fear of conceiving a child was greater than her lust for him, Rapskal had surprised her by nodding gravely.

"It is a concern. I will take it on myself to find out how Elderlings once prevented conception, and when I know it, I will tell you. After that we can enjoy ourselves without fear." He had said these words as they walked hand in hand along the riverbank, only a few evenings ago. She had laughed aloud, both charmed and alarmed, as she always was, by his childlike directness about things that were definitely not childish.

"So easily you set aside all the rules we grew up with?" she asked him.

"Those rules don't apply to us anymore. If you'd come back to Kelsingra with me and spend a bit more time with the stones, you'd know that."

"Be careful of the memory stone," she had warned him.

It was another rule they had grown up with. All Rain Wild children knew the danger of dallying in the stored memories in the stones. More than one youngster had been lost to them, drowned in memories of other times. Rapskal had shrugged her concerns aside.

"I've told you. I use the stones and the memories they hold as they were intended. Some of it, I now understand, was street art. Some of them, especially the ones in the walls of homes, were personal memories, like a diary. Some are poetry, especially in the statues, or histories. But there will be a place where the Elderlings stored their magic and their medicines, and when I discover it, there I think I will find what we need. Does that comfort you?"

"Somewhat." She decided that she did not have to tell him right then that she was not sure if she would take him into her bed even if she knew it was safe to do so. She was not sure she could explain her reluctance. How could she explain to him what she did not understand herself? Easier not to talk about it.

Easier not to discuss Rapskal with Tats as well. So she turned to him now with a half smile and an apologetic, "I was just about to go hunting. Carson has given me Willow Ridge today."

"And me, also," Tats answered easily. "Carson wants us to hunt in pairs for safety. It's not just Alise's pards. Less chance that we'll be spooking each other's game away too."

She nodded dumbly. It had been bound to happen sooner or later. Since the keepers had gathered to discuss how best to encourage the dragons to fly, Carson had come up with a number of new ideas. Dividing the hunting territory to prevent conflicts and hunting with a partner for added safety had been one of them. Today, some keepers would be hunting Long Valley, others High Shore, and some would be fishing. Willow Ridge paralleled the river and was, as they had named it, forested mostly with willow. It was prime range for deer to browse, and Carson had reserved it for his best bow hunters.

She had her gear and Tats had his. There was no excuse not to set out immediately. After the morning's conflict, Thymara had wanted to flee. Even though Sintara had taken no notice of her, had possibly not even seen her watching from the riverside, Thymara felt shamed by her dragon. She had not wanted to be around the other keepers; she didn't want to hear what they would be saying about her spoiled queen. Worse was that she kept trying to find a way to justify Sintara's arrogance and spite. She wanted to be able to defend her dragon. Sintara cared little to nothing for her. She knew that. Yet every time she thought she had divorced her feelings from the blue queen, every time she was sure she had made herself stop caring about her dragon, Sintara seemed to find a new way to wring emotions from her. Today, it was shame.

She tried to shake herself free of it as Tats fell into step beside her. It wasn't her fault. She had done nothing, but it did not help to know that. As they crossed the face of the meadow and passed the other keepers and the dragons, she told herself she was imagining that they were staring after her.

Kase, Boxter, Nortel, and Jerd had drawn grooming duty for the day. They were going over the earthbound dragons, checking for sucking parasites near their eyes and ear holes while encouraging them to stretch out their wings. Arbuc was cooperating in his sweet but rather dim way while Tinder paced impatiently while awaiting attention. Ever since the lavender dragon's colors had started to develop, he had shown a dandyish side that had several of the keepers chuckling about his vanity. Alise was smoothing deer tallow into the new scratches that Kalo had given Baliper.

Once the dragons had been groomed, the keepers would encourage each of the remaining dragons to make an effort at flight. Only after they had complied, at least nominally, would they be fed. Carson insisted.

Thymara did not envy them their tasks. Of the dragons, only Mercor was patient when hungry. Spit was as foul tempered, obnoxious, and rude a creature as she'd ever met. Even Carson could barely manage him. Nasty little Fente had been able to take flight, thank Sa, but gloriously green-and-gold Veras remained earthbound, and she was as vindictive as her keeper, Jerd. Kalo, the largest of the dragons, was almost suicidally determined to fly. Davvie was his keeper, but today it was Boxter tending the dragon's numerous cuts and scratches after his spat with Baliper. The spat that Sintara had provoked. Thymara walked faster. A day spent hunting and killing a deer and dragging it back to camp was definitely preferable to a day spent dealing with the other keepers and their dragons.

At least she no longer had to deal with her own dragon. She cast her eyes skyward as she thought of Sintara and tried to deny the pang of abandonment she felt.

"Do you miss her?" Tats asked quietly.

She almost resented that he could read her so clearly. "I do. She doesn't make it easy. She touches my thoughts sometimes, for no reason that makes sense to me. She will suddenly be in my mind, bragging about the size of the bear she has killed, and how he fought but could not lay a claw on her. That was just a couple of days ago. Or she will suddenly show me something that she sees, a mountain capped with snow, or the reflection of the city in that deep river inlet. Something so beautiful that it leaves me gasping. And then, just like that, she's gone. And I can't even feel that she's there at all."

She hadn't meant to tell him so much. He nodded sympathetically and then admitted, "I feel Fente all the time. Like a thread that tugs at my mind. I know when she's hunting, when she's feeding . . . that's what she's doing now. Some sort of mountain goat; she doesn't like how his wool tastes." He smiled fondly at his dragon's quirkiness, and then, as he glanced back at Thymara, his smiled faded. "Sorry. I didn't mean to rub salt in the wound. I don't know why Sintara treats you so badly. She's just so arrogant. So cruel. You're a good keeper, Thymara. You always kept her well groomed and well fed. You did better than most at that, at feeding her. I don't know why she didn't love you."

Her feelings must have shown on her face, for he abruptly said, "Sorry. I always say the wrong thing to you, even when I think I'm stating the obvious. I guess I didn't need to say that. Sorry."

"I think she does love me," Thymara said stiffly. "As much as dragons can love their keepers. Well, perhaps *values* is a better word. I know she doesn't like it when I groom one of the other dragons."

"That's jealousy. Not love," Tats said.

Thymara said nothing. It was getting dangerously close to a prickly topic. Instead, she walked a bit faster and chose the steepest trail up the ridge. "This is the shortest path," she said, although he hadn't voiced an objection. "I like to get as high as I can, and then hunt looking down on the deer. They don't seem as aware of me when I'm above them."

"It's a plan," Tats agreed, and for a time the climb took all their breath.

She was glad not to talk. The morning air was fresh, and the day would have been cold if she had not been putting so much effort into the climb. The rain remained light, and the budding branches of the willows caught some of it before it touched them. They reached the crest of the ridge, and she led them upriver. When she struck a game trail she had not followed before, she took it. She had decided, without consulting Tats, that they needed to range farther than usual if they were to find any sizable game. She intended to follow the ridge line, scouting new hunting territory as well as, she hoped, bringing home a large kill today.

Silence had enveloped them since the climb. Part of it was the quiet of the hunter; part of it was that she didn't wish to talk about difficult things. Once, she recalled, her silences with Tats had been comfortable, the shared silences of friends who did not always need words to communicate. She missed that. Without thinking, she spoke aloud. "Sometimes I wish we could go back to how things were between us before."

"Before what?" he asked her quietly.

She shrugged one shoulder and glanced back at him as they walked in single file along the game trail. "Before we left Trehaug. Before we became dragon keepers." Before he had mated with Jerd. Back when romance and sexuality had been forbidden to her by the customs of the Rain Wilds. Before Tats had made it clear that he wanted her and stirred her feelings for him. Before life had become so stupidly complicated.

Tats made no response, and for a short time she lost herself in the beauty of the day. Light streamed down through breaks in the overcast. The wet black branches of the willows formed a net against the gray sky. Here and there, isolated yellow leaves clung to the branches. Under their feet, the fallen leaves were a deep sodden carpet, muffling their footfalls. The wind had quieted; it would not carry their scent. It was a hunter's perfect day.

"I wanted you even then. Back in Trehaug. I was just, well, scared of your father. Terrified of your mother. And I didn't know how to talk to you about it. It was all forbidden then."

She cleared her throat. "See how the trail forks there, and the big tree above it? If we climb it, we can have a clear view in all directions, and a good shot at anything that comes that way. Plenty of room for both of us to have a clear shot if we get one."

"I see it. Good plan," he said shortly.

Her claws helped her to make the ascent easily. The trees of this area were so small compared to those of her youth that she'd had to learn a whole new set of climbing skills. She had one knee locked around a branch and was leaning down to offer Tats a hand when he asked, "Are you ever going to talk to me about it?"

He had hold of her hand and his face was inches from hers, looking up at her. She was mostly upside down and could not avoid his gaze. "Do we have to?" she asked plaintively.

He gave her some of his weight and then came up the tree so easily that she suspected he could have done it by himself all along. He settled himself on a branch slightly higher than hers, his back to the trunk, facing in the opposite direction so he could watch a different section of trail. For a short space of time, both of them were quiet as they arranged arrows to be handy and readied their bows. They settled. The day was quiet, the river's roar a distant murmur. She listened to birdcalls. "I want to," Tats said as if no time had passed at all. "I need to," he added a moment later.

"Why?" she asked, but she knew.

"Because it makes me crazy to wonder about it. So I just want you to tell me, just so I know, even if you think it will hurt me. I won't be angry . . . well, I'll try not to be angry and I'll try not to show I'm angry if I am . . . but I have to know, Thymara. Why did you choose Rapskal and not me?"

"I didn't," she said, and then spoke quickly before he could ask anything. "This probably won't make sense to you. It doesn't make sense to me, and so I can't explain it to you. I like Rapskal. Well, I love Rapskal, just as I love you. How could we have been through all we've been through together and not love one another? But it wasn't about what I felt for Rapskal that night. I didn't stop and think, 'Would I rather be doing this with Tats?' It was all about how I felt about *me*. About *being* me, and that suddenly it was something I could do if I wanted to. And I did want to."

He was quiet for a time and then said gruffly, "You're right. That makes no sense to me at all."

She hoped he was going to leave it at that, but then he asked, "So. Does that mean that when you were with me, you didn't want to do it with me?"

"You know I've wanted you," she said in a low voice. "You should know how hard it's been to say no to you, and no to myself."

"But then you decided to say yes to Rapskal." He was relentless.

She tried to think of an answer that would make him understand. There wasn't one.

"I think I said yes to myself, and Rapskal happened to be the person who was there when I said it. That doesn't sound very nice, does it? But there it is and it's the truth."

"I just wish . . ." His voice tapered off. Then he cleared his throat and made himself go on, "I just wish it could have been me. That you'd waited for me, that I'd been your first."

She didn't want to know why, yet she had to ask. "Why?"

"Because it would have been something special, something we could have remembered together for the rest of our lives."

His voice had gone husky and sentimental, but instead of moving her, it made her angry. Her voice went low and bitter as venom. "Like you waited for your first time to be with me?"

He leaned forward and turned his head to look at her. She felt him move, but would not turn her head to meet his gaze. "I can't believe that still bothers you, Thymara. After all the time we've known each other, you should know that you've always meant more to me than Jerd ever could. Yes, that happened between us, and I'm not proud of it. It was a mistake. There. I admit it; it was a huge mistake, but I was stupid and, well, she was right there, offering it to me, and you know, I just think that it's different for a man. Is that why you went to Rapskal? Because you were jealous? That makes no sense at all, you know. Because he was with Jerd, too."

"I'm not jealous," she said. And it was true. The jealousy had burned away, but she had to acknowledge the hurt that remained. "I'll admit that there was a time when it really bothered me. Because I had thought there was something special between us. And because, in all honesty, Jerd rubbed my face in it. She made it seem like if I had you, then I was picking up her leavings."

"Her leavings." His voice went very flat. "That's how you think of me? Something she discarded, so I can't be good enough for you."

Anger was building in his voice. Well, she was getting angry, too. He'd wanted her to tell him the truth, promised he wouldn't get angry, but obviously he was now looking for any excuse to show her the anger he'd felt all along. Making it impossible to admit that, yes, she had since then rather wished it had been him rather than Rapskal. Tats was solid and real in her life, someone she had always felt she could count on as a partner. Rapskal was flighty and weird, exotic and compelling and sometimes dangerously strange. "Like the difference between bread and mushrooms," she said.

"What?" The tree branches creaked as shifted his weight. A distant scream sounded.

"Quiet! Listen!"

The sound came again. Not a scream. At least, not a human scream, and not a sound of distress. A sound of excitement. A call. The hair prickled up on the back of her neck and arms. The sound came again, longer, rising and falling, a wailing noise. As it started to die away, another voice took it up, and then another. She gripped her bow tightly and set her back firmly to the tree. The sounds were coming closer. And there was another noise, a heavy thudding of hooves.

Tats moved through the tree, clambering around until he was above her and staring in the same direction. She could almost feel the hoofbeats; a very large animal was running in their direction. No. Two. Three? She hunched down to grip the tree and peer along the game trail.

They were not elk, but they were perhaps kin to them. Antlerless, with large hummocks of flesh on their front shoulders, and taller at the shoulder than Carson. They were running flat out, throwing up chunks of forest floor as they came. They were too large for this game trail; they were running down it because they'd been driven. Low branches slapped against them and broke as they fled. The nostrils of the creature in front were flared wide and blood-red. Flecks of foam flew from his mouth as he came on. The animals behind him were as frantic. They breathed out shrill terror as they ran, and the stench of their fear hung in the forest after they'd thundered past. Neither she nor Tats had even nocked an arrow, Thymara realized in disgust.

"What were they . . . ?" Tats began, and then a long wailing cry rose and fell again. Another answered, and it was not distant now, but coming closer.

Thymara knew what wolves were. They did not live in the Rain Wilds, but even so, in the old tales that people still told, wolves were the ravening predators that made people shiver in the night. Her imagination, she now saw, had been insufficient for the task. They were huge creatures, red tongued and white toothed, shaggy and joyous in their blood-thirst. They poured along the game trail, five, six, eight of them, running flat out, and yet somehow still managing to give tongue to their hunt. It was not a howl, but a yipping, wailing call that told all that meat would soon be theirs.

As the intervening trees and branches blocked them from

sight and their hunting calls began to fade, Tats climbed down past her, and then jumped with a thud to the ground. She sighed and shook her head. He was right. After that cacophony, no game animal would remain anywhere in their vicinity. She followed him down and called out in annoyance, "You're going the wrong way!"

"No, I'm not. I've got to see this." Tats had been walking. Now he broke into a jog, following the same trail the elk and the wolves had taken.

"Don't be stupid! They'd be just as happy to tear you to pieces as those elk, or whatever they were!"

He didn't hear her or he didn't care. She stood a moment, wondering if her fear or her anger was stronger. Then she started after him. "TATS!" She didn't care how loud she yelled. There was no game left in this area anyway. "Carson told us to hunt in twos! Those wolves are exactly what he warned us about!"

He was out of sight, and she stood still for one indecisive moment. She could go back and tell Carson and the others what had happened. If Tats came back, it would seem childish tale carrying. If he didn't, she would have let him go to his death alone. Teeth clenched, she put her bow on her back and took an arrow into her hand as if it were a stabbing spear. She hiked her tunic up and tucked it into its belt and set out running.

Running was not a skill the tree-raised children of the Rain Wilds practiced much. She'd become a better runner since coming to this place, but it still felt almost dangerous. How did one run and remain aware of one's surroundings? How could she listen when her heart was pounding in her ears, or scent anything when panting through her mouth?

The game trail wound along the ridge, avoiding the densest brush and threading its way through the groves of trees. Tats, she discovered, was a strong and swift runner. She did not even see him for a time, but followed the trampled trail the immense deer had left.

When the game trail left the ridge and plunged across a steeper slope toward the river, she caught her first glimpse of Tats. He was running, bow gripped in one hand, head down, free hand pumping. She lifted her eyes and saw, not the hunt, but swaying brush that told of the fleeing animals. The whining excitement of the wolves carried back to her and infected her with something of their frenzy. She tucked her chin to her chest, tightened her wings to her back, and ran, bounding in leaps as the slope of the trail became steeper. "Tats!" she called again, but breathlessly and without carrying power. The trail suddenly twisted, heading up the slope again. She gritted her teeth and pounded on.

Lifting her head, she saw Tats ahead of her. He had paused at the crest of the hill. "Tats!" she yelled, and this time she saw him turn his head. He stood still, and much as she would have liked to slow down, or even to drop to a walk and catch her breath, she pushed herself to run up the hill.

As she reached his side, she found herself both breathless and speechless. Tats, too, stood staring down and across the hillside before them.

The hunt had gone on without them. The deer and their pursuers must have leaped across the extremely steep slope before them. The whole hillside was pocked with hoofprints and flung earth. Below them, the remains of an Elderling road paralleled the game trail for a short distance before turning toward the river. From their vantage point, Thymara could see that the road ventured out onto the ruins of a bridge, where it ended abruptly in jagged timbers and tumbled stone. Once that bridge must have spanned the river, a feat that seemed impossible now: she could glimpse the other end of the bridge on the far side of the river, similarly truncated.

Far below the ragged end of the bridge's arc, the river foamed and boiled. On the near shore, the road that once must have joined to the bridge approach was a succession of broken surfaces. Trees had encroached, and parts of the road had broken and slid down as the river gnawed at the shores. Of the roadway that should have led to their current village, there was no sign. Long ago the river had shifted in its bed to devour it, and then shifted back, ceding its place to tussocky meadow.

"They've got them cornered," Tats announced. "The wolves must know this place. They're driving the deer right out to the end."

He was right. Her eyes found first the fleeing animals and then, through a screen of trees, the wolves behind them. She glanced back at Tats, only to discover that he was sliding down the steep slope. He'd started out in a crouch, but soon sat down abruptly and slid. He vanished from sight in the rough brush that cloaked the lower slope.

"Are you STUPID?!" she yelled angrily after him. Then, cursing herself for a bigger fool than he was, she followed him. His passage had loosened the scree, and rain had made the earth slippery. She kept her feet longer than he had, but eventually fell over on one hip and slid the rest of the way, earth and brambly brush bunching up against her as she went down. He was waiting for her at the bottom.

"Be quiet!" he cautioned her, and then held out a hand. Grudgingly she took it and let him pull her to her feet. They scrambled up a short slope and suddenly found themselves out in the open on a section of the old road.

Nothing now blocked their view of the drama in front of them. The wolves were indeed driving the deer. Decorative stone walls framed the bridge's approach, funneling the deer out onto it. The lead animal, swifter than the other two, had already realized his error. He'd reached the end of the sheared-off bridge and now moved unsteadily, his huge head casting back and forth as he looked for some safe passage down. There was none. Far below him, the waters raged past.

One of the other animals was limping badly and had fallen behind. The second beast was still running, apparently unaware that they had been driven to a drop-off. As they watched, the pack of wolves poured out onto the bridge. Unlike their prey, they did not slow or hesitate.

The lagging animal was engulfed. It went down, a single shriek its only protest. One of the wolves clamped its jaws onto the staggering animal's throat, as two others seized its hind legs. A fourth jolted into its shoulder and it went down and then over as yet another wolf went for its belly. It was all over then, long legs kicking hopelessly as it vanished under its attackers.

The second deer, spurred by the scream of the dying animal, raced forward. Oblivious, or blinded by panic, it reached the end of the bridge and leaped off.

The lead deer had come to bay. The largest of the three, he rounded on his pursuers. There were only three of them now, for the rest of the pack were engrossed in the creature they'd already pulled down. The immense deer shook his head, menacing them with the memory of his antlers, and then stood tall, waiting. As the first wolf slunk in, the deer spun and kicked out with his hind legs, scoring a hit on the first wolf, but a second rushed in, to get under him and then turn his ravening jaws up to his belly. The deer hopped awkwardly, but he could not break the wolf's grip, and as he struggled to get away, the last wolf sprang for his throat. By then, the first wolf was on his feet again. Thymara was astonished when he sprang from the ground, landed on the deer's back, and then darted his head in to bite right behind his prey's head. The great deer staggered another two steps, and then folded onto its front knees. He died silently, trying to walk away even as his hindquarters collapsed. As he fell over, Tats let out a pent breath.

Thymara realized she still had hold of his hand. "We should get out of here," she said in a low voice. "If they turn around, there's nothing between them and us. And no place for us to run where they can't run faster."

Tats didn't take his eyes off the scene before him. "They'll gorge themselves and they won't be interested in us." He suddenly snapped his gaze skyward. "If they get a chance," he added.

Sintara fell on them like a blue thunderbolt, striking the thick huddle of wolves tearing at the first deer they had downed. The weight of her impact sent carcass and wolves sliding across the bridge deck to fetch up against the stone wall. She rode them, her rear talons set firmly in the carcass, her front claws tearing at the wolves as they went. By the time they slammed into the wall, she had closed her jaws on a wolf and lifted it aloft. Others, yelping in pain, sprawled in a trail behind her. None of them would hunt again.

A fraction of a breath behind her, Fente hit the other deer and the three wolves that had killed it. Her strike was not as fortuitous. One wolf went spinning off the end of the bridge, and her impact sent the carcass flying after him. The other died in a screaming yelp while the third, *ki-yi-ing* in fright, fled back the way they had come.

"Tats!" Thymara shrieked the warning as the creature galloped toward them, but in one motion he swept her behind him with one arm while brandishing his bow like a staff. As the animal came on, it grew impossibly large, until she abruptly realized it truly was that big. If it had stood on its hind legs, it would have been taller than Tats. Jaws wide, tongue hanging red, it raced directly at them. Thymara sucked in a breath to scream, but then held it as the terrified wolf suddenly veered past them and scrabbled up the steep slope, to disappear in the brush.

Belatedly, she realized she had a tight grip on the back of Tats's tunic. She released it as he turned and put his arms around her. For a time they held each other, both shaking. She lifted her face and looked over his shoulder. "It's gone," she said stupidly.

"I know," he replied, but he didn't let her go. After a time, he said quietly, "I'm sorry that I slept with Jerd. Sorry in a lot of ways, but mostly that it hurt you. That it made it harder for us to . . ." He let his words trail away.

She took a breath. She knew what he wanted to hear and what she couldn't say. She wasn't sorry she had been with Rapskal. She didn't think it had been a mistake. She wished she had considered the decision more coolly, but she found she could not tell Tats she was sorry for having done it. She found other words. "What you and Jerd did had nothing to do with me, at the time. At first I was angry about it because of how I found out, and how stupid I felt. Then I was angry because of how Jerd made me feel. But that's not something you could have controlled or—"

"Of course! We've been so stupid!"

She stepped away from him to look up at his face, affronted. But he wasn't looking at her, but past her, at the truncated bridge. She tried to see what had startled him.

Sintara was still there, feeding on deer and wolf carcasses. Fente was gone, as was the sole dead wolf that had been the only fruit of her strike. She'd probably gulped it down and taken flight. As she watched, Fente came suddenly into view, rising up from beyond the tattered end of the bridge. The slender green dragon beat her wings steadily, rising as she flew across the river. Halfway across, she banked her wings sharply and flew upstream, gaining altitude as she went.

"Why are we stupid?" Thymara demanded, dreading his answer.

He took her by surprise when he exclaimed, "This is what the dragons have needed all along. A launching platform. I bet that half of them could fly across the river today if they launched from here. At the very least, they'd get close enough that even after they hit the water, they could wade out on the other side. They can all fly a bit now. If they could get across, soak in the baths, chances are that they could relaunch from that end of the bridge and have a better chance of flight. And hunting."

She thought carefully about it, measuring the bridge ends with her eyes and thinking over what she'd seen the dragons do. "It would work," she agreed.

"I know!" He seized her in his arms, lifted her up against his chest, and whirled her around. As he set her down, he kissed her, a sudden hard kiss that mashed her lips against her teeth and sent a bolt of heat through her body. Then, before she could react or respond to his kiss, he set her down and stooped to pick up the bow he had dropped when he embraced her. "Let's go. News like this is more important than meat."

She closed her mouth. The abruptness of the kiss and Tats's assumption that something had just changed between them took her breath away. She should have pushed him away. She should run after him, throw her arms around him, and kiss him properly. Her hammering heart jolted a hundred questions loose to rattle in her brain, but suddenly she didn't want to ask any of them. Let it be, for now. She drew a long breath and willed stillness into herself. Let her have time to think before either of them said anything more to each other. She chose casual words.

"You're right, we should go," she agreed, but she lingered a moment, watching Sintara feed. The blue queen had grown, as had her appetite. She braced a clawed forefoot on the deer, bent her head, and tore a hindquarter free of the carcass. As she tipped her head back to swallow, her gleaming glance snagged on Thymara. For a moment she looked at her, maw full of meat. Then she began the arduous process of getting the leg down her gullet. Her sharp back teeth sheared flesh and crushed bone until she tossed the mangled section into the air and caught it again. She tipped her head back to swallow.

"Sintara," Thymara whispered into the still winter air. She felt the briefest touch of acknowledgment. Then she turned to where Tats waited and they started back for the village.

"This is NOT what you promised me." The finely dressed man rounded angrily on the fellow who held the chain fastened to Selden's wrist manacles. The wind off the water tugged at the rich man's heavy cloak and stirred his thinning hair. "I can't present *this* to the Duke. A scrawny, coughing freak! You promised me a dragon man. You said it would be the offspring of a woman and a dragon!"

The other man stared at him, his pale blue eyes cold with fury. Selden returned his appraisal dully, trying to rouse his own interest. He had been jerked from a sleep that had been more like a stupor, dragged from belowdecks up two steep ladders, across a ship's deck, and down onto a splintery dock. They'd allowed him to keep his filthy blanket only because he'd snatched it close as they woke him and no one had wanted to touch him to take it away. He didn't blame them. He knew he stank. His skin was stiff with salt sweat long dried. His hair hung past his shoulders in matted locks. He was hungry, thirsty, and cold. And now he was being sold, like a dirty, shaggy monkey brought back from the hot lands.

All around him on the docks, cargo was being unloaded

and deals were being struck. He smelled coffee from somewhere, and raised voices shouting in Chalcedean besieged
his ears. None of it was so different from the Bingtown
docks when a ship came in. There was the same sense of
urgency as cargo was hoisted from the deck to the docks, to
be trundled away on barrows to warehouses. Or sold, on the
spot, to eager buyers.

His buyer did not look all that eager. Displeasure was
writ large on his face. He still stood straight, but years had
begun to sag the flesh on his bones. Perhaps he had been a
warrior once, but his muscles had long turned lax and his
belly was now heavy with fat. There were rings on his fingers and a massy silver chain around his neck. Once perhaps his power had been in his body; now he wore it in the
richness of his garb and his absolute certainty that no one
wished to displease him.

Certainly the man selling Selden to him agreed with that.
He hunched as he spoke, lowering his head and eyes and
near begging for approval.

"He is! He's a real dragon man, just as I promised. Didn't
you get what I sent to you, the sample of his flesh? You must
have seen the scales on it. Just look!" The man turned and
abruptly snatched away the blanket that had been Selden's
sole garment. The blustery wind roared its mirth and blasted
Selden's flesh. "There, you see? See? He's scaled from head
to toe. And look at those feet and hands! You ever see hands
like that on a man? He's real, I promise you, lord. We're just
off the ship, Chancellor Ellik. It was a long journey here.
He needs to be washed and fed up a bit, yes, but once he's
healthy again, you'll see he's all you want and more!"

Chancellor Ellik ran his eyes over Selden as if he were
buying a hog for slaughter. "I see he's cut and bruised from
head to toe. Scarcely the condition in which I expect to find
a very expensive purchase."

"He brought that on himself," the merchant objected.
"He's bad tempered. Attacked his keeper twice. The second
time, the man had to give him a beating he'd remember, or
risk being attacked every time he came to feed him. He can
be vicious. But that's the dragon in him, right? An ordinary

man would have known there was no point starting a fight
when he was chained to a staple. So there's yet another proof
for you. He's half dragon."

"I'm not," Selden croaked. He was having trouble standing. The ground was solid under his feet; he knew that, and
yet the sensation of rising and falling persisted. He'd lived
too long in the hold of a ship. The gray light of early morning seemed very bright to him, and the day very chilly. He
remembered attacking his keeper, and why he'd done it.
He'd hoped to force the man to kill him. He hadn't succeeded, and the man who had beaten him had taken great
satisfaction in causing him as much pain as he could without
doing deadly damage. For two days, he'd scarcely been able
to move.

Selden made a lunge, snatched his blanket back, and
clutched it to his chest. The merchant fell back from him
with a small cry. Selden moved as far from him as his chains
would allow. He wanted to put the blanket back around his
shoulders but feared he would fall over if he tried. So weak
now. So sick. He stared at the men who controlled him,
trying to force his weary brain to focus his thoughts. He was
in no condition to challenge either of them. To which would
he rather belong? He made a choice and changed what he
had been about to say. He tried to clear his throat and then
croaked out his words. "I'm not myself right now. I need
food, and warm clothes and sleep." He tried to find common
ground, to wake some sympathy from either man. "My
father was no dragon. He was from Chalced, and your coun-
tryman. He was a ship's captain. His name was Kyle Haven.
He came from a fishing town, from Shalport." He looked
around, hoping desperately as he asked, "Is this Shalport?
Are we in Shalport? Someone here will recall him. I've
been told I look like him."

Glints of anger lit in the rich man's eyes. "He talks? You
didn't warn me of this!"

The merchant licked his lips. Plainly, he had not expected
this to be a problem. He spoke quickly, his voice rising in a
whine. "He is a dragon man, my lord. He speaks and walks
as a man, but his body is that of a dragon. And he lies like a

dragon, as all know that dragons are full of lies and deception."

"The body of a dragon!" Disdain filled the chancellor's voice and eyes as he evaluated Selden. "A lizard perhaps. A starved snake."

Selden debated speaking again and chose silence. Best not to anger the man. And best to save what strength he had for whatever might come next. He had decided he stood a better chance of survival if he were sold to the courtier than he did if he remained with the merchant. Who knew where the man might try to sell him next or to whom? This was Chalced and he was considered a slave. He'd already experienced how harsh the life of a slave could be. Already known the indignity and pain of being something that someone owned, a body to be sold. The sordid memory burst in his mind like an abscess leaking pus. He pushed it aside and clung instead to the emotion it brought.

He clutched at his anger, fearing it was giving way to resignation. *I will not die here,* he promised himself. He reached deep into the core of his being, willing strength into his muscles. He forced himself to stand straighter, willed his shivering to cease. He blinked his rheumy eyes clear and fixed his stare on the rich man. Chancellor Ellik. A man of influence, then. He let his fury burn in his gaze. *Buy me.* He did not speak the words aloud but arrowed the thought at the man. Stillness grew in him.

"I will." Chancellor Ellik replied as if Selden had spoken his words aloud, and for one wild moment, he dared to hope he yet had some power over his life.

But then the chancellor turned his gaze on the merchant. "I will honor our bargain. If a word such as *honor* can be applied to such deception as you have practiced against me! I will buy your 'dragon man.' But for half the agreed price. And you should count yourself fortunate to get that."

Selden more felt than saw the repressed hatred in the merchant's lowered eyes. But the man's response was mild. He thrust the end of Selden's chain toward the chancellor. "Of course, my lord. The slave is yours."

Chancellor Ellik made no move to take it. He glanced

over his shoulder, and a serving man stepped forward. He was muscled and lean, dressed in clean, well-made clothes. A house servant, then. His distaste for his task showed plain on his face. The chancellor didn't care. He barked out his order. "Take him to my quarters. See that he is made presentable."

The servant scowled and gave a sharp jerk on the chain. "Come, slave." He spoke to Selden in the Common Tongue, then turned and walked briskly away, not even looking back to see how Selden lurched and hopped to keep up with him.

And once again, his fate changed hands.

✧ ✧ ✧

Day the 25th of the Fish Moon

Year the 7th of the Independent Alliance of Traders
**From Reyall, Acting Keeper of the Birds,
Bingtown
To Detozi, Keeper of the Birds, Trehaug**

Enclosed, an offer of a reward for any new information regarding the fate of either Sedric Meldar or Alise Kincarron Finbok, members of the Tarman expedition. Please duplicate the enclosed message of a reward and post widely in Trehaug, Cassarick, and the lesser Rain Wild settlements.

To Detozi, Keeper of the Birds, a brief greeting from her nephew and an explanation of this new packaging for messages. I will write this directive on an outer envelope of fabric, and afterward stitch it shut and dip it all in wax. Within is a tube of hollowed bone, sealed with wax, and within that an innermost tube of metal. The Guild leadership insists this will not overburden the birds, but I and many other keepers have reservations, especially concerning the smaller birds. Clearly something must be done to restore confidence in the privacy of messages sent and received, but this seems to me a measure that will punish the birds rather than root out any corrupt keepers. Could you and Erek add your voices to the opinions given on these new message holders?

✧ ✧ ✧

CHAPTER FOUR

OPENING NEGOTIATIONS

W ho knew that a room this dismal could smell even worse than it looks," Redding observed with cheerless sarcasm.

"Do be silent," Hest told him, and pushed past him into the small room. It swayed alarmingly under his tread as he entered. It was not an inn room: Cassarick had no proper inns, only brothels, taverns where one might pay extra to sleep on a bench for the night, and accommodations like this, rooms the size of a birdcage rented out by working families as a secondary source of income. The woman who had taken their money was some sort of a tailor. She had assured them that they were most fortunate to find any lodgings this late in the day. Hest had tried not to snarl at her as she had taken the exorbitant sum and then sent her young son to escort them to the small, unlocked chamber that dangled in the wind several branches away from her own.

Redding had clung to the ridiculous piece of knotted line that pretended to be a handrail as they negotiated the narrowing branch to their lodgings. Hest had not. He would far rather have plunged to his death in the forested depths below than make such a timid spectacle of himself. Redding, however, had no such reservations. He had whined and gibbered with tittering fear every step of the way along the rain-wet bridge until Hest had been sorely tempted to simply push him off the branch and move past him.

Now he looked around the room and then grunted. It would have to do. The bed was small, the pottery hearth unswept, and he doubted that the bedding had been laundered since the last guest had used the pallet in the corner. It mattered little to him. He had a fine traditional inn room waiting for him back in Trehaug. He intended to conclude the Chalcedean's business here as quickly as possible, and then he had no doubt he could bribe some riverman to give him passage back to Trehaug tonight. Once there, he could begin his own business, that of tracking down his errant wife. True, she had left from Cassarick, but he saw no reason not to conduct his search for her from a comfortable room in Trehaug. After all, that was what runners were for, to be sent to ask questions and take messages to unpleasant places.

He gritted his teeth as he abruptly realized that was how the Chalcedean was using him; he was his runner, sent to an unpleasant place to deliver a nasty message. Well. Get it over with. Only then could he get back to his own life.

He had sought a rented room only for the privacy it would afford him for his meeting. The Chalcedean villain back in Bingtown had emphasized, over and over, that he must be more than discreet in these meetings and that the "message" must be delivered in private. The process for setting up the meeting had certainly been ridiculous in the number of steps it required, for it had involved leaving a written message at an inn in Trehaug, waiting for a response, and then obediently visiting a certain lift operator in the same city to ask for a recommendation for a room here in Cassarick. He had assumed the fellow would have had the sense to pick a decent place. Instead, he had been directed here. His only piece of good fortune had been that, by great coincidence, the impervious boat was also moving to Cassarick on the same day. He had not had to completely vacate his cabin there.

He set down his modest pack and watched Redding lower his larger case to the floor. His traveling companion straightened up with a martyred groan. "Well. Here we are. Now what? Are you ready to share a bit more with me about this mysterious trading partner of yours and the reason for his need for absolute confidentiality?"

It had not suited Hest to betray too much of his mission to Redding. He had explained their journey as a trading trip with the unfortunate extra mission of resolving the situation of his vanished wife. He had not mentioned Sedric's name; Redding was irrationally jealous of the man. There was no sense in provoking him with it right now; he'd save it until such an outburst would be more amusing and to his advantage. Jealousy truly spurred Redding's efforts to be entertaining.

Of the Chalcedean blackguard, he had said nothing, letting Redding assume that all their furtive messages and odd contacts had to do with extremely valuable Elderling merchandise. The mystery had excited Redding, and it had been enjoyable to thwart his efforts at questioning him. Nor had Hest mentioned the possibility that, if his mission succeeded perfectly, he'd be establishing a rather large claim to Kelsingra. No sense in stimulating the little man's greed too much. He'd reveal all at the proper moment, creating a tale of Trader cleverness that Redding would bark and bray all over Bingtown.

Since Hest had arrived in the Rain Wilds every bit of news he had heard had convinced him that such a Kelsingra claim would mean wealth beyond imagining. Trehaug had been buzzing with secondhand rumors about Leftrin's visit and precipitous departure. There were rumors that the expedition had formed an alliance with the Khuprus family; certainly the captain of the *Tarman* had freely relied on their credit to restock his ship. Leftrin had flung accusations of treason and broken contracts and then fled Cassarick without his money. That made no sense. Unless, of course, there was so much money to be made from another trip up the river that his pay from the Council no longer mattered to him. Now there was a thought.

Most of the small vessels that had tried to follow the *Tarman* had since returned, but one ship, twin to the one that Hest had traveled on, had not come back. Sunk in the river or still in pursuit, he wondered. If that ship could follow and survive the trip, then so could the vessel he had come on. He wondered how much it would cost him to hire it for a journey to Kelsingra. In Bingtown, the captain had been surly and secretive as if he did not even want to sell Hest passage to Trehaug. Hest had had to bundle Redding aboard at the last minute when the captain was so eager to leave that Hest could push the issue of an extra passenger through. The captain might not be open to a trip farther up the river. But the captain of a ship was often not the owner. Perhaps the owners would be bold enough to speculate, perhaps to make the voyage for an offer of one-tenth of whatever share in the city it ultimately gained for Hest?

So far he had not mentioned his possible claim to anyone. Only two Traders had dared to ask him if his visit to the Rain Wilds was in connection with his vanished wife. He'd stared them down. No sense in saying anything to anyone that might prompt them to come sniffing after the fortune that was rightfully his. Then he pushed that consideration from his mind. Much as he longed to distract himself from the business at hand, he knew he must finish it first before pursuing his own interest. Finish it and be done with the damned Chalcedean.

So, "Now we wait," he announced, gingerly taking a seat in the only chair in the room, a contraption woven of dried vines. A rather flat cushion was the only protection for his bottom, and the drape of canvas on the back added little or no comfort. But at least he could rest his legs after the interminable stairs. Redding looked around the room in vain and then, with a groan, squatted on the low bedstead, his knees jutting up uncomfortably. He crossed his arms on them and leaned forward, looking grumpy.

"Wait for what?"

"Well, I should have said that *I* wait. I'm afraid that my first meeting must be conducted in an extremely confidential manner. If all goes well, then soon I will receive a visit from a fellow responding to the note you left with Innkeeper Drost at the Frog and Oar Tavern in Trehaug. I will deliver certain items to him. In the meanwhile, you, dear fellow, should go out and amuse yourself for a time. When my business is concluded, I'll ask our landlady to send her boy for you."

Redding sat up straighter, and glints of dismay came into his eyes. "Amuse myself? In this monkey village? Where, I ask you? It's getting dark, these tree branches they call paths are becoming slippery, and you want me to go out and wander about on my own? How will you send a boy for me when you won't know where I am? Hest, really, this is too much! We've come on this ridiculous journey together, and up to now, I've done it all your way, climbing through trees, dropping off secret notes in filthy taverns, and even toting that box for you as if I were some kind of treetop donkey! I am hungry, wet through, chilled to the bone, and you want me to go back out in this foul weather?" He lunged to his feet and attempted to pace the small room angrily. He looked more like a dog turning round and round before settling to sleep. His movements made the room sway. He halted, looking dizzy and angry. Hest watched his fury build to the popping point.

"I don't think your business is 'confidential.' I think you don't trust me. I am not going to be your lapdog the way Sedric was, dependent on you for everything, never making a move on my own! If you want my company, Hest, you'll have to respect me. I came on this jaunt with the aim of acquiring Rain Wild goods, as an independent trader. I brought my own funds for that purpose. I had thought that as we had become such good friends, I could avail myself of some of your business contacts as well. Not to compete with you or bid against you for anything you wanted, but only to make small investments of my own, in items you found unworthy of your time. And now that I am here and have come all this way and served you like a runner-boy, you intend to dismiss me as if I were some sort of brainless lackey or servant. Well, it won't do, Hest Finbok. It won't do at all."

The chair was very uncomfortable. And he was as chilled and weary as Redding. Sedric would have had the good sense not to pick a quarrel with him at a time like this. Hest regarded the pink-cheeked man with his lower lip jutting like a petulant child, puffing away like a pug-nosed dog, and, at that moment, seriously considered abandoning him there in Cassarick. Let him see just how well he managed as an "independent trader."

Then a far more appealing plan occurred to him.

"You're right, Redding." At this concession, the man looked so startled that Hest was hard put to keep from laughing. But he put a serious expression on his face and continued, "Let me show my confidence in you quite clearly. I'm going to put you in charge of this meeting, and leave you to it. The men you will meet today represent some powerful trading interests. You may be a bit surprised to discover they are from Chalced—"

"Chalcedean traders? Here in the Rain Wilds?" Redding was indeed shocked.

Hest raised his brows. "Well, certainly you know that I've made trading trips to Chalced, so you must know I've contacts there. And three Chalcedean trading houses have established offices in Bingtown since the end of our hostilities with them. Indeed, I've heard several members of the Bingtown Traders' Council say that they believed establishing trade relations with Chalced may be our best path to a lasting peace with them. When economic goals and benefits align, countries seldom go to war."

Hest spoke smoothly. Redding's brow was wrinkled, but he was nodding. Hest made the leap, trusting that Redding would accept whatever he said now. "So it should be no surprise to you that some Chalcedean trading concerns have been making efforts to establish connections here in the Rain Wilds. There are, of course, backward elements that frown on such things. That is our reason for keeping the negotiations absolutely confidential. One of the individuals, Begasti Cored, you may recognize. He had made several journeys to Bingtown, before transferring his operation here to Cassarick. The other fellow, Sinad Arich, I have not met before. But he comes to me, of course, with the best credentials and references. I, that is *we,* have been entrusted with messages from home for both these gentlemen. Gifts, as it were, in the form of two small boxes inside the very case you have handled so conscientiously for me since we left Bingtown." Hest leaned forward and lowered his voice. "These gifts and the message that accompanies them come from someone very close to power in Chalced. Begasti Cored will perhaps be expecting me, though in the past Sedric was his contact. And the message we must deliver has to do with goods that Sedric promised to deliver to him. And has not, of course. So you see how delicate a position we are in, do you not? We must deliver the message and the gift, and encourage our Chalcedean counterparts to contact Sedric, if indeed they have any means of doing so, and impress on him the utmost importance of delivering his promised goods quickly."

Hest took in a deep breath through his nostrils and then confided to Redding, "I fear Sedric's failure to keep his end of the bargain has reflected very badly on me. A large part of my willingness to undergo the rigors of this journey was due to my need to retrieve my reputation! One of the things I need to request from Begasti Cored is a signed statement that his agreement was solely with Sedric, and not with me. And if he has the original document, well, having him surrender that to us would be even better."

Hest's thoughts were racing as he marveled at the brilliance of his inspiration. Redding would do the dirty work for him. Having Redding ask Cored for such a statement might free Hest from the Chalcedean's attention. And if there were any repercussions from meeting with Chalcedeans in Rain Wild territory, they would fall on Redding, not him. If need be, he could disavow any knowledge of the transaction. After all, it had been Redding who had taken the message to the tavern. Let him finish the errand, and leave Hest well clear of any later accusations of treason.

Redding was still nodding, his eyes alight with interest. The unusual aspects of the transaction had seized his imagination. Hest took a long breath, trying to evaluate if his plan had any flaws. True, the Chalcedean had told him to deliver the message himself, but how would he know he had not? It would be all right. And it would serve Redding right for him to be the one who was there when the Chalcedeans opened their grim little tokens. Let him see just what demanding a share of Hest's business would gain him. He found a smile for Redding and leaned forward confidentially. "I know that you compare yourself to Sedric and wonder if I am satisfied with you. Well, I will let you prove your worth to me now. Correct Sedric's errors in our dealings with these men, and you will clearly prove your superiority to him. I think you are worthy of this sort of trust, Redding. And having you demand it of me proves to me that you have the teeth to be a Trader and partner to me."

Redding's cheeks had grown pinker and pinker. Beads of sweat had started on his brow, and he was breathing through his mouth now. "The message for them? Is it with the boxes?" He asked the questions eagerly.

Hest shook his head. "No, it is to be delivered by you. This is what you are to say." He cleared his throat and the memorized words came easily. "Your eldest sons send you greetings. They are prospering in the Duke's care. This is not something that every member of your families can say, but for your eldest sons, it is still true. For it to remain true, all you must do is complete your mission to prove your loyalty to the Duke. These tokens are sent to you to remind you that the promised shipment from you is still eagerly awaited. The Duke wishes you to do your utmost to see that it arrives swiftly."

Redding opened his eyes wide. "Must I use those exact words?"

Hest considered for a moment. "Yes. You must. Have you paper and ink? I'll dictate them and you can read them if you cannot memorize them quickly."

"I've, well, not with me, no, but . . . say it again. I can memorize it, or come close enough as will make no difference. The Duke? Sweet Sa, the Duke of Chalced! Oh, Hest, that is a high connection indeed! We do tread a fine line here, and now I understand all your calls for discretion. I won't fail you, my friend. I truly will not fail you in this! Oh, sweet Sa, my heart is pounding to think of it! But where will you be? Cannot you simply remain here and be the one to give the message?"

Hest cocked his head at him. "But I've told you, the meeting was to be highly confidential. They are expecting one man to be here, not two. I will step out for a time, find a hot cup of tea for myself or some sort of amusement while you conduct this bit of business." He paused and then asked abruptly, "Surely that was what you wanted?"

"Well, no, I never meant to drive you away from your own—"

"No, none of that now, no!" Hest interrupted Redding's apologetic stuttering. "No regrets! You've drawn a line with me, and I respect you for that. I'll just step out and give you some time to try your wings with this. But before I go, I'll repeat the message one more time for you."

THEY SPOTTED THE first dragon when Leftrin knew they were still at least three days from Kelsingra. The ship had alerted him to it, not in any overt way, but as a sudden shivering that ran up Leftrin's spine and ended in a prickling on his scalp. He'd scratched his head, turned his eyes skyward to see if Tarman was warning him of an approaching squall, and seen instead a tiny chip of sapphire floating against the gray cloud cover.

It vanished, and for a moment he thought it had been an illusion. Then it appeared again, first as a pale blue opal, winking at him through a haze of cloud, and then abruptly as a sparkling blue . . . "Dragon!" he shouted, startling everyone, as he pointed skyward.

Hennesey was suddenly beside him. All knew he was the keenest eyed of the crew, and he proved it when he asserted, "It's Sintara! See the gold-and-white tracery on her wings? She's learned to fly!"

"I'm lucky I can make out it's a dragon," Leftrin grumbled good-naturedly. He could not keep the grin from his face. So. The dragons were flying now, or at least one was. The elation he felt surprised him; he was as proud as a father watching a child's first steps. "I wonder if the others are flying, too."

Hennesey had no chance to reply.

"Can you call to her? Signal to her that we need her?" Reyn shouted the question as he pounded down the deck to Leftrin's side. Terrible hope lit his face.

"No." Leftrin offered him no lies. "And even if we could, there's no place along this stretch where she could alight. Still, it's good to see her, Khuprus. Take heart from that. We're only a few days out from Kelsingra now. Soon, very soon, we'll be where there are dragons, and perhaps we can get the help your boy needs."

"You are sure that Tarman can go no faster?"

It was another familiar question, and much as the captain sympathized with the young man, he was tired of answering it. "The ship has his heart in what he's doing. Neither of us can ask more of him than that."

Reyn looked as if he might say more, but he was interrupted by faint shouts from downriver. Both men turned and looked aft.

The vessel from Bingtown still pursued them. Their lookout had just spotted the dragon, probably after wondering what the crew of the *Tarman* was pointing and shouting about. Leftrin sighed. He was tired of seeing the "impervious" ship off his stern. Time after time, Tarman had outdistanced it by traveling at night, only to have it catch up with them a day or so later. The speed the narrow vessel could maintain was uncanny. Leftrin suspected that the crew were risking their lives by rowing day and night to keep up with him. Someone had paid them very well indeed. Or perhaps they were treasure hunters, dreaming of making a fortune.

That would account for their tireless efforts. He wished with all his heart that they would give up and go back. Now that they'd seen a dragon in flight, it was a forlorn hope.

If Sintara was aware of any of them, she gave no sign of it. She was hunting, ranging far to either side of the river in slow arcs. Leftrin made a mental note to add that to his growing collection of notes, charts, and sketches of the river. If a dragon was hunting here, he suspected that it meant that there was solid ground back there somewhere. He could not imagine Sintara diving on anything that would require her crashing through layers of trees and ending in a swamp, nor that she would willingly dive on prey in the river. No. Back behind those layers of tall trees, there must be low meadows or perhaps even rolling foothills, precursors to the meadows and hills of Kelsingra. That would bear more exploring. Someday.

"Is she coming? Was it Tintaglia?"

Reyn looked down and away from the hope in Malta's blue eyes. He shook his head. "She's not our dragon. I think if she were, we could feel her. No, it's one of the youngsters, a blue female called Sintara. Leftrin says that even if we could call out to her or signal her, there is nowhere she could land. But we are only a few days from Kelsingra at worst now. We'll be there soon, dear. And Phron will be fine."

"A few days," Malta said dejectedly. She looked down on their sleeping child. She did not utter the words they were both thinking. Perhaps their boy did not have a few days.

In his first few days onboard *Tarman,* he had prospered. He had nursed and slept, wakened to stare at both of them intently with his deep blue eyes, stretched and wiggled and grown. His legs and arms had fleshed out to plumpness, and his cheeks had become round. A healthy pink had suffused his body, making him appear much less lizardlike, and they had both dared to hope that the danger to the child had passed.

But after those first few days, his improvement had faded. His sleep had become fitful, interspersed with long wailing fits when nothing could comfort him. His skin became dry, his eyes gummy. Reyn had schooled himself to endurance, though holding the screaming child for hours so that Malta could isolate herself in their cabin and get a bit of sleep had been one of the most maddening experiences of his life. A wide variety of possible solutions had been offered and tried, from wrapping him more securely in his blankets to offering him a few drops of rum to settle his stomach. Phron had been walked, joggled, bathed in warm water, rocked, sung to, left to cry it out, and wept over. None of it had affected his thin, incessant wailing. Reyn had felt hopeless and frustrated, and Malta had sunk into a deep sadness. Even when the child slept, someone kept watch over him. All feared the moment when he would exhale a breath and not draw in another.

"Let him sleep by himself for just a few moments. Come with me. Stand and stretch a bit, and breathe the wind."

Malta unfolded herself reluctantly, leaving Phron asleep in his basket. Reyn put his arm around her to guide her out of the canvas shelter and onto the open deck. The wind was chill, laden with the promise of more rain to come, but not even it could put color into Malta's cheeks. She was exhausted. Reyn took her hand, feeling the fine bones beneath the thin flesh. Her hair was dry, fraying out of the golden braids pinned to her head; he could not recall the last time he had seen her brush it. "You need to eat more," he told her gently, and saw her wince as if he criticized her.

"I have lots of milk for him, and he nurses well. But he does not seem to take any good from it."

"That wasn't what I meant. I meant for your own sake. As well as his, of course." Reyn fumbled through his words, and then gave up. He pulled her to him, put his cloak around her to shelter her, and looked out over her head. "Captain Leftrin told me that the last time they made the upriver journey through this area, the water got so shallow that they wandered for days trying to find a channel to follow. Hard to believe, isn't it?"

Malta looked out over the wide stretch of water and nodded. It seemed more lake than river here, reaching out in all directions. This section of the river moved more slowly, supporting more floating plant life. And the plants, at least, seemed to believe that spring was around the corner. New fronds twisted up from the water, waiting for warmer weather to unfurl into pads. Blackened strands of trailing weed showed green buds along their length.

"Once, Elderlings built grand homes along this water-front, with special places for dragons to enjoy themselves. Some of the houses were on pilings: this time of year, they would have been little islands. Others were farther back, on the shore. They offered all sorts of comforts to visiting drag-ons. Stone platforms that became warm at a dragon's touch. Rooms with walls of glass and exotic plants where a dragon could sleep comfortably on a wild winter night. Or so the captain says the dragons told him." He gestured at a distant rise covered with naked birch trees. Pink had begun to suffuse the white trunks, a sure sign of spring. "I think we shall build our mansion there," he told her grandly. "White pillars, don't you think? And an immense roof garden. Rows and rows of decorative turnips." He looked into her face, hoping he'd wakened a smile there.

His ploy to distract her with a daydream failed. "Do you think the dragons will help our baby?" she asked in a low voice.

He gave up his ruse. The same question had been torturing him. "Why wouldn't they?" He tried to sound surprised at her question.

"Because they are dragons." She sounded weary and discouraged. "Because they may be heartless. As Tintaglia was heartless. She left her own kind helpless and starving. She made my little brother her singer, enchanted him with her glamour, and then sent him off into the unknown. She did not seem to care when Selden vanished. She changed us and left us and never cared what it did to our lives."

"She is a dragon," Reyn conceded. "But only one. Perhaps the others are different."

"They were not different when I visited them at Cassarick. They were petty and selfish."

"They were miserable and hungry and helpless. I don't think I've ever met anyone who was miserable, hungry, and helpless who was not also petty and selfish. The situation brings out the worst in everyone."

"But what if the dragons won't help Phron? What will we do then?"

He pulled her closer. "Let's not borrow trouble from tomorrow. For right now, he lives and he sleeps. I think you should eat something, and then you should sleep, too."

"I think you should both eat something and then go sleep together in the cabin. I'll stay here with Phron."

Reyn lifted his eyes and smiled over Malta's head at his sister. "Bless you, Tillamon. You truly don't mind?"

"Not at all." Her hair was loose around her shoulders and a gust of wind blew a stray lock across her face. She pushed it back, and the simple gesture of baring her face caught his eye. There was color in her cheeks, and it suddenly came to Reyn that his sister looked younger and more alive than she had in years. He spoke without thinking, "You look happy."

Her expression changed to stricken. "No. No, Reyn, I fear just as much as you do for Phron!"

Malta shook her head slowly. Her smile was sad but genuine. "Sister, I know you do. You are always here to help us. But that doesn't mean you should not be happy with what you have found on this journey. Neither I nor Reyn resent that you've . . ."

Malta's voice tapered off as she glanced at him. Reyn knew that his face was frozen in confusion. "Found what?" he demanded.

"Love," Tillamon said simply. She met her brother's stare directly.

Reyn's thoughts raced as his mind rapidly reinterpreted snatches of overheard conversations and moments glimpsed between Tillamon and . . . "Hennesey?" he asked, caught between amazement and dismay. "Hennesey, the first mate?" His tone conveyed all that his words did not say. His sister, a Trader-born woman, taking up with a common sailor? One with the air of a man used to womanizing?

Her mouth went flat and her eyes unreadable. "Hennesey. And it's none of your business, little brother. I came of age years ago. I make my own choices now."

"But—"

"I am so tired," Malta suddenly interjected, turning in his embrace. "Please, Reyn. Let's take this chance Tillamon is giving us to share a bed and some rest. It's been days since I've slept beside you, and I always rest better when you are near me. Come."

She tugged at his arm, and he turned unwillingly to follow her. Getting her to rest was more important than quarreling with his sister. Later, they could talk in private. In silence he followed Malta toward the chamber they would share. It was little more than a large cargo crate secured to the deck. Within was a pallet that had served them alternately as a bed. He did look forward to rest and to holding Malta as she slept. He had come to hate sleeping alone.

It was as if Malta could read his thoughts. "Let her be, Reyn. Think of what we have and how it comforts us. How can we resent Tillamon seeking the same?"

"But . . . Hennesey?"

"A man who works hard and loves what he does. A man who sees her and smiles at her rather than grinning mockingly or turning away. I think he's sincere, Reyn. And even if he is not, Tillamon is right. She is a woman grown and has been for years. It is not for us to say to whom she should entrust her heart."

He drew breath to voice objections, then sighed it out as Malta lifted the latch on the door. The airless little compartment suddenly looked inviting and cozy. His need for rest and for holding her flooded up through his body.

"Time enough later to worry. While we can sleep, we should."

He nodded his agreement to that and followed her in.

✦ ✦ ✦

Day the 25th of the Fish Moon

Year the 7th of the Independent Alliance of Traders
**From your friend in Cassarick to Trader
Finbok, Bingtown**

The need for caution has increased greatly and with it my expenses. I will expect my next payment to be double what the previous one was. It must all be in coin and delivered discreetly. Your last courier was an idiot, coming directly to where I work and delivering to me only a writ of credit rather than the cash payment we agreed upon.

For this reason, the information I send you today is but the bare bones of what I know. Pay me, and you will know what I know.

The traveler arrived, but not alone. His errand does not seem to be what you suggested it would be. Another stranger offered me substantial money for information about him. I was discreet, but information is what I sell. Or do not sell, if that is more profitable.

The news from upriver is scarce. It might interest you, but for me to deliver it to you, I would have to receive hard coin, taken to the inn in Trehaug that was mentioned to you before and given only to the woman with red hair and a tattoo of three roses on her cheek.

If any of this is done otherwise, our business will be over. You are not the only one who would like to know the inside secrets of Trader news before others do. And some of those others might be very interested to learn what I know of your business.

A word to the wise is sufficient.

CHAPTER FIVE

TAKING THE LEAP

Getting the dragons from the riverside meadow to the bridge had taken more time and much more effort than anyone had expected. Sedric stood beside Carson and watched the last of the large dragons go down the steep slope to the old road below them. They had eroded a trough in the steep bank, setting off slides of mud, rock, soil, and branches that now spattered out in a fan across the old road below. Tinder was the last to go. By the time he reached the road surface, Nortel's lavender dragon was dirty brown from his shoulders down.

Only the two smaller dragons, Relpda and Spit, remained. "Nasty cold wet mud," Relpda complained.

"I tried to get you to go first, before the others loosened the slope," Sedric reminded her.

"Did not like. Do not like. It's too steep."

"You'll be fine. You'll slide down and then you'll be at the bottom." Sedric tried to reassure her.

"You'll roll like a rock and be lucky not to break both your wings," Spit suggested spitefully. His silvery gray eyes were tinged with red as they spun slowly. He seemed to relish the distress he was triggering in Relpda. Sedric wanted to hit him with something large. He smothered the thought before Relpda or Spit could react to it and tried to suffuse his thoughts and voice with calmness.

"Relpda, listen to me. I would not ask you to do anything that I thought would hurt you. We have to get down from here, and there's only one way. We need to slide down the hill, and then we can join the other dragons on the bridge."

"And once you're there, he wants you to jump off the bridge and into the water and drown." Spit sounded absolutely enthused with the idea.

"Dragon," Carson warned him sternly, but the little silver was unrepentant. "My keeper wants me to drown, too," he confided to Relpda. "Then he won't have to hunt as often to feed me. He'll have more time to jostle around in his bedding with your keeper."

Carson didn't respond with words. He simply lunged forward suddenly, his shoulder striking his dragon's haunch with the full force of his weight behind it. Spit had been loitering too near the edge, peering with disapproval at the long, steep drop. The small silver dragon scrabbled wildly to regain his clutch on the hillside, but succeeded only in loosening more earth. He lashed his tail, knocking Carson's feet from under him and then they were suddenly both sliding down the hill, fishtailing in the muddy chute, with Carson lunging and getting a grip of the top of Spit's wing. The dragon trumpeted wildly as they went, but it was only when Carson added a whoop of his own that Sedric realized neither of them was truly upset at the abrupt descent.

"They like it? The being dirty and going fast down the hill?" Copper Relpda echoed his confusion.

"Apparently," Sedric replied dubiously. Carson and Spit reached the bottom and rode a spray of loosened earth out into the road. Getting to his feet, Carson brushed uselessly at his clothing and called back up the hill, "Not so bad, really. Come on down."

"I suppose there's no help for it," Sedric replied. He scanned the hillside below him, trying to see if there were not an easier, safer, cleaner way to descend. The other dragons and their keepers were already making their way out onto the broken bridge. Carson waited for them, looking up at them. Spit had opened his wings and was shaking them out, heedless of how he spattered his keeper with mud.

"Don't take all day!" Carson called up good-naturedly.

"She is always the slowest," Spit complained.

"I'm coming!" Sedric shouted reluctantly. He turned sideways to the slope, resolving to walk at a slant across the steep face.

"No dirt!" Relpda replied stubbornly.

"My copper beauty, I don't like it any better than you do. But we must get down." He didn't even want to think of the upcoming challenge he'd face when he tried to persuade her to leap from the bridge in flight. He thought she could do it. All the dragons had practiced so earnestly of late, and most had shown some skill at gliding at least. He was almost certain that she could take flight and safely reach Kelsingra. Almost. He pushed his worry aside. Carson had been warning him about that. He could not doubt Relpda without making her doubt herself.

Moving to one side of the mud chute the larger dragons had created, he began a cautious descent, cutting across the steep face of the hill at a slant. He had gone perhaps five steps when his braced lower foot abruptly slid out from under him. He slammed hip-first to the ground, rolled onto his belly, and made a frantic grab for some nearby coarse grasses, only for them to tear free from the earth in his grasp. He was sliding. The suppressed guffaw from Carson and the wild trumpeting of amusement from Spit did not ameliorate his predicament. Twice his body almost stopped, but as soon as he tried to come to his feet, he slid again. By the time he reached the bottom of the slope and managed to sit up, Carson was at his side, offering him a hand up.

"That wasn't funny," Sedric began indignantly, but

the merriment dancing in Carson's eyes above his tightly pinched mouth could not be denied. Sedric came to his feet grinning, and he spent a few moments brushing gravel, burrs, and mud from his Elderling tunic and trousers. When he had finished, his hands were dirty, but the garments gleamed just as deep blue and silver as they had before. He looked up at Carson. The hunter's stained leathers were still streaked with mud.

"I told you that you should try these garments. Rapskal brought back plenty of them."

Carson shrugged sheepishly. "Old habits die hard." Then, at the disappointment in Sedric's eyes, he added, "Perhaps after we all transfer to the city. I feel a bit awkward, calling attention to myself in bright colors."

"You don't like them on me?"

Carson smiled wickedly. "I like them better off you. But, yes, I like them on you. But it's different. You're beautiful. You should wear beautiful things."

Sedric shook his head at the compliment even as it warmed him. Carson was Carson, and in the greater scheme of things, Sedric had no desire to change him. If pressed, he would have to admit now that there was a special rough attraction to Carson in his coarse clothing. There was something comfortingly competent in the way he wore the product of his hunts.

"I like them, too," Spit observed abruptly. "They make him smell like killing and meat. A good way to smell."

Sedric turned away from the knowledge that the silver dragon sometimes seemed a bit too aware of his innermost thoughts. He looked up the steep hill at Relpda, who had ventured to the edge and was looking down at them, shifting her front feet nervously as she did so. Save for Carson and Spit, the others had gone on without them. "Make haste, my copper queen, or we shall be left behind!"

"And you will be the last to leap, as you've been last at everything else!" Spit mocked her unfairly. "Come, copper cow, find one straw of courage and tumble down the hill to join us."

"Make him stop mocking her," Sedric complained angrily to Carson. "He'll make her angry and then I can't persuade her to do anything." Even at this distance, Sedric could see red anger sparking in Relpda's whirling eyes. She lifted her head, her neck arching and the frills along it standing erect with fury. Her colors grew brighter; her whole body gleamed with her anger like a copper kettle on an overheated stove.

"The last?" she cried out. "You shall be last, and mateless forever, you shiny toad!" She transferred her angry gaze to Sedric. "No mud!" she proclaimed, and abruptly whirled away from the edge and vanished from his sight.

"Now see what you've done!" he rebuked the unrepentant silver. "She'll go all the way back to the village and it will take me another whole day to bring her—"

He never completed his sentence. He heard her thunderous tread and looked up to see her race up to the edge and leap into the air.

"Run!" Carson bellowed; but Sedric couldn't. He stared up in sheer terror for her and for himself.

Relpda snapped her wings open and he cowered, hands over his head, as the little copper dragon fell toward them. Her wings spread wide and as he peered up at her in terror, he saw her beat them frantically. He closed his eyes.

A moment later, uncrushed, he opened them again. Carson was looking up, his mouth opened in astonishment. Spit's triumphant shout penetrated his brain. "She flies! The copper queen flies!"

Sedric strained to see what Carson watched. Then the big man put his arm around him and pointed out at the river. It took Sedric a moment to make sense of what he was seeing. His dragon. The day was overcast but still she glittered, copper against the dull pewter of the river's surface. Her wings were stretched wide, and she was in a glide. She was losing altitude, and Sedric could predict exactly where she would contact the river's surface, well short of the middle. "Fly!" he shouted, his voice a hoarse roar. "Beat your wings, Relpda! Fly!"

Carson's grip tightened on his shoulders. The hunter was silent, but Sedric knew he shared his agony. Down by the bridge, he could hear the voices of the other keepers raised in anxious questions. Dortean trumpeted wildly, and Veras echoed him more shrilly.

"FLY!" It was a roar of command, full of fury, and it came from silver Spit. The silver dragon capered up onto his hind legs, opening his own wings and beating them in futile frustration. "Fly!"

Sedric could not watch and yet he could not tear his eyes from her. He could feel Relpda's terror and her excitement at how the wind swept past her. He knew how she struggled to pull her body into alignment. Then, beat and beat and beat, she began to work her wings. Her leap from the embankment had thrown her into a long swoop, and she had had to do little more than outstretch her wings to ride the air. But now ancient memories were stirring. She had been a queen and once she had ruled these skies.

"Don't think! Just fly!" Spit roared at her. And then he took off in a lumbering run.

"Spit!" Carson shouted and set off in pursuit. Sedric could not stand still. He raced after them, feeling the wind on his own face and the rush of air past Relpda's outstretched neck and how the air over the moving water buffeted her. He forced himself to halt. He closed his eyes tightly.

"With you, Relpda. Fly, my beauty. Nothing else. Only flying."

Ever since he had drunk her blood, he had shared her awareness. Sometimes it had been merely distracting, and at other times it had been overwhelming. He had not stopped to think that being linked to him might be not just a distraction but a source of doubt for her. No doubts now. Nothing but a copper queen and the free air and Kelsingra in the distance, calling to her. He poured himself into her, willing strength to her wings and confidence to her heart.

"Spit, NO!" Somewhere in the distance, he heard Carson's voice. With steel resolve, he kept his focus as it was. Wings beating steadily now. The sound of the water rushing by below him was only a sound; it could not pull him down and under. Ahead, the gleaming stone walls of Kelsingra beckoned him. There would be warmth there, he promised

her, warmth and shelter from the endless rain and wind.
There would be hot water to rest in, to ease away the endless
ache of cold.

I come, copper queen. We rise in flight together.

The thought pushed into the mind they shared. It was
Spit. He had leaped from the bridge, pushing past the larger
dragons to be the first to make the jump. *I have caught the
wind itself beneath me and I come to you. We rise together!*

The beating of Relpda's glittering wings suddenly surged
to a new level. The rhythm was slower, the downward push
more powerful. She rose, the river receding beneath her,
and for a long giddying moment, Sedric shared her dragon's
view of the countryside that spread out below her. He had
never imagined that any creature could see such a distance
in such detail. A human standing upon a mountain might
see such a panorama but could never detect the elk drows-
ing on the hillside or the movement in the deep grass of
a meadow that was not wind but the passage of a herd of
small, goatlike creatures. Abruptly, he could smell them, the
musky male that led them and five, no, six females that followed him. Detailed information poured into his mind in
a way he had never experienced. When he abruptly broke
free of his contact with Relpda, he was not sure if she had
pushed him away or if he had fled.

He stood, blinking at the day around him, feeling as if he
had just awakened from an extraordinary dream. His vision
seemed hazed, and he closed his eyes and then rubbed them
before he could accept that his problem was merely a return
to ordinary human sight. He gave his head a shake and
looked around. The other dragons and keepers were all gathered at the end of the road on the bridge approach. Carson
was running back toward him, a strange look between joy
and terror on his face. Motion on the bridge caught his eye
and he saw orange Dortean suddenly gallop up the bridge
approach, pause for a heartbeat, and then vault off. As he
did so, he snapped his wings wide open, revealing markings
like large bright blue blossoms on them. He pulled his body
into perfect alignment, making himself an arrow. As Sedric
watched, Dortean did not drop at all, but rose on power-

ful strokes of his wings. On the bridge approach behind him, Kase capered and danced in wild joy at his dragon's triumphant launch. His cousin, Boxter, raced out to join him, pounding him on the back and laughing wildly as Kase pointed up at his dragon. Then they abruptly halted their celebration and fled to one side to be clear of Skrim as the long, skinny dragon made his own dash for the end of the bridge. He did not hesitate, but flung himself out, a second orange arrow in flight. His long narrow body undulated like a snake as he fought his way higher and higher into the sky.

"Sedric!" Carson's shout distracted him from Skrim's successful launch. "Sedric, did you see him? Do you see them now?"

His partner was suddenly in front of him, seizing him and lifting him off his feet, to whirl him joyously about. "Did you see our dragons?" he demanded by Sedric's ear.

"NO! Put me down, what are you talking about?" Sedric demanded. But when Carson dropped him back onto his feet, he had to hold on to his arm to keep vertigo from felling him. "What? Where?"

"There!" Carson declared proudly, and he pointed to the distant sky over Kelsingra.

Sedric's highest hope had been that Relpda would manage to land safely on the far shore. He had never imagined her spiraling up above the city. She tilted and tipped into each wild turn, and if she was not as graceful as a skylark, she was still as joyous in her flight. Below her, beating his silver wings hard in a frantic bid to match her ascent was Spit. He flew more heavily than she did and his effort was obvious, but so was his achievement. As the two men watched, Spit gained on her and then surpassed her. Abruptly, he dived down on her, and Sedric gave a useless cry of warning to his distant queen. But Relpda had seen Spit coming. At the last moment, she tucked her wings tight to her body and plummeted toward the ground, only to smoothly level out to a glide. She opened her wings and gained speed, shooting toward the distant foothills. But Spit had copied her and was not far behind her. He trumpeted wildly as he pursued her. As Relpda dipped from sight behind a far ridge, Sedric cried out, "Why does he harry her so? Carson, call him back! Do something. I fear he means her harm!"

Carson tightened his arm around Sedric's shoulders and then seized his chin to turn Sedric's worried gaze from the sky to meet his own. He smiled down at him. "City boy," he mocked gently. "Spit means Relpda exactly as much harm as I mean to you." Then he turned his head and lowered his face to kiss Sedric hard.

HEST WAS SURPRISED. The tea was hot and excellent, spicy and warming. The shopkeeper had given him a little table near a fat blue pottery stove. He had served Hest pastries with the tea, some filled with peppered monkey sausage and others with a soft pink fruit that was both tart and sweet. Hest did not hurry his repast. He wished to give Redding plenty of time to complete his encounter with the Chalcedeans, and lots of time afterward to contemplate his foolishness in pushing him. He suspected that by the time he returned to the dismal little room, he would have achieved two goals. The nasty messages would have been passed without Hest dirtying his hands with them, and Redding would be very submissive to his will once more.

Hest had extended himself to be charming and witty to the shopkeeper. As it always did, it had worked well. The tea man had proven affable, but busy. He'd passed a few pleasantries with Hest, but Hest's gambit that "I've just arrived on one of the impervious boats; I think they will transform travel on the river" had led to nothing. But a young woman with a tattoo of four stars on her cheek had been attracted to him, and she had proven very chatty. It had not been too difficult to steer the conversation. He'd taken it from impervious boats to liveships to the *Tarman* and the *Tarman* expedition. There'd been no lack of gossip. She knew all about Captain Leftrin's visit to Cassarick and his abrupt departure and even that he seemed to have formed a partnership with one of the daughters of Trader Khuprus. The daughter had not been seen since the *Tarman* left the docks and some speculated she had fallen in love with the captain and run off with him. There was gossip, too, about Reyn Khuprus and his pregnant wife, Malta. Rumors said that they had come to the Rain Wild Traders' meeting about the time that Leftrin appeared, and then he had given Malta Khuprus some sort of secret message and possibly an extremely valuable treasure from the Elderling city of Kelsingra. Neither of the so-called Elderlings had been seen in Cassarick since then. By the curl of her lip, he deduced her prejudice against Reyn and Malta, and once he implied that he shared her disdain, they got along famously and she was very forthcoming with all she knew. The Khuprus family matriarch had been reticent about their whereabouts or if the pregnancy had culminated in a viable child. The lack of information had become very noticeable, as had the haggard and anxious appearance of Jani Khuprus. The girl suspected the birth of a monster, kept hidden from all lest it be destroyed.

It had taken some little time for Hest to steer her away from the internal politics of the Rain Wilds and back to what interested him. He wanted gossip about Kelsingra and specifically his wife but could not ask for it directly. At last he maneuvered her back to the first time Leftrin had spoken to the Council about the expedition. She had not been there, but she went on at length about how "that Elderling Malta" had pushed her way into Council business, all on the claim of representing her missing brother, Selden, who in turn was supposed to speak for the dragons, as if the dragons had any right to representation before the Council! She suspected Selden's claim to know the dragon's will had simply been another Khuprus Elderling ploy to seize more power. All knew they dreamed of being king and queen and lording it over everyone else in the Rain Wilds. Her diatribe had become dreary to him long before she tired of it. Still, she did not leave until she had eaten the last of the cakes. It had cost him an afternoon and several coins to discover that no one seemed to know just what the *Tarman* had discovered up the river.

He glanced out of the small window. Dark. But as it had seemed dark to him since he had arrived, he concluded that it was a poor way to estimate the time. The dense canopy of the rain forest stole what little sun the late winter had offered. It was better to go by his personal inclination, and he believed it was now an appropriate time for him to return. He stacked silver coins in a short pile by his cup and then rose to leave. Outside the snug little tearoom, the wind had come up substantially. Old leaves, brown needles, and bits of moss rained down through the branches. It took him a few moments to get his bearings and make his way to a smaller tree, up two stairways, and then out on a limb to the tatty swinging structure that held his room. As he reached it, the rain that had been battering the upper reaches of the canopy worked its way down to his level. It fell in a very large collective drop, laden with the twigs and earth it had picked up along the way. He was glad he would not be spending the night here: he suspected the swinging of the chamber would be just as bad as being on a ship at sea.

He tried the door but found it blocked from the inside. "Redding?" he called out in annoyance, but got no response. How dare he! So Hest had played a bit of a prank on him, giving him the grisly rebukes to deliver. That didn't merit him barricading Hest out in the wind and rain. "Damn it, Redding, open the door!" he insisted. He hammered on it, but still got no response. The rain began to fall in earnest. Hest put his shoulder to the door and succeeded in pushing it a handbreadth open.

He peered into the dim room. "Redding!" His cry was cut short by a tanned and muscular hand that shot out to seize him by the throat.

"Quiet," commanded a low voice that he knew too well.

The door was dragged partially open, and he was pulled into the darkened room. He stumbled over something soft and heavy and fell to his knees. The hand released its grip on his throat as he fell; he coughed several times before he could drag in a full breath. By then, the door had been pushed shut. The only light in the room came from the coals in the small hearth. He could just make out that the object blocking the door was a man's body. The Chalcedean stood between him and escape. The body on the floor was still. The room stank.

"Redding!" He reached out to the body and touched a coarse cotton shirt.

"No!" The disdain in the Chalcedean's voice was absolute. "No, that is Arich. He came alone. Your man did not do too badly with him at first. He delivered the parcel, and Arich understood its significance before he died. That was necessary, of course. For him to have died with hope would have been intolerable after his terrible failure. Of course he had questions that your man could not answer, so I had to intrude on their meeting. He was so surprised to see me, almost as surprised as your man. Before I dispatched Arich, he said several things that make me believe that Begasti Cored is no more. A shame. He was cleverer than Arich and perhaps would have held more information. Not to mention that the Duke had so cherished the idea that Begasti would recognize the hand of his only son."

"What are you doing here? And where is Redding?" Hest had recovered himself slightly. He staggered to his feet and moved back toward the wicker wall of the chamber. The flimsy chamber swayed sickeningly under his tread, or perhaps that was vertigo brought on by the horror of the situation. A dead man on the floor of a room he had paid for; would he be blamed?

"I am doing here my mission for the Duke. I am getting him dragon parts. Remember? That was the whole reason I sent you here. As for 'Redding' . . . your man's name, I take it? He is there, on the bed where he fell."

In the gloom, Hest had not noticed the mound on the low bed. Now he looked and his eyes showed him details, a pale hand dangling to the floor, the lacy cuff dark with blood. "Is he hurt? Will he be all right?"

"No. He is all dead." There was absolutely no regret in the man's voice.

Hest gasped unevenly and stepped back until his hands met the woven wall. His knees shook and there was a roaring in his ears. Redding was dead. Redding, a man he had known his whole life, his on-and-off partner for bed play since they had discovered their mutual interest; Redding who had breakfasted with him this morning. Redding had

died here in sudden violence. It was incomprehensible. Hest
stared, and his eyes gathered the moment and burned it into
his mind. Redding sprawled belly down on the pallet, his
face turned toward him. The uneven light from the hearth
danced over the outline of his open mouth and staring eyes.
He looked mildly startled, not dead. Hest waited for him to
laugh suddenly and sit up. Then the long moment for it to be
some bizarre prank concocted between the Chalcedean and
his friend passed. Dead. Redding was dead, right there, on a
grubby pallet in a tiny Rain Wild hut.

Suddenly it seemed extremely possible that the same fate
could befall him. He found his voice. His words came out
hoarsely. "Why did you do this? I was obeying you. I did all
you asked me."

"Almost. But not quite. I told you that you were to come
alone. You disobeyed. See what you caused?" The Chalcedean's tone was the mild rebuke of a schoolmaster with a
pupil who had failed a lesson. "But not all was lost. You and
your merchant friend lured them out for me."

"So, you are finished with me? I can go?" Hope surged
in him. Get away from this. Flee. Get back to Bingtown as
swiftly as possible. Redding was dead. *Dead!*

"Of course not. Hest Finbok, fix this in your mind. It
is a simple idea. Your man Sedric said he would get us
dragon parts. We have not yet received what was promised.
Your part is over when you fulfill his agreement, which
in reality is *your* agreement, as he was your servant and
speaking on your behalf." The assassin lifted his hands
and let them fall. "What is so difficult for you to understand about this?"

"But I did all you asked. I can't make dragon parts just
appear! If I don't have them, I don't have them! What do you
want? What else can I give you? Money?"

The Chalcedean advanced on him. The scar on his face
was not as livid as he had been, but he seemed more haggard, both hair and beard gone ragged. "What do I want?"
He put his face close to Hest's and his hazel eyes lit with
fury. "What I do *not* want is my son's hand delivered to me
in a jeweled box. I want to take back to my duke the flesh

and blood and organs of a dragon so that he will return to me my flesh and blood that he holds hostage. I want him to reward me richly and then forget that he ever saw me or my family. So that I and my family can live in safety to the end of my days. Money will not buy that, Bingtowner. Only dragon's flesh."

"I don't know how to get that. Don't you think that if I could give you that, I would have done so by now?" Hest's voice shook. His entire body was shaking. Not fear, but something deeper than fear rattled him. He clenched his teeth to keep them from chattering.

"Be quiet. You are useless, but you are the only tool I have. I have done here what could be done with these wretched fools. Sinad Arich and Begasti Cored had failed; I was almost sure of that when I was sent to see what delayed them. So I have removed them from my path. I have also removed your Redding; you chose poorly when you selected him as your hands. He vomited when Arich opened his gift. When I entered the room, he very nearly fainted. Then he screamed like a woman when I killed Arich. This is the sort of man you choose as a companion?"

"I knew him all our lives," Hest heard himself say. He spoke numbly, scarcely able to comprehend that Redding was no more. Redding clambering up on a table to offer a toast. Redding trying on cloaks at their favorite tailor's shop. Redding, one eyebrow lifted as he leaned close to share an absolutely scandalous bit of gossip. Redding on his knees, lips wet, teasing Hest. Redding on his belly, eyes going dull. All their lives, and now Redding's life was ended. No more Redding. "I have no idea how to get dragon parts for you," he said flatly.

"I'm not surprised," the Chalcedean replied. "But you'll find out."

"How? What are you talking about? What can I possibly do?"

The Chalcedean shook his head wearily. "Did you think I didn't ask questions about you? Do you think I don't know all about your wife? And your connections here as the future Trader for your family? I brought you here to use you, to find out all that can be discovered of the dragons and your dear little woman. When we know, we will follow them—"

"No boat will carry us up the river!" Hest dared to interrupt.

The Chalcedean barked out a laugh. "Actually, it was all arranged before we departed from Bingtown. Did you think it all a coincidence that one of the new impervious boats should happen to be departing at such an auspicious time for you? That it had but one cabin left for a passenger? Fool."

"Then . . . you were on the same ship as we were?"

"Of course. But enough of the obvious. We have still a task here tonight, and that is to make things less obvious before we sleep."

"Less obvious?"

"You have bodies to dispose of. First, you must strip them of all clothing, the better to destroy their identities." The Chalcedean paused thoughtfully. "And it would be better if their faces were not easily recognized by anyone." He drew out one of his nasty little knives as he crouched by Arich's body. "You can be stripping him while I take care of this one's face." He did not turn as he added, "And we must be quick. This is but the first of our tasks tonight. Hest Finbok has some letters to write, notes offering a very profitable association with his family, but one of a most confidential nature. That, I think, will draw our hidden friends out of their lairs and to the edge of the precipice. Just where we want them."

◇ ◇ ◇

Day the 26th of the Fish Moon

Year the 7th of the Independent Alliance of Traders
**From Ronica Vestrit of the Vestrit Traders,
Bingtown
To Whatever Incompetent Bird Handler is
accepting messages in Cassarick**

The patron requests this be posted in the Bird Keepers'
Guild Hall.

*Once might be an accident. Twice might be
coincidence. Four times is deliberate spying. You have
been tampering with all messages sent to me from
Cassarick. Messages sent to me from Malta Vestrit
Khuprus have been received with seals damaged or
missing, as well as a very recent message sent from
Jani Khuprus. It is obvious to us that you are targeting
messages moving between the Khuprus and Vestrit
Trader families.*

*It is also obvious that you think us both stupid and
ignorant of how the Guild employs birds and bird
keepers. You will note that this message reaches you
attached to the leg of one of the birds from your cote,
birds you are personally responsible for. Although
the Guild has refused to name you by name, I know
that they now know who is responsible for at least
some of the tampering. I have filed a complaint
against you specifically, citing the leg-band marks
of the birds that have arrived bearing damaged
messages for me.*

*Your days as a keeper are numbered. You are a
disgrace to the Rain Wild Traders and to the family*

that bore you. Shame upon you for betraying your oaths of confidentiality and loyalty. Trade cannot prosper where there is spying and deception. People like you do damage to us all.

CHAPTER SIX

DRAGON BLOOD

H e looks sick," the Duke objected.

Chancellor Ellik lowered his eyes silently, humiliated that his duke would publicly disparage the gift he had brought, but he would bow his head and accept it. He had no choice in that, and it pleased the Duke to keep him aware of that.

The private audience room was warm, possibly stifling to some of those in attendance. The Duke had lost so much flesh that he felt cold all the time, even on a fine spring day. Fires crackled in both the large hearths, the stone floors were thickly carpeted, and the walls were draped with tapestries. Soft, warm robes swaddled the Duke's thin body. Still, he felt chilled, though sweat stood on the faces of the six guardsmen who attended him. The only others in the room were his chancellor and the creature he had dragged in with him.

The chained dragon man, the Elderling who stood before him, did not sweat. He was thin, with sunken eyes and lank hair. Ellik had allowed him only a loincloth, doubtless the better to show off his scaled flesh. A pity it also showed his ribs and how the knobs of his elbows and knees stood out. A bandage was bound to one of his shoulders. Not at all the glorious being that the Duke had anticipated.

"I *am* sick."

The creature's voice startled him. It was not just that he could speak; his voice was stronger than the Duke would have expected it to be, given his condition. Moreover, he spoke in Chalcedean. It was accented but clear enough.

The Elderling coughed as if to illustrate that he spoke the truth, the light sort of throat clearing one did when afraid that coughing hard enough to clear the mucus would hurt more than it was worth. The Duke was familiar with that sort of cough. The creature drew the back of one slender blue-scaled hand across his mouth, sighed, and then lifted his eyes to meet the Duke's stare. When he let his hands drop back to his sides, the chains on his wrists rattled. His eyes were human, in this light, but when he had first been brought into the chamber, his gaze had seemed lambent like a cat's, gleaming blue in the candlelight.

"Silence!" Ellik spat the word at his creature. "Silence and on your knees before the Duke." He expressed his frustration with a sharp jerk on the dragon man's chain, and the creature stumbled forward, falling to his knees and barely catching himself on his hands.

The dragon man cried out as he slapped the floor and then, with difficulty, straightened so that he was kneeling. He glared hatred at Ellik.

As the chancellor drew his fist back, the Duke intervened. "So. It can talk, can it? Let it speak, Chancellor. It amuses me." The Duke could see that this did not please Ellik. All the more reason to hear what the dragon man would say.

The scaled man cleared his throat but still spoke hoarsely. His courtesy was that of a man on the crumbling edge of sanity. The Duke was familiar with that sort of final clutching at normality. Why did desperate men believe that logic and formality could restore them to a life that had vanished?

"My name is Selden Vestrit of the Bingtown Traders, fostered by the Khuprus family of the Rain Wild Traders, and singer to the Dragon Tintaglia. But perhaps you know that?" The man looked up into the Duke's face hopefully. When he saw no recognition there, he resumed speaking. "Tintaglia chose me to serve her, and I was glad to do so. She gave me a task. The dragon bid me go forth, to see if I could find others of her kind or hear any tales of them. And I went. I journeyed far with a group of Traders. I went for love of the dragon, but they went in the hope of gaining her favor and somehow turning that favor to wealth. But no matter where we went, our search was fruitless. The others wanted to turn back, but I knew I had to go on."

Once more, his eyes searched the Duke's impassive face for some sort of sympathy or interest. The Duke allowed his face to betray no interest in the tale. The dragon singer's voice was more subdued when he went on. "Eventually, my own people betrayed me. The Traders I traveled with dismissed our quest. I think they felt I had betrayed them, had led them on a foolish venture that had used up their money and gained them nothing. They stole everything I had, and at the next port, they sold me as a slave. My new 'owners' took me far to the south and displayed me at markets and crossroads fairs. But then, when my novelty waned and I began to get sick, they sold me again. I was shipped north, but pirates took our vessel and I changed hands. I was bought as a freak to be displayed to the curious. Somehow your chancellor learned of my existence and brought me here. And now I have come to you."

The Duke had known nothing of that. He wondered if Ellik had, but he did not look at his chancellor. The dragon man held his attention. He spoke persuasively, this "dragon singer." His voice was rough, the music gone from it, but the cadence and tone of his words would have been convincing to a less susceptible man. The Duke made no response to him. Desperation broke into his voice on his next words, and the Duke wondered if he were younger than he appeared.

"Those who claimed to own me and sold me were liars! I am *not* a slave. I have never committed any crime to be punished with slavery, nor ever been a citizen of any place where such a punishment is accepted. If you will not free me on my own word that my imprisonment is unjust, then let me send word to my people. They will buy my freedom back from you." He coughed again, harder this time, and pain spasmed across his face with each rough exhalation. He barely managed to remain kneeling upright, and when he wiped his mouth, his lips remained wet with mucus. It was a disgusting display.

The Duke regarded him coldly. "Now I know your name, but who you are does not matter to me. It is *what* you are that brings you here. You are part dragon and that is all I care about." He considered his options. "How long have you been ill?"

"No. You are wrong. I am not part dragon. I am a man, changed by a dragon. My mother is from Bingtown, but my father was a Chalcedean, Kyle Haven. He was a sea captain. A man just like you."

The creature dared to knot his fists as he advanced on his knees. Ellik jerked on the leash he held, and the Elderling gave a wordless cry of pain. Ellik spurned him casually with a booted foot, pushing him over on his side. The creature glared up at him. The chancellor set his boot on the chained Elderling's throat, and for a moment the Duke recognized the warrior Ellik had once been.

"You had best find some courtesy, Elderling, or I will teach you some myself." Ellik spoke severely, but the Duke wondered if it was truly out of respect for him, or if he wanted to silence the creature before his "gift" could deny his bloodlines again. It didn't matter. The fine scaling, the blue coloration, even the gleaming eyes proved he was not human. A clever lie, to pretend his father was Chalcedean. Clever as a dragon, as the saying went.

"How long have you been ill?" the Duke demanded again.

"I don't know." The Elderling had lost his defiance. He

did not look up at the Duke as he spoke. "It is hard to tell the passage of time from inside a dark ship's belly. But I was already ill when they sold me, and sick when the pirates took the ship I was on. For a time, they feared to touch me, and not just because of my appearance." He coughed again, curling inward where he lay.

"He is down to bone," the Duke observed.

"Such, I believe, is their natural shape," Ellik suggested cautiously. "To be long and thin like that. There are some few images of them in old scrolls that depict them that way. Tall and scaled."

"Has he fever?"

"He is warmer perhaps than a man, but again, such may be the way of his kind."

"I am *sick*!" the creature declared again, with more force. "I've lost flesh, I cannot take a deep breath, and yes, I burn with fever. Why do you care to ask me such questions? Will you or will you not let me send word to those who would ransom me? Ask what you wish for me; I wager it will be paid."

"I do not eat the flesh of sick animals," the Duke said coldly. He fixed his gaze on Ellik. "Nor do I appreciate having one brought into my presence, to give off contagious vapors. Perhaps you meant well, Chancellor, but this does not fulfill your portion of our agreement."

"Your Excellency," Ellik acceded. He had to agree, but there was the slightest bit of stiffness in his voice. "I apologize for inflicting his presence on you. I will remove him immediately from your sight."

"No." The Duke gathered his wits carefully. The tiny sample of flesh that Ellik had given him weeks ago had been invigorating. For almost two days after he had consumed it, he had digested his other food well, and he had even been able to stand and walk a few steps unaided. Then the sense of well-being had passed and his weakness had returned. So the flesh of a dragon man had not cured him, but it had given him strength for a few days. He narrowed his eyes, appraising. The creature was valuable, and to disappoint Ellik too much at this juncture would be a serious mistake. He needed to accept the Elderling as a gift, to let Ellik feel he remained high in his favor. He knew that Ellik's strength was what currently supported his throne. But he must not give too much power over to the chancellor. He could not yet surrender his daughter to him in marriage. For once Ellik had got a belly on the daughter, what need would he have of the father?

The Duke pondered his options, taking his time, not caring how his guardsmen shifted in the heat or how Ellik's face darkened with shame and perhaps anger. He considered the Elderling. One could become ill from eating a sick animal. But a sick animal could be cured and become useful again. The Elderling's vitality seemed strong even if he was ailing. Perhaps he could be cured.

He considered putting the creature in Chassim's care. Among his women, her skills as a healer had been well known, and it would certainly keep Ellik off balance. At present, his daughter was securely confined and isolated. Daily she sent messages to him, demanding to know what she had done, to be treated so. He had not replied to any of them. The less she knew, the fewer weapons she had to turn against him. The Elderling would have to be confined in similar circumstances to keep him safe and reserve him for his sole use. And he certainly would not entrust his care to his bumbling healers. They had not been successful in healing him; why give them the chance to sicken this creature further? Pure jealousy that the chancellor had procured for him what they had not might lead them to poison the dragon man.

He nodded to himself as he fitted the pieces together. The plan pleased him. The Elderling would be put into Chassim's care. He would let her know that if she cured him, she might win her freedom. And if he died . . . he would leave her to imagine the consequences of such a failure. For now, he would not ingest any of the creature's blood until he was sure it was healthy. And if the Elderling could not be made healthy enough to consume, there was still the possibility that it could be traded for what he did desire. The dragon man had implied that he was valuable to his own kind. The

Duke leaned back on his throne, found it no more comfortable for his jutting bones, and curled forward again. And all the while the fallen creature stared up at him defiantly and Ellik seethed.

Enough of this. Be decisive. Or at least appear that way. "Summon my gaoler," he said, but even as his guards flinched at his command, he lifted a finger and gestured that Ellik was to be the one to obey his wish. "When he arrives, I will speak to him and tell him that this Elderling is to be confined with my other special prisoner and treated just as gently. I think that in time, he will recover his health and we will have a good use for him. You, good chancellor, will be allowed to accompany him and be sure he is put where he will be warm and comfortable and that good food reaches him." He waited a moment, giving Ellik time to fear that the Duke was simply going to make off with his exotic gift and return him no recompense. When he saw the sparks of anger begin to kindle, he spoke again.

"And I will convey to my gaoler that you are to have the privilege of visiting both my prisoners, when and as you wish. It seems only right to reward you with some privilege. Access to what will eventually be yours, so to speak . . . Does that seem fair to you, Chancellor?"

Ellik met the Duke's gaze and very slowly, understanding dawned in his eyes. "It is beyond fair, Excellency. I will fetch him immediately." He tugged at his prize's chain, but the Duke shook his head. "Leave the dragon man here while you fetch the gaoler. I have my guards, and I think I have little to fear from such a rack of bones."

An expression of uneasiness flickered over the chancellor's face, but he bowed deeply and then backed slowly from the room. When he was gone, the Duke sat regarding his prize. The Elderling did not look as if he had been severely abused. Starved a bit, perhaps, and his fading bruises spoke of a beating. But there were no signs of infected injuries. Perhaps he just needed to be fattened up. "What do you eat, creature?" he demanded.

The Elderling met his gaze. "I am a man, despite my appearance. I eat what you would eat. Bread, meat, fruit, vegetables. Hot tea. Good wine. Clean food of any kind would be welcome to me."

The Duke could hear some relief in the creature's voice. He had understood that he was to be treated well and given time to heal. There was no need to put any other thought in his mind.

"If you will but give me ink and paper," the creature said, "I will compose a letter to my family. They will ransom me."

"And your dragon? Did not you say you sang for a dragon? What might he give for your safe return?"

The Elderling smiled, but there was a wry twist to his mouth. "It is hard for me to say. Nothing at all, perhaps. Tintaglia does not act by predictable human standards. At any moment of any hour, her fancy toward me might change. But I think you would win her goodwill if I were returned safely to where she could eventually find me again."

"Then you do not know where she is?" The possibility of holding this Selden hostage and luring his dragon in to where it could be slain and butchered faded a bit. If he was telling the truth at all. Dragons were notorious liars.

"Held in captivity as I was, I was carried far from where I might expect to see her. Possibly she believes I have abandoned her. In any case, it has been years since I have seen her."

Not the most encouraging news. "But you come from the Rain Wilds? And there they have many dragons, do they not?"

The creature drew breath to speak, seemed to waver in his resolve, and then said, "The rumor of the dragons hatching went far and wide when it happened. I have not been home for a long time. I cannot say with certainty how the dragons that hatched there have fared."

Did the creature sense that there was a bargain to be struck? Let him think on it, then, but best not to let him know the Duke's life depended on it. He heard the footfalls of the gaoler and Ellik as they approached the doorway and nodded gravely to the creature.

"Farewell for now, Elderling. Eat well, rest, and grow

strong. Later, perhaps, we will speak again." He looked away from the creature. "Guards. Bear me to the sheltered garden. And mulled wine is to await me there when I arrive."

IN LATE MORNING, Tintaglia smelled wood smoke on the wind. The breeze had carried it a long way; nonetheless, it lifted her heart. Trehaug was not far now and the day was still young. The thought that soon she would see her Elderlings again lifted her hearts. Pumping her wings more strongly, she braced herself against the pain. It was endurable now that an end was in sight. She would summon Malta and Reyn and they would attend to her injury. It would not be pleasant, but with their clever little hands, they could search the wound and pull out the offensive arrowhead. Then a soothing poultice and perhaps some grooming by them. She made a small sound of longing in her throat. Selden had always been the best at grooming her. Her small singer had been devoted to her. She wondered if he was still alive somewhere and how much he would have aged. It was hard to understand how quickly humans aged. A few seasons passed and suddenly they were old. A few more and they were dead. Would Malta and Reyn have aged much?

Useless to wonder. She would see them soon. If they were too old to help her, she would use her dragon glamour to win others to her service.

As the afternoon sun began to slant across the river, the smells of humanity grew stronger. There was more smoke on the wind and the other stenches of human habitation. Their sounds reached her sensitive ears as well. Their chittering calls to one another vied with the sound of their endless remaking of the world. Axes bit wood into pieces and hammers nailed it back together. Humans could never accept the world as it was and live in it. They were always breaking it and living among the shattered pieces.

On the river, bobbing boats battled the current. As her shadow swept across them, men looked up, yelling and pointing. She ignored them. Ahead of her were the floating docks that served the treetop city. She swept over them, displeased at how small they seemed. She had landed on them before, when she was not long out of her cocoon. True, planks had split and broken free under her impact, and the boats tethered to them had taken some damage and some had floated away down the river still attached to a broken piece of dock. But that was scarcely her fault; humans should build more sturdily if they wanted dragons to come calling.

She grunted in pain as she banked her wings and circled. This was going to hurt no matter whether she landed in the water or on the dock. The dock, then. She opened her wings and beat them, letting her clawed feet reach toward the dock. On the long wooden structure, humans were yelling and running in all directions.

"OUT OF MY WAY!" she warned them, trumpeting the thought as well as impressing it on their tiny brains. *"Malta! Reyn! Attend me!"* Then her outstretched front legs struck the planking. The floating dock sank under her; tethered boats leaned in wildly and shattered pieces of wood went flying. Gray river water surged up to drench her, and as she roared in outrage at its cold and acid touch, the buoyancy of the dock suddenly asserted itself. The structure rose under her until the water barely covered her feet. She lashed her tail in disgust and felt wood give beneath the impact. She looked over her shoulder at a boat that was now listing and taking on water. "A foolish place to tie that," she observed, and moved down the dock that swayed and sank beneath her every tread until she emerged onto the muddy, trodden shore. As she left the dock, most of it bobbed back up to the surface. Only one boat broke free and floated away.

On the solid if muddy earth, she halted. For a time, all she did was breathe. A wave of heat swept through her, flushing her hide with the colors of anger and pain. She bowed her head to her agony and kept very still, willing it to pass. When finally it eased and her mind cleared, she lifted her head and looked around.

The humans who had fled shrieking at her approach were now beginning to gather at a safe distance. They ringed her like carrion birds, chattering like a disturbed flock of rooks. The shrillness was as annoying as her inability to separate any one stream of thought from any of them. *Panic, panic, panic!* That was all they were conveying to one another.

"Silence!" she roared at them, and for a wonder, they stilled. The pain of her injury was beginning to assert itself. She had no time for these chittering monkeys. "Reyn Khuprus! Malta! Selden!" She threw that last name out hopefully.

One of the men, a burly fellow in a stained tunic, found the courage to address her. "None of them here! Selden's been gone a long time, and Reyn and Malta went to Cassarick and haven't been seen since! Nor Reyn's sister Tillamon. All vanished!"

"What?" Outrage swept through her. She lashed her tail and then bellowed again at the pain it cost her. "All gone? Not a Khuprus to attend me? What insult is this?"

"Not every Khuprus is gone." The woman who shouted the words was old. Her facial scaling proclaimed her a Rain Wilder. The hair swept up and pinned to her head was graying, but she strode swiftly down the wide path from the city toward the dragon. The other humans parted to let her through. She walked fearlessly, though with one hand she motioned for her daughter, trotting uncertainly behind her, to stay well back.

Tintaglia lifted her head to look down on the old woman. She could not quite close her wing over her injury, so she let both her wings hang loose as if she did it intentionally. She waited until the woman was quite close, then she said, "I remember you. You are Jani Khuprus, mother of Reyn Khuprus."

"I am."

"Where is he? I wish for him and Malta to attend me at once." She would not tell this woman she was injured. Beneath the humans' fog of fear she sensed a simmering anger. And she was still hearing shouts and curses from the area of the flimsy dock she had landed on. She hoped they'd repair it sufficiently for her to safely launch from it.

"Reyn and Malta are gone. I have not seen or heard from them in days."

Tintaglia stared at the woman. There was something . . . "You are lying to me."

She felt a moment of assent, but the words that came from the woman's lips denied it. "I have not seen them. I am not sure where they are."

But you suspect you know. Tintaglia spun the silver of her eyes slowly while she fixed her thought on the upright old woman. She reached for strength and then exuded glamour at Jani. The woman cocked her head and a half smile formed on her face. Then she drew herself up very straight and fixed her own stern gaze on the dragon. Without speaking, she conveyed to Tintaglia that attempting to charm her had made her more wary and less cooperative.

Tintaglia abruptly wearied of the game. "I have no time for this. I need my Elderlings. Where did they go, old woman? I can tell that you know."

Jani Khuprus just stared at her. Plainly she did not like to be exposed as a liar. The other humans behind her shifted and murmured to one another.

"Half my damn boat's smashed!" A man's voice.

Tintaglia turned her head slowly; she knew how sudden movements could wake pain. The man striding toward her was big, as humans went, and he carried a long, hooked pole. It was some sort of boatman's tool, but he carried it as if it might be a weapon. "Dragon!" He roared the word at her. "What are you going to do to make it good?"

He brandished the object in a way that made it clear he intended to threaten her. Ordinarily, it would not have concerned her; she doubted it would penetrate her thickest scaling. It would do damage only if he found a tender spot. Such as her wound. She moved deliberately to face him, hoping he would not realize that her slowness was due to weakness rather than disdain for him.

"Make it good?" she asked snidely. "If you had 'made it good' in the first place, it would not have shattered so easily. There is nothing I can do to 'make it good' for you. I can, however, make it much worse for you." She opened her jaws wide, showing him her venom sacs, but he obviously thought that she threatened to eat him. He stumbled back from her, his pike all but forgotten in his hand. When he thought he was a safe distance, he shouted, "This is your fault, Jani

Khuprus! You and your kin, those 'Elderlings,' are the ones who brought the dragons here! Much good they did us!"

Tintaglia could almost see the fury rise in the old woman. She advanced on the man, heedless that it brought her within range of the dragon. "Much good? Yes, much good, if you count keeping the Chalcedeans out of our river! I'm sorry your boat was damaged, Yulden, but don't throw the blame on me, or mock my children."

"It's the dragon's fault, not Jani's!" A woman's voice from back in the crowd. "Drive the dragon away! Send her off to join the others!"

"Yes!"

"You'll get no meat from us, dragon! Get out of here!"

"We've had enough of your kind here. Be off!"

Tintaglia stared at them incredulously. Had they forgotten all they'd ever known of dragons? That she could, with one acid-laden breath, melt the flesh from their bones?

Then, from back in the crowd, the pole came flying. It was the trunk of a sapling, or a branch stripped of twigs, but it had been thrown at her as if it were a spear. It struck her, a feeble blow, and bounced off her hide. Ordinarily, it would not even have hurt, but any jarring movement hurt now. She snapped her head on her long neck to face her attacker, and that hurt even more. For an instant, she began to rise on her hind legs and spread her wings, to terrify these vermin with her size before spitting a mist of venom that would engulf them all. She resisted that reflex just in time: she must not bare the tender flesh beneath her wings, and above all she must not let her attackers see her injury. Instead, she drew her head back and felt the glands in her throat swell in readiness.

"TINTAGLIA!"

The sound of her name froze her. Not for the first time, she cursed the moment that Reyn Khuprus had so callously gifted the humans gathered in Bingtown with her name. Since then all humans seemed to know it—and use every opportunity to bind her with it.

It was the old woman, of course, Jani Khuprus, moving in a stumbling run to put herself between the dragon and the mob. Behind her, her shrieking daughter was held back by the others. She halted, swaying, in front of the dragon and threw up her skinny arms as if they could shield something.

"Tintaglia, by your name, remember the promises between us! You pledged to help us, to protect us from the Chalcedean invaders, and we in turn cared for the serpents that hatched into dragons! You cannot harm us now!"

"You have attacked me!" The dragon was outraged that Jani Khuprus dared to rebuke her.

"You wrecked my boat!" The man with the boat hook.

"You've destroyed half the dock!"

Tintaglia turned her head slowly, shocked to find how careless she had been. There were other humans behind her, humans who had come out of the damaged boats and from the shattered docks. Many of them carried items that were not weapons but could be used as such. She still had no doubt that she could kill them all before they did her serious harm, but harm they could do in such tight quarters. The trees that leaned over her would prevent an easy launch, even if she were not injured. Abruptly, she realized that she was in a very bad situation. There were other humans, looking down on her from platforms and walkways, and some were moving down the stairways that wound around the immense trunks of the trees.

"Dragon!"

She swung her attention back to the old woman. "You should leave," Jani Khuprus cried out in a low voice. Tintaglia heard fear in it, but also a pleading. Did she fear what would happen if the dragon had to defend herself?

"You should follow the rest of your kind and their keepers, who are turning into Elderlings. Go to Kelsingra, dragon! That is where you belong. Not here!"

"Elderlings. In Kelsingra? I have been there. The city is empty."

"Perhaps it was, but no longer. The other dragons have gone there, and the rumor is that the keepers who went with them are becoming Elderlings. Elderlings such as you seek."

Something in the old woman's voice . . . no. In her thoughts. Tintaglia focused on her alone. *Kelsingra?*

Go there! As Malta and Reyn have gone there. Go, before blood is shed! For all our sakes!

The old woman had caught on quickly. She stared silently at the dragon, projecting the warning with all her heart.

"I am leaving," Tintaglia announced. She turned slowly, deliberately back toward the docks. The men in front of her muttered angrily and gave way only grudgingly.

"Let her leave!" Jani's voice rang out again, and surprisingly, other voices echoed hers.

"Let the dragon go! Good riddance to her!"

"Please, let her pass, with no one killed!"

"Let her be gone, and let us be done with all dragons!"

The men were giving way to her as she moved toward the damaged dock. They cursed her in low voices and spat on the ground as she passed, but they let her go. Within, she seethed with hatred and disdain for them, and she longed to kill them all. How dare they show their petty tempers to her, how dare they spit at her passing, the puny little monkeys! She swung her head slowly as she passed, keeping as many of them in view as she could. As she had feared they might, they closed ranks behind her and moved slowly after her. They could corner her on the dilapidated docks and possibly drive her off into the cold swift river if she was not careful.

She loosened her wings slightly and steeled her will. This was going to hurt, and she would have only one chance. She studied the long wooden dock before her. Loosened planks sprawled at odd angles and yes, two tethered boats foundered there, listing at odd angles as they tugged at their moorings. She gathered her strength in her hind legs.

Without warning, she sprang forward in a great leap. Behind her, human voices were raised in roars of fear and dismay. She landed on the dock, and it gave to her weight. And then, as she had hoped, it recovered buoyancy and began to rise. Not much, but it would have to be enough. She flung her wings open, shrieked in harsh fury at the pain, and drove her wings down hard as she leaped up.

It was enough. She caught the wind above the moving river water and, beat by painful beat, rose into the sky. She thought of circling back, of diving on them and sending them scattering, perhaps even driving them into the river. But her pain was too great and her growing hunger stabbed her. No. Not now. Now she would hunt, kill, eat, and rest. Tomorrow she would fly on to Kelsingra. Perhaps one day she would return to make them sorry. But first she must find Elderlings to heal her. She banked and turned and resumed her painful journey upriver.

"It won't be long now," Leftrin said, and felt vast relief at being able to utter the words. He stood on the roof of the deckhouse. The wintry day was winding down to an early close, but he had sighted the first buildings of Kelsingra. They were nearly home, he thought, and then chuckled. Home? Kelsingra? No. Home was where Alise was now, that was clear for him.

The journey had been long but not nearly as long as his first trip to Kelsingra. This time he had not been slowed by the need to hold his boat to the pace of plodding dragons or to stop early every night so that the hunters might bring meat for the dragons and the keepers could rest their weary bodies. Nor had they wasted days in a shallow swamp trying almost in vain to find their way back to the true course. But even so, the thin wailing of the sickly infant had made each day seem to last a week. He was sure he was not the only one to have been unable to sleep through Phron's colicky cries. Looking at Reyn's gaunt face and bloodshot eyes, he knew that the baby's father had shared his unwilling vigil.

"That's Kelsingra? That scatter of buildings?" Reyn seemed incredulous.

"No. That's the beginning of the outskirts. It's a big city, and it sprawls along the riverbank and maybe extends up into those foothills. With the leaves off the trees, I can see that it's even bigger than I thought it was."

"And it's just . . . deserted? Empty? What happened to all the people? Where did they go? Did they die?"

Leftrin shook his head and took another long drink from his mug. The steam and aroma of the hot tea swirled up to join the mist over the river. "If we had answers to those questions, Alise would be ecstatic. But we don't know.

Maybe as we explore the city more, we'll find out. Some of the buildings are empty, as if people packed all their belongings and left. Other homes look as if people pushed back from the table, walked out the door, and never came back."

"I should wake Malta. She'll want to see this."

"No, you shouldn't. Let her sleep and let the baby sleep. It will all still be here when she wakes up, and I think you should let her get whatever rest she can." It would have shamed Leftrin to admit that he wasn't thinking of Malta so much as his own peace. He doubted that Reyn could wake her without disturbing the baby and setting off another long spate of crying. The child was quiet only when he was asleep or nursing, and he seemed to do little of either of late.

"Is that another dragon?" Reyn asked suddenly.

As Leftrin turned his eyes toward the sky, he felt a tingle of interest from his ship. He squinted, but the only color he could make out was silver. "When I left, only Heeby had made it aloft. The others were trying, but none of them were doing too well. It's one reason I was so startled to see Sintara a few days ago. Still, it doesn't seem likely . . ."

"It's Spit!" Hennesey shouted the news from the afterdeck. "Look at that little bastard fly! Can you see him, Tillamon? He's silver, so when he's in front of the overcast, he's a bit hard . . . there! See him? He just broke out from those clouds. He's one of the smallest and, to start with, one of the stupidest of the dragons. Looks like he can fly now; but even if he's smart enough to get off the ground, he's still a mean little package of trouble. When we get to the village, you'd best avoid him. But Mercor, now there's a dragon you'll enjoy."

Tillamon, her shawl clasped around her shoulders, shaded her eyes with her free hand and nodded to every word. Her cheeks were pink with the chill wind and excitement. And perhaps with something more? Hennesey had seemed more garrulous and social of late. Leftrin glanced at Reyn a bit warily, wondering if the Elderling had noticed that the mate was perhaps just a bit too familiar with the lady. But if Reyn had noticed, his objection was drowned by the sudden shrill wail of his son.

"Damn the luck," he said quietly, and he left the captain's side.

The effect of the baby's crying on the crew seemed a palpable thing to Leftrin. He wondered if it was because it also seemed to distress the liveship. A shivering of anxiety, probably undetectable to some of the crew members but definitely unnerving to him, ran through the ship. Almost as if in response, Spit dipped one wing to circle overhead, dropping lower with each revolution. Of all the dragons that could take an interest in their arrival, Spit was his least favorite. He was as Hennesey had described him: dim-witted when they had first taken the dragons on, and mean since he had acquired a mind of his own. His temper was uneven, and it seemed to Leftrin that he was the most impulsive of the lot. Even the larger dragons seemed to give him a wide berth when he was in a foul mood.

As he watched, Spit left off circling above Tarman and sped off downriver. Leftrin hoped he'd spied some prey and that he'd hunt, kill, eat, and leave them alone. But in a moment, he heard distant shouts and realized that Spit was now circling the Bingtown boat that still stubbornly shadowed them. Leftrin smiled grimly. Not the sort of prey he'd had in mind for Spit. Well, they'd been curious as to what had become of the cast-out dragons that had left Cassarick in midsummer. Let them have a good look at what one of them had become.

Spit descended another notch, tightening his circle so that no one could mistake the object of his interest. Leftrin watched in amusement tinged with alarm as the distant deck of the pursuit vessel suddenly swarmed with human figures. He could not make out what they were shouting. From the very beginning of their pursuit, they had kept their distance from the *Tarman,* never hailing the other ship or coming close to tie up beside them in the evenings. They had enacted that quarantine, not Leftrin, but he had chosen not to challenge it.

Now, as Spit circled ever closer to them, he regretted the decision. Regardless of their eventual intent, they were fellow Traders and humans. He wished now that he knew

who captained the Bingtown vessel and the temperament of
the crew. He wished he had seized an opportunity to caution
them against provoking the dragons. They were no longer
the earthbound beggars they had been.

"I never thought they would follow us this far up the
river. I thought sure we would lose them along the way."

Hennesey had joined him on the roof of the deckhouse.
When the baby had begun to wail, Tillamon had hastened
to see if she could be of any help to Malta, leaving the first
mate to recall his duties to the ship. Leftrin glanced over
at him. He'd known Hennesey since he was no more than
a scupper plug on the ship when Leftrin himself had first
come aboard to share that lowly status. Was there a light in
his eyes that had never been there before? Hard to tell. Right
now, he stared raptly at the drama unfolding downriver.

"Who could have predicted this? No one." Leftrin wondered if he were trying to evade responsibility. For onto the
other ship's deck had come a man who now assumed the unmistakable stance of an archer. They were too far away for a
warning shout from him to carry to the men on the deck or
the circling dragon. They could only watch disaster unfurl.

"Oh, don't do it . . ." Hennessey groaned.

"Too late." Leftrin could barely make out the arrow that
took flight, but he tracked it by Spit's response. The dragon
evaded it easily and then shot skyward, beating his wings
hard to gain altitude.

The fools on the Bingtown vessel cheered, thinking they
had warded off the dragon's attack. But as Spit reached the
top of his arcing flight, he trumpeted out a wild summons.
A strange thrill shot through the liveship; Leftrin saw Hennesey feel it as much as he did. Before either man could
comment, distant answering cries came from all directions.
Then, in less than a breath, half a dozen dragons, including
gleaming Mercor and shimmering Sintara, hove into view.
Some came from the city; some simply seemed to appear
in the sky as if the clouds had hidden them. Kalo, black as
a thundercloud and as threatening, shot toward the circling,
keening Spit.

"Like crows gathering to harry an eagle," Hennesey

pointed out, and in an instant, he was proven right. Instead of one dragon circling the hapless ship, a funnel cloud of avengers was forming. Leftrin was left breathless with wonder. How they had grown since last he had seen them, and how their ability to fly had transformed them! He felt awe that he had walked among such fearsome creatures without terror, that he had doctored their injuries and spoken with them. To see them now, glittering and gleaming even in the dimmed sunlight of the overcast day, transformed them from the crippled and wounded creatures he had shepherded into knife-edged predators of incredible power.

On the ship below them, men were bellowing commands and warnings to one another. Their archer had set an arrow to his bow and stood, muscles taut, ready to fire should any dragon descend within range. Leftrin could hear the dragons calling to one another, wild trumpets, distant rumbles of thunder and shrill cries.

"They're disagreeing about something," Hennesey guessed.

"Those dragons . . . can you call to them? Can anyone here persuade one to come to us?" Malta had joined them. Leftrin turned to look at her, shocked that in the midst of the dragons threatening the other vessel, she still thought only of her child. Then he really saw her, and his heart filled with pity.

The Elderling woman looked terrible. The colors of humanity had fled from her face, and the overlay of bluish scaling made the rest of her seem gray, as if someone had ornamented stone. There were lines by her mouth and under her eyes. Her hair had been brushed, braided, and pinned up. It was tidy, but it did not gleam. Life was draining out of her.

"I can't call them, I'm afraid. But we are close to Kelsingra, Malta. As soon as we arrive the keepers will be able to summon them. Even if we could call one here, it could not land and speak with us. Once we are off the river—"

"Dragon fight!" Hennesey interrupted them. From *Tarman*'s deck, there were shouts of amazement. Leftrin turned in time to see Spit diving on the distant ship. He seemed luminous, his silver sparkling like a tumbling coin, and by that the captain knew that his poison glands would be swollen and ready. Matching him in his dive was Mercor: as Spit swept over the ship, the golden dragon came up suddenly beneath him and knocked him off his course. The golden dragon beat his wings strongly, bearing the smaller silver up and away before tilting sideways and away from him, leaving Spit flapping wildly as he fell. As he went down, a pale cloud of sparkling venom shone. Just short of the water, the silver dragon recovered, but not well. He flew, his wings flinging up splashes at the tips, to land awkwardly at the river's edge. The venom fell too, dispersing as the light wind touched it, landing harmlessly in the river rather than on the ship. From the shore, Spit's vocalizations were savage and furious.

The crew of the other ship bent energetically to their sweeps. It was moving downriver as fast as the current and its oars could carry it. Overhead, the circling dragons took it in turns to feint dives at the fleeing boat, their trumpeted calls conveying merriment and mockery to Leftrin. After a time, he realized that the boat was scarcely their target anymore; they appeared to be competing to see who could dive fastest and swoop closest to it before rising back to join the others. Spit managed to launch himself back into the air, but he did not join the others. He flew laboriously, possibly injured from his collision, back toward the heart of Kelsingra. Leftrin continued to watch the Bingtown boat as the dragons harried it out of sight down the river. He waited, but even after it was out of sight, the dragons did not return.

"They've changed," Hennesey observed quietly.

"Indeed they have," Leftrin agreed.

"They're real now," the mate said. More quietly he added, "They frighten me."

✦ ✦ ✦

Day the 27th of the Fish Moon

Year the 7th of the Independent Alliance of Traders
From Keffria Vestrit, of the Bingtown Traders
To Jani Khuprus of the Rain Wild Traders,
Trehaug

Jani, as we both well know, there is no privacy to bird-sent messages anymore. If you have anything of great confidentiality, please send it in a packet by any of the liveships that ply the Rain Wild River. I have far more confidence in them than I do in the so-called Bird Keepers' Guild. I will do the same, save for tidings that must reach you immediately and thus must, unfortunately, be subject to spying and gossip.

Herewith, the bones of what you must know. My messages to Malta are going unanswered. I am gravely concerned, especially since she was so close to giving birth. If you can send me any tidings to put my mind at ease, I would greatly appreciate it.

Other information also too grave to delay sharing: I have finally heard from Wintrow in the Pirate Isles. You may recall I wrote to him months ago to ask if he knew anything of Selden. As is often the case with letters sent through that region, both my message and his response were greatly delayed. He had no tidings of Elderlings but was alarmed at gossip of a "dragon boy" exhibited in a traveling display of freaks and oddities that had been journeying through his territory. Efforts on his part to learn more were fruitless. He fears that those he has queried have been less than frank for fear of incurring the wrath of the Pirate Queen's consort.

I beg you to use your contacts to ask if anyone has heard of such a traveling exhibition, and where they were last seen.

With great anxiety,
Keffria

CHAPTER SEVEN

CITY DWELLERS

Moving to the city had proved more challenging for the keepers than the dragons, Thymara thought. Kelsingra was a city built for dragons. The broad streets, the immense fountains, the scale of the public buildings all proclaimed that dragons had resided there. Entries were tall and wide, steps were set for a dragon's tread, and every dimension of every chamber dwarfed humans to insignificance. For keepers who had grown up in the tiny tree houses of Trehaug and Cassarick, the differences were stunning. "It doesn't feel like I'm inside," Harrikin had observed the first time he entered the dragon baths. All the keepers had clustered together, looking up in wonder at the immense frescoes on the ceiling far overhead. Sylve, Thymara, Alum, and Boxter had held hands and tried to measure the diameter of one of the supporting pillars. The first night that all the keepers had spent in the city together, they had slept in a cluster in the corner of an immense room, as if the building were a new kind of wilderness in which they had to huddle together against unknown dangers.

For the dragons, it was different. The dragons had prospered since they had gained access to as much warmth as they wanted. After soaking in the baths, they had gone on to recall and visit other sites in the city that had been created for the enjoyment of their kind. At the crest of one of the hills, there was a structure where sections of stone wall alternated with glass beneath a domed roof. The ceiling was a strange patchwork of glass and stone as well, while the heat-radiating floor contained shallow pits of sand in varying degrees of coarseness.

The building would have been incomprehensible to her a few years ago. Now she knew at a glance that it was a place for dragons to sprawl on heated sand while watching the life of the city below them or the slow wheeling of the stars by night. She had first seen it when Sintara had summoned her there a few days ago, much to Thymara's surprise, and bade her search through the cupboards and shelves to see if the tools for dragon grooming remained in their old storage places. While she had looked, Sintara had writhed and wallowed in the sand, near burying herself in the hot particles. She had emerged gleaming like molten blue metal fresh from a furnace.

Time had rendered most of the grooming tools into rust and dust, but a few remained intact. There were small tools with metal bristles of something that rust had not eaten, and brushes like scrubbing brushes, but with the handles crafted of stone and the metal bristles set in clusters. There were metal rasps with the wooden handles long gone, glass flasks with a thickened residue of oil in the bottom, and a gleaming black case that held an assortment of black metal needles and other items she did not comprehend. Specialized tools for grooming dragons, she supposed, and she wondered if one day all the niceties of that lost skill would be recalled.

With the smaller brushes, Thymara had performed the delicate grooming around Sintara's eyes, nostrils, and ear holes, scrubbing away the remnants of messy meals. They had not spoken much, but Thymara had noticed many things about her dragon. Her claws, once blunted from walking and cracked by too much contact with water and mud, were now longer and harder and sharper. Her colors were stronger, her eyes brighter, and she had grown, not just putting on flesh, but gaining length in her tail. Her shape was changing as her muscles took on the duties of flight and forgot the long earthbound years of slogging through mud. This was no great lizard that she groomed, but a raptor, a flying predator that was both as lovely as a hummingbird and as deadly as a living blade. Thymara privately marveled that she dared touch such a being. It was only when she noticed Sintara's eyes whirling with pleasure that she realized the dragon was a party to all her thoughts and was relishing her wonder.

As she realized it, the dragon acknowledged it. "I awe you. Perhaps you cannot sing my praises with your voice, but reflected in you, I know I am the most magnificent of the dragons you have ever seen."

"Reflected in me?"

Dragons did not smile, but Thymara felt Sintara's amusement. "Do you fish for compliments?"

"I don't understand," Thymara replied both honestly and resentfully. The dragon's response had somehow implied she was vain. About what? About having the most beautiful of the queen dragons? One that alternated ignoring her with mocking or insulting her?

"The most beautiful of *all* the dragons," Sintara amended her thought for her. "And the most brilliant and creative, as is clearly reflected in my having created the most dazzling Elderling."

Thymara stared at her wordlessly. The brush hung forgotten in her hand.

Sintara gave a small snort of amusement. "From the beginning, I saw you had the most potential for development. It was why I chose you."

"I thought *I* chose *you*," Thymara faltered. Her heart was thundering. Her dragon thought she was beautiful! This soaring she felt, was it merely Sintara's beguilement of her? She tried to ground herself but was certain this was not the dragon's effortless glamourizing of her. This was what Sintara actually thought of her. Extraordinary!

"Oh, doubtless you thought you chose me," Sintara went on with casual arrogance. "But I drew you to me. And as you see, I have employed a keen eye and a sure skill to make you the loveliest and most unusual of the Elderlings that now live. Just as I am the most glorious of the dragons."

Thymara was silent, wishing she could deny the dragon's self-aggrandizing, but knowing only a fool would claim to have lied in her thoughts. "Mercor gleams like liquid gold," she began, but Sintara snorted contemptuously.

"Drakes! They have their colors and their muscles, but when it comes to beauty, they have no patience for detail. Look at Sylve's scaling some time and then compare it to your own. Plain as grass she is. Even in coloring their own scales, the other dragons lag far behind me." She shook herself and then came suddenly to her feet, erupting out of the hot sand and opening her wings in a single motion. "Look at these!" she commanded proudly, flourishing her wings so that the wind from them sent particles of sand flying into Thymara's face. "Where have you seen such intricacy, such brilliance of color, such design?"

Thymara stared. Then wordlessly, she dragged her tunic up and over her head, to unfold her own wings. A glance over her shoulder told her that she had not imagined it. The differences were of scale only. She mirrored Sintara's glory. Dragons did not laugh as humans did, but the sound Sintara made was definitely one of amusement.

The dragon settled herself onto the sand, leaving her wings open over the heated beds. "There. Next time you are moaning and sniveling that your dragon has no time for you, look over your shoulder and realize you already wear my colors. What more could any creature ask?"

Thymara had looked back at her basking dragon, torn between emotions. Did she dare trust any display of kindliness from her? "You seem different," she ventured hesitantly and wondered what the dragon would read more strongly, her suspicion or her hope. She braced herself for mockery. It did not come.

"I *am* different. I am not hungry. I am not cold. I am not a crippled, pitiable thing. I am a dragon. I don't need you, Thymara." Sintara shook herself, and excess sand that had been trapped beneath her scales went runneling down her sides in streams. Without being asked, Thymara found a long-handled brush. The handle was of a strangely light metal, as were the bristles. She studied them for a long moment; they gleamed like metal but flexed at her touch. More Elderling magic, she supposed. She began to apply it to Sintara, working from the back of her head down, dislodging particles of sand that had wedged at the edges of her scaling. Sintara closed her eyes in pleasure. By the time she reached the end of her tail, Thymara had formed her question. "Needing me made you dislike me?"

"No dragon likes to be dependent. Even the Elderlings came to realize that."

"Dragons were dependent on Elderlings?" She sensed that she trod in dangerous territory, but she formed the question anyway. "For what?"

The dragon looked at her for a long moment and she wished she had not dared to ask, sensing how resentful Sintara was of her question. "For Silver." She spoke the word and stared at Thymara, eyes whirling as if the girl would deny what she said. Thymara waited. "For a time Silver ran in the river here and was easy to find. Then, there was an earthquake, and things changed. The Silver ran thinly for a time. Some dragons could find it by diving into the shallows and digging for it. Sometimes it welled up abruptly and showed as a silver streak in the river. But mostly it did not. Then we could get it only from the Elderlings."

"I don't understand." Thymara kept her words as soft and neutral as she could. "Silver? A treasure of some kind?"

"Neither do I understand!" In a fury, the dragon erupted fully from the sandpit. "It's not a treasure, not as humans think of such. Not metal made into little rounds to trade for food, nor decorations for the body. It's *the* Silver, precious to dragons. It's here. It was here, first in the river near this city, and then, when the Elderlings lived, here in the city, some-where. Everything else we can find here. All the pleasures we recalled from Kelsingra are here: the hot water baths, the winter shelters, the sand grooming places—everything else we recall so clearly is here. So the Silver should be here too. Somewhere. But not one of us can find it. There were places in the city where the Elderlings helped us get the Silver. None of us recall them clearly. All of us find that strange, as if a memory has been deliberately withheld from us." Sintara lashed her tail in frustration. "One place, we think, is gone with the collapsing street along the riverside. An-other may be where the earth split open and the river flowed in. Gone and lost. Baliper tried to dive for it there, but that chasm is deep, and the water got colder the deeper he went. There is no Silver there for us.

"There were other places. We think. But those memories are lost to us, lost since we hatched, along with all manner of information we cannot even guess at. We will not be full dragons, nor you real Elderlings, until we can find the Silver wells. But you refuse to remember! No Elderling dreams of the wells. And try as I may, I cannot even make you dream of a Silver well!"

With these words, Sintara had given a final shudder and a lash of her tail. Thymara jumped back and watched her wade out of the sandpit and then stalk out of the doors that opened for her and then closed behind her, leaving Thymara staring after her.

Thymara had pondered the dragon's words in the days that followed. Sintara had spoken true. She had often en-countered a dragon wandering the streets, snuffing and searching. Thymara's curiosity was piqued. She had asked Alise if she knew of any silver wells in Kelsingra, but Alise had only looked puzzled. "There is a fountain called Golden Dragon Fountain. I read of that, once, in a very old manu-script. But if it remains intact, I haven't found it yet." She had smiled and then commented as if vaguely amused, "But I dreamed a few nights ago that I was looking for a silver well. Such an odd dream." She had cocked her head and furrowed her brow with the faraway look of someone who tinkers with the threads of a mystery. A strange thrill ran through Thymara. It was the same look Alise had worn so often earlier in the expedition, when she had been putting pieces together to understand something about Elderlings or dragons. She had not seen it on her face for some time.

Alise mused aloud, "There are odd mentions in some of the old manuscripts, things I was never able to make sense of. Hints that there was a special reason for Kelsingra to exist, something secret, something to guard . . ." A slow look of wonder had dawned on her face. She spoke more to herself than to Thymara as she muttered, "Not so useless, perhaps. Not if I can ferret out what they mean."

Alise's look had gone distant. Thymara had known that any further conversation with her that day would consist of her own questions and the Bingtown woman's distracted replies. She had thanked her, decided she had delivered the mystery to someone better suited to handle it, and put silver wells out of her mind.

But Sintara's remark about dependence she did not forget. She watched the other dragons grow and yes, change, some becoming more affable and others more arrogant as they gained independence of their keepers. It was odd to watch the ties between them loosen. Different keepers adapted to the dragons' dwindling interest in them in various ways. Some relished having leisure time and a beautiful city to explore. Suddenly the keepers could put their own well-being first. They made their first priority comfortable lodging. Although the city offered a vast array of empty dwellings, Thymara was amused that she and her fellows ended up in three buildings that fronted onto what they had begun to call the Square of the Dragons after a very large sculpture in the middle of it. They could have moved into what Alise called villas or mansions, structures that were larger than the Traders' Concourse back in Trehaug. Instead, most of them had chosen the smaller, simpler quarters above the dragon baths, housing obviously designed for those who tended dragons. It was wonder enough to Thymara to have as her own room a chamber twice as large as her family home had been. It was wealth to possess a bed that softened under her, a large mirror, drawers and shelves of her own. She could soak in a steaming bath as often as she wished and then retire to a room so comfortably warm that she needed no blankets or garments at all. She had time to study herself in the mirror, time to braid and pin up her hair, time to wonder who and what she was becoming.

But such luxuries did not mean that daily life was all leisure. There was no game in the city, and few green growing plants and no dry wood for cooking fuel. Gathering those demanded daily hikes to the outskirts of the sprawling city. Carson had suggested that they needed to create some sort of a dock for Tarman. The liveship would need a safe place to tie up when he returned, and they needed a place for unloading the supplies they hoped he would bring. "We will need docks and wharves, too, for our own vessels. We can't always assume Tarman and Captain Leftrin will ferry our supplies for free."

That comment had drawn startled looks from the gathered keepers. Carson had grinned. "What? Do you think we are reclaiming this city for only five years, or ten? Talk to Alise, my friends. You may live a hundred years or more. So what we build now, we had best build well." With that, Carson had begun to sketch out the tasks before them. Hunting and gathering for their daily needs, building a dock for the city, and, to Thymara's surprise, sampling the memories stored in stone to try to understand the workings of the city.

Thymara had volunteered to bring in food and hunted almost daily. As early spring claimed the land, the forested hills behind the city yielded greens and some roots, but their diet was still mostly flesh. Thymara was heartily weary of it. She did not relish the long hike to the edge of the city, nor the return journey burdened with firewood or bloody meat. But her days in the hills with her bow or gathering basket were now the only simple times in her life.

On the days when she remained in the city, she contended with both Tats and Rapskal. Their rivalry for her attention had eclipsed the friendship they once had shared. They had never come to blows, but when they could not avoid each other, the awkwardness between them froze any hope of normal conversation. Several times she had been trapped between them, besieged by Rapskal's endless chattering from one side as Tats sought to win her attention with small articles he had made for her or stories of his discoveries in the city. The intensity of the attention they focused on her made it impossible for her to speak to anyone else, and she winced whenever she thought of how it must appear to the others, as if she deliberately provoked their rivalry. If Tats had noticed something about the city and wondered about it, Rapskal was sure to claim knowledge of what it was and explain it endlessly while Tats glowered. As the keepers still gathered for most of their meals, it had begun to cause a rift in the group. Sylve sided with Thymara, sitting with her no matter which of her suitors claimed the spot on her other side. Harrikin made no effort to disguise his support for Tats, while Kase and Boxter were firmly in Rapskal's camp. A few of the others expressed no preference and some, such as Nortel and Jerd, resolutely ignored the whole issue when they were not making snide comments on it.

If one had work duty, the other took advantage of his absence to woo her. When Tats worked on the docks, Rapskal would insist on going hunting with her, even if Harrikin was her assigned partner for the day. Worse were the days when both she and Rapskal were free. He would lurk outside her chamber door. The moment she appeared, he would beg her to accompany him back to the villa and the memory columns, to join him in learning more of their Elderling forebears.

She felt a trace of shame when she thought how often she surrendered and joined him there. It was an escape to a gloriously elegant time. In that dream world she danced gracefully, partook of extravagant feasts, and attended plays, living a life such as she had never imagined. But Amarinda's passing observations of life allowed Thymara to gain an understanding through the eyes of an Elderling of old about how the city had once worked. Conservatories had furnished fruits and greens year-round, while the humans in outlying settlements and across the river had traded what they manufactured, raised, and grew with the Elderlings for their magical items. With Carson and Alise she had visited several of the immense greenhouses. They were sized for a dragon to stroll through, with chest-high beds for soil and gigantic pots for trees. Yet whatever had once flourished there had perished long ago, leaving only a shadowy tracery of long-vanished leaves on the floor and hollow stumps in the soil. The earth in the containers looked usable, and water still spilled from leaks in the system of pipes that had once heated and irrigated the plant beds.

"But without seeds or plant stock, we cannot start anything here," Alise observed sadly.

"Perhaps in spring," Carson had said. "We might move wild plants here and tend them."

Alise had nodded slowly. "If we can find seeds or take cuttings from plants we know, then the new Elderlings could begin to farm for themselves again. Or if Leftrin could bring seeds and plant starts to us."

In other memory walks, Thymara glimpsed gauntleted Elderlings at work. They stroked sculpture from stone, imbued wood with mobility, and persuaded metal to gleam, sing, and heat or cool water. Their shops lined some of the narrow streets and they called greetings to Amarinda as she passed. Thymara felt an odd kinship with them, an almost recall of what they did but not how. Amarinda merely strolled past amazing feats with scarcely a glance, accepting them as part of her everyday world. But there were other places and times when Amarinda focused her attention intently and relentlessly, drowning Thymara in her emotions and sensations. The Elderling woman's infatuation with Tellator continued, deepened, and became a lifelong passion. In the space of a single afternoon of memory walking, Thymara experienced months of her life. She would emerge from those hours with dimmed eyes and dulled senses, her hand clasping Rapskal's as he sprawled on the steps beside her. She would turn her head and see him wearing Tellator's smile, and the thumb that rubbed sensuously against the palm of her hand was not Rapskal's at all. Only slowly would his gaze become Rapskal's again, and she wondered who he saw when he looked at her, which parts he remembered as they rose, stiff and chilled. Rapskal always wanted to speak of the shared memories afterward. And she always refused. After all, they were only memories. Dreams.

Did it matter what she experienced as a memory walker? If the food she ate there did not nourish her, did the sex she enjoyed in that world matter in this one? She was of two minds. Certainly, it had changed her attitude toward many things that people could do in a cozy bed on a winter's eve or in a meadow under a summer sky. Could she claim she was not being intimate with Rapskal when she knew that he wore Tellator's skin? Certainly, she assured herself. Sometimes. For he could change nothing that Tellator did or felt, just as she had no control over Amarinda. She could not prevent their lovers' quarrels, and she could not sidetrack their sensuous reunions. It was as if they watched the same play or heard the same story told. That was all.

Sometimes she could almost believe that. Certainly, that puppetry of intimacy did not seem to completely satisfy Rapskal. Often, as they walked back to their lodgings he would drop hints or outright beg her to come with him to some private place where they could reenact what they had just experienced. She always refused. Over and over, she had told him that she did not want to risk a pregnancy. Yet she could not deny that she longed for the excitement of being the woman in control of the situation. Or a woman being loved by a man.

And today, as she strolled with Tats down to the riverside to visit the dock construction, the same thoughts were still on her mind. What would it be like to have Tats as a lover? She had experienced Tellator any number of times now and shared one long night with Rapskal. Would Tats be as different from both of them as Rapskal had been from Tellator? It was an unsettling thing to wonder and she tried to push the thoughts aside. She gave the young man beside her a sideways glance. His face was grave and thoughtful. A question popped out of her mouth before she considered the wisdom of asking it.

"Have you dream-walked in any of the memory stones yet?"

He squinted at her as if she were a bit odd. "Of course I have. We all have. Boxter and Kase go to a whorehouse and linger with the sampling they offer there. Some of the others join them there from time to time. Don't look at me like that! What else would you expect them to do? Neither Kase nor Boxter have any hope of finding a mate unless other women move to Kelsingra, and that certainly won't be any time soon. Alum, Harrikin, and Sylve found a place where some of the famous Elderling minstrels immortalized their performances. And you yourself lingered with us when we watched the puppet show and the juggler and then the acrobats that night the Long Street was remembering a festival there. So, yes, we've all memory-walked in the stones. Hard to avoid it when we live here."

That wasn't what she had meant, but she was relieved he had taken her question that way.

"I know. How can you walk down one of the broad streets at night and not share the memories there?" She snorted. "Sylve told me that when Jerd finds a street memory of a festival night, she follows the richly dressed women home and then searches their dwellings for any jewelry or garments that have survived. She has amassed quite a wardrobe." She shook her head, wondering if she thought Jerd was greedy or envied her expert looting. Then in a low voice, she admitted, "That isn't the kind of memory walking I was talking about."

Tats gave her a long level look. "Do I ask you questions like that?"

She looked away. After a time had passed when she did not respond, he added, "There are a lot of reasons to memory-walk that have nothing to do with sex or eating or listening to music. Carson tries to discover how the city works. He asked me to see what I could find out about the original docks. Not that we can replicate them, lacking the sort of magic the old Elderlings had. But to see what sort of things they considered when they were building them, as people who had known this stretch of river for a long time."

He sighed and shook his head. "I went to places where I thought they would have kept records of things like that. That big building with the map tower, and then that one with all the faces carved above the doors. We thought maybe that was an important place. But nothing. Or actually, much too much. I learned things that I still don't understand. Do you know why so much of this city is still standing? Why grass hasn't grown in the streets, or cracks started in the fountains? It's because stone remembers here. It remembers that it's a building façade, or a street, or the bowl of a fountain. It remembers, and it can repair itself, on some level. It can't fix itself if a quake makes a gigantic crack. But tiny cracks and crumbles just don't happen. The stone holds on to itself. It remembers."

He shook his head in wonder at the thought and then added, "And they could do more than that, it seems. You know how some of the keepers swear they have seen a statue move? The Elderlings knew how to do that. They breathed life into the stone, and the stone keeps a part of them and can move. Sometimes. When it's awakened by . . . something. Something that I could not understand, even though an old man was remembering it clearly. It made me realize that Alise was right, *is* right. We need to know what she knows about the history of this city, and then we need to apply it. You know what she told me a few days ago? That when Rapskal confronted her that day and said she wasn't an Elderling and that the city didn't belong to her, she was so discouraged that she nearly burned all her work! Can you imagine it? I knew I felt angry at him that day, but I'd no idea how badly he had hurt Alise."

He paused, and she sensed he hoped she would share his anger. He waited for her to say something, and she knew that if she did, it would be saying much more than that she thought Rapskal had been thoughtlessly cruel. Tats watched her stillness. But she could not find a way out of her silence. Rapskal hadn't said it to hurt Alise; he'd said it to assert his right to the city. A silly thought danced in her brain. *Alise is a grown-up. Can grown-ups really have their feelings so badly hurt? So hurt they think of burning all their work or killing them-*

selves? But by the time she realized how childish her reaction was, Tats had shaken his head at her silence and moved on.

"We need to map this city. Not just the streets, but where the springhouses are, and the drains. And we need to make maps that show what information is stored where. Right now, it's like a huge treasure house, full of thousands of boxes of treasures, and we have thousands of different keys. The wealth is here, right under our feet, but we can't make sense of it. Like that silver well that Sylve was talking about the other day."

She looked at him, surprised. He mistook it for confusion.

"I guess your mind was elsewhere. She says she keeps having dreams about a silver well. She's wandered through the city looking for it, but hasn't seen anything like what she dreamed. She thinks she's remembering something that Mercor knows about. She says he mentioned something about the silver wells of Kelsingra, a long time ago when we first began our journey here. She wants to talk to him, but she's like the rest of us. Since her dragon took flight, he doesn't have a lot of time for her. And she said another odd thing. She says it feels like he avoids the topic, as if it makes him uncomfortable."

"Sintara spoke to me once of a silver well. It seemed very important to her. But she said her memories of it were fragmented." She put the words out casually.

"The well isn't silver," Tats said slowly. He gave her a sideways glance as if he expected her to mock him. "I dreamed of it last night. The structure around it was old and very fancy. As much wood as stone, as if it had been built at the very beginning of the city. Inside there was this mechanism . . . I couldn't see it well. But when you cranked up the bucket from the depths, it was full of silver stuff. Thicker than water. Dragons can drink it and love it. But I had the feeling it was dangerous to humans."

"Humans? Or Elderlings?"

He looked at her for a long moment. "I'm not sure. In the dream I knew I had to be very careful of it. But was I dreaming it as if I were a human or an Elderling?"

It was her turn to sigh. "Sometimes I don't like what this place is doing to me. Even without touching memory stones, I have dreams that don't quite belong to me. I turn a corner and just for an instant I feel like I'm someone else, with a whole lifetime of memories and friends and expectations for the day. I pass a house and want to visit a friend, one I've never had."

Tats was nodding. "Those standing stones, the big ones in the circle in that plaza, they remind me of different cities when I pass them. You know, the other Elderling cities . . ."

She shook her head at him. "No. But I walk through a memory of a market and suddenly I want a fish cake spiced with that hot red oil. And then, just as abruptly, I'm me again and I know that I'm sick of fish, with or without red oil."

"The memories tug at me, too. I don't like it—" Tats halted suddenly. He took her arm, pulling her to a stop.

Down by the river, work progressed under Carson's supervision. A crude wooden dock made of logs had been roped to some of the old support columns. The river tugged at it and gray water bulged and flowed over the end of it. Harrikin, stripped to worn trousers and securely roped against the current, was in the water, trying to force one log into alignment with another. Carson was shouting directions to him as he kept tension on a line tied to the opposite end of the timber. Lecter, muscles bunching with effort, crouched over a log on the shore, slowly turning a drill to put a hole through it. Not far away, Alum was smoothing straight pieces of sapling into dowel. The sound rode thin on the spring wind. Nortel, ribs bandaged from a log-setting mishap earlier in the week, crouched on the dock with a mallet and pegs, waiting to fasten the log. It was cold, wet, dangerous work. And it was Tats's assignment for the afternoon. He tugged at her hand and she met his gaze. "I've heard what Rapskal says. That we have to plunge ourselves into the city's memories if we are to learn how to live here as Elderlings. But I also remember all the warnings I heard in Trehaug. What Leftrin told us before he left, that lingering too long near memory stone can drown you. That you can lose your own life in remembering someone else's."

Thymara was silent for a moment. Tats had put a precise finger on her own fear, the one that she didn't like to admit. "But we are Elderlings. It's different for us."

"Is it? I know Rapskal says that, but is it? Did the Elderlings prize having their own lives, or did they grow up so saturated in other people's experiences that they didn't realize what was theirs and what they'd absorbed? I like being me, Thymara. I want to still be Tats, no matter how long I live and tend my dragon. And I want to share those years with Thymara. I don't need to soak you in someone else's life when I'm with you." He paused, letting her feel the sting of that little barb. Then he added, "My turn for a question. Are you living your life, Thymara? Or avoiding it by living someone else's?"

He knew. She hadn't confided in him about the memory columns and her visits there with Rapskal. But somehow he knew. A deep blush heated her face. As her silence became longer, the hurt in his eyes deepened. She tried to tell herself that she'd done nothing wrong, that his hurt was not her fault. He spoke while she struggled to find words.

"It's pretending, Thymara." His voice was low but not gentle. "It's not plunging into this life in Kelsingra. It's letting go of now, and living the past, a past that will never return. It's not even really living. You don't make decisions there, and if the consequences become too dark, you can run away. You take on a style of thinking, and when you come back to this world, it sways you. But worst of all is, while you are swimming in memories, what are you *not* doing here? What experiences are you missing, what chances pass you by? A year from now, what will you say about these seasons, what will you remember?"

She was moving from embarrassed to angry. Tats had no right to rebuke her. He might think she was doing something foolish, but she hadn't hurt anyone with it. Well, only him, and only his feelings. And wasn't that partially his own fault, for caring about such things?

He knew she was getting angry. She saw how he tightened his shoulders and heard his voice deepen a notch. "When you're with me, Thymara . . . if you ever decide to be with me . . . I won't be thinking of anyone else except you. I won't call you by someone else's name, or do something to you because it's what someone else liked a long, long time ago. When you finally decide to let me touch you, I'll be touching you. Only you. Can Rapskal say that to you?"

Her mind swirled with conflicting thoughts and emotions. Then, from the riverbank, Carson shouted, "Dragon fight! Keepers, get down here!"

She spun away from Tats and ran, as much toward danger as away from it.

"WHY DO YOU hate me?"

She gave two final snips with her shears before she spoke, then ran her slender fingers through his hair, loosening it as she checked for any more mats or tangles. It sent a shiver up his back and he shuddered to cast it off. Another woman might have smiled at his reaction. Chassim's eyes remained cold and distant. She replied with a question of her own. "Why do you suppose I hate you, dragon man? Have I treated you with anything less than respect? Been less than attentive and subservient to you in any way?"

"Your hatred shimmers around you like heat from a fire," he replied honestly. She stepped away from him to fling handfuls of his damp hair out of a barred window. That task done, she closed the window and then folded down the elaborate wooden cover. Even though the cover was painted white and bore images of birds and flowers, it still plunged the room into gloom. Selden sighed at the loss of sunlight: his body craved it after the long months of deprivation.

The woman halted, her hand on the screen. "I have displeased you and now you will tell my father." It was not a question.

He was startled. "No. I just miss the daylight. I was kept for months inside a heavy tent and journeyed here in the hold of a ship. I've missed fresh air and daylight."

She moved away from the window without opening the cover. "Why look on what you cannot have?"

He wondered if that was why she had draped herself,

head to foot, in a shapeless white shroud. Only the square of her face was visible; he had never seen a woman attired so and suspected it was her own invention. All Rain Wild folk went veiled when they visited other places. Even when they went to Bingtown, where folk should have known better, their scales and wattles drew the curious eyes and invited fear or mockery. But a Rain Wild woman would have veiled her face as well, and her gloves and robes would have been rich with embroidery and beading. Her garments would have displayed her wealth and power. This woman was swathed as plainly as if her body had been wrapped for a pauper's grave. Her bared face, though fair, was a window into the anger and resentment she felt. Almost he wished she had hidden those eyes from him.

Yet the fury in her eyes had not reached the gentleness of her touch. He lifted his hands to his hair and ran his fingers through it. She had left it to his shoulders. It felt light and soft, and for the first time in months his fingers moved freely through it. Such a wonder to be entirely clean and warm. She had trimmed his nails, hands and feet, and scrubbed his back and legs and arms with a soft brush until his skin blushed pink and his scaling shone. His wounds had been cleaned and bandaged with salves and clean linen. It had felt odd and uncomfortable to be groomed as if he were a prize animal, but he had neither the strength nor the will to resist her. Even now, wrapped in soft blankets and enthroned before a fire, he felt it took all his strength just to hold his head upright. He gave up and let it loll back on the cushions. He could feel the drag of his eyelids. He struggled to stay awake: he needed to think, to put together the pieces of information they had given him.

The chancellor had brought him here, apparently at great expense, and presented him to the Duke. The Duke had spoken kindly to him and had placed him here with this woman who tended him with both gentleness and disdain. What did they want of him? Why had his presentation to the Duke seemed so formal and portentous? Questions, but no clear answers. Life was suspended, his existence dependent on the whims of others. He had to decipher the mystery. In this woman's care, he had the chance to regain his health. Could he manipulate that into a chance to regain his freedom?

Stay awake. Ask questions. Make plans. He fixed a smile on his face and inquired casually, "So. Chancellor Ellik is your father?"

She turned back to him, startled. Her upper lip was lifted like a cat's that smelled something bad. He could not tell if she were pretty or even how old she was. He saw her pale blue eyes and sandy lashes, a face sprinkled with faded freckles, a small mouth and a pointed chin. All else was hidden. "My father? No. My suitor. He wishes to marry me, to gather power to himself, so that as my father fails, he may assume it."

"Your father is failing?"

"My father is dying and has been for a long time. I wish he would accept that and do it. My father is the Duke of Chalced. Antonicus Kent."

Selden was doubly startled. "Your father is the Duke of Chalced? That is his name? I've never heard it."

She turned away from him again, hiding her face from his honest stare. "No one speaks it anymore. When he made himself duke, years before I was born, he declared that was all he would ever be, for the rest of his life. Even as a child, I did not refer to him as 'Father' or 'Papa.' No. He is always 'the Duke.'"

Selden sighed, all hopes of an alliance fled. "So. Your father, the Duke, is my captor."

The woman gave him an odd look. "Captor. That is a kind word for someone who intends to devour you in hopes of prolonging his own life."

He stared at her without comprehension. She met his gaze. Perhaps she had intended to jab him with her words, but as he looked at her, her face changed slowly. Finally she said, "You don't know, do you?"

His mouth had gone dry at the look on her face. She didn't like him, so how could she feel so much horror and pity at his fate? He drew an uncertain breath. "Will you tell me?"

For a moment, she bit her lower lip. Then she shrugged.

"My father has been ill for a very long time. Or so he says. Others, I think, would simply accept it as aging. But he has done all he could to stave off death. Many a learned healer he has brought here, and many rare cures he has consumed. But over the last few years, all efforts have failed him. Death beckons, but he will not answer its call. Instead, he threatens his healers and in turn, fearing death just as much as he does, they have told him that they cannot cure him unless he can procure for them the rarest of all ingredients for their medicines. Powdered dragon liver to purify his blood. Dragon blood mixed with ground dragon's teeth to make his own bones stop aching. The ichor from a dragon's eye to make his own eyesight clear again. The blood of a dragon, to make his own blood run hot and strong as a young man's."

He shook his head at her. "I don't even know where my dragon is right now. In the past three years, I have felt her mind brush mine only twice, and never have I been able to reach out to her. She does not come at my call, and even if she did, she would not give up her own blood to save me. I feel sure she would be roused to killing fury at the thought of a man wishing to drink her blood or make medicine from her liver." He shook his head more strongly. "I am useless to him! He should ransom me and demand his healers find other cures for him."

She cocked her head, and the pity in her eyes became unmistakable. "You did not hear me out. He could not get his dragon's blood, but what my suitor gave him woke his curiosity. A small square of scaled flesh. Flesh cut from your shoulder, if I am not mistaken. Which he ate. And it made him feel better than he had in months. But not for long."

Selden sat up. The room began a slow turn, rotating around him in a sickening way. He shut his eyes tightly, but it only became worse. He opened them again, swallowing against the vertigo. "Are you sure?" he asked her hoarsely. "He told you such a thing, that he ate my flesh?"

"My father did not tell me, no. My suitor . . . Chancellor Ellik bragged of it. When he . . . came to . . . tell me that you would be put in my care." The smoothness had gone out of her speech. Her words hitched along, and he sensed a terrible story behind them.

Her eyes had gone distant and dark. He reached out to touch her arm. She gave a small shriek and leaped away from him. She stared at him wildly. "What is it?" he demanded. "Tell me what you know."

She retreated from him, reached the covered window, and halted there. He feared suddenly that she might fling the cover wide and throw herself against the barred window. Instead, she turned back to face him, a cornered animal, and flung the words at him as she might fling stones at hounds baying after her. "He cannot have dragon's blood, so he will have yours! He will consume you, as he consumes every living being that comes near him. Consume and destroy, for his own dark ends!"

To hear her speak the words made the unthinkable something he must confront. A strange coldness filled him slowly, flowing out from his bones. When he spoke, his voice was higher than usual, as if air could not quite reach the bottom of his lungs. "It won't work," he said desperately. "I am as human as you are. My dragon has changed me, but I am not a dragon. Drink my blood, eat my flesh, it will not matter. He will die just as surely as I will."

Full knowledge of the fate the Duke intended for him penetrated his mind. He had not, at first, comprehended why they had taken a sample of his flesh and skin when he was being sold. He had thought then that it was to prove that he was scaled. The wound on his shoulder from that "sample" still oozed through the clean bandaging the woman had applied to it. He had thought it was healing and left it alone, but the girl had abraded away the thick scab to reveal the festering infection beneath. He wrinkled his nose as he recalled how bad it had smelled.

Even the meaning behind the Duke's words when he had first been brought before him had slipped past Selden's cognizance. But this woman who had been entrusted with his care seemed determined to make him confront it. She studied him from across the room; then, as abruptly as she had taken flight, she calmed. Her voice was low as she crossed the room to sit by his couch. "The Duke knows that your flesh and blood will not serve him as well as a dragon's would. Knows it—and does not care. He will spend you ruthlessly, using you as a stopgap measure to keep himself alive until he can procure the genuine cure."

She tugged his blanket straight, her lips folded. Then she spoke without hope. "And so I must heal you of infection, and clean your body, and ply you with food and drink, just as if you were a cow being fattened for the slaughter. We are both his cattle, you see. Chattel to be used however it best suits him."

He stared into her face, expecting to see anger or at least tears. But she looked wooden, her eyes fixed on a hopeless future. "This is monstrous! How can you just accept what he does to me? To you?"

She gave a bitter laugh and slumped on the simple wooden stool and gestured around the little room. It was small and comfortably appointed, but the bars on the window and the stout door proclaimed what it was: a gilded cage. "I am as much his captive as you are, and as human as you say you are, but it will make no difference to him. He will consume us both. I am the bribe that he offers Ellik in return for the chancellor doing all he can to preserve my father's miserable life. It gives me a little comfort that you say that if he consumes you, your death will not buy him more life." She looked down at her hands and confided hopelessly, "Once, I had planned to outlive him and then to proclaim myself his rightful heir. All my brothers are dead, either at my father's hands or of the blood plague. And I am eldest of my sisters and the only one not wed away in trade. The throne should be mine upon his death."

He looked at her incredulously. "Would his nobles support you in such a claim?"

She shook her head. "It was a silly dream. Those I attempted to rally to my cause are, ultimately, as powerless as I am. It was the fancy I concocted to give purpose and hope to my life. Now it's gone. I have no way left to reach out to those who also shared my ambition. Instead I shall comfort myself with the knowledge that he will not outlive me by much, if at all."

Selden furrowed his brow. "But you are a young woman. Surely you shall outlive your father by many years."

"My father's daughter might have a long life span, but not Ellik's wife, I think. His last wife gave him heir sons for his own fortune and name. That was all he needed of her, and when he was finished with her, her life was finished, too. He needs but one son from me to establish a regency the other nobles will not challenge. I am sure that is why the mother of his sons died so suddenly: to make space for me." She looked at him. "I did not know her but I mourn her. His last woman has scarcely begun to rot in her grave, and Ellik is ready to begin on me. No. I will be consumed just as you are. But not, I am told, until I have restored you to health. So. To hasten our ends, you should eat." Her tone became falsely light, a mockery of the tragedy in her eyes.

She rose and brought a little table to his bedside. On it was a tray with a large covered dish set beside two smaller ones. She lifted the lid on the large dish. Selden stared at a mound of raw meat cut into chunks. An inadvertent sound of disgust welled from his throat. She stared at him. "Are you not hungry?"

"If it were cooked," he said faintly. At the prospect of food, his mouth had begun to water, but the bloody red chunks of flesh only reminded him of his ultimate fate. He turned away, swallowing. His wakened hunger was making him feel nauseated.

"I can remedy that," she said, and for the first time, her voice seemed free of bitterness. "I can toast it over the hearth here, and I will welcome whatever you leave. My father does not think it fitting that women consume flesh. This is my provender." She uncovered the two smaller dishes. One held grain porridge with a generous pat of butter still melting in the center of it, and the other a heap of boiled vegetables in an orange, yellow, and green heap. At the sight of them, Selden's stomach growled loudly. The homely smell of stewed turnips, carrots, and cabbage almost brought tears to his eyes.

Chassim was silent for a moment. "If we share all, there is enough for both of us to dine well." Her voice was hesitant, her eyes downcast.

"Please," he begged, and something in that simple word woke the first shadow of a smile he had seen on her face.

"Please," she said softly to herself, as if the word were foreign to her. "Yes. And with thanks."

✧ ✧ ✧

Day the 28th of the Fish Moon

Year the 7th of the Independent Alliance of Traders
From Sealia Finbok, wife of Trader Finbok
To Hest Finbok, beloved son

A message to be held for him at the Trehaug Traders'
Concourse.

*My dear boy, you left Bingtown with scarcely a word
to us! I do not even know where you lodge in Trehaug.
Still, I need you to know that your father is quite angry
to learn that Trader Redding's son accompanied you. He
says that he expressly forbade you to take a companion
with you, something that I regard as quite ridiculous.
How could anyone tolerate an extended journey to a
place as backward as the Rain Wilds without a cultured
and witty fellow to help pass the tedium? To calm his
wrath, I told him a bit of a story, that is, that I insisted
you take Redding with you as I was concerned for your
safety, traveling alone in such an uncivilized place. So,
when you return, you must agree with my story when
your father asks you.*

*Most Important! Lissy Sebastipan has broken her
engagement to Trader Porty's son Ismus! She discovered
that he had a bastard daughter with a girl from a
Three Ships family. The whole town has been buzzing,
for their wedding was to have been the social event
of the year. I am in an agony of sympathy for Lissy's
mother, yet at the same time, I confess that I do see a
wonderful opportunity here for you! I am sure you take
my meaning!*

*Please do not waste too much time on what I perceive
as a useless mission. Come home, annul your contract*

for abandonment, forget that eccentric and ungrateful woman, and let me find you a faithful and appropriate wife.

Should you have time to do any trading, I have heard that some absolutely amazing deep purple flame jewels have recently been unearthed. Do look into this rumor, and feel free to use the family credit if they prove worthy of purchase.

With all affection, and the desire that you use your travel time to revive your poor broken spirit and renew your enjoyment of life,

Your loving mother

CHAPTER EIGHT

CITY OF ELDERLINGS

A lise! Alise, are you in there?"

Alise straightened up slowly. She had been hunched over a tabletop inlaid with very detailed illustrations of dragon anatomy. She now realized she had been hearing shouts in the distance for some time but had blocked them from her mind, assuming they were only the city's memories trying to invade her. Most often the city's whispers were a distraction. Today, cleaning and studying the diagrams, the whispers had been informative. She prayed she might never *need* to know how to remove a broken tooth from a dragon's jaw, but she valued the knowledge all the same.

"I'm here," she called, wondering who needed her for what now. The interruptions always seemed to come when she was in the most interesting part of something, and for what? So that she could identify a stove part or something that someone had found. Earlier in the week, it had been Rapskal with an armful of very large buckles set with sparkling stones. "I know these are important," he had said without preamble. "I know that I know what they are, but when I reach for the memory, it slides away. It isn't something I used to deal with directly, but I know that someone did it for me and it was important to me and my dragon." He had taken a breath and added mournfully, "I found them in a pile of rubble behind my house. Something bad happened there, Alise. I know it."

She'd looked at him dispassionately. He would never be her favorite person, but he seemed artlessly unaware of how devastating his comments had been to her. He was the one who had pointed out that she was not an Elderling and never would be. He was the one who had told her that she had no say over what they did with the city, that the city belonged to the new Elderlings, not her. True as those statements had been, they had still devastated her and turned her life upside down. She'd had to change her image of herself from the very bones out. Ultimately, she knew, it had been good for her. That did not mean she enjoyed being reminded of it.

"*You* never touched one of these before today," she pointed out to him. "But you may have sampled the memories of someone who did." An understatement if there was one. All knew how obsessed Rapskal was becoming with his "other" self's memories. She took one of the buckles from him and turned it slowly in her hands. "It's from a dragon's harness. Not for battle armor but for show. Perhaps as part of a victory parade or other celebration—"

"Battle harness?" he had interrupted her. "Battle harness? YES! Yes, that's it, that's what this reminded me of. But . . . but . . ." Mouth slightly ajar, his eyes went distant and the light went out of his face. "I don't remember all of it. I should, but I don't know . . ."

"Go to the Hall of Records, the building with the map tower. Climb up, oh, I think it was on the third story. There are many wall decorations there that you can study to see how the harness was made and fitted."

"Yes. Yes, now I remember. Heroes were honored there.

Valiant men and dragons of great battle prowess . . ." Absently, he took the buckle from her hands. Clutching it to his chest, he'd left her standing without even a thank-you as he hurried off to try to recover a piece of a self he'd never been. She sighed. Leftrin had warned them all, but nothing she could say now would dissuade any of them. Lingering too long in memory stone was dangerous.

And exciting.

She might not be an Elderling, but privately she still believed she was the one best suited to extract the city's secrets. The knowledge she had gleaned from her studies prepared and anchored her. It was not so foreign to her, and yet she could hold tight to her humanity and not be swept away. Still, it was frightening to let her own life and thoughts be swept aside in the stream of memories stored in the city's stones. She had learned a new discipline in this city. When she ventured into her memory sampling, it was for a specific purpose and she kept her attention tightly focused on what she wanted to know, refusing all other tugs at her attention. It was like diving into deep cold water to retrieve a sparkling stone.

"Alise!"

The voice came again and she recognized it as Sylve's. Before she could respond, the keeper called once more, "Alise? Are you in here? Tarman's coming. They're back!"

"I'm back here, Sylve!" Then the meaning of the girl's shout penetrated her distracted mind. Tarman had been sighted. Leftrin! He was back! And she was on the wrong side of the river. He'd be expecting to find everyone at the village site, not in the city. She scrambled to her feet, dragon dentistry discarded. Leftrin was coming, and she looked a fright! She hurried to the door of the chamber and peered out into the tall, wide corridor. "Where's Relpda?" she demanded as Sylve came barreling toward her. Behind the girl, the tall double doors stood open to the gusty wind of the spring day. Alise hoped the little dragon and her keeper would carry a message to the ship for her.

"She and Rapskal are guiding Tarman in! Carson says he thinks our dock will hold, but it might not be very good for unloading yet. He's worried about it, but I think it will be a good test of what we built."

"Tarman is coming directly here?" She had even less time to prepare for him.

"Yes! We sighted them coming on the river, not long after the dragons had their quarrel."

"Dragon quarrel?" Alise interrupted in alarm. "Was anyone hurt?" She must have been tightly focused on the city to have remained unaware of that!

"No, no injuries among the keepers. It happened in the air, downriver. We couldn't see much of it, but we did see Mercor give Spit a good tumble. But Spit rose again, so he couldn't have been much hurt, and then the whole flock of dragons moved farther away down the river. So we still don't know what that was about. But shortly after that, we spotted Tarman!"

Alise's hands flew to her hair. Then she laughed at the instinctive gesture of a Bingtown woman. It would be silly to fuss over her appearance. Leftrin knew the conditions she'd been living under! Well, at least he would find her in better circumstances than when he had left. Since the keepers had moved across the river and into Kelsingra, they were all cleaner and better groomed. Nonetheless, she found herself pulling the precious few pins she still possessed from her hair and letting it down. She shook her hair out as she hurried after Sylve. Her hands moved as she strode along, smoothing the stubborn red ringlets, rebraiding it, and then pinning it back up. She wondered what it looked like and then discovered that, truly, she didn't care. And if Leftrin did, well, then he wasn't the man she thought he was. She found herself smiling confidently. He wouldn't care.

"I wonder what upset the dragons. Was it the beginning of a mating battle?"

"I don't think so. Didn't you hear them? There was a lot of trumpeting from Spit, and then the others came to see what he wanted. That was what caught Carson's eye, all the dragons converging. At least six of the dragons went to Spit, in a big circling swarm. Then I saw Mercor clash with him!

Why, we don't know; and they haven't been paying much attention to us since then. But Mercor went up under him as Spit was diving down and then he just tipped Spit off sideways. We saw him fall and then the trees were in the way and everyone was terrified that he would land in the river. Well, except a few of us who were rather hoping the little beast would get a good cold dunking. But then we saw him come up again. I still have no idea what it was about." Her voice dropped on her last words and Alise heard the hurt in it that Mercor had not spoken to her since the fray. Since the dragons had become capable of feeding themselves, they had taken little interest in their keepers. Of course, any dragon might still summon a keeper at a moment's notice for special grooming, but few of them made daily contact with the young Elderlings. Some of the keepers seemed as affronted as snubbed lovers over this. Others, like Sylve, were sad but resigned to their loneliness. She and Boxter seemed to take the abandonment the hardest. Some of the others, notably Jerd and Davvie, seemed relieved to be free of their demanding dragons. Last night as the keepers had shared a sparse dinner in the back room of the dragon baths, Sylve had bravely spoken the truth that the others preferred to ignore.

"Nothing's changed, really. They feel about us as they always have. From the beginning, they were honest. They wanted to get away from Cassarick and become dragons again. They tolerated us because they needed us."

The keepers gathered around the ancient table had grown still, food forgotten.

"And now they don't. So, they tolerate us still, but they prefer their own kind. Or they prefer their solitude."

She was right, but it had not lifted the gloom that had fallen over the company since the dragons achieved flight. Alise could sympathize. She recalled how heady it had been to be the subject of Sintara's attention. And when the dragon had taken the trouble to cast her glamour over her? She smiled and swayed slightly at the thought of it. It had been all-encompassing. The delight and joy of being the object of a dragon's attention had been surpassed only by the giddiness of her infatuation with Leftrin, and then the swirl of excitement at realizing he reciprocated her admiration. Now that was something no one ever got from a dragon!

When she had first met the blue queen, she had felt lightheaded each time the dragon deigned to speak to her. She had been willing to do anything, any task no matter how menial, to keep that regard. She had felt such a sense of loss when the dragon had recognized that Thymara was a better provider and had chosen the girl over her. If Leftrin had not been there to cushion the blow, she probably would have been devastated to lose Sintara's regard. She smiled now as she thought how well he had distracted her.

In the days since the dragons had stopped paying attention to their keepers, some of them seemed to have chosen similar distractions for themselves. She had watched, uncomfortably, as Thymara swung between Rapskal and Tats. She pitied all three of them; yet at the same time, she reflected that each of the young men knew of his rival. Thymara did not deceive them as Alise had been deceived. Thymara respected her suitors and struggled to treat them well.

Jerd had plunged herself into yet another torrid romance; Alise did not know which keeper she had chosen this time, and she wondered wearily if it truly mattered.

It was strange to watch Davvie and Lecter be so absorbed in each other. In Bingtown, it would have been a scandal for two young men to be so openly passionate. Here, their relationship was accepted by their fellow keepers, much as they accepted that Sedric and Carson were partnered. Perhaps once one realized how deeply one could bond with a creature as foreign as a dragon, all forms of human love seemed more acceptable. The two young keepers could often be seen wandering the town together. Their laughter at the smallest shared joke made others smile, while their tempestuous quarrels, it sometimes seemed to Alise, were only because both of them so enjoyed the drama of parting and the relief of coming together again.

Others of the keepers, such as Harrikin, had immersed

themselves in hunting. Tats seemed as fascinated by the engineering of the city as Carson was. A few, such as Nortel and Jerd, had become devoted treasure seekers; while Rapskal spent his free time when he was not trailing after Thymara in a different sort of exploration of the city. Since he had asked her about the buckles, he spoke often of weaponry and techniques of fighting and how the city had once defended itself from the dragons of another city. It frightened and alarmed her to hear that once there had been such rivalries among Elderling cities and the dragons that inhabited them, but when she asked what was at the base of their quarrel, Rapskal had gone silent and looked confused. It worried her.

Alise and Sylve emerged into the streets; the fresh spring wind bludgeoned them, whipping Alise's freshly confined hair out into wild red strands. She laughed aloud and reached up to salvage the last of her pins before they could be scattered. Her hair flounced free onto her shoulders. So be it.

"Hurry!" Sylve called over her shoulder and broke into a run.

Alise set off in a dogged trot, but the Elderling girl ran effortlessly away from her. Sylve had shot up taller than Alise, and her face was beginning to be that of a woman rather than a child, but she had growing still to do and not just her body. Alise was glad that Harrikin apparently had the patience to wait for her. The girl obviously enjoyed his company, and all spoke of them as a couple, but Alise had seen no indication that he had attempted to gain more than her promise from her. They walked hand in hand sometimes, and she had witnessed a few stolen kisses, but he was not pressing her. For now, he was her true friend, and Alise did not doubt that in time he would win all that he sought.

As Leftrin had.

The thought warmed her suddenly and she abandoned her reserved jog, stretching her legs into a run and astounding herself and Sylve by catching up with the girl. They glanced at each other, windblown hair netting their faces, and then both burst into laughter. The final hill before the run down to the docks fell away before them, and they both raced down it.

LEFTRIN RISKED ONE backward glance. The gyre of dragons had dispersed, or perhaps they had descended below the tree line to harry the hapless Bingtown ship. He felt sorry for that crew but knew he could do nothing for them. The dragons would probably be content with just chasing the boat away, and good riddance to it. Surely the dragons could not have changed so much as to casually slaughter humans. Could they?

He pushed that thought out of his mind. Focus on the problems that he could do something about. He had some very immediate worries. Tarman was struggling as he approached the Kelsingra docks. The steady current pushed the barge on relentlessly. The water that swept past the city was deep and swift, eating away at the bank and the structures on it. Obviously, it had been doing so for a number of winters. In some stretches, the current foamed and crashed over the stony bones of recently conquered masonry. Leftrin gritted his teeth at the sight and refused to imagine Tarman suddenly slammed against it by a trick of the current.

As the ship approached the heart of the city's waterfront, Leftrin could see that the keepers had attempted to rebuild the dock. Rough logs had been roped or pegged to the standing stone pilings that were all that remained of the ancient docks. It did not look very sturdy and he questioned his wisdom in listening to Rapskal. Right after they had witnessed the dragon attack on the boat, Heeby had flown over them, Rapskal on her back. The keeper had shouted down to them, over and over, to come to Kelsingra, not the village. When Swarge had waved that he understood the message, the dragon and boy had flown off. It had taken the combined efforts of Tarman and the full crew to battle their way across the river and work their way along a shore where the water ran deep and swift. The village side of the river had offered slower and more shallow water, and a wide and sandy bank for the ship to wedge itself against. Here, they had only the makeshift new dock and a strong deep current pushing against them. Leftrin was aware of how stubbornly his liveship paddled against that rush, how his hidden tail thrashed as his crew pulled valiantly at their oars, steering him toward the dock.

The keepers had come down to greet them. Wisely, most of them remained on the shore. Carson was on the dock, ready to catch a line as soon as it was thrown to him. Harrikin was with him, and, to Leftrin's amazement, so was Sedric, looking more muscular and fit than when Leftrin had last seen him. Harrikin and Sedric were clad in bright clothing, as were the rest of the keepers; evidently the city had yielded up a bit of its treasure to them. His brow furrowed as he wondered how Alise felt about that.

The tethered logs of the dock moved with the current, rising and falling steadily. On the crumbling street behind the docks, the other keepers were massed. Much as he longed to scan that crowd for Alise's face, he knew that his ship required all his attention just now. He kept his place on top of the deckhouse, bellowing course corrections while Tarman fought the seething current as they moved toward the dock and pushed steadily upstream until they were past it.

"Drop anchor!" Hennesey roared and Big Eider obeyed, deploying a kedge anchor first on the port and then another on the starboard side of the barge. Chain and then line played out swiftly as the crew continued to fight the current. Then the anchors caught and the liveship curtsied to the water as the lines took the ship's weight. A moment later, there was a lurch as the port anchor dragged a short distance before lodging firmly on the bottom.

"Even them out!" Leftrin bellowed to Hennesey, but the mate was already in motion, assisting Big Eider in that very task. As the ship came into alignment, they began the careful process of paying out line to let the current carry them downstream to a position parallel to the docks.

Leftrin prayed there were no concealed pilings from the old dock hiding beneath the river's rush. The space between Tarman and the dock narrowed and still the ship's unseen legs and tail fought to gain a place alongside the dock and hold there. Plainly Tarman did not trust the kedge anchors completely. It made the task of docking him more difficult, but Leftrin allowed the liveship to follow his own instincts. Finally, they were close enough for lines to be flung. Sedric caught the first one and quickly wrapped it around one of the few remaining stone supports from the fallen dock. Carson caught the next and took it a quick wrap around a wooden upright. It groaned, swayed slightly, and then held. Other lines were tossed, caught, and tied. As soon as Tarman was somewhat secured, longer lines were run out, past the dock and up onto dry land. With a fine disrespect for the city's antiquity, one was tied off around an Elderling statue, while another was taken in the window of a small stone structure and then out of the door before being made fast. It was a sloppy tie-up, as if an immense spider had trapped the liveship in a web. Leftrin waited, but the lines held. He breathed out.

"It will do for now," he told Hennesey. "But I don't like it, and neither does Tarman. I want you or me on board at all times, and I don't want the crew to go far. At least three hands on board at every moment. Once we get off-loaded, then we'll head back across the river and beach Tarman there. Jaunting back and forth in the ship's boats from the village to Kelsingra won't be fun, but at least he'll be safe there."

Hennesey nodded grimly. Leftrin continued, "Let's unload right away then. As soon as we see our passengers safely ashore. Get it started. I want a word with the ship."

Hennesey jerked his head in a nod and was gone. In a moment, he was shouting the orders that would get the cargo moving onto the deck for off-loading. A chorus of greetings rose from the waiting crowd onshore. Leftrin gave a single wave as he made his way forward. He saw Hennesey leaning over the side, exchanging words with Carson. The big hunter could move with alacrity when he needed to, and as if by magic, the keepers were suddenly lining up like ants as they readied themselves to act as stevedores. Big Eider was personally assisting Malta across the deck and down onto the wobbly dock. She clutched her baby, refusing to surrender him to anyone while Reyn followed closely behind her, looking anxious. Leftrin noticed that Hennesey was waiting to perform the same service for Tillamon. He compressed his lips, and then decided that it was up to Reyn to intervene if he thought anything improper was going on. And perhaps not even Reyn, given that Tillamon was a woman grown.

He reached the foredeck and leaned on the wizardwood railing. "Ship. You going to talk to me?"

He felt the familiar thrumming of a liveship's awareness. Tarman was the eldest of the liveships, built long before anyone had any idea that wizardwood was anything other than finely grained and excellent quality timber. He'd been built as a barge, with the traditional painted eyes for watching the river's current, but no figurehead such as the other liveships boasted. While his "painted" eyes had become ever more expressive over the years, he had no carved mouth with which to speak. Usually Leftrin shared his ship's feelings on an intuitive level, or when Tarman intruded directly into his dreams. Only rarely did the captain have the sensation that the ship was speaking to him in actual words. He had always respected however little or much Tarman chose to share with him. Only rarely, when he felt there was a direct threat to his vessel, did he make such a request. Now he leaned on the railing and waited, hoping.

He felt the ship's uneasiness, but he would have had to be stone to be unaware of that. Every one of the crew was moving with a quick nervousness that said that at any moment they could spring into action to save the ship if the anchors dragged or the dock gave way. "Not safe here, is it, Tarman? We need a better place than this to tie up on this side of the river if we want you to be here for any length of time. But once we're unloaded, we'll get you out of here and across and onto the beach. It will be good to rest, won't it?"

As he spoke, Leftrin glanced up at the sky. Working with experienced longshoremen on sturdy docks at Trehaug, it had taken most of a day to get supplies aboard. Now crates were being wrestled down a gangplank and onto a rickety, bobbing dock, and then hauled from the dock to the shore. At a quick glance it appeared to Leftrin that about ten of the keepers were present, and all seemed frantically engaged with the unloading. He saw that Reyn and Malta had made it ashore and that Tillamon was standing with them. And there, in a familiar gown, her red hair an unruly cascade down her shoulders, was his Alise, taking charge of them. He gave a small groan, longing to be there, to pick her up and hold her against him and smell again her sweet scent.

Not yet.

I know, ship. Not yet. My duty is here. And I'll stay aboard you until you're safe on the other side. He glanced up at the sky, calculating time, and realized that he might have to spend the night tied up here. He wondered if Alise would join him, and he smiled to guess that she might be very willing. The ship's anxiety pulled his attention back.

Not yet. The child is not yet safe.

Alise will help them. She'll get them to a dragon, perhaps Mercor. Maybe Heeby. One of them will certainly be willing to help the baby.

Maybe. If they can. I have done what I could.

If they can? Leftrin didn't like the feel of that thought. He had believed that bringing the baby here for one of the dragons to treat would solve everything. Persuading a dragon to take it on had been the only obstacle he had foreseen. *Do you think all the dragons will refuse us?*

The right one must be there and must agree. The response was slow and Leftrin sensed that his ship struggled to convey something. He decided to let it go. Mercor had been the most communicative among the dragons in the past. Perhaps he would be willing to shed more light on the creation of Elderlings and what the baby might actually need. Yet the captain was heavyhearted at the thought of breaking this news to Malta. He ventured another query to his ship. *Would the baby be better off if it remained on board for now? Could you continue to help him?*

The response was reluctant. *As much as could be done, I have done.*

And our thanks to you, Tarman.

He felt no acknowledgment from the ship, and no further touch upon his mind. It was Tarman's way, and for himself,

Leftrin was grateful that his liveship was more taciturn than most. He did not think he could have enjoyed a chatterbox like the *Ophelia* or a moody and dramatic ship like the *Paragon*. But there, it was probably like it was for children. Each parent thought his was the best, and doubtless every captain would prefer his own liveship to any other.

That brought a tiny nudge from Tarman.

I am the best. Eldest, wisest, best.

Of course you are. I've always known that.

And again, there was no acknowledgment of Leftrin's remark. But that was what he'd expected.

MALTA LOOKED AROUND her in a daze. A long corridor led off into gently lit dimness. At intervals, doors opened off it, most closed but a few ajar. "Any open door?" she asked wearily.

"Any open door," Alise Finbok affirmed. "If a keeper has already claimed a room, then the door is closed. And most of them were long ago locked by their previous owners, and we haven't found any way to open them. I'd suggest one of those last three at the end of the hall. They are larger with several chambers and beds. We think that perhaps they were for visiting delegations from other cities. Of course, we have no basis for that theory, other than it was the only one any of us could imagine."

"Thank you." The two words were almost more than Malta could manage. Her body was still flushed from a hot bath, and her hair was damp on her shoulders. They had been the only inhabitants of the dragon baths. Malta vaguely appreciated that at any other time she would have been awed by the immense chamber with the distant ceilings and the magic of the hot flowing water. But sorrow and weariness had driven all wonder from her heart. In a daze, she had rubbed days of salty sweat from her body. The hot water had drained away the aches from her bones, but also the last of her stubborn strength.

Alise had been so kind as to hold the wailing Phron while Malta bathed and washed her hair. He was quiet now in her arms, but Malta could feel that his little body was slack with weariness, not sleepy and content. He had cried himself out in Alise's arms and come back to his mother as limp as a rag doll. He had seemed to be asleep when she had gently lowered his little body into the water. But his eyes had opened at its embrace, and she had been pleased to see him stretch out in the steaming bath and wave his little arms and legs about in it. He had patted the water's surface and looked first startled and then pleased at the splashes he made. She had smiled to see him behave so much like an ordinary child. But as the colored scales on his body had flushed and then deepened in hue, she had known a wave of uneasiness. "Something is happening to him!"

"That happened to the keepers, too," Alise had assured her. She had waited at the edge of the immense tub, a drying cloth open and ready to receive the baby. Malta had smiled up at her. The Bingtown woman had not changed nearly as much as the other members of the expedition. It took a discerning eye to notice the scaling behind her eyebrows and on the backs of her hands. Her words still held the intonation of the scholar. "The hot water made the dragons grow quite a bit and seemed to ease their aching. We could literally see the colors spreading on their wings and then deepening. They stretched, and their bodies seemed to take on a new alignment. And they grew, some startlingly. Tinder went from pale lavender to a deep purple with gold tracery. Spit had always had a rather stubby tail. Now it seems the appropriate length for his body. After a day or two of access to the water and warmth, almost all the dragons could take flight from the ground. And now, of course, they all can. The keepers experienced similar changes: brighter colors, lengthening limbs. Thymara's wings are astonishing now."

"Wings?"

The older woman nodded. "Wings. And Sylve may be growing a crest on her brow."

"Did I change?" Malta had asked her immediately.

"Well, you seem to shimmer more brightly to me. But perhaps that is a question better asked of your husband, who knows best how you usually look." Politeness ruled Alise. She would not say what Malta knew was true. She had been so unkempt from her constant vigilance over little Ephron during the journey that Alise could not tell if the changes in her scaling were merely that she was clean now, or if her dragon characteristics had advanced. Malta found she didn't care and smiled wearily. *Look what it had taken to erode girlish vanity,* she thought to herself. *Merely threaten my son's life and none of it mattered anymore.* She looked down into his little face. He was silent but not asleep. His face did not look like the face of any baby she had ever seen before. His little mouth was pinched up as if he were in pain, and his breath whispered through his narrow nostrils. She tried to see him impartially; was he an ugly child, doomed to be rejected by other children as he grew? She had found she could not tell. He was Ephron, her little boy, and his differences were part of who he was, not points to be compared with others. With a forefinger, Malta had traced the fine scaling that outlined his brows, and he closed his eyes. She had handed him to Alise, who wrapped him in the waiting towel while Malta waded wearily out of the water.

Her skin had dried quickly in the warm chamber, and Alise had supplied her with an Elderling gown of shimmering pink. The gleaming color reminded Malta of the inside of a conch shell. At another time, she would have longed to see herself in a mirror, to admire the supple fall of the soft fabric. But at the pool's edge all she had wanted was her child back in her arms. Now she stared numbly down the hall of closed and opened doors. Choices, some she might make and others closed forever to her. How did one ever know how one small choice might forever change the course of one's life?

"Let me show you a chamber I think you'll like and settle you there for the night. In the morning, after you've rested, if you don't like it, you can change it."

Malta realized that she hadn't moved nor spoken in several minutes. Had she fallen asleep standing up? "Please," she said faintly, and did not mind when Alise took her arm and guided her down the hall. It was a relief to be away from the keepers' noisy and joyous welcome. When they had introduced themselves, several had seemed stunned.

"The king and the queen of the Elderlings!" someone had whispered.

Malta had shaken her head, but it had not seemed to affect their awe. They had pelted them with hundreds of questions, and Reyn, knowing her exhaustion, had tried to answer them. The girls had seemed entranced by her baby, and even the boys had come to look on him in amazement.

"Like Greft," one of them had exclaimed as he stared at her boy. A taller keeper on the verge of manhood had bade him hush and pulled the scarlet-scaled boy aside. Reyn had read her anguished look and drawn the keepers off, while suggesting strongly that Alise help her find a place to bathe and rest. Now here she was, barely able to make sense of things as the evening drew to a close. She had come all this way, hoping to be greeted by dragons. None had appeared. Now all she wanted was Reyn back, wanted her little family close at hand again.

At the end of the hall Alise escorted her through a door that swung wide at her touch. The room had been dark, but it lit as they entered, gaining sourceless light slowly until a warm glow suffused the room. There was no hearth, Malta noticed with dismay, and almost as if Alise heard her, she said, "The rooms stay comfortably warm. We don't know how. The chairs and the beds soften as you sit on them, and we don't know how that works either. There is still so much to learn about Kelsingra. There is no bedding. Perhaps the Elderlings had no need for it when the rooms stayed warm. Some of the closets had clothing in them, and a few of the shelves and cupboards held personal items. Some things were of obvious use, such as brushes and necklaces and others we didn't understand at all. I've urged all the keepers to leave nonessential items in place until we can learn more. But"—a small sigh—"they do not listen to me very well. Jerd is the worst, treasure-hunting from building to building and amassing more jewelry than one woman could wear in a lifetime, with no thought as to where it came from or who wore it before her. Goblets made of gold, as if we had wine worthy of them. A mirror that shows what it should have reflected the moment before, so she can examine the back of her head. And useful items as well. A pot that warms whatever is put into it. Stockings with sturdy soles that adjust to the wearer's foot . . . Oh. I'm sorry. I'm chattering away while you stand there. Come. This room has only a table and chairs, as if for a gathering of people, as you can see. But here is a bedchamber, and those other two doors also go to bedchambers. As soon as you sit down on one of the beds, it will start to soften to your form."

Malta nodded dumbly. "Reyn?" she asked wearily, and Alise promised, "I'll see that he knows where you are. You are exhausted, my dear. Go to bed right away, for the sake of your child, if not yourself."

Alise patted the bed, and Malta carefully set Phron down on it. He squirmed, and with a sinking heart, she knew he was going to wail again. Then, as the bed softened around his tiny form, his cross expression eased. As she watched him, his eyes sagged slowly closed. Reflexively, she leaned down, putting her cheek and ear near to his face, to assure herself he was breathing. She wanted so to follow him into slumber, but not yet. Not yet. A sad smile twisted her mouth as she recalled how her own mother had always seen to her children's needs before she allowed herself to rest.

"His things," she said, turning to Alise. "Will my trunks be brought here? There is a blue case that has all Phron's things in it, his extra napkins, his little robes and soft blankets . . ." She let her voice trail away as she wondered what was wrong with her, to be so stupid as to leave such things behind. She could not seem to focus her thoughts; her mind seemed to buzz with a thousand half-remembered ideas . . .

"Malta!" Alise's voice was almost sharp, and the Bingtown woman gave her elbow a gentle shake. "This city is full of Elderling memories. This building does not seem to be as heavy with them as some, but still, it is easy to let your mind drift here and lose track of what you were thinking and doing. Will you be all right sleeping here tonight? Do you think you should return to the ship?"

The moment Alise mentioned it, Malta recognized it for what it was. Memory stone, full of stored lives and thoughts. She squinted her eyes tight and opened them again. "I'll be fine, now that I'm aware of it. I've been around it before. The first time was when I went into the buried part of Trehaug, to try to find Tintaglia and plead with her to leave Reyn alone."

Alise looked intrigued and Malta had to smile. "It's a long tale, but if you wish, I'll tell it to you. But not now. I'm exhausted."

"Of course you are. And I heard Tarman's crew say that everything on board would be off-loaded tonight so that they could move him to a safer place across the river. I'll go and make sure your things are brought here. Now. Before I leave, is there anything else you need?"

"Only Reyn," Malta replied honestly.

Alise laughed, the sort of laugh that women share. "Of course. It was so clever of him to keep the keepers occupied. All of them are buzzing with curiosity about why you are here and all you can teach them of Elderling ways. The king and queen of the Elderlings. Did you ever think those titles would come to mean so much? For here, they do. I heard the youngsters talking."

Malta stared at her. Alise smiled and spoke more softly. "They think you've come to lead them. To use your power and stature to establish Kelsingra. I heard Rapskal say, 'They will call us the Dragon Traders, and we will stand on an even footing with Bingtown or the Pirate Isles or even Jamaillia. They'll respect us now that our king and queen are here.'" Alise dropped her voice. "I know it isn't why you came. But you need to know that. Every word you speak here carries weight with these young Elderlings. They'll be gathered around Reyn now, hanging on his every word. But I'll free him from them and send him up to you. And I'll let them know that their queen wishes her trunks delivered tonight. And it will happen."

"Alise, I can't deal with this," Malta replied feebly. "I never thought . . ." Words failed her. Useless things. She was so tired. Stupidly tired. She'd forgotten all about Tillamon. "Reyn's sister . . . will you help her find us here? She must be as tired as I am, and I just left her there at the docks. So rude, but I'm just so tired."

Alise looked a bit surprised. "Well, I thought Tillamon said that she wanted to stay on board Tarman tonight and help take him across to the village tomorrow. But if you wish, I'll ask after her."

"Sleep aboard Tarman? Well, as she wishes. I thought she might want to join us here where things are so comfortable. But perhaps the memory noise would bother her." Malta was suddenly too tired to think about it anymore. "Please, just ask Reyn to come up. And good night to you, and many, many thanks for your welcome here."

"Good night. And by tomorrow morning, I am sure we can persuade one of the dragons to speak to you. I'll ask every keeper to summon his dragon, to speak with the king and queen of the Elderlings. Surely one will be able to help your babe."

King and queen. It made her ridiculously sad. The dreams of Malta the girl might come true even as the longings of Phron's mother were destroyed. She had no words for it. "Alise, you have been too kind. I have been thoughtless . . ."

"You are just tired," Alise replied firmly, with a smile. "Get some rest. I'll free Reyn from the keepers and send him up."

ALISE SLIPPED FROM the room, pulling the door closed quietly behind her. It was a relief to let the false smile fade from her face. Tragedy. She had never seen such a bony baby. And despite what the keepers said, Malta the Elderling queen was gone, replaced by a grieving mother with a lined face. The hot water had brightened her scale colors, but her once-golden hair reminded Alise of the dead straw after harvest, and her hands were clawlike. Beauty had fled before life's harshness. She wondered if it would ever return.

Alise hurried down the hall and then down the spiraling stair. The dragon baths, with their hot water and comfortable lodgings, were a popular gathering place for the keepers. At the back of the entry hall, behind the stairs, a door led to a gathering space. A long table and chairs and benches that became comfortable after one sat on them filled that room.

Beyond it, there was a kitchen area. It illuminated when one entered, and the cupboards and worktables reminded Alise of the cooking space in many a Bingtown mansion. But there was no hearth, only stone ovens and several mysterious workbenches. There was a large basin with a drain in it, and a mechanism that possibly should have furnished water, but no one had deduced how to make it work.

So cooking took place in an alley behind the building. It had pained her heart to see the keepers build a large hearth of rubble where they cooked game meat on spits over driftwood hauled up from the riverbank. She knew it was a necessity, but the mess it created in the formerly pristine city shamed her. In this, Rapskal was right. There was a way to use this city, and the sooner they learned it, the better for both city and keepers. For now, she felt as if she were part of a barbarian invasion rather than settlers reclaiming a beautiful place.

She opened the door to conversation and the smell of cooked food and almost swooned when she smelled hot tea. She had not tasted tea for months! And bread, there were rounds of hard bread in baskets on the table. It seemed no less than a miracle. She made her way to the table, past a jumble of stacked crates and barrels, the foodstuffs unloaded from the *Tarman*. With relief, she saw a number of large trunks and cases that probably belonged to Malta

She made her way through the hodgepodge of crates and barrels to where Reyn sat at the head of the long table. Six keepers clustered about him, and Lecter was telling the tale of how they had treated the dragons for rasp snakes on their way to Kelsingra. Reyn was leaning forward on the table, the picture of a rapt listener, or a very weary man who might otherwise collapse. Alise spoke crisply. "Enough! It's time to let this man join his wife and child in some well-earned rest after such a journey. There will be plenty of time to exchange news and tales tomorrow."

"After you summon the dragons for us," Reyn ventured.

The smiles around the table faded a bit. "I'll try," Sylve volunteered quickly. The others exchanged glances. Their thoughts were plain to Alise. Their king and queen wished to speak with their dragons, but no one could promise the dragons would come.

"Let the poor man get some rest!" she insisted again, and Reyn seized the opportunity to stand up.

The gathered keepers groaned at losing him. He gave them a weary smile. "I would greatly welcome a bit of assistance with our trunks," he said gently, and the response was overwhelming.

Alise took the opportunity to slip out of the gathering. Her heart beat faster at the thought of her own reunion. She paused only to get her cloak and then hastened out of the door.

It was raining, yet she wasn't cold. She pulled up the hood of her midnight blue Elderling cloak. It was spangled with yellow stars at the hem. Her feet and legs were warmly covered in Elderling garb as well. Sylve had been the one to bring it to her, telling her that everyone thought it ridiculous that she went clad in leaking boots and a ragged cloak while they walked in warmth and finery. "But . . . I am not a true Elderling like the rest of you," she had said. It was as close as she had come to admitting to anyone how much of an outsider she had become.

Sylve had scowled, her scaled brow wrinkling, first in puzzlement and then in annoyance. "Rapskal," she sighed in disgust. "Think of all the peculiar things that boy says, and then tell me why any of them should be taken seriously. Not an Elderling . . . Oh. I suppose that technically he was right. But only in that you have no dragon to demand ridiculous tasks on a moment's notice. Not that Sintara would hesitate to do so! But, Alise, please, you have come all this way with us, done so much for us. Without you, do you think we would be here? Would we ever have dared believe this place existed? Look. I chose these for you, the colors will suit you. I've seen you wear the Elderling robe that Leftrin gave you, so why not dress as one of us?"

Alise had had no response to that. Not sure if she felt humbled or honored, she had taken the garments from Sylve's hands. And worn them the next day.

Now she pulled her Elderling cloak tighter around her as she strode through the windy streets, and it was like wrapping herself in Sylve's friendship. Winter had loosened its harsh grip on the land, and the last few days had seemed almost springlike, but every evening the chill settled again and wind swept through the city.

The streets of Kelsingra were like the streets of no other city in the world. She hurried along, the sole living figure on a thoroughfare wide enough for two dragons to pass each other. The buildings soared on either side of her, structure after structure with steps, porticoes, and entries scaled to dragons. Empty and dark, the broad streets still teemed with remembered Elderlings and occasional dragons, all bathed in an imaginary light. To that remembered illumination was added the light that spilled from the awakened city windows, now white, now golden, now a muted blue. A few of the larger buildings gently glowed in the darkness, acting as beacons within the city. She turned her face toward the waterfront.

She had seen Leftrin from the shore, shouted a greeting to him, and saw on his face all that she longed to hear him say. He had glanced around, agonized by the conflict between duty and longing, and she had suddenly known that she did not want to be something that required that sort of decision. He had to think only of his ship now, not arrange to have her board and become a distraction.

She remembered how the voice of Malta the Elderling had broken into her dilemma. "Alise? Alise Finbok? Is that you?" She had felt startled and honored that the Elderlings had seen fit to come to Kelsingra. Until she had seen the woman's haggard face and skeletal child, and then a very different emotion had filled her. She had glanced back only once at Leftrin as she took charge of them and had been proud to see the relief on his face. She had lifted a hand, waved a reluctant farewell, and seen him echo the gesture. And then she had left the docks to escort Malta, Reyn, and her child to what comforts they could offer them.

She and Leftrin had needed no words. Now there was a novelty; a man who assumed she knew what she was doing and was willing to wait for her. A smile broke out on her face. She was willing to wait no longer.

She crested one of Kelsingra's rolling hills and suddenly saw the riverbank scene before her as if it were a Jamaillian puppet play. The keepers had borrowed tethered light globes that graced some of the more elaborate gardens. The spheres gleamed golden and scarlet, and their light ran away in spills across the streaming river water. She stood staring; never had she beheld anything like it. The yellow light bounced off Tarman's deck and then faded into a halo around the ship against the black night. Men still moved there as shadowed silhouettes. The crew called to one another as they worked, the sound carrying oddly over the water. She saw squat and bulky Swarge moving across the deck, graceful for a man of his size. A moment later, she realized she had become accustomed to the slender silhouettes of the keepers. Ordinary folk looked strange to her now.

A hastily rigged tripod lifted and swung crates from the ship's deck to the rudimentary dock where men grunted and swore as they caught them and guided them down. She spotted Carson's silhouette, and Lecter's, and then she saw Sedric among those dragging the crates from the dock to the shore. That made her smile. Alum was there, working alongside Skelly, and she suspected she knew why he had volunteered to stay and help with the last of the unloading. Once the crates were off the dock, they were loaded onto barrows and shuttled off to their temporary warehouse. The work proceeded in a steady, orderly fashion, the deck and shore crews moving in their concerted efforts as if in a careful dance.

She caught sight of Thymara working alongside the men, and Nortel. There was Tats, shouting to Davvie to come lend a hand with the final crate he was struggling to shift. It came to her to wonder when a ship had last unloaded supplies for this city. What had this river port looked like in the days of the Elderlings? Too careless a thought. She knew a dizzying moment of double vision and saw a sprawling dock system and a score of vessels moored to it. Lights on tall poles streamed golden rays down on the broad-beamed, brightly painted vessels, and all manner of people came and went on the wharves. Some were Elderling by their dress and tall silhouettes, but others seemed to be foreigners to these shores. They wore tall hats and were garbed in long furs. She blinked and then squinted her eyes, willing herself back to the present. The Elderlings faded and the ships became fog until only the *Tarman* rode at anchor on the river's tugging current.

"And that's the last of it, boys!" Hennesey shouted as four netted casks landed with a thump on the dock. A ragged cheer went up from the crew and the keepers. "Still got to get it all under cover, so don't think the work is all done yet!" the mate reminded them.

Alise had to agree. It looked like so much cargo, crates and kegs stacked in rows in the street as the keepers struggled to move it to shelter. But when she thought of the long months that remained and all the work that must be done before the keepers could create their own food supplies, her heart sank. Food from Trehaug would still have to be managed carefully, and wild game and forest greens would remain the bulk of their diet.

So much to do, such a long distance to go before the city would function as a real city. Kelsingra needed seed for crops, plows to break the meadow soil, and horses to draw those plows. Most difficult of all was that the keepers would have to learn how to provide for themselves. Sons and daughters of hunters and gatherers, merchants and traders, former residents of a city that had never been able to feed itself, would they adapt to tilling fields and raising kine?

And even if they did, were there enough of them to sustain it? The male-to-female ratio was worrisome and had been from the beginning.

Resolutely, she pushed it all from her thoughts. Not tonight. Tonight was hers, finally. She reached the bottom of the hill and threaded her way through the crates and boxes and out onto the dock. "Watch your step!" Carson cautioned her with a grin. "We've given these timbers a real test tonight, and some are starting to split. One of the hazards of building with green logs."

"I'll be careful," she promised him.

The emptied *Tarman* rode high, and the taut anchor lines

hummed a quiet song of vigilance. She eyed the makeshift gangplank, steep and worn. No. She wouldn't ask for help. She started up it, her Elderling shoes surprisingly sure on the wet wood, but was scarcely three steps up before Leftrin came leaping down to her. Heedless of the treacherous surface, he seized her in a hug that lifted her off her feet. Close by her ear, his unshaven cheek prickling hers, he told her, "I have missed you like I'd miss air in my lungs. I can't leave you again. Just can't, my lady."

"You won't," she promised him, and in the next gasped breath, demanded, "Put me down before we both go overboard!"

"Not a chance!" As casually as if she were a child, he swung her up into his arms and in two steps thudded her down on Tarman's deck. He set her on her feet but did not release her. His embrace warmed her as nothing else could. Perhaps her days in the Elderling city had sensitized her, but she felt Tarman's welcome of her as a warmth that flowed up from where her feet touched his deck to engulf her whole body.

"That's amazing," she murmured into Leftrin's shoulder. She lifted her face slightly to ask him, "How do I let him know that it's mutual?"

"Oh, he knows, trust me. He knows it just as I know it."

She could smell his scent. Not cologne such as Hest had often worn, but the scent of a man and the work he had done that day. His hands held her firmly against him; she surrendered to the rush of arousal that suffused her and turned her face up to his to be kissed.

"Sir. Captain Leftrin."

"What?" His bark was more demand than question. Alise turned her head to find Skelly stifling a grin. Her hair gleamed from being freshly brushed, and she had abandoned her trousers and tunic for a flowered skirt and a pale yellow blouse and looked, Alise thought to herself, more like a girl than she ever had before.

"Everything is tidied away, and the mate says he has no more tasks for me. Permission to go ashore for the night, sir?"

Leftrin straightened. "Skelly. As your captain, I'll grant you a night's leave. But you are to be back here by dawn's light, to help take Tarman across the water. Be late, and you won't see this city again for a month. Are we clear on that?"

"Yes, sir. I'll be here, I promise."

As she spun excitedly away, he cleared his throat. Skelly halted to look back at him.

"As your uncle, I'll remind you that we had no opportunity to speak to your parents or your fiancé. They all still have assumptions about commitments from you. You are not free. Even if I thought it was wise to do so, I couldn't give you that sort of permission. You know what I'm talking about. I'm responsible for you. But even more so, you are responsible for yourself. Don't risk either of us."

Skelly's cheeks had gone red. The smile flattened from her face. "I know," she said sharply, and then, "sir," she added, as if fearful he would revoke her shore time.

Leftrin shook his head, then shrugged. "Go see your friends. Wander the city. Sa knows, I'm as curious as you are about this place. And if I were a deckhand instead of the captain of this vessel, I'd want to get off and take a good look. But I'm not. So I'll be staying aboard, and I'll expect to find you at the galley table when dawn breaks, ready for a day's work."

"Sir," she agreed and spun on her heel. In a twinkling, she was down on the dock and hurrying up the street. As they watched, Alum waved a farewell to Tats and Sedric and hurried after her.

"Are you sure that was wise?" Alise asked, and then wondered at her own temerity.

"I am sure it was not," he told her. "Come."

Together they began the slow circuit of Tarman's deck that always presaged bed and rest for them. Bed. No rest tonight, and a sudden shiver of desire rushed through her. A moment later, Leftrin smiled. "That's an odd reaction for a lady to have to a poor sailor checking his knots."

"This ship keeps none of my secrets from you." She laughed and walked to the next cleat to inspect the lines for herself. As Leftrin came to join her, she said more quietly,

"I fear for your niece. While you have been gone, I have watched this place change all the young keepers. Alum is no exception. Skelly may not find him the same young man she left behind."

Leftrin smiled wryly. "That is ever the fate of sailors! And if you are correct, the sooner she discovers it, the better. And then she may be glad that she did not break her engagement with her beau in Trehaug." He shook his head and in response to her unasked question, added, "There were many things I did not get done there. Did Malta and Reyn tell you the full tale of how the Council received me, and of the dastardly attack on Malta and her babe?"

"I had the bones of it. I do not think Malta wanted to relive it, and Reyn strikes me as a man who always speaks less than he knows."

Leftrin made a wry face. "They are private people. Despite their beauty, I think they have lived a life apart. Perhaps because of it. Or it may be caution. They may fear treachery still. Who would ever have imagined Malta the Elderling attacked by Chalcedeans in a Rain Wild city? It speaks to me of a duke who is very determined to get what he wants, and Traders corrupt enough to help him in that insanity. Alise, I know you have feared for the city. But the treasure that seems to be sought most at this time is not Elderling artifacts but dragon flesh. The rewards for it must be very high indeed if two men were willing to murder a woman and a newborn child in the hope of passing off their bodies as dragon meat. The dragons have shown already that they can drive off approaching ships. But what I fear is what will eventually happen if they feel they must continue to defend themselves. Sooner or later, human lives will be lost. Possibly many of them. And if there is war between humans and dragons, where will the Elderlings stand?"

Alise walked with him in silence as they checked the last three lines. She heard the low murmur of voices and glanced up. On the roof of the deckhouse, Hennesey was standing, a wide smile on his face as he told some sailor story to a strange woman. Her scaled face reflected light from the tethered globes. So. That must be Tillamon, Reyn's

sister. She seemed captured by the mate's tale. The Rain
Wild woman was well bundled against the night's damp
chill. Someone had thought to bring her an Elderling gown.
Probably Sylve, Alise thought to herself. In the reflected
light of the failing torches, it glimmered copper and bronze.
She was smiling up at Hennesey as he concluded his story,
and they both laughed aloud at the finish of it. Much as she
wanted to meet Reyn's sister, Alise knew that now would
not be a good time for pleasantries.

Leftrin halted beside her. His eyes were narrowed, and
a slight scowl bent his lips. She took his arm and drew him
along with her as she approached the galley door. "They do
as we do, my dear. They take what joy they may find in life
as they can. As you well know that Skelly has run off to do
tonight, also. The shadows of harsh times creep over us. For
in a battle between dragons and men, my love, it is not only
the Elderlings who must decide where they stand, but you
and me as well."

They stepped into the cramped little galley of the ship.
The room was deserted. A single mug, half full of coffee,
graced the table. The small room smelled of coffee and
cooking grease, tar and people living in close quarters.
Alise felt her heart lift. "It's so good to be home," she said.

He folded her into his arms, his hand sleeking her Elderling robe to her body. His mouth found hers and he kissed
her, slowly and gently, as if all the time in the world belonged to them. When he finally lifted his mouth from hers,
she was breathless. Words came in a whisper. "Now is all
we really have, isn't it?"

He tucked her against him, his chin resting on top of her
head as if she were an instrument he was preparing to play.
"Now is enough," he murmured. "Now is enough for me."

✧ ✧ ✧

Day the 2nd of the Plough Moon

Year the 7th of the Independent Alliance of Traders
From Reyall, Keeper of the Birds, Bingtown
To Detozi, Keeper of the Birds, Trehaug, and
Erek

Standard message tube, wax applied.

I am sure you are aware of the unhappiness of many of our patrons. The Bingtown Traders' Council has now filed a formal petition asking that the Bird Keepers' Guild accept a Committee of Traders to look into allegations of corruption, spying, and the selling of secrets. Messages and even birds have gone missing now. I think it likely we can blame some of the missing birds on the unwieldy message tubes and attachments that we are now being required to use!

Three of our apprentices have reported being approached by Trader families wishing to breed and use birds of their own to establish private message flocks. I do not need to explain to you how this would undermine the Guild. A whole way of life and livelihood will be lost if this comes to pass.

We have been directed here to adhere strictly to all rules about messages between keepers. Appending an additional message to an official message sent by a client is now cause for dismissal from the Guild. We must do bird counts three times a day, including eggs and fledglings, and any bad eggs or young birds that die in the nest must be witnessed by three keepers of journey level or higher before they can be disposed of. Bird handlers in Bingtown are allowed to touch only birds specifically registered to their own coops.

Informally helping one another, allowed in the past, is now forbidden.

Have these measures also been enacted in Trehaug or Cassarick or the lesser settlements? I will tell you that there are rumors that the Guild is sending out "testers," but the gossip does not tell if these are men attempting to bribe bird handlers, or if they are messages designed to tempt those who tamper and spy. It saddens me that I rise to being a full Keeper of the Birds in these distrustful times.

In happier news, Erek, your swift birds appear to be breeding true. Two of the offspring set records this last week in a race back to Bingtown after being released from a ship that was four days out of port. I have submitted the breeding records to the Guild masters, noting that you were the one who saw the potential and began specifically breeding this line. I hope they will recognize your expertise.

With respect and affection,
Reyall

CHAPTER NINE

PASSING SHIPS

Hest was trapped in someone else's life. This was not the existence of the heir-son of a Bingtown Trader! He had never lived in such miserable conditions, let alone traveled in them. He'd lost count of the days he'd been confined belowdecks. He still wore the same garments he had been wearing when the Chalcedean had abducted him. Now they hung on him, their tailoring a victim of his greatly reduced diet and heavy labor. He knew he stank, but his only option for washing himself was cold river water, and he knew the dangers of using it. The chores the Chalcedean gave him put him out on the deck in the weather as often as not. His hands and face were chapped and sore from exposure to rain and chill and sun; his clothes were fading and tattering. He could not remember the last time his feet had been dry. He was starting to develop sores under his toes, and the wind-reddened skin on his face and hands stung constantly.

He still had nightmares about disposing of Redding's body. Dragging Arich's body out along the narrow walkways in the dark and rain and eventually shoving him over the edge had been disgusting and unpleasant work. They had heard his falling body crashing through branches, but there had been no final sound. It had made Hest queasy, but it paled in comparison to his final parting with Redding. The Chalcedean had made him carry Redding's body, and they had gone quite a distance, choosing always the tree paths that seemed least used. Eventually they had been balancing along a limb that had no safety ropes at all. Redding's body was slung across Hest's shoulders as if he were a hunter bearing home a deer. The familiar fragrance of Redding's pomade mingled with the smell of the blood that dribbled down Hest's neck. With every step, his limp burden had grown heavier and more horrific. Yet he had no choice but to lurch along in front of the man with the knife at his back. He suspected that if he had fallen while carrying the body, the man would have thought it of little consequence. The Chalcedean had finally chosen a spot where the narrowing limb of their tree crossed branches with another. Hest had propped Redding there and left him for the scavengers to find. "Ants and such will take him down to bones in just a few days. If he is found, which I doubt, no one will be able to tell who he was. Now we go back to your room and obscure all sign that you were ever in Cassarick."

He had meant it quite literally. He'd burned the children's hands in the pottery hearth and destroyed the elaborate boxes that had held them. Redding's cloak became a sack to hold the precious stones he'd salvaged from the boxes. He'd departed briefly, warning Hest not to leave. Hest suspected that he went to murder the woman who had rented him the room. If he did, he accomplished it very quietly. Perhaps, Hest told himself as he gritted his teeth to keep them from chattering, he had only bribed her well. But he was gone a very long time, leaving Hest alone in the room that smelled of burned flesh and spilled blood. Sitting in the dimness, he could not shake the image of Redding's ruined face peering back at him from the crook of the tree. The Chalcedean had slashed it repeatedly, crosshatching it with cuts until his familiar features were eradicated. Redding's eyes had stared out from the dangling tatters of his once-handsome face.

Hest had always thought of himself as a ruthless Trader. Deception, spying, sharp deals that bordered on theft; he had never seen any advantage to being fair, let alone ethical. Trade was a rough game and "every Trader needs to watch his own back," as his father often said. It had pleased him to think of himself as rough-and-tumble, a man hardened to everything. But never had he been a party to murder. He hadn't loved Redding, not as Sedric overused that tired word. But Redding had been an adept lover and a jolly companion. And his death had left Hest alone in this mess. "I didn't mean for any of this to happen," he had told the dying flames. "It's not my fault. If Sedric had never made his insane bargain, I wouldn't be here now. It's all Sedric's fault."

He had not heard the door open, but he had felt the draft and seen the hearth flames flicker. The Chalcedean was a black shadow against the blackness beyond. He pulled the door quietly closed. "Now, you will write a few letters for me. Then, we shall deliver them."

Hest had been beyond questioning what was happening to him. He wrote the letters as he was told, to names he did not recognize, signing his own name to them. In the notes he bragged of his reputation as a clever Trader and directed the letter recipients to meet him before dawn at the impervious boat that was tied up at the docks. Every letter was identical, stressing discretion and hinting that a great fortune awaited them now that "our plans have come to fruition," and citing names of Traders that Hest had never even met.

Each letter was neatly rolled, tied with twine, and sealed with a drop of wax. Then the Chalcedean smothered the fire in the hearth and they left the stripped room, carrying the missives with them.

The long night had become endless as they moved through Cassarick. The Chalcedean was spry but not absolutely certain of their way. More than once, they retraced their steps. But eventually, the six scrolls had been delivered, tied to door handles or wedged into door frames. Hest had been almost grateful to follow the assassin down the endless stairs to the muddy road at the bottom of the city. His well-appointed stateroom, a clean warm bed, and dry garments awaited him on the impervious ship. Once he was there and alone, surely he could put the night's events into focus and decide what he must do next. Once there, he would be Hest again and this evil adventure would become no more than an episode in his past. But when they reached the vessel, the Chalcedean had prodded him along at knifepoint, forcing him into a cargo compartment belowdecks, and then dropping the hatch shut behind him.

The indignity had astonished him. He'd stood, arms crossed sternly on his chest, and waited in silence, certain that the Chalcedean would return at any moment. As time passed, the discomfort had infuriated him. He groped his way around the freight compartment but found only rough timber walls with no hope of egress. The hatch was just out of his reach, and when he climbed the short ladder to push at it, he found it secured. He pounded on the hatch but could achieve no real force, and his shouting roused no one. He had paced, cursing and roaring, until he was exhausted. Eventually he had sat down to wait for the Chalcedean, but awakened to darkness. How long he had been held there, he did not know.

Time passed. Hunger and thirst afflicted him. When the hatch was finally lifted, the wan daylight flooded down and blinded him. He immediately started up the ladder.

"Out of the way!" someone shouted at him. And other men were pushed pell-mell down the hatch. Three landed well, cursing and trying to fight their way back to the ladder even as others were being forced down. Hest recognized some of them as his fellow passengers from the trip up the river, and others as members of the ship's crew. Some were Jamaillians who had invested in the boat's construction, the last a pair of Bingtown Traders. The men who looked down at them, mocking and threatening, were unmistakably

Chalcedeans, with their embroidered vests and the curved knives they favored.

"What's going on?" Hest demanded, and one Trader shouted, "It's a mutiny!" while another said, "There were Chalcedeans hiding belowdecks for the whole voyage. They've taken over the ship!" The cargo hold was crowded with men, at least ten of them. One was holding his shoulder, and blood seeped between his fingers. Several of the frightened and confused merchants bore signs of a struggle.

"Where's the captain?" Hest asked through the shouting and taunts.

"In on it!" someone shouted at him, as angry as if it were his fault. "Well paid to let these bastards on board and hide them. Claims they invested just as much as we did, and paid him more on the side!"

The hatch cover began to slide shut. Men surged toward the ladder, shouting defiance and pleas, but in moments, the light was gone.

If being alone and locked below the deck was bad, then being crowded in with two dozen strangers in the dark was worse. Some were irrational with anger or fear. Others argued heatedly about exactly what had happened and who was at fault. Some of them were not former passengers but Rain Wild Traders "tricked into coming down to the ship by a false message." Hest kept his mouth shut and was grateful for the darkness that kept him anonymous.

The Chalcedeans who now commanded the ship had apparently killed at least three crewmen in taking over the ship, and possibly four, as a woman who had come aboard had been flung over the side bleeding but still alive. Hest suddenly grasped the full ruthlessness of the assassin and the gravity of his own situation. When one of his fellow prisoners speculated that they'd probably all be dead before long, someone roared at him to shut up, but no one contradicted him. Two of the men climbed the ladder and exhausted themselves trying to force the heavy hatch open while the others shouted encouragement and suggestions. Hest had retreated to the corner of the compartment and put his back to the wall.

While they were pounding, a new motion started. It took Hest a moment to deduce what it was, and in that second, one of the crewmen shouted, "You feel that? They've shoving off. We're under way. Those bastards are kidnapping us!"

A roar of voices rose, the angry cries underscored with wild wailing from one man. The victims pounded on the walls and shouted, but the rhythmic rocking of the ship only increased as it picked up speed in its battle with the current.

"Where are they taking us?" Hest demanded of everyone and no one.

"Upriver," someone responded. "Feel how she fights the current."

"Why? What do they want from us?"

His question was drowned in the outcry the others raised as they realized they were being carried away from any hope of outside aid.

The swearing and the shouting went on for a long time, to be replaced gradually by angry discussion and then muttering and the sound of someone weeping harshly. Hest felt dazed by his situation. He crouched in his spot in the darkness, smelling sweat and piss. As time trudged by and moving water whispered past the sides of the vessel, he wondered what had become of his organized and genteel life. None of this seemed possible, let alone real. How furious his mother would be when she heard of this outrage to her son!

If she ever heard of it. And in that moment, Hest suddenly realized how completely he had been severed from his old life. His name, his family's money, his roguish reputation, his mother's love for him meant nothing here. All shields, all protections, had fallen away. In a caught breath, he could become a body, his face slashed beyond recognition, food for ants or fish. He gasped, his chest hurting. He subsided onto the deck and sat in the darkness, his face resting on his knees. The thunder of his heart filled his ears. Time passed, or perhaps it did not. He could not tell.

When the hatch was finally slid open, it admitted a yellow slice of lantern light. Night reigned. A voice Hest recognized warned them, "Stand back! If any man starts up the ladder, he'll fall back with a knife in his heart. Hest Finbok! Come to where I can see you. Yes. There you are. You. Come up. Now."

Back in the corner of the hold, someone bellowed, "Hest Finbok? Is that Hest Finbok? He is here? He's the traitor that lured me here with a note left on my doorstep, even signed his own name to it! Finbok, you deserve to die! You're a traitor to Bingtown and the Rain Wilds!"

By the time Hest reached the top of the short ladder, he was fleeing the ugliness below as much as reaching toward space and air. As he scrambled out onto the deck on all fours, curses and threats followed him. Two sailors slid the hatch shut, cutting off the cries of those trapped below. He found himself at the feet of the Chalcedean. The assassin was holding a lantern and looked very weary. "Follow me," he barked and did not wait to see if Hest obeyed. He trailed behind him to the door of his erstwhile stateroom.

The scattered contents of Hest's plundered wardrobe littered the floor of his compartment, his garments mingled carelessly with Redding's. The chest of wine, cheese, sausages, and delicacies that Redding had so carefully packed stood open, and the sticky table attested to the enjoyment of its contents. Obviously the Chalcedean had settled in and availed himself of all the room's comforts. The bedding on Hest's bunk was rumpled, half dragged to the floor. Redding's was undisturbed. The shock and loss of his friend's death swept through him again and he drew a breath, but before he could speak, the Chalcedean spun to confront him. The look on his face drove the breath from Hest's lungs and he stumbled back a step. "Clean it up!" he barked, and then flung himself, boots and all, onto Redding's bed and reclined there, eyes half lidded, face lined with weariness. When Hest just stood, staring at him, he spoke quietly. His scarred lips bulged and stretched with the words. "I don't really have a need for you anymore. If you are useful, I may keep you alive. If not . . ." His hand lifted and one of his little knives had appeared. He waggled it at Hest and smiled.

Ever since that moment Hest had lived as the Chalcedean's

slave. He served not only the assassin, but any Chalcedean who barked an order at him. He was given the lowliest and most disgusting tasks: from emptying chamber pots overboard to clearing the galley table and washing the dishes. As Hest had scrubbed the blood of slain crewmen off the deck, he had decided he would offer no resistance. He lived hour to hour. Of his fellow prisoners he saw no sign and heard only their angry shouts and pleas that weakened daily. He ate the leavings from his masters' meals and slept belowdecks in a locker full of spare line and shackles. He was glad not to be lodged with the other prisoners, for he knew that they blamed him for their predicament and would tear him to pieces if they could. His was a solitary existence, in which he was despised by the Chalcedeans and reviled by the Traders.

He learned little that he didn't already know. The impervious ships were being built in Jamaillia, and the shipbuilders cared little who paid for them, as long as they paid well. Chalcedeans might be prohibited by the Traders from the Rain Wild River, but their obsession with slaughtering dragons conquered all concerns they might have had. The Chalcedean "investors" had remained hidden on the very ship on which he had traveled up the river. And now, a bribed captain and a Chalcedean crew were taking the vessel up the Rain Wild River, into unexplored territory in the hopes of finding Kelsingra and dragons to butcher.

It was insane. Just because the ship would not be eaten by the river, it could not be assumed that the forgotten city could be found or that the malformed dragons were actually there. And if they did find Kelsingra and the dragons were there, what then? Had any of them ever witnessed the fury of an enraged dragon? When Hest had dared to voice that question, the Chalcedean had stared him down with cold, still eyes. Dread had uncoiled in Hest's belly, and he had steeled himself not to scream as he died. But the man had said only, "You have never witnessed the fury of our duke when thwarted. Insanity and impossible missions are to be preferred to disappointing him." He cocked his head. "Do you think a jeweled box with my son's hand in it is the worst thing I can imagine?" He shook his head slowly. "You have no idea." Falling silent, the assassin had stared out of the window at the passing view of the forested riverbank, and Hest had been relieved to resume his menial duties.

Hest knew little about the dragons and even less of Alise's theories about lost Elderling cities. Time and again he had been interrogated, with stern warnings that lies would bring great pain. He had never lied, being too convinced of the Chalcedean's utter willingness to punish him for any false-hood. It had been hard to stand and repeat, "I do not know," to the man's whispered or shouted questions, but from the beginning, he had known that the truth was his only protec-tion. Any lie he might have invented to please him would surely have tangled around his tongue later.

Over and over, the Chalcedean came back to one thing. "Was not this the mission your father sent you on? To re-trieve your runaway wife? And did not you tell me she had run off with your slave? So. How were you going to do that? You must know something of how to find the city and the dragons?"

"No. NO! I don't. He said I must go to the Rain Wilds, and so I went. I know no more than you do, and probably less. The people I would have spoken to are back in Tre-haug, or maybe in the cargo hold of this ship! You should ask them, not me!"

So although the Chalcedean had several times slapped him hard enough to bloody the inside of his cheek, and once backhanded him off a chair, Hest had not suffered any ex-treme physical hurt or damage. Unlike some of the Trader captives in the hold of the ship. But there was no good to be had of dwelling on that. It was none of his doing, and solely their misfortune. Confined to his gear locker, he had blocked his ears against the sounds of torture. And when he had been ordered to clean up the aftermath, he did only what he was told.

And assured himself that despite his hardships, he hadn't really been hurt. Some bruises and cuts. Some hunger. He had suffered only the utter humiliation of living at the man's beck and call. Only the complete destruction of his good name among those Traders imprisoned aboard the vessel.

Only the death of his lover and his forced participation in concealing the murder. He tried not to let his thoughts dwell on the greater impact of the terrible things that had befallen him. Sometimes his thoughts strayed to his father and mother. Did they yet know he was missing? Had they taken action, offered rewards, sent out birds hiring searchers? Or would his father grumpily assume that Hest was deliberately out of contact, having taken his lover along on his trip to the Rain Wilds? Probably the latter, he admitted to himself. He could not even dream of escaping and returning to Bingtown. This would follow him for the rest of his life unless he could find some way to redeem himself.

HEST GRITTED HIS teeth and wrung out the shirt. It was a chill and blustery day. He had started the washing with hot water, but the wind had quickly cooled it. It was one of his own shirts, he'd noted with grim silence, appropriated by the Chalcedean, as had been most of his possessions. He wore Hest's fur-lined cloak out onto the deck even in pouring rain, while Hest shivered in his shirtsleeves as he went about his tasks. He had never so hated a man as he hated the Chalcedean. He hated, too, the moments in which he wondered if this was how Sedric had sometimes felt about him, when he had indulged in utter domination of the younger man. As the boat bore him on, ever closer to a possible reunion with Sedric, he found his feelings about him were in turmoil. When he slept on the wooden planks that floored his cargo compartment, it was hard not to recall how the young man had once been eager to assure every aspect of Hest's comfort. He would have gently rubbed Hest's aching shoulders and back and exclaimed in horror over Hest's ruined hands. Sedric's devotion to him had actually begun to grate on Hest toward the end of their relationship. He recalled now how deliberately he had challenged his affection, trampling on Sedric's sentimental gestures, turning his tender advances into rough encounters and mocking his efforts to discover how he had displeased his lover. At the time, it had all been so amusing, and Redding's suggestions as to how he might test his lover's ardor had resulted in many anecdotes that he had later used to regale Redding and stimulate his rivalry with Sedric. How they had laughed together during their early assignations. With his clever tongue how Redding had mocked Sedric's gullibility and trusting nature!

And yet, despite all Sedric's declarations of devotion, he was responsible for this disaster. It was all Sedric's fault that Hest had been reduced to scrubbing out someone else's laundry, his life daily endangered and his reputation as a Bingtown Trader in tatters. In the dark hold at night, during the hours when he had the most leisure to pity himself, Hest sometimes imagined the poignancy of a possible reunion. When Sedric looked at his friend and benefactor and saw him bruised and thin, worn with hardship and unjust imprisonment, would he then realize how badly he had wronged Hest? Would he grasp the magnitude of the evil he had done with his pathetic efforts to become a Trader in his own right? Would he perhaps risk his own life to save Hest's? Or would he turn aside selfishly and leave him to his fate?

Sometimes Hest played through the possible outcomes in his mind. Sedric risking his life to save him, and Hest magnanimously welcoming him back into his life. Sometimes he ground his teeth in fury as he imagined Sedric rejoicing at the mischief he had done. But perhaps Sedric himself was already dead, the victim of his own foolishness. It was certainly the fate he hoped had befallen Alise!

At other times, when bitterness and desolation weighed him most heavily, he simply hoped he would die quickly. He had no illusions as to why the Chalcedean had preserved his life and those of the other Bingtown Traders. "Having a few valuable hostages is always a nice bit of security," the man had told him as Hest waited for him to finish eating one evening. "We've no idea what we'll encounter when we come back past Trehaug. Hostages may buy us safe passage. The only ones we have taken are those with the misfortune to have been on board our ship, and those Traders who had agreed to help us obtain dragon parts for the Duke. Since they broke their word to us, they deserved to come with us and aid us however they may in getting what they promised us. But even if they are useless at that, hostages can be offered for ransom from Chalced once we are home again. Waste not, want not."

And then, just as Hest was reflecting that his mother, at least, would pay handsomely for his return, the man added, "But don't think of becoming more trouble than you're worth. Right now, you are useful. Continue in that role, and I'll continue to spare your life. Become any sort of a nuisance, and I won't."

Hest wrung the shirt out a final time, feeling the mild sting of the acidic water on his hands. The fabric was a paler blue than when he had begun; the river was only mildly acid right now, but given enough exposure, it would eat the shirt to a rag. Too bad. It had been one of Hest's favorites. Sedric, he recalled bitterly, had chosen the fabric and the tailor for it.

He gave the wet shirt a shake, snapping it out in the crisp breeze. Clean enough. He carried the bucket to the side to dump it overboard. He sighted the other vessel at the same moment as one of the Chalcedean deckhands. "There's a boat headed toward us!" the lookout shouted. "It's an impervious vessel, twin to our own!"

Hest watched it come toward them, carried on the river's swift current and pushed by the wind against its single square sail. He stood as he was, holding the rail, listening to the shouts from the other ship, and the round of orders issued by both captains. Each appeared surprised to see the other vessel. Hest thought of calling out and warning him that there had been a mutiny, that Chalcedean pirates now held the ship, but in the end he chose caution and silence. The captain and crew of the sister ship were Jamaillian, and as the vessels maneuvered closer to each other, it was obvious to him that they had already faced some sort of trouble.

"Dragons!" someone on the other ship shouted. "We were attacked by dragons! Have you a surgeon aboard? We have need of one."

There were gouges in the ship's hull, and part of one deck railing was completely gone. The lookout who shouted carried one arm in a sling, and his head was bandaged in a turban. Hest craned his neck, trying to see more, but suddenly the Chalcedean was at his elbow. "Go below. Now."

And Hest went, like a beaten dog, followed by his master, to be shoved down into the storage compartment again. The hatch closed and he heard it secured. He went and sat down in the corner of the locker and leaned his head back against the bulwark. Sound, he had discovered, carried oddly throughout the ship. He listened. He could not make out individual words, but there was some sort of a shouted conversation, and then, as he had dreaded, running feet on the deck above him and loud commands, heavy thuds and men yelling in anger or fear, and one clear scream of agony that was cut short. The thunder of pounding feet on the deck and the shouting went on for some time and he sat hunched in suspense, wondering what was happening and how it would affect his chances of survival.

A brief quiet fell, and then noises resumed. He heard the cover of the other hatch being dragged open. The prisoners there no longer shouted and pounded on the walls as they once had; he suspected they were given enough food and water to keep them alive, but little more than that. But now the sounds he heard made him suspect the Chalcedeans had just added fresh specimens to their collection of ransomable captives. Did that mean they had captured the other vessel, or simply taken prisoners in some sort of skirmish? And why, in Sa's name, would they do that?

He drew his knees up to his chest and huddled onto his side, shivering in the chill. His mind raced, trying to think as they would. Of course. The other ship had shouted a warning to them about dragons. The other captain had found the way to wherever the dragons were. And now the Chalcedeans would use his knowledge to go where they must. To where dragons had attacked them. And Hest would go with them into that danger.

TINTAGLIA FLEW AGAIN. Not gracefully, not easily, but she flew. With every flap of her wings, fluid pulsed in a slow dribble from her toxic wound. Pain echoed each beat. The infection was spreading, taking a toll on her whole body. All around the wound area, her scales were beginning to slip, leaving the bared area of skin soft and painful. When she slept long, she awoke with her eyes gummed shut and had to snort mucus from her nostrils. She was hungry constantly, but no matter how much she ate, she took no strength from her food. Everything was a task; all pleasure had fled from her life.

Her landing in Trehaug had been disastrous. She had exhausted her strength quickly, and foolishly stooped to attack a herd of riverpigs in the shallows. She caught one, but it was small, and she had eaten it standing in the fast-flowing water. Her efforts to take to the air after that had failed. Three times she had beaten her wings furiously, and each time she had fallen back into the icy river. She'd been forced to spend a night in the cold water.

By daylight's dawning, she'd been scarcely able to stand. The thick canopy of trees leaning out over the river had made it impossible for her to take flight from the shallows. It had taken all her will to force herself to wade upriver. Only luck had delivered a basking tusker to her jaws that evening, after which she had slept on a narrow strip of reeds and mud. Two more days of sluggishly toiling up the river, eating whatever she could find, carrion included, had taken a toll on her. On the night she found a broad sandbar to sleep on, one that protruded beyond the overreaching trees, she had wondered if she would wake the following day.

But she had. Lightened by privation, driven by desperation, knowing it was her final chance, she had leaped, beating her wings. And flown again.

It took all her concentration to keep to her path. Each stroke of her wings now demanded a conscious effort and an iron will as she defied both pain and weariness to drive herself on. Soon she would have to divert from her course and find something to kill and eat. Only then would she allow herself to sleep. Already her body nagged her with weariness. She wanted to stop now, but every day she flew less and rested more. One day she would not be able to rouse herself and make the immense effort to rise once more to the skies. If that day came before she reached Kelsingra, then she would die. And dragonkind would die with her, her immature eggs never laid. Ever since she had seen the

incompetent weaklings that had emerged from the last serpents' cases, she had known that she was the sole hope of
her race.

Until, that was, the single arrow of a treacherous human
had doomed her dreams. Sometimes, as now, when the pain
blossomed brighter and brighter in her side and made every
muscle in her body ache with its echoes, she took refuge in
hatred. She fed it with plans and dreams of how she would
take vengeance on those humans, how she would return to
Chalced when she had her strength back, to sear their paltry
cities with dragon fire and dragon might. She would kill
hundreds, *thousands* of them in her revenge, and teach them
forever more to fear the wrath of a dragon.

With every downward stroke of her wings she renewed
her vow to fill the streets of those cities with screaming
humans.

Kelsingra. Not far now, she promised herself. Much farther than Trehaug, true, but she could make it. She could
because she must. Sometimes, just as sleep claimed her,
she heard the distant dragons. They had found Kelsingra
and created Elderlings for themselves and wakened the
city. Awake, she could not reach their minds. It was only
when she was on the verge of exhaustion that their distant
thoughts intersected with hers. Once she had even thought
that Malta reached out to her, her thoughts full of anxiety
and reproach. She had tried to respond to her Elderling,
tried to command her to be ready to serve her dragon. But
awake, the pain fogged her mind and made tasks as simple
as flying and hunting challenges for her. Still, that their
thoughts could brush hers meant that it could not be much
farther.

At least the rain had stopped for a time. At least she was
not flying against the wind. Such small comforts were all
she had. She beat her wings steadily but flew lower over
the river, watching for game and thus heard the cacophony
of sound before she saw the source. When she saw the two
boats below her, she knew a moment of fury. The two vessels were locked together, their crews shouting at one another and throwing each other into the river. Not a hunt for

meat, just killing each other, as usual. Noisy, useless smelly humans! Their uproar would have driven all game from the area. Just when she needed her hunting to be effortless, they had complicated it. No game of any size would venture within earshot of their useless squabbling. If she could have spared the energy, she would have circled back and spat venom at them for the trouble they had caused her. She flew low over them, hearing their cries as the wind of her passage rocked both vessels. As she did so, she caught a scent that lifted her hearts.

Dragon venom.

Grunting with the effort, she banked her wings and circled back. Yes. There were acid runs and scorches on the deck of the one vessel. It was clearly the work of an angry dragon. Or dragons? She took a long snuff of the air as she passed over the ship. Possibly more than one. Certainly it was not the work of Icefyre. She knew his rank musk well. No, the vengeance below did not reflect his temperament either. The boat still floated and the crew had been allowed to escape. Not Icefyre then. Other dragons. Other dragons that could fly! Fly, and spit acid fire. *Real dragons.* Hope blazed up within her and she resumed her course, her will to ignore the pain and live reinforced. Other dragons. Her dreams had steered her true. Other dragons lived and flew in the sky over Kelsingra. A future awaited her.

She followed the river, leaving the humans and their noise behind, around a lazy bend and then on, until she came to a long muddy spit covered in winter-dead rushes. Fortune favored her in the form of a herd of riverpigs that had emerged from the water to snout and dig in the rushes. Some ancient memory or perhaps a more recent experience alarmed them as her shadow swept over them, for they squealed and began to rush back toward the water. She answered their squeals with a scream of her own, expelling pain and hunger as she banked far too sharply on her injured side. She more fell than dived on the herd, coming down with every taloned foot extended wide. Her chest hit a large pig, pinning him to the muddy bank, and her left claws raked another wide open. With her right she convulsively seized an animal, pulling it in close to her body and uniting his squeals to the cries of the one trapped under her chest. Her eyes spun with red fury at the pain it had cost her to make her kill, and she savaged the two trapped pigs to a messy death, tearing them into pieces.

When their dying squeals faded, she remained as she was, sprawled upon her kills, trying to draw breath. Stillness was her only hope of making the pain subside. And after a time, it did, but not to its previous level. It was something she had noticed: every day it hurt more, and every day the sudden spikes of agony that a wrong movement could deliver became more debilitating. Yet the spilled blood smelled so good, and the warmth of the freshly killed prey beckoned her. As cautious as if she were woven of glass strands, she extended her neck to pick up a chunk of pig. She gulped it down, waking her hunger. Need warred with pain. She could scarcely stand, but managed to maneuver herself over the mucky ground to reach her kills.

As soon as the last piece was swallowed, lethargy rose up to claim her. It was still early in the afternoon. There was plenty of light to fly by still, but she had no strength for it. Pain still ruled her, but the muddy bank was chill and damp. She dragged herself to slightly higher ground, to where the rushes had not been crushed and dirtied by her battle. She considered, regretfully, that if she slept now, she would be here all through the night. She would not wake in time to fly more today. It was as it was, she decided. She settled, gently arranging her body in the position that hurt least and closing her eyes.

$$\diamondsuit \quad \diamondsuit \quad \diamondsuit$$

Day the 3rd of the Plough Moon

Year the 7th of the Independent Alliance of Traders
From Reyall, Keeper of the Birds, Bingtown
To Detozi, Keeper of the Birds, Trehaug

Enclosed, a transcription of a hand-carried message from Wintrow Vestrit Haven, captain of the liveship *Vivacia* and consort to the Pirate Queen Etta Ludluck.

Please note that dates indicate this message has been delayed by several months, through no fault of the Bird Keepers' Guild. It is addressed to the Khuprus household, but appears intended for Reyn and Malta Khuprus.

To my sister, Malta Vestrit Khuprus, and her husband, Reyn Khuprus, of the Rain Wild Traders:
  Sister, Brother, if you can summon that dragon of yours, there was never a better time for you to do so. My efforts to locate Selden have been fruitless. I wish he had contacted me before he undertook a journey in this direction, for I would have made sure that a suitable escort was provided to an Elderling lord and dragon-poet such as he. For now, I am heartsick to tell you that I have received tidings of a "dragon boy" that somewhat matches a description of Selden since his Elderling changes. I both hope and fear that this is indeed our little brother. My hope is that at least he was alive when this gossip reached me, and my fear is that he is in dire need of help as he has been taken as a slave of sorts, displayed as a wonder for the ignorant gawker. I pray to Sa to keep him safe wherever he may be, but I have also offered a substantial reward if he is brought safely

to me. I regretfully add that I have promised a reward also for reliable news of his demise, with evidence, for I would know what has become of him, no matter how much sorrow it brings me.

What was our mother thinking, to let him go off on his own like this? Did no one there think of how valuable a hostage he was to any that cared to take him?

Vivacia sends greetings to Althea and Brashen, if you should see them. Etta earnestly desires them to know that our Paragon wishes to see the ship whose name he bears. I myself think he is still young to hear of that part of his heritage, for doubtless the Paragon would disagree and would impart far more information than a boy of his years needs to understand just yet.

Please remember you are always welcome here and that we all most earnestly desire to see you again.

And if Selden has since wandered home, in the name of Sa herself, send me word by the swiftest means possible.

When I think of him, I still imagine him as a boy with his front teeth just beginning to grow in.

My love to both of you, and my hope that this finds you both in good health.

Your loving brother,
Wintrow

CHAPTER TEN

TINTAGLIA'S TOUCH

But we came so far!" Malta protested. "There must be something you can do! Please!"

The golden dragon once more lowered his muzzle and drew his breath in as he nearly touched her child with his nose. The dragon's head was so large that she could see only one of his eyes at a time when he was this close. That black eye seemed to whirl as he slowly lidded it and then opened it again. The wind off the river rose in a gust and swept past them. And Malta waited, hope painful in her chest.

A number of the dragons had converged on the baths late last night. Alise had cautioned her that they would not be patient of questions when they were soaking lethargically. So Malta had risen at dawn and waited in the Square of the Dragons, knowing they must pass her before they could take to the skies to hunt. They were hungry. One after another, she had importuned them to help her babe. A few had simply passed her by as if she were a mad beggar woman. Others had paused to snuff the baby. "She smells of Tintaglia," a green queen dragon had told her, and a tall cobalt dragon had said, "Would that I were of Tintaglia's lineage!," before he passed on. One after another, she had stopped them, sometimes with the aid of their keepers. Hunger flared in them, and she shared their relentless appetites when she spoke to them.

Now only one remained. His slender, golden-haired keeper stood with her hand on his mountainous shoulder, almost as if her touch could restrain him. Hunger blazed inside him, but fondness for the little creature at his side tempered it. Malta felt how impatience simmered in the dragon, but desperation boiled in her own heart. She reached for courtesy, reviewed all she knew of dragons, and sank down in a low curtsy. "Please, O Glorious One. Please, proud lord of the Three Realms. Please help me understand."

Golden Mercor drew his head back and looked down on her once more. He was almost patient as he repeated what he had already told her. "No one here is sufficiently related to Tintaglia to accomplish what you ask. Her marks are on you and on your mate. She made you the Elderlings that you are. Your child has inherited from you the distinctive traits of the dragon who made you. For him to survive, the one who left her marks upon you must alter them so he can grow." He snorted, and his rank carrion-scented breath smelled to Malta like death and despair. Perhaps he tried to be gentle as he said, "You should not have bred without the permission of your dragon."

"What?" Reyn demanded, fury scarcely caged in his voice.

Malta made a small and hasty motion with her hand, trying to caution him to calmness, but as he stepped forward, his anger was like a cold cloud around him. Malta more felt than saw several of the dragon keepers who had accompanied them step closer to them. Plainly what she was now hearing was news to them as well. She glanced back over her shoulder and saw flecks of fury in one girl's eyes. Thymara, yes, that was her name.

"Permission?" the winged girl repeated in a low voice full of outrage.

Alise suddenly held up her hands as if by doing so she could quell the mood of the Elderlings or at least bid them suppress their frustrations. "Please. Malta, if you will, allow me to ask a few questions." She stepped between Reyn and the dragon, as if her small body could shelter him from the dragon's wrath. Mercor's eyes were spinning faster, with tiny flecks of red in them. Malta held Ephron closer and reached out to seize Reyn's hand. He put his arm around both of them, but he did not allow her to retreat. Mercor's keeper stood biting her lip.

Alise glanced back at them nervously and then lifted her voice. "Mercor, most gracious and golden of all dragons, font of wisdom and power, have patience with us, we plead. What you tell us confounds us, and we seek only to understand."

Even in an Elderling robe, standing as tall as she could before the dragon, the Trader woman looked short and round now. Her body had not changed, Malta realized. It was her contrast to the tall and willowy Elderlings who surrounded her that made her seem like a creature different from them. Yet all the dragons seemed to treat her with respect. Certainly she seemed most adept at speaking to them. Malta was as frustrated as she was frightened, but bit back her anger and made not a sound. Alise had kept the golden dragon's attention when he had seemed on the point of dismissing them all. He looked at her, and pleasure at her praise seemed to shimmer off his golden scales like heat from a stove.

"Ask your question, then," he invited her.

Malta clutched at Reyn's arm. She could feel the ridged muscles in his forearms and knew how difficult it was for him to restrain himself. After days of waiting for the dragons to converge and have speech with them, it seemed that all the creatures could tell them was that Ephron must die. Had they come so far and waited so long just to hear what she had most feared from the moment of his birth? She looked down into the little face she held so close to her breast. Her son was swaddled in an Elderling tunic to keep the cold and damp from him, but even so, he never seemed warm to her touch. His dragon scaling was bright where it outlined his brow and the line of his nose, but his human flesh below it seemed grayish, and he was so thin. The little hand that had ventured outside his coverings clutched at her with fingers more like a bird's bony talons than a child's fat fingers. An ache sharper than any physical pain she had ever endured stabbed her every time she looked at him. So tiny and so brief a life, and he had never known a moment of ease or contentment.

Alise was speaking. "For generations, the folk of the Rain Wilds have suffered the deaths of their children, children born too changed to survive. Those who have lived have taken on some aspects of Elderlings that we have seen depicted on ancient tapestries, but they too go to early graves. All these things the Rain Wild Traders have accepted as the cost of living where they do. Yet in all those days, there were no dragons to wreak changes on them. Why, then, wise Mercor, did they have to endure such hardships?"

The dragon's head was held high, and he appeared to be looking off into the distance. Was he thinking, or merely wishing the puny humans would leave him alone so that he could safely launch himself back into the air and return to hunting?

He spoke reluctantly. "Humans are vulnerable to dragons. Of old, we changed some of you deliberately, to better fit you to be companions and servants to our kind. You lived such a short time that it was nearly impossible for us to achieve full communication with a human before it died. And so we allowed and shaped change for those who seemed most fit to live alongside us. But soon humans learned that any exposure to dragons and the things of dragons could change any human, and that those changes were not always beneficial. So those who took pleasure and found purpose in serving the dragons built their cities and their works, lived alongside us, and took joy in serving us. They cherished the ways we could change them.

"Those who wished to remain unchanged ventured into those cities but seldom and knowing the risk involved. Here, in Kelsingra, Elderlings lived. Humans lived and worked in a different settlement, across the river. Others lived outside the city, where they tended herds or grew crops far from the silver-streaked stone walls of the city. Risks were known, and those who took the risks did so of their own will. We did no willful harm to humans; if harm was done, they brought it on themselves."

Was it the dragon's words alone or did he summon memories from the stone? Malta felt entranced, as if she saw and heard the things he related. She could see this square thronged with folk, talking together in the spring sunshine. A silver-gloved Elderling with three elaborate marionettes dangling from his hands shouted to three tall, slender women carrying gleaming pipes. One lifted hers to her lips and tweetled a reply to him, and several passersby laughed at the exchange. Through the Elderlings came a lumbering violet dragon, his wings chased with silver, wearing an elaborate golden harness covered with a thousand tiny round bells. The crowd parted for him and many an Elderling shouted a greeting or made an obeisance to him as he passed. The bells made a sweet, shrill jingling. Mercor's ancestor? The glorious scene of prosperity and plenty faded and she once more stood in the windy plaza hearing his words.

"While dragons were gone from the world and Elderlings, too, humans came into the lands where once we had prospered. You discovered the magic creations of the Elderlings and the places they had shared with dragons. You handled their works and lived where dragons had walked and lived. Enough influence remained that those who lived there changed. But the changes were random, not shaped by a dragon, and often displeasing or dangerous.

"So you keepers were when you first came to serve us. Contorted by proximity to the things of dragons, but not on the path to being true Elderlings. But, with a bit of blood to bond you to us, we could shape you to be more pleasing. For there is Silver in dragon blood, and we are most powerful when our blood is rich with it. Deprived of Silver as we have been, each of us yet still has the power to shape an Elderling to our service. So we have changed you, made you Elderlings, and if later you attempt to have children, we may shape them as well. But no dragon can change what another dragon has begun, any more than a human can change the aspects of another human's child. Tintaglia herself might be able to aid your baby, but none of us can."

There was nothing of apology in his tone, and a cold part of Malta wondered if dragons could even grasp the concept of regretting something they had done, or feeling responsible for the pain their carelessness could cause. Her fear vanished suddenly, leaving only her fury. If her son could not live, what did it matter what this dragon might do to her? She stepped forward suddenly, almost shouldering Alise aside to stand before Mercor. She felt her skin flush with her anger and knew that the crest on her brow and her scaling took on brighter colors as she did so.

"I never asked for this!" Her low voice was swollen with anger and sorrow. "Tintaglia never sought our permission for the changes Reyn and I have experienced, let alone warned us that our baby might suffer for them. Our changes brought beauty and pleasure to us, but we would not have accepted them if we had known the price! Nor did I ever take blood from Tintaglia! So how can this change in me be her doing?"

The dragon tucked his head and looked down on her. His black eyes were spinning with silver glints that seemed to ride that ominous whirlpool. But his response was thoughtful rather than angry. "You were near her at some point. Did you run your hands over the cocooned dragon? Share long thoughts with her, perhaps breathe the warmth of her breath?"

Reyn spoke quietly, to her rather than the dragon. "Selden and I were there when she melted her way out of her case. The air was thick with the stench of dragon; we both breathed it in."

"I was there, too, in that same chamber. And Sa knows I shared thoughts with her during that time. But—"

Mercor made a sudden sound of impatience, cutting her

off. He looked up at the morning sky, as if he longed to take flight and begin his day's hunt. The other dragons had already left. He alone remained, and she sensed he would not stay much longer. When he returned his gaze to Malta, the ebon liquid of his great eyes spun more slowly. A long moment passed as he studied her. Great puzzlement and curiosity were conveyed as he asked, "Why do you ask so many questions, Malta Vestrit Khuprus?" Malta could feel how he tried gently to compel a truthful answer by the use of her full name. "You have been touched with Silver in a purposeful way. The smell of that magic is all over you and wakes my thirst for it. Why do you ask questions when it seems to me you must know the answers very well indeed?"

"Me? Tintaglia marked me with red, not silver!" She looked at the scaling on her arms, trying to discover the meaning of his words.

Mercor snorted out his disdain. "You bear the mark of Silver, on the back of your neck. I can smell it on you still, even though you have worn it for years. Someone touched you, with skill and purpose, and sent you on your way to fulfill a great task." The dragon leaned close to her, and she saw her own shocked face reflected in his gleaming black eye. "Whence came the Silver that marks the back of your neck? You must know how great our need for it is! You come to us, asking this favor, but hide from us the source of your Silver that began your change."

Malta's hand flew to the back of her neck. "I don't know what you are talking about!" she proclaimed in confusion. But she did know of the faint silvery scaling there, each mark the size of a fingerprint. Never before had she associated it with a dragon. The marks had been there since the day her family had launched the *Paragon,* long before the fall of Bingtown had sent her fleeing to the Rain Wilds and ultimately to the cocooned dragon's chamber. No dragon had put them upon her. She held Tintaglia responsible for many things in her life, but not those marks.

Reyn spoke out in her defense. "She has always had those marks. Birthmarks when first I glimpsed them, just dusky smudges, now made silver by her changes. That is all they are. We keep nothing from you, great dragon. Whatever we have is yours, if you will just save our child. Take my life, eat me now if you wish, but let my son know a moment of peace and calm!" And then the man Malta loved more than life fell to his knees before the dragon and offered the golden dragon his bent neck.

"Oh, please," she moaned, knowing how ravenous the dragon was. But Mercor did not move to strike. If anything, his stillness became that of stone. All around her the gathered keepers kept silent. Sylve kept her hand on her dragon's shoulder, and Alise stood with both her hands clasped over her mouth as if to seal in a scream of terror.

Then the dragon slowly swung his head away. "You speak those words as if you believed them true. You know nothing useful, I fear. Tintaglia's Elderlings, I cannot help your babe. But if you have any loyalty to dragonkind . . ." He lifted his head high and suddenly trumpeted the words loud, issuing his command to every keeper there, "Find the Silver well for us! She is proof that one still exists somewhere! In her lifetime, someone has touched Silver and shared that touch with her. If you care for us at all, make this your quest now. For until it is found, no Elderling magic can be done, no dragon can prosper! Find the Silver well for us."

"If we find this Silver well for you, will you then save my baby?" Malta tried recklessly for a bargain. She knew nothing of Silver. Offering it was her last hope.

The dragon looked at her a final time. "I have told you. Only Tintaglia can save your child. Reach for her, Elderling. Tell your dragon of your plight and perhaps she will come to aid you." He turned away, and Sylve lifted her hand and stepped out of his way. He did not look at her as he added, "But do not have great hopes. Tintaglia did not come to us when we needed her. If she would not come for dragons, I doubt she will come for an Elderling."

Malta could not breathe. Did the dragon know he had just condemned her child to death? Did he understand what it meant to them? He looked at her, and his slender keeper shook her head slowly. A sense of Mercor's sympathy reached Malta, but it was the same sort of sympathy she

would have extended to a child with a wilted flower. The
dragon did not grasp her agony.

"But cannot one of you—" Reyn began, but Malta was
already turning away from them all.

"Let's just go," she said quietly. "If this must be, let us
just go somewhere private and be with him while we can."
She walked away, not so much from Reyn as from the gathered keepers and the dragons. Some things were too hard to
bear, and the scrutiny of outsiders only made them worse.
She began to tremble as she walked, a shuddering she could
not control. Reyn was suddenly at her side, putting his arm
around both of them and guiding her staggering steps. Behind
her, the muttering of voices rose, but she did not look back.
She and Reyn could do nothing for Ephron except be with
him as his little life ended. So that was what they would do.

"GET UP HERE. Now." The Chalcedean barked the order as
if it had been Hest's idea to stay belowdecks after the sun
was up.

He had awakened from his chill and cramped sleep as
soon as the locker was opened. Even so, it was hard to move
quickly. Hest was still blinking at the light as he emerged
onto the deck. Early morning, he estimated, and for a bless-
ing, it was not raining at the moment. He looked about
hastily, trying to gauge the situation quickly. The boat was
moving slowly upriver, the rowers steady at their oars. The
other impervious boat was following them. He stared at the
other craft for a moment, wondering if they followed under
duress or if they were allied now.

The Chalcedean had no patience with his curiosity. "Not
there!" He cuffed Hest, then pointed ahead of them and
Hest's jaw dropped at what he saw. Ahead of them was a
low spit of grassy mud projecting into the river. Amid the
rushes, the dragon was curled like a huge blue cat, asleep
and glittering in the wan afternoon light. The Chalcedean
spoke in a low voice. "We are going to kill it. But we need
to know everything you know about dragons. Does it have
a vulnerable spot? If it awakens before we manage a quick
kill, how will it respond to our attack?"

Hest shook his head. "I don't know. I've never tried to kill a dragon! Look at the size of that animal. You'd have to be mad to attack it!" The assassin gave him a dangerous look and Hest reconsidered his tack. What did he know? Only what he had heard. He cleared his throat and spoke more calmly. "When the Chalcedeans invaded Bingtown, a dragon helped us fight them off. A blue one, like that one but much smaller. She was able to spit acid, sometimes as a mist that rained down on ranks of men and sometimes in a spray aimed at one man. She also used her wings and her tail to lash at the ships and the warriors. She had clawed feet, too. But what I am telling you is what I was told. I never actually saw her fighting. I wasn't in that part of the city." He hadn't been in Bingtown at all for those weeks, in truth, but had fled with his mother to their country house. The marauders had never penetrated that far inland.

"Useless!" The Chalcedean dismissed him, turning away to speak to another of his party. They conversed in Chalcedean, and they were either unaware that Hest was a fluent speaker of that tongue or did not care if he overheard them.

"We will put in here, downriver of it, and approach on foot. The creature is far larger than expected from what our spies have told us of the Rain Wild dragons. We have two archers, and they must go first. Aim for an eye and perhaps we will kill it as it sleeps. If it awakes, then send in everyone else with pikes."

The other man shook his head. "Lord Dargen, it is too dangerous. When we captured the other vessel as you commanded, we lost men we could not afford to lose. We are already spread too thin manning both vessels. If you take most of our men off both ships to attack the dragon and the attack fails, there will not be enough of us left to man one ship. We will all die here."

The assassin—Lord Dargen—stared at his companion as if he were stupid. "This is why we came. To kill a dragon, to butcher it, and to return to Chalced as swiftly as we can." He shook his head, and then smiled. "We may all die here, or we may all die somewhere else, or all our families may die while we are here thinking of ways to save our own lives.

It is done. We are marching toward death as soon as we are born. The only hope a man has is that his family line will remain, that his sons will go forward to father more sons, and that his name will be remembered by them. If I do not soon bring to the Duke's feet that which he desires, all futures will be lost to me. So I risk my life today in the hopes that my memory will go on forever if I succeed. Put in to shore. I myself will lead the men." He jerked his head at Hest. "Put my servant back in his den. He is useless, and I do not want him underfoot."

The man seized Hest by the arm and jostled him along. As he was shoved unceremoniously and without benefit of ladder belowdecks, Hest knew that he was receiving the treatment the man longed to inflict on Lord Dargen himself.

"Lord Dargen," he muttered as he stood up. "Now I have his name! A thread I can follow to deliver vengeance to his door." He spoke the words aloud, but in the cold wooden space they sounded as hollow as a child's threats against the father who has sent him to his room. He folded himself into the corner, his arms wrapped around his knees and tried not to think what would become of him if the dragon attacked the ship. He'd be helpless, trapped like a rat in the bilge as the ship went down. Cold water. He never imagined he'd die drowning in cold water.

TINTAGLIA LIFTED HER head and unlidded her eyes. Outrage that anyone dared approach her while she was sleeping flooded her. Humans, clustering close, weapons raised! She surged to her feet, tail lashing, and roared at the sudden pain that swept her as her injury opened and fresh fluid ran down her side.

"Leave me!" she demanded, and as her command washed against the men facing her, the first barrage of arrows struck. She was in motion, but three still struck her face. They rattled off her, one striking her ridged brow, and the two others hitting just below her eye. Plainly her eye had been the target, and in that instant she realized fully that they intended to kill her. She turned her shoulder and flank to them, showing them only the most heavily scaled parts

of her body. At the same time, she slashed her tail and men
tumbled, either victims of her blow or of their own frantic efforts to avoid it. She became aware of the other men
moving up on her: they were trying to surround her!

One man ran forward, a pike in his hands. His face was
set in a rictus of fear and determination. One of her ancestors had known such a charge, and so she did not rear back
onto her hind legs and expose her softer belly. Her wings
she kept clapped tight to her sides lest they see her swollen
wound and know her vulnerability. Instead, she threw her
head back on her long neck and then snapped it forward,
opening her mouth to hiss out a cloud of venom.

But nothing emerged from her wide open jaws. Her
poison sacs were empty, victim to her long illness. The warriors cowered and one man screamed as the mist of saliva
engulfed them. When, a few instants later, they realized
they were unhurt, they whooped triumphantly and surged at
her in a wild charge.

She willed herself to spin tightly, to meet their attack
with a savage lash of her tail. Instead, she moved as ponder-
ously as a wounded buffalo, limping as she slowly wheeled
away from them. They were on her, jabbing at her with
their spears and shrieking. All she could sense from their
thoughts was fear and triumph and bloodlust, just as if she
were battling jackals for the rights to a kill. She swept her
tail, knocking some of them down while others leaped back
and jeered at her.

"You will pay!" she roared at them, and one or two of
their minds registered astonishment that an animal could
speak. But the others were deaf to her words as so many
humans were. They came at her again, thudding their useless spears against her heavy scaling. She turned toward
them again, thinking of charging at them and crushing as
many as she could with her jaws. But a spear flew, striking
dangerously close to her eye, and she knew a sudden jolt of
fear. These humans *could* kill her. They were not shepherds
trying to drive her away from their flock, or hunters trying
to defend their prey from her. They had come here to kill
her.

She roared again, and there was a small satisfaction in seeing some of them hastily retreat. But others set their spears at the ready and ran toward her.

Tintaglia had no choice. She staggered toward them, stiffly and then in a lumbering charge, whipping her head from side to side, sending one man flying into the rushes and flattening another. She trod on her screaming victim as she passed, vindictively flexing her foot to be sure her nails scored him well.

Once past them, there was no escape save the river in front of her. She could not take flight; she needed time to limber her muscles and space to gather herself for that first painful vault into the air. She lashed her tail as she thundered past them and knew the satisfaction of feeling it connect and hearing a man scream. She did not look back. Better to appear that she was merely stalking off rather than fleeing.

The river awaited. She did not pause, but waded into it. Her enemies had nosed their vessels onto the bank downstream of her. So the humans had abandoned whatever quarrel they had with each other to unite in coming after her! She thought about destroying the ships in passing, but doubted her strength. Instead, she waded chest-deep in the water and started upriver. If they wanted to come after her, they'd have to reboard their vessels and man the oars. And if they did come up on her in the water, she thought she could possibly tip a boat over, or at least destroy a bank of oars.

She heard them shouting in frustration on the bank behind her. A spear splashed into the water beside her, and an arrow struck her back plates, lodged briefly between two of them and then fell. Stupid insects, daring to attack her! If she hadn't already been injured, there would have been nothing but smoking meat and shattered wood left of them and their ships!

She took another step and then the river water penetrated beneath her tightly clasped wings and she trumpeted in furious pain as the icy water found her wound with an acid kiss. Lurching on, she stumbled to her knees as the agony stabbed into her deeper than the spearhead had ever penetrated. The men on the shore screamed and whooped like monkeys as they watched her sink, her legs collapsing under her. She turned to look back at them, and shrieked a thought out on a wild blast of anger. *"You will all die! I give you a dragon's promise unending. All humans who attack dragons die!"*

She sent that blast of anger winging wide, a desperate message to the distant dragons of Kelsingra. As the pain stabbed deeper into her and the cold water sucked the warmth from her flesh, she wondered if any heard it.

✧ ✧ ✧

Day the 5th of the Plough Moon

Year the 7th of the Independent Alliance of Traders
From the Bird Keepers' Guild
Notice of Commendation

To be posted at all Guild Halls.

We are most pleased to announce this honor for Erek Dunwarrow, formerly a keeper of the birds in Bingtown and a master bird handler in good standing with the Guild. With this commendation, we recognize his significant contributions to the bird-breeding program at Bingtown, specifically the program for breeding birds for hardiness and swiftness.

A prize of sixty silvers is hereby awarded to him, and the further honor that birds of this particular lineage and coloration will now be formally named as Dunwarrows.

✧ ✧ ✧

CHAPTER ELEVEN

SILVER

There were some wonderful places up near the foothills. Smaller, but with sweeping views. Closer to hunting." Carson added the last in a lower voice, knowing that hunting was not really one of the criteria that topped Sedric's list. He turned his eyes toward the hills and cliffs that backed the city and stared wistfully at their forested flanks.

"Closer to the wild lands. And farther from everything else," Sedric pointed out with a wry smile.

"From the river, perhaps," Carson countered. "But closer to everything else that we need right now to live independently. The hunting is good in the wooded hills; the dragons prefer to hunt the more open lands. And there are trees that may bear nuts or fruit. There will almost certainly be wild berries. The supplies that Captain Leftrin brought back from Cassarick won't last forever. We shouldn't be waiting until they run out before we worry about it. We should be stocking up on meat now, and scouting for other food sources."

"I think I've heard this before," Sedric said quietly, and Carson suddenly stopped in midbreath.

Then he laughed. "I know. I say the same things over and over. Usually to you, because I sometimes think you're the only one listening to me. The others act like children, thinking only of this day, this hour."

"The others listen too. They're just enjoying a brief respite from daily hunts and work on the dock and every other task you urge them to undertake. They *are* young, Carson. And suddenly they have tea and jam and ship's biscuit again. Give them a few more days, and then I'll help you persuade some of them to go on an extended hunt again. But for now, can't we take a bit of time for ourselves? There's a house I want to show you. I think you'd like it."

"A house?" Carson cocked his head and grinned. "Or a mansion?"

It was Sedric's turn to shrug ruefully. "Well, any house in Kelsingra is bound to seem a mansion to you. The Rain Wilds taught all of you to build small. But there's a street of houses I walked through a few days ago that intrigued me. And yes, they are large, even by Bingtown standards. But the one I went into had garden rooms in it, with transparent ceilings. So, although we might be a long way from the forest or foothills, we might be able to grow food right in our home."

"If we had seed— Oh, very well. Let's look at it," Carson conceded as Sedric shot him a long-suffering look. "I suppose you are right, and Leftrin did say that he put in an order for seed and chickens and so on. I just never imagined myself tending a garden. Or raising birds to eat."

"I never imagined myself as an Elderling," Sedric countered. "Carson, I think we are going to have a lot of years to explore many kinds of lives. We may farm, or raise cattle . . ."

"Or hunt."

"Or hunt. Here. I think this is the right street. Kelsingra is so big and so spread out. Every time I think I've learned the city, I find another street to explore. Up this way I think. Or was it downhill from here?"

Carson chuckled tolerantly. "Did you notice if there was a view? If so, that would be uphill." He halted and watched Sedric look up and down the street. He straightened the collar of his tunic. He had to admit that the clothing Sedric had chosen for him was comfortable. And warm. And weighed less than his leathers. He glanced down at himself, at his legs clad in a blue that reminded him of a parrot's wings. Elderling garb. At least the boots were brown. They were so light he felt as if he had nothing on, and yet his feet weren't cold and the stones underfoot didn't jab him. The wide brown belt he wore was of Elderling make, as was the sheathed knife he wore on it. The blade wasn't metal. He wasn't sure what it was, but it had been razor sharp from the moment he drew it from the sheath and it had stayed that way. It looked like blue, baked pottery to him more than anything else. Yet another Elderling mystery.

The more the keepers explored the city, the more artifacts they found. True, most of the houses and shops and buildings were empty, as if the people who had lived here had packed and left. But in some sections of the city, they were finding mansions and homes that held all sorts of Elderling items. Most items of wood had crumbled to dust, and scrolls and books had likewise decayed. But some of their fabrics had survived, especially of the sort that his tunic was made from, and it was not unusual anymore to see keepers ringed and necklaced as if they were wealthy Bingtown traders. It made Carson uneasy, though he had difficulty expressing why. Just as deciding which house to take over as their own made him uncomfortable. He and Sedric had been sharing chambers above the dragon baths, and even these had seemed a sybaritic luxury to him. He wasn't sure that he understood why Sedric wanted a large and elaborate home. But he deserved one, if that was what he wanted.

He glanced over at him and had to smile. Sedric looked so intent, as alert as any hunter, as he prowled down the street studying the grand houses that fronted it. The move to Kelsingra had agreed with him. Carson was a fastidious man about cleanliness, when such a state was possible, but Sedric elevated it to an art form. His hair gleamed gold, touched with the metallic sheen that Relpda had awarded to every part of him. To his eyes and his skin, his nails, and even his hair she had lent coppery warmth. Today, Sedric had chosen to echo that gleam with metallic blues in his tunic and hose, while his belt and boots were black. The Elderling garb wore so well, Carson thought no one needed more than one extra change of clothing. But Sedric had appropriated a rainbow for his wardrobe and took unutterable joy in varying his garb, sometimes several times a day. Even if Carson did not understand his partner's infatuation with clothing, it did not diminish his delight in watching him exercise it. Sedric felt Carson's scrutiny and turned to the hunter with a questioning look.

"What?" he demanded.

Carson's smile widened. "Just you. That's all."

A blush suffused Sedric's face, rendering him both more boyish and yet more charming. And that he blushed because he was overwhelmed by Carson's compliment only magnified the effect for the hunter. He jostled Sedric with an elbow and then put an arm around him. "Which house?" he asked him genially, knowing that if, at that moment, Sedric declared he wished to live in all of them at once, he'd have done his best to make it possible.

"Wait!" Sedric said sharply. He shrugged out from under Carson's arm and strode briskly away. For a moment, Carson felt hurt; then he recognized the intensity of Sedric's stalking. An odd prickle of premonition ran up his own spine as he stared around.

This was a district of elaborate houses, and almost every intersection boasted a fountain or a statue or plaza of some sort. Any of the structures were palatial by Carson's standards, but Sedric was moving steadily downhill, ignoring their allure. He strode through a small square with a statue of a woman pouring water and turned deliberately into a street of humbler houses. The thoroughfares went from broad avenues fit for a parade of dragons to wide but wind-

ing streets, and the buildings changed to a more human
scale as they moved along it. Odd. Carson had never imagined that such simple dwellings might attract his peacock
lover. Sedric moved strangely, peering from side to side,
not like a man who considers the houses he passes but as if
trying to find something he'd lost. No. Like a man who had
lost his way, Carson suddenly realized, and was looking for
a landmark. He lifted his own eyes and scanned the area.
Like all of Kelsingra, it was built of stone, and here a bluish-
gray stone predominated. He noticed nothing noteworthy.
Cautiously, he opened his awareness of the city and let the
impressions of Elderlings long dead touch his thoughts.

He had always felt a bit squeamish about this aspect of
being an Elderling. A private man himself, he felt strange
wallowing in the personal memories of others. The other
keepers seemed to take it in stride, and personally he did
not blame those who chose to enjoy the sensual memories
of another time. In such a small population, it was better
for them to satisfy their needs that way than to jostle and
fight for the available partners. And he knew there was valuable information to be gained in sharing memories from the
stones, technical information on the workings of the city in
addition to knowledge of the ways of dragons and the surrounding lands. He knew that Sedric enjoyed tapping the
memory stones in the same way that he had enjoyed going
to plays or listening to minstrels. The stones of the city were
full of stories, some dramatic, some poignant. But no other
part of the city had felt the way this one did. It was quiet.
No memories stirred here, no brief waft of scent or echo of
someone's laughter from a long-ago summer day. Here the
city was mute, hoarding its secrets in silence. Sedric glanced
back at him, bafflement on his face, and Carson sensed his
partner had just shared the same realization.

"What are you looking for?" he called to Sedric, and his
words bounced back to him from the silent stone.

"I'm not sure." Sedric stared all around him like a man
wakening from a dream. "The streets just suddenly seemed
very familiar. As if I'd been here before, and often. For an
important reason. But every time I try to remember that part

of the memory, it fades out of reach. But in an odd way. The Elderling memories I've taken from stone usually stay with me clearly. But this is like fog . . ."

"In a purposeful way." Carson finished the thought for him.

"Yes. As if something were being deliberately concealed."

The buildings that they passed now were no longer homes or mansions but were designed to allow dragons to enter as freely as humans. They walked quietly past them, their softly shod feet whispering on the paving stones.

"It's older here," Sedric said suddenly. "The way the streets are paved, the buildings . . . this is older than the part of the city where the dragon baths are, or that grand Hall of Records with the map tower."

"I suspect this is where Kelsingra began." Carson nodded to where worn steps went down into a building's entrance. "It seems to me it would take a lot of feet walking down stone steps before they were worn like that. And these buildings are actually lower than the street, if you look at it. As if the streets have been repaired and raised." In reply to Sedric's startled glance, Carson looked aside. "I've never been there, but I've heard that Old Jamaillia is like that. One fellow who had been there told me that openings that used to be first-floor windows are doors now, the streets have been built up so much."

Sedric nodded, a slow smile curving his lips. "I have been there, and you're right. Strange. I was looking right at it and not really seeing it."

For a time, they walked in silence. The streets grew narrower and the buildings humbler, as if when people had first settled here, they had not known the full ambition of Elderlings. Carson found that Sedric had drawn closer to him. Carson linked arms with him and felt himself more alert than he usually was in this city. The din of memories simply didn't exist in this part of the city. Perhaps it had been built before the Elderlings had gained the magic of storing memories in stone. The scuff of their footsteps on the cobblestones seemed louder, the warmth of Sedric's skin under his fingers more intimate. All his senses were keener here. He

felt more himself and wondered uneasily who he had been
before.

"There!" Sedric said suddenly, and pointed.

"What is it?" Carson asked. Recognition tickled at the
back of his mind, but he could not summon the memory.

"I don't know," Sedric admitted. "I only know it's important."

Carson shivered suddenly but not with a chill. Something
else. Danger? Anticipation? He lifted his head and sniffed
the air, wondering if the scent of a predator had triggered it.
Nothing. But an almost sexual excitement infused him suddenly, and as it tingled through his body, he recognized it
was not his own. Spit, never far from him in thought, knew
something about this place. Or almost did. Somewhere, the
little silver dragon had tipped his wings, ignoring the dozing
deer below him. He was winging back to the city as fast as
he could. Carson stared around him, trying to see what his
dragon had glimpsed through his eyes.

"It" was an open plaza, not as wide or as grand as many
in the newer part of the city. In the center of it was a tumble
of rubble. The destruction looked both deliberate and recent—or at least much more recent than the other quake
damage to the city. A length of black chain coiled like a
dead snake. Timbers of green and gold and red had been
rendered to kindling. They approached the collapsed structure slowly, and Sedric was the first to speak. "It's sticking
out of a hole there. See the low wall around it, or what is
left of it? It looks like a well, for drawing water, but much
wider. But with a river so close by, why would they dig a
well here?"

"It wasn't for water," Carson said quietly. He listened
to his own words as if someone else were speaking them,
then he fell silent, chasing an elusive idea. At last he spoke
a single word. "Silver," he said aloud, echoing his dragon's
thought, and then shook his head in denial. "It makes no
sense."

But Sedric seemed to grow taller, as if he were a puppet
and someone had just drawn his head string up. His eyes
opened wider. "Silver? SILVER!" He shouted the word.

"This is it, Carson. From my dreams. The Silver place. Sweet Sa, you're right. This is the Silver well, the whole reason Kelsingra was first built. Remember, a long time ago, you wondered why they'd built such a grand city here. What was the reason for it, what trade, what industry, what port anchored it? Why build a city for dragons in a place so chill and damp in the winters? Why did the Elderlings stay here? And here's our answer. The Silver well. The secret heart of Kelsingra."

Carson blinked. Sedric's words had filled his ears, flooding his mind with vague memories, linking half thoughts and hints into an almost recognizable network. "Secret, indeed. Knowledge kept from outsiders. Only Elderlings were allowed to come here, to this part of the city." He breathed deeply, and it was as if he inhaled information. He frowned as another thought drifted into his mind. "And not all Elderlings. Only a few had the privilege of this duty. It was a closely kept secret, not just from the outside world, but even within the city. Memories of it were never preserved in the stone, at least not intentionally. It was passed down, from one generation of well tenders to the next. Silver was so rare, so precious, that the well sites could not be mapped or recorded in memory stone. Like a guild secret that only masters could know. A secret so precious that even the dragons did not speak of it to dragons from other hatching grounds." His gaze went sad and distant. "A resource so precious it was probably the only things dragons would war over with one another."

"How do you know?" Sedric demanded curiously.

Carson lifted his shoulders and let them fall in a slow shrug. "Some of it comes from Spit, but even he didn't have enough to puzzle it out. I've been deliberately seeking out the places where people stored memories of how the city worked. The water system, the heated buildings, how the stones were fitted so well to one another. I like to know how things are done, how things *were* done. I have found a lot of information about what they did, but little about how. I think those same people who left stone memories of what they did tended this well, and . . . did something else here.

It's not clear to me. But I think that, without intending to, they stored bits of those memories with the other ones. Enough for me to puzzle it together and get a feeling for it. Like following a game trail with no tracks. A bent stick, a torn leaf . . ."

For a moment, his vision dimmed. He blinked and shook his head, and then he realized he hadn't imagined it. The day was darker. He glanced up to find the reason. Overhead, the dragons were gathering in a gyre that spiraled up to block the sun's thin rays. They circled overhead, coming lower. Spit led the way. In the distance, golden Mercor was coming fast, growing larger. He trumpeted and the others answered. Wordlessly, they were summoning all the keepers to converge here. Carson looked at Sedric; his friend was smiling. "I think they heard me."

But as Carson looked up at the circling creatures, he felt a premonition. It became a flood of sensation, jubilation and anticipation making his heart hammer. He knew he felt only an echo of the emotions of the dragons. "Sedric. What is the 'Silver well'? What is it about the stuff that comes out of it?"

"I'm not sure exactly. Mercor said to Malta that all dragons have some Silver naturally, in their blood, that it helps them change us to Elderlings. There has to be more to it than that, given how anxious they are to find it. I think we'll soon find out just why it's so important."

THYMARA JERKED AS if jabbed with a needle. An instant later, Tats followed her example. She had been dozing in the crook of his arm. They had fallen asleep in the glass-roofed atrium of a building that had once been devoted to flowers. The bas-reliefs on the walls depicted flower blossoms of a kind she had never seen before, and of a size that seemed completely impossible, until Tats had gently suggested to her that the images were made so large in order to show detail. The room they were in was at the top of the building. A flat section of the roof would have allowed dragons to alight and enter through an archway. A maze of large pots and vessels of earth surrounded benches where once

Elderlings had sat and discussed the plants. She had tried to imagine having the leisure hours in her life to spend a whole day just looking at flowers, and could not. "Did they eat them?" she had wondered aloud. "Did they work here, growing them for food?"

By way of response, Tats had wandered over to a statue of a woman holding a basket of flowers and set his fingertips to her hand. His face grew bemused, his gaze distant. She watched his awareness recede from her, slipping into the memories of the woman with the flowers. His eyelids drooped and the muscles of his face loosened as he wandered through her life. His expression became vacant and slack, almost idiotic. She found she didn't like how he looked, but knew it was useless to speak to him. He'd come back to her when he willed it, and not before.

Almost as soon as she had the thought, she saw his eyes twitch, and then he blinked. Tats came back into his face and then smiled at her. "No. The flowers were cultivated simply for their beauty and fragrance. They came from far away, from a land much warmer than here, and only inside this room could they flourish. This Elderling wrote seven books about them, describing them in detail and giving directions for their care, and telling how one might force larger blossoms or subtly change the colors and fragrances by using different types of soil and adding things to the water."

Thymara had drawn her knees up to her chin. The benches were like the bed in her room; they appeared to be stone, until one had been seated for a time. Then they softened, slightly. She shook her head in wonder. "And she devoted months of her life to this work."

"No. Years. And was well respected for it."

"I don't understand."

"I'm starting to. I think it has to do with how long one expects to live." He paused and then cleared his throat uncomfortably. "When I think about how long we may have to live, how many years I may be able to spend with you, it lets me think about things differently."

She shot him a strange look, and he came over to sit on the wide bench next to her. He met her gaze for a time, and then he lay back on the bench and stared up at the sky through the dust-streaked glass. "Rapskal and I had a talk. About you."

Thymara stiffened. "Did you?" She heard the chill in her own voice.

A small smile tweaked Tats's mouth. "We did. Would you be more pleased if I'd said we'd had a fistfight? I think we both knew it might come to that. Rapskal is changing as he takes on the memories of that Elderling. He's becoming more . . ." He paused, seeking a word. "Assertive," he said, and she sensed it was not quite the word he wanted.

"And he was the one who was wise enough to come to me and say he didn't want us to end up fighting. That we'd been friends too long to end it for any reason, but especially over jealousy over you."

She sat stiffly beside him, trying to decipher not only what she felt but why she felt it. Hurt. Angry. Why? Because she felt they had gone past her, perhaps decided between themselves something that should have been discussed with her. She imposed calm on her voice. "And what did the two of you decide?"

He didn't look at her, but he reached over and took her hand. She let him hold it but did not return the pressure of his fingers. "We didn't decide anything, Thymara. It wasn't that kind of a conversation. Neither one of us is Greft, thinking that we can force you to make a decision. You've proven your point to both of us. When or even if you want to be with one of us, you will. And until then . . ." He gave a small sigh and then finally looked at her.

"Until then you wait," she said, and felt a small thrill of satisfaction at his understanding that she controlled the situation.

"I do. Or I don't."

Startled, she met his gaze. It was strange to look at his face now and recall the smooth-skinned boy he had been. His dragon had incorporated his slave tattoo into his scaling, but the horse on his cheek looked more dragonish now. She almost lifted a hand to touch it but held herself back. "What does that mean?"

"Only that I'm as free as you are. I could walk away. I could find someone else—"

"Jerd," she growled.

"She's made it plain, yes." He rolled onto his side and tugged at her hand. Reluctantly, she lay down beside him. After a time, the bench adapted to her wings, cradling her. She looked into his eyes, her gaze cold. He smiled. "But I could also be by myself. Or wait for others to come and join us here. Or go looking for someone else. I have time. That's what Rapskal and I talked about. That if, as seems likely, we may live two or even three hundred years, then we all have time. Nothing has to be rushed. We don't have to live as if we were children squabbling over toys."

Toys. Her, a toy? She tried to pull away from him.

"No, listen to me, Thymara. I felt the same way when Rapskal first spoke to me. Like he was making what I feel a trivial thing. Like he was telling me to wait and that when he was finished with you, I could have you. But that wasn't it at all. I thought it was stupid of him, at first, all the time he spent with memory stone. But I think he's learned something. He said that the longer life is, the more important it is to keep your friends, to not have quarrels that can be avoided." His smile faded a bit, and for a time he looked troubled. "He said that, as a soldier, he had learned that a man's deep friendships were the most important thing he could possess. Things can be broken, or lost. All a man can keep for certain are the things in his mind and heart."

He lifted his free hand and traced the line of her jaw. "He said that no matter what you decided, he wanted to stay friends with me. And he asked me if I could do the same. If I could resolve that what you decided was your decision, not something we should blame on the other fellow."

"I think that's what I've been trying to tell you," Thymara said quietly, but in her heart she wondered if that were so.

"He said something else, something I've been thinking about. He said that from what he's remembered from the stones, some of the Elderlings had the same sort of problem. And they solved it by not being jealous. By not limiting each woman to one man. Or each man to one woman." He turned to look up at the sky again. She wondered what he didn't want her to read in his eyes. Did he fear that she would agree to that? Hoping? It was not the first time she had heard such an idea. Jerd had made it plain of late that she would share her favors where she willed, and that none of the male keepers should think she was his simply because she'd shared one night with him. Or a month of nights. Three or four of the keepers had seemed to accept this relationship with her. Thymara had heard a few disparaging remarks from them about her, but she seemed to be gaining a genuine partnership with several of them, one in which her partners seemed as bonded to each other as they were to her. Thymara was skeptical that it would work long term but had resolved to ignore the situation.

But if that was what Tats was broaching as a solution . . . She spoke stiffly. "If that's what you're hoping for, I'm sorry, Tats. I can't be with both you and Rapskal, and be glad of it. Nor can I share you with another, even if she weren't Jerd. My heart doesn't work that way."

He heaved a sudden sigh of relief. "Neither does mine." He rolled to face her, and she let him take her hands. "I was willing to compromise if it was the only future you saw. But I didn't want to. I want you all to myself, Thymara. Even if it means waiting."

The depth of feeling in his words took her by surprise. He read it on her face. "Thymara, it's no accident I'm here in Kelsingra. I came here because of you. I told you and your father that I just wanted the adventure, but I was lying. I was following you, even then. Not just because there was no real future for me in Trehaug, but because I knew that there was no future for me anywhere if you weren't there. It's not because you just happen to be here, and I just happen to be here. It's not because you're a good hunter, nor even because of how beautiful you've become. It's you. I came here for you."

She had no words to reply to him.

He spoke as if he had to fill the silence. "Some of the others have made me feel like an idiot because I can't compromise. The other night, after dinner, when you went out walking with Rapskal, Jerd called me aside. She said there was something on a high shelf in her room, something she couldn't reach. It was a ploy. There was nothing there, but once we were alone, she said that she didn't have the problems you did with men. That if I wanted her, I could be with her, and then still court you if I thought I wanted you as well. She said she could keep it secret, that you'd never know." He looked into Thymara's eyes and quickly reminded her, "Jerd said it, not me. I didn't agree to it, and I walked away from what she was offering." In a lower voice, he added, "Trusting her is not a mistake I'd make twice. But she did manage to make me feel childish. Foolish that I couldn't just dispense with the 'old rules' and 'live our lives as we pleased.' She laughed at me." He paused for a moment and then cleared his throat. "Rapskal made me feel that way, too. And while he didn't laugh at me, he told me that in a few decades I'd change my mind. He's so comfortable with these ideas. But I'm not."

"Then I suppose I'm as childish and rule bound as you are. Because I feel the same way." She moved her head onto his shoulder and spoke hesitantly. "But if I say that I still don't feel ready, will you change your mind?"

"No. I've thought it through, Thymara. If I have to wait, then, well, I have the time. We don't have to rush. We don't have to rush to have children before we're twenty because we may not live past forty. The dragons changed that for us. We have time."

Then maybe I am ready. She almost said the words aloud. Hearing that he would no longer pressure her to decide, hearing that he understood that, with her, it had to be exclusive had affirmed something about him. Instead, she said, "You are the man I thought you would be."

"I hope so," he'd said. And then they had been still, so still that she had started to doze off, until Sintara's excited jab awoke her.

"Silver!" she exclaimed and Tats's voice almost echoed hers. His dragon's excitement came through in his inflection. But he gave Thymara a puzzled look. "A silver well? *The* Silver well?" He was incredulous. "Did we dream it?"

She shook her head at him and grinned. "Sintara says

that Carson and Sedric have found it. She showed me where." She blinked, the location of the well suddenly reordering her mental map of the city. Of course. It all made sense now. Knowledge seeped up from buried memories; the secret that only Elderlings and dragons must know, the one bit of knowledge that must never be shared with the outside world. The very reason for Kelsingra's location and existence. She did not smile: it was too immense for that. "It's dragon Silver. The source of all magic."

SELDEN AWOKE TO low voices. A man's voice, insistent and almost mocking, a woman's voice, indignant and venturing toward anger. "I will tell my father."

"Who do you think gave me the key? Who do you think ordered the guards to allow me to come and go as I please?"

"You have not married me! You have no right to touch me! Get away! Stop!"

It took Selden a time to realize that he was awake, that this was not a dream, and that he recognized the woman's voice. He dragged himself to a sitting position on the narrow divan. The fire in the little hearth had burned low: it was late at night, then. He looked around the small study. No one was there. A dream, then?

No. A man's voice, low and angry. "Come here!" From the next room.

He clutched his head to make the room stop spinning, then went off into a coughing fit, and abruptly the voices in the other room were stilled.

"You've wakened him," Chassim exclaimed. "I have to see if he is all right. You would not want him to die before my father has the chance to kill him." Her voice was full of disgust for whomever she addressed.

"He can wait until I'm finished," the man replied abruptly. His words were followed by a crash of falling furniture, and then a woman's shriek, suddenly muffled.

The long robe she had given him to wear was twisted around his hips and swaddled his legs. Selden swung his legs off the bed and then struggled to free himself. "Chassim!" he called, and then choked on his coughing. He stood,

feeling too tall, swaying like a reed in the wind. His knees
started to buckle under him. He grabbed the back of the
divan and took two staggering steps until his outstretched
hands met the stout wood of the door. He had not been out
of this room since he arrived here; he had no idea where
the door led. He slapped at the heavy panels and then found
the handle and tugged at the catch. The door swung open,
and he followed it in a stagger. Chassim was pinned on the
bed by a heavy man. His one hand clutched her throat while
with the other he was dragging her nightrobe up her body.
Her hands tugged hopelessly at the hand that choked her.
Her head was flung back, her braided hair coming loose, her
mouth wide open, and her eyes bulging with terror at not
being able to breathe.

"Let her go!" he shouted, but the words took all his
breath. He staggered forward, coughing. He caught at a pot
of flowers and threw it at the man. It bounced off his back
and fell to the floor, unbroken, rolling in a half circle, spilling soil as it went. The man glanced over his shoulder; his
face, already red with passion, went purple with fury. "Out!
Get out, or I kill you now, you freak!"

"Chassim!" Selden shouted, for her tongue was beginning to protrude from her mouth. "You're killing her! Let
her go!"

"She is mine to kill! As are you!" Ellik shouted. He released her, lifting his body off her to come at Selden.

A brass figurine was at hand. Selden threw it at the chancellor and watched it sail past him to land with a thud on the
floor. Then Ellik seized him by the front of his robe, lifted
him off his feet, and shook him like a rag. Selden could
not control the wild whipping of his head. He rained blows
on his attacker, but there was no strength in his hands or
arms. An angry child would have fought more effectively.
Ellik laughed, mocking and triumphant, and flung Selden
aside. He struck the door and clutched at it as he slid down
it. Darkness made the room small—and then it did not exist
at all.

SOMEONE GRIPPED HIS shoulders, rolling him onto his

back. He flailed, trying to land a telling blow until he heard Chassim say, "Stop it. It's me. He's gone."

The room was in darkness. As his eyes adjusted, he made out the paleness of her nightrobe, and then the faded gold of her tattered braids hanging around her face. Seeing her face with her hair half loosened around it made him realize she was younger than he had thought. He pushed his own hair back from his face and suddenly realized that he hurt. All over. Badly. It must have showed on his face, for she said wearily, "He saved a few kicks for you, on his way out."

"Did he hurt you?" he asked, and saw small sparks of rage light in her eyes at the stupidity of his question.

"No. He only raped me. Not even in a very imaginative way. Just plain old-fashioned choking, slapping, and rape."

"Chassim," he said, shocked; he almost rebuked her for how callously she dismissed it.

"What?" she demanded. Her mouth was swollen, but her lip still curled in dismay. "Did you think it my first time? It was not. Or will you pretend to surprise and claim that this is not the way of your kind?"

She touched him kindly as she spoke so harshly, taking him by the shoulders and pulling him to a sitting position. He coughed again and was ashamed when she lifted the corner of her sleeve and wiped his mouth with it. When he could speak, he said, "Among my people, rape is not condoned."

"No? But I am sure it still happens all the same."

"It does," he had to admit. He gently pulled free of her. If she had not been watching, he would have crawled back to the divan. He could feel where Ellik had kicked him. Once in the ribs, once on the hip, and once in the head. It hurt, but it could have been worse. During his captivity, he had seen a man beaten down and then stamped upon. It had happened right outside his cage when he had first been put on display. The attackers had all been drunk, all mocking spectators, and he had not felt kindly toward any of them, but he had still screamed at them to stop and yelled for help, for anyone to come and make it stop.

No one had.

"I tried to make him stop," he said. Then he wondered why he pointed out his own failure to her. He got himself to his feet and crossed the short space to the divan, catching at furniture as he went. When he reached it, he fell more than sat on it.

Chassim watched him accomplish this, then went to the hearth's edge and added a stick or two of wood. In a few moments, flame woke and ran along the stick. In the additional light, he could see her cheek starting to purple. "Yes. You did," she said, as if there had been no gap in their conversation. Then she turned to look at him directly. Sitting on the floor, with her braids falling down, her pale nightdress catching light and shadow from the fire, she looked more childish than ever. Like Malta, when she was a girl and he a small boy and they had sometimes crept down to the kitchen at night to see what treats the cook might have tucked away in the pantry. It had been a very long time ago, he suddenly realized. A tiny bit of a pampered childhood that had lasted only a short time before war and hardship had shattered it forever.

Chassim's eyes were not a child's as she asked him, "Why? Why did you do that? He might have killed you."

"He was hurting you. It was wrong. And you had been kind to me . . ." He was shocked that she would ask him why he had tried to help her. Was it such a strange act? He reached deeper, pulled up a painful honesty. "It happened to me once." He blurted out the words and then was horrified. He had never intended to speak of it to anyone. Having someone else know about it made it real.

She stared at him, her blue eyes wide, and he wondered what she thought of him now. How much less human did it make him in her eyes?

"How?" she said at last, and he saw that she did not grasp what he was saying.

He spoke roughly and suddenly understood her own callousness when she had spoken of what Ellik had just done to her. "There was a man who wanted me. As a novelty, I think, as when some men mate with an animal, just to see what might be different. He paid the man who kept me captive well. My keeper let him into my cage and walked away. And . . . it was like he was insane. Like I was a thing, not even an animal. I defied him, and I fought him, and then, eventually, I pleaded, when I knew he was far stronger than I was. It didn't help. He hurt me. Badly. And then he got off me and walked away. There is something about knowing that someone is taking pleasure in giving you incredible pain . . . with no remorse. It changes how you see yourself; it changes what you can believe of other people. It changes everything." His words ground to a halt.

"I know," she said simply.

A silence fell. The fire crackled, and he felt more naked than he had when he was displayed bare for all to see. "I was sick for days afterward. Really sick. I had so much pain. I bled and I had a fever. I don't think I've been completely healthy since then." The words tumbled out of him. He lifted his hand, covered his own mouth to stop them. Tears he had not shed then nor since burned in his eyes. The tears of a torn and battered child, helpless against violence done to him. With his last shred of manhood, of dignity, he fought to hold them back.

"Flesh rips when you are forced." She spoke the harsh fact quietly. "I have heard people, other women, make mock of it. As something that some women deserve, or as a fillip of excitement to the act. Something to pretend, for titillation. I cannot understand it. It makes me want to slap them and choke them until they understand." She stood up slowly and he could see the pain it cost her. She took a few breaths and then leaned over him to pull a blanket around him. "Go to sleep," she suggested.

"Maybe tomorrow will be a better day," he dared to say. He coughed again.

"I doubt it," she said, but without bitterness. "But whatever it is, it will be the only day we have." She left the room slowly, pausing at the door. "Your dragon," she said. She cocked her head at him. "Did it hurt when she changed you?"

He shook his head slowly. "Sometimes the changes are uncomfortable. But what we shared was worth it. I wish I could explain it better."

"Does she know where you are now? Does she know how they hurt you?"

"I don't think so."

"If she did, would she come here? To help you?"

"I'd like to think so," he said quietly.

"So would I," she replied. And on those odd words, she left him.

✧ ✧ ✧

Day the 5th of the Plough Moon

Year the 7th of the Independent Alliance of Traders
**From Jani Khuprus, of the Rain Wild
Traders, Trehaug
To Ronica and Keffria Vestrit of the
Bingtown Traders, Bingtown**

Keffria, I have taken your advice. A lengthy explanation of Malta's absence is on its way to you in a wax-sealed packet sent on the liveship Ophelia and entrusted to Captain Tenira. He is, as we all well know, a man of impeccable honor.

I beg you to hold the information in deepest confidence. I myself am still awaiting more tidings, but I have shared what I know with you. I regret that I must be so evasive and leave you to endure the wait for the packet's arrival. Right now I share your reluctance to entrust information about confidential family business to Guild birds.

I share your agony over Selden's fate. Would that we had even one scrap of certainty of what has befallen him. We have sent a response to Wintrow, telling him we still await news.

All else here is the best that it can be, given the daily worries that we share for Selden.

I pray you, if you receive good tidings about our boy, send them as swiftly as possible, by bird. That would be a message I would wish to share with the world.

May Sa shelter us all!

Jani

✧ ✧ ✧

CHAPTER TWELVE

DRAGON WARRIOR

The endless pursuit dragged on and on and on. Hest was sickened by it. It was not that he felt any sympathy for the creature they hunted. It was the utter boredom spiked with sudden uncontrollable danger that roiled his belly.

The Chalcedean and his fellows were determined to take the dragon, to harvest blood, scale, eyes, flesh, tongue, liver, and spleen. And whatever other bits of her they salivated over each night as he waited on them at the galley table. To-night, the Chalcedean and his cohorts were full of wild optimism. They slammed their mugs on the table for emphasis and praised their own cleverness and courage in persevering so long. The dragon was theirs, and with her death, fame and glory would come to them. They would kill her, plunder her body, and go home to fame and riches and, sweetest of all, safety for themselves and their families. The Duke would cease his threats and shower them with gifts and favors. Cherished sons long held hostage in horrific conditions would be restored to them.

So they spoke by night when darkness forced them to cease their drudging hunt and tie up for the night. By dawn, they would once more stalk the dragon. The damned beast refused to die. She trudged away from them, day after day and possibly long into the night. Each day, the impervious ships battled the current until they caught up with her. Twice she had lain in wait for them and sprung out in a wild attempt to capsize their vessels. She had splintered oars, and eaten two rowers who had fallen or been flung overboard by her attacks. She seemed to take great pleasure in crushing them slowly in her jaws as they shrieked in agony.

It had not discouraged the Chalcedean. Lord Dargen was relentless.

Captives had been taken from belowdecks to replace the rowers who had been lost, chained to oars as if they were slaves. The merchants and Traders were poor replacements for the work-hardened slaves and sailors that had perished. Yet the Chalcedean and his followers seemed not to care that nineteen of twenty arrows shot at the dragon either missed or splashed uselessly into the river. If the twentieth one loosened a scale or stuck for even a moment in a tender part of her body, they roared and screeched victoriously.

Hest did not see why they put so much effort into it. It seemed plain to him that the dragon was dying. Daily she looked more dilapidated. She was obviously incapable of flight. She carried one of her wings partially open at an odd angle. Her colors were faded and the smell of her was terrible, a stench of rotten meat. Rousted from wherever she had finally taken rest at night, she now put most of her energy into staying out of range of their arrows. Sometimes she sought refuge in the marshy reed beds at the swampy edge of the river. Lying down, she became almost invisible to them. Then Lord Dargen would force some of his men over the side to harry and taunt her into showing herself. Some of those men became food. Privately, Hest believed that if the Chalcedean would stop feeding his henchmen to the dragon, she would sooner succumb to her injuries and die.

But he did not say so. He did not wish to end up on the end of an oar. Yet he feared that, at the rate the Lord Dargen was spending men, it would be inevitable. The Chalcedean seldom gave him an order anymore. Hest kept himself busy and out of the man's sight, making every effort to be both useful and invisible. For hours every day, he carried out menial tasks, wiping tables, stirring porridge or soup, and any other work he could find to occupy himself. He had, he thought bitterly, adapted himself into the ideal slave, endlessly laboring without need of direction.

The only thing worse than the constant drudgery were the times of absolute terror when the dragon attacked the ship. Those could happen at any moment, he had discovered. Pestered and poked enough, she would turn and lash out. Her roars lacked spirit, more the response of a cornered rat than an enraged predator. Yet even so, every attack damaged one ship or another and often enough claimed a life.

"Hest!"

He jerked at the sound of his shouted name, and the men gathered at the table roared with laughter. The Chalcedean did not. He was scowling, displeased with his servant. Hest tried not to cower. He had several reasons to fear. He had stolen two pieces of bacon that morning on the pretense of cleaning the pan. And he had purloined a water-stained cloak that one of the Chalcedeans had thrown to the deck after the dragon had given them an unexpected drenching. It served as his bedding now and he was pathetically grateful for its thin comfort. But now, as dread rose in him, he cursed himself for a fool. He had not been that cold nor were the deck planks that hard. That discomfort was not worth his life!

The Chalcedean's cheeks and nose were red with drinking, or perhaps just from recent splashes of river water. They all looked the worse for wear by now, and Hest dared not imagine how he appeared. His hands and arms were scalded red to the elbows just from his cleaning tasks. But his master only took a heavy brass key from the pouch at his belt and said, "Go to the second aft hatch and bring us back that little keg of Sandsedge brandy." He looked around the table at his men, swaying slightly. "I don't think it's too early for us to celebrate. Tomorrow she will surely fall to us. That spear from Binton went deep today, did it not? Did you see how her blood bubbled as it met the water? Dragon blood! Soon enough, we'll have plenty of it. So emptying the keg to hold it tonight might be a wise course of action!"

Two men cheered, but the others at the table shook their heads. Hest's heart sank as one of them snatched the key back from him and stuffed it back into his master's pouch. Anger blossomed on the Chalcedean's face, and Hest knew he would bear the brunt of it. "Your master is drunk. Only a fool celebrates a victory before it is in his hands. Take him back to his bed for the night. Tomorrow, perhaps, you will have to bring us that cask."

Lord Dargen rose unsteadily. His hand hovered over one of his vicious little knives. "You are not in command here, Clard. It is something for you to remember."

The man did not lower his gaze. "I know it well, Lord Dargen. You lead us, and you have borne the hardship of doing so. But I follow you, and not the wine in your belly!" He grinned as he added this, and after a moment, the fury melted from the Chalcedean's face. He nodded slowly, and relieved smiles broke on the faces of the other men at the table.

Lord Dargen turned to Hest. "I am going to bed. Take a candle and precede me, Bingtown Trader. When we go back to Chalced, perhaps I will make you my valet. I have never had a valet, but you appear well suited to the task. As long as you keep your hands to yourself."

The men at the table roared with laughter. Fury burned in his heart, but Hest bent his mouth in an approximation of an appreciative smile. Dismay that such a fate could await him warred with hatred for the man. Would it be much worse to be eaten by the dragon or drowned in the river? As he sheltered their candle from the wind on the way back to the deckhouse and his stateroom, he wished he had the courage to push the drunk overboard, even as his wiser self reminded him of how his companions would react to the loss of their leader.

DEATH WAS NOT far away. They knew it, the carrion eaters and blood drinkers, and they swarmed around her. Some did not wait, but darted forward to try for a chunk of her flesh or the opportunity to latch onto one of her wounds. She longed to shake them off, to dart her head down and make her predators her own meal, but she did not. Let them come. Tintaglia moved in silence, ignoring the swarms of small vampire worms and the fish that kept trying to take a bite of her. They might feed on her tonight; they would almost certainly feast on her tomorrow. But no human would draw her blood or slice her scales free; no human would lay her belly open and take her heart with bloody hands. No. If she could not escape them, she would at least ensure that they joined her in death.

She had taken some rest earlier in the day, if it could be called that. As evening fell, she had found a gap in the forest wall and crept back among the trees. She could not go far, but she had stiffly wound her aching body among the trunks and tree roots and, for a short time, closed her eyes.

And dreamed.

That had surprised her. Of late, when she found a place and a moment to sleep, exhaustion dragged her under into a dark cavern that could scarcely be called rest. *More like a bite of death,* she thought to herself. But that brief rest had brought her a gobbet of an idea. Some ancient ancestral memory had uncoiled in her mind, and when she awoke, it awaited her. Ships had a vulnerable point. Every ship needed a rudder, be it a sweep or a steering oar. Destroy those, and neither vessel could maneuver well.

She had been stupid to flee them, to let them attack and chase her. The only times she had gained any blood from them was when she had lain in wait and attacked them. But they had learned to anticipate those ambushes. She had attacked them when they were awake and alert, their arms ready to hand, and the light helping them to see. Now as she paced slowly and silently through the water back toward the ships, she hissed in silent satisfaction. The lights of the anchored vessels beckoned her, spilling a pale betrayal of their silhouettes onto the river's face. But she would be almost invisible to them, a black shape in the black water.

She did not deceive herself. This was her last bid at survival. If she did not destroy or at least disable her foes tonight, she did not think she could live through another day of their harrying. The infection from her original wound seemed to have spread to all the minor injuries they had dealt her since then. She was not healing; daily her injuries worsened and she weakened. If she could only rest, make a kill, eat and rest, then perhaps she could muster the strength to plod on toward Kelsingra. Flight was beyond her now. She could scarcely move one wing, and the thought of springing into the air, snapping it open, and beating her way up into the sky seemed no more than a long-ago dream.

They had moored their boats with their noses upstream. She would have to pass them as silently as possible, then turn and attack. She hoped to disable both ships and then flee before they could retaliate. It was not a dragon's way of fighting, to strike and then run, but she was not living in ordinary times for dragons. She carried within her eggs that would mature and eventually be ready for laying. She had caught the scent of dragons on the one damaged vessel; there was a faint chance that there was a colony of viable dragons at Kelsingra. But it was hard to believe, and until she knew, she felt that the fate of her race rested on her. If these stupid men so bent on killing her succeeded, they might well eradicate dragons forever.

The thought steeled her resolve. She would disable their ships and escape. And when she was healed, she would return to destroy not just them but the evil nest that had bred them. She had heard their speech and recognized words from her ancient memories. *I know where you spawn,* she thought at them. *I and my offspring will fall upon your land and leave not one of your nests standing. We will feast on your kine and your children, and foul your drinking places with carrion. You will be the ones eradicated, and no memory of your ways will descend from you.*

She was so close now that she could hear their muffled voices and stupid laughter. *Laugh well, for a final time,* she thought at them. Her path would take her between the two moored vessels, in water deep enough to conceal her and shallow enough that her claws would not lose their grip on the river bottom. She bent her legs slightly, crouching so that only her eyes and nostrils remained above the water and began her stealthy approach.

LORD DARGEN BREATHED out the fumes of Hest's own wine as he staggered along beside him. He gripped Hest's shoulder and leaned on him, cursing him when his stumbling feet jostled him against the railing. "Stop. Stop!" he commanded Hest suddenly. "Need to piss. Stay and watch, Bingtown Trader, and see the weapon a Chalcedean bears." He was, Hest thought, very drunk indeed.

He kept his grip on Hest's shoulder as he staggered to the railing and Hest had perforce to move with him. He moved aside in distaste as the man made lewd comments about Hest's supposed desire for him and Hest's lack of endowment. The night was not peaceful. Animals called to one another in the nearby forest, and ghostly gleams of luminescent hanging moss made mad ghosts in the trees. The yellow lamplight from the windows of the ship streamed in long bars of light on the river's face. A ripple in the water's surface caught Hest's eye. He stared, wondering what disturbed the slack current between the two vessels. A large gleaming eye glared up at him and then was lidded abruptly.

"The dragon!" Hest shouted. "She is right alongside us! The dragon is in the river!"

"Idiot!" The Chalcedean cursed him. "What is frightening you? A riverpig? A floating log?" Lord Dargen staggered to Hest's side and looked down. "There is nothing there! Just water and a coward's imagining." He seized Hest's wrist and with shocking strength dragged him closer. "Look down, Bingtown coward! What do you see? Nothing but black water! I should throw you in so you can see for yourself!" With his free hand, he seized the back of Hest's neck and shoved him forward so that he leaned far out over the railing. Hest shouted wordlessly and struggled, but even drunk, the Chalcedean had a madman's strength. Worse, as Hest stared, a gleaming blue eye looked up at him from the depths. The rest of the creature was invisible, cloaked in the black water, but he knew it was the dragon that looked up at him with hatred. And waited.

"It's there! Look for yourself, there! See the eye, look!" His voice rose and cracked into a woman's squeal.

The Chalcedean laughed, drunk and guttural. "Over you go, Bingtowner!"

The boat gave a sudden wild heave sideways. The shrieking of splintered wood competed with the harsh cries of the men in the galley and the terrified screams of the hostages trapped belowdecks. Hest clutched at the railing, and a wordless scream escaped him. The Chalcedean staggered free of him, shouting, "Arms! The dragon attacks us. Kill her, kill her now!"

As the boat tipped again, the Chalcedean lord was flung against the railing. For a long moment he clung there, and Hest dared to hope to see him tip over the edge. But the next onslaught from the dragon flung the ship in the other direction, and he slammed against the ship's house. "Attack!" he roared, fury and fear diminishing his drunkenness.

The door of the galley was flung open, and men poured out onto the deck, weapons in their hands.

"I WISH THE city would light itself here," Rapskal complained.

Privately, Thymara agreed with his sentiment even as she recognized the impossibility. Even this magical city had limits. Only certain bands of metal woke to light, and not all of them still worked. How they worked at all was still a great mystery, but she now recognized Elderling magical works when she saw them. And in this part of the city, they seemed to have chosen to use it as little as possible. Almost, she remembered why. She turned away from the memory tug. The statues in the nearby squares were only statues, silent and unmoving. They were of lovingly worked stone, but no shining silver threads of memory gleamed in them.

The keepers had gathered at the well plaza to bend their backs to clearing the debris. Alise was there and, for the first time in weeks, she carried her case of paper and pencils. She seemed to take immense satisfaction in the new supplies that Leftrin had brought her. She clambered through the stack of broken timbers and sketched a copy of the lettering on one. The timbers had been amazingly well preserved, and Thymara had heard her speculate to Leftrin that the thick glossy paint that coated them had something to do with it. Leftrin had grudgingly agreed even as he muttered his disappointment that his work crew was here instead of applying their efforts to reinforcing Tarman's dock.

Thymara stretched her aching back and tried to see the plaza as Alise did. It was not easy to mentally piece it together. A graceful and lavishly decorated roof of carved wood supported on stout wooden pillars had sheltered the walled well at one time. The roof had been pyramidal, and painted green and gold and blue. It had given way to time and possibly violence. Carson had pointed out that some of the timbers were torn while others had rotted. Mixed in with the timbers were chains and pulleys, the remnants of a windlass that had once cranked up a large bucket from the depths. Carson had directed the keepers to pull the metal parts to the side and to preserve every piece they found. "We may be able to reassemble at least part of it."

Leftrin had looked at the heaped sections of broken chain and whistled low. "Can the well have been that deep?"

And to that question Mercor had replied, "The level of Silver receded over time. It was indeed that deep."

The dragons had all gathered to watch them in a hopeful shifting circle. They came and went as hunger drove them away to hunt, gorge, and sleep, but they always returned to the plaza as evening was shifting into night rather than seeking the baths or the sand wallows. Thymara privately reflected that this was the most time any of the dragons had spent with their Elderlings in weeks.

The palpable anticipation of the dragons had infected all the keepers. Every one of them, as well as Leftrin's entire crew, had put aside all other work to labor at clearing the site. Leftrin had insisted that a skeleton crew must remain aboard his beloved liveship, but the crewmen had alternated duties so that each one had spent some time at the well plaza. Big Eider's incredible strength had been indispensable to moving the larger pieces of timber, while Hennesey and Skelly had sorted usable lengths of chain from short sections. Thymara had marked well how Hennesey grinned as he worked, jesting and good-natured as she had never seen him before. Perhaps it had something to do with how Tillamon, well attired in Elderling dress now, was always the one to bring him water and to stand beside him asking earnest questions as he affably explained all to her. Tillamon was not pretty; her scaling and the wattles along her jaw reminded Thymara more of an armored toad from the rain forest than of a graceful Elderling. But then, Hennesey with his scars and work-roughened hands was not a gem of masculine beauty. And neither of them seemed to care much what anyone else thought of them so long as they were pleased with each other. Tall, slender Alum looked more out of place as he struggled to find tasks in Skelly's vicinity while enduring the solemn scrutiny of every other crew member. Bellin in particular watched him with measuring eyes and a flat mouth.

And so the long workday had gone, with Alise scribbling and the others sorting and moving broken things. Before long, a round hole, bigger across than a tall man's height, gaped up at them from the center of the simple plaza. The remains of a brick wall encircled it. The well was wedged full of more wreckage. "Going to have to rig a hoist to clear that," Swarge observed dourly. "Almost looks like it was stuffed down there apurpose," he opined, and Carson had agreed, with several colorful profanities added.

It had not just fallen; debris had been deliberately packed into the well until it lodged there. Even after a tripod of salvaged timbers had been erected over the well mouth, the task of removing it included breaking it free before it could be hauled up out of the mouth. As the level of debris receded, Leftrin insisted that any keeper climbing into the hole must wear a harness and have a tender. "No telling when that wreckage could all give way and fall in, Sa knows how deep. Don't want a keeper or crew hand going down with it."

And so the hard work of clearing the packed wreckage had begun. From dawn until dark the keepers toiled, and all the while the dragons had watched, pacing eagerly and sometimes crowding so close that keepers were forced to plead, with much flattery, for them to move back and give them all room to work. Even as night stole the colors from the sky, the dragons clustered there. Some merely stood; others prowled as if they expected game to erupt from the well shaft. Spit nosed through the heaped piles of chain, undoing most of a day's work. Carson heaved a great sigh. "Dragon. Leave off that, unless you want it to take us even longer to solve this puzzle."

Spit stopped his rummaging and lifted his head. His eyes gleamed. "Silver is everything. In traces we gain it when we drink from the river or eat prey that has done so. It is threaded through the stones and bones of this place and moves deep beneath the earth here." His words were measured and spoken calmly. "All creatures that live here gain some Silver from what they eat and drink, and once dragons had to be content with that. We knew that the prey of this land and the waters of this land were more rejuvenating to us than anywhere else we hunted. We heard one another more clearly when we hunted here, and we could hear humans as well . . ." His words trailed off, and it felt to Thymara as if the night darkened around them.

"Spit?" Carson asked as the extraordinary flow of thought dwindled and ceased. He was not the only one staring at the mean little silver. Spit was standing stock-still, staring sightlessly at the crumpled walls of the old well. The silence stretched.

Mercor broke it. "I feel that Spit spoke true. I cannot remember all the events he spoke of, but what I can remember fits with what he said."

"Give me that!" Carson commanded suddenly. He advanced on the small dragon and peered at him sternly. After a long pause, Spit's jaws opened slightly. A length of chain dangled from his mouth, and then spooled out to clank to the stones of the plaza. Carson crouched down to examine it but did not touch it. "What just happened?" he demanded of no one and everyone.

Mercor blew air from his nostrils. "There must have been a trace of Silver left on the chain, and Spit found it."

"Only a tiny bit," Spit admitted blissfully. "I smelled it. And I took it while the rest of you were standing and staring like cattle." His satisfaction was poisonous.

"Now there's the Spit we know," Carson muttered, and then he and the other keepers dodged away as the other dragons surged forward to investigate the well wreckage. But their snorting and shuffling of the chains and broken timbers evidently yielded nothing to them. They dispersed slowly, going back to their watch, and Thymara knew that every keeper shared her wonder. If a tiny amount of Silver could work so great a change in Spit, even temporarily, what would a flowing supply of it do for the dragons? And what would they be willing to do for it?

Sintara had visited the work site no less than three times. She had spoken little to Thymara but radiated approval at how hard the girl was working to clear the well. Thymara resented how the dragon's enthusiasm could warm and energize her, but she could not resist it. She knew she worked harder when the blue queen was watching over her. She was not the only one. Even Jerd had come to lend a hand with an enthusiasm she seldom showed for hard labor on a chilly day. Thymara had avoided her, preferring to work alongside Tats and Rapskal. It warmed her in a different way to see how easy they were with each other now. Tats had evidently been sincere about setting his jealousy aside, and Rapskal had never shown signs of feeling any. *Could it be that easy?* she wondered, and she found that she hoped so. She had been able to relax and be more herself. When they paused in late afternoon to eat a simple meal that blessedly included hot tea with sugar and hardtack as well as their perpetual smoked meat, Jerd had strolled by behind them and made a smiling remark that the three of them seemed to have found something to enjoy together.

Thymara had let it go by and told herself that she was proud of having done so.

But with night coming on and the cold rising from the earth to chill her hands and face, she wanted only to go home. *Yes, home,* she affirmed to herself. Her cozy room with her small hoard of personal items was home now. *Clearing the well would have to wait for tomorrow and daylight,* she thought to herself, but the others did not seem to share her desire for rest. Carson and Big Eider and Leftrin had moved to the well's edge and were staring down into it.

"Too dark to work any more tonight," Leftrin declared.

"I'm too cold to do more right now," Tats called up from the depths.

Kase and Boxter were on the line for the hoist. As they pulled him up to the lip, Nortel and Rapskal were standing by to grasp his harness and swing him to sure footing. Even through his Elderling scaling, his face was red with cold and his hands looked like claws: Rapskal had to untie the knots of his harness.

As Tats stepped clear, he added, "I think we're nearly there. That last chunk of timber you hauled up, the one with the piece of chain attached to it? After you hauled it out of the way, I felt around and there was a partial hole. There's still some clearing to do, but I think there's only two more chunks blocking it. After we jerk them out, we'll have a clear way to the bottom of the shaft."

"Was there Silver at the bottom?" Veras asked eagerly. Her nostrils were flared, and the spikes around her neck stood out like a ruffle. Jerd stood by her queen dragon, her face echoing the question.

"Can you reach it?" Sintara demanded. She pushed to the front of the circle and, ignoring Leftrin's shout to be careful of his hoist, stalked over to peer down the hole. "I can't see it," she said after a few moments. "But I think I smell it!"

"The wreckage smells of Silver. That's all." Spit was pessimistic as always. "All the Silver wells have gone dry, and we are doomed. I'm glad I took what I found on that chain."

Heeby gave a mournful call, and Rapskal dropped the harness he had been holding to run to her side. "No, my

beauty, my darling. We are not giving up. Far from it!"
He spun back to face the men standing by the shaft. "Can
we not lower a light of some kind? To give the dragons an
answer tonight?"

Despite the deepening night and the cold, the attempt had
been made. It had taken several tries. The first torch they
dropped landed on the blockage and rested there, burning
and blocking their view of anything below it. But by its light,
they dropped two more torches, and one fell through the gap.

Thymara had lain on her belly, part of a circle of keepers peering down the hole, as the first burning torch fell. It
briefly lit the gleaming walls. The shaft was perfectly circu-
lar and smooth: she saw no sign of individual bricks facing
it. The flames made a shimmering reflection as they fell.
And fell. Thymara was impressed with how deep her fellow
keepers had descended to clear the blockage. She glanced
over at Tats. "I couldn't go down into the darkness like you
did. I just couldn't."

Rapskal was on the other side of her. "Surely you could,"
he asserted quietly. His words irritated her, but she could
not think why. Usually, when he said she was stronger or
braver than she thought she was, she felt flattered. But not
tonight, looking down into blackness.

"I could, perhaps, but I wouldn't," she countered, and he
was silent.

When the third torch fell through the gap Tats had seen,
it seemed to fall forever. But it did not go out.

It was keen-eyed Hennesey who said, "There's something silvery down there. But not much, I don't think. I see
what might be a bucket turned on its side. But it's not floating and neither is the torch. Looks like it's resting on the
bottom. The bucket is what I can mostly see. It's huge."

"Why so large a bucket?" Thymara wondered aloud.

"Big enough for a dragon to drink from," Rapskal asserted quietly.

In the uneven, flickering light they studied what they saw
at the bottom of the shaft. Carson summed it up: "Looks
like the well filled up with sediment and went dry, and then
someone broke the mechanism and dumped it down there,

blocking the shaft. If there's any Silver down there still, it's not standing visible. I'm not sure this is worth our time." He gave a weary sigh and stretched. "My friends, I think we should give this up."

"Clear the rubble away."

"It can be dug deeper again. Elderlings can go down that hole."

"Can any of the Silver be brought to the surface?"

The dragons trumpeted their anxious queries. Thymara felt their longing for the precious stuff. It was like a thirst for water, only deeper.

"NO!" Spit's furious roar drowned out all others. "Must have the Silver! We must! Kill you if you stop trying!"

Mercor slowly moved until he stood between Spit and the keepers. He favored him with a long black stare. The small silver dragon lowered his head until his muzzle pointed at the ground. He hissed low, but he also stepped back.

"Dragons don't just want the Silver. They need it," Thymara said quietly. The knowledge had simply risen in her, some common bit of Elderling lore. But her words were spoken into the shocked lull that followed Spit's outburst, and all seemed to hear them. The keepers waited, bewildered by the intensity of the dragons' response until at last Mercor spoke, his words measured and slow. As he often did, he ignored Spit's outburst.

"Once, there were places in the river where the Silver ran just beneath the water. And dragons could get what they needed for themselves. There were seasons when it ran shallow, and sometimes, after an earthquake, one place would lose its Silver, but we would scent it out in another. It was precious stuff, and the best seeps were protected jealously by the strongest drakes."

He was silent for a time, as if he sought the most ancient of memories. Kalo made a deep chuffing sound, a territorial warning. Thymara had never heard any dragon make such a sound before but instantly recognized what it was. Baliper, who so seldom spoke, added, "Many a bloody battle was fought for a Silver seep. Dragons were less touched by humans then. We were different creatures."

"A savage time," Mercor agreed, but he sounded almost wistful for such conflict. "We made few Elderlings then . . . only singers, I think. But some settled here, brought by their dragons. They made a little village. They did not go near the seeps or know of Silver. It was not for them. But then, after a quake much stronger than any we recalled, Silver rose in one of the human-dug wells. The first humans who discovered it died from touching it. But the dragons that ate their bodies became powerful of mind. It was a pure, true flow of Silver, much better than any we had ever tasted. All learned to drink long and deep of the pure Silver pulled up from that well. We began to speak with humans and to use the power of the Silver to shape them into forms more suitable to attend us. They became true Elderlings. From dragons, they gained the power of the Silver, and they built this place, a city for dragons and Elderlings to share. When another quake closed that well, our Elderlings found other sources for us. Some lasted a long time, while others failed quickly. I do not have a memory of how or when this Silver well was dug. But I do have ancestral recollection that once this well near brimmed with Silver.

"Here a dragon could come and drink his fill. And that was well, for the Silver seeps grew less predictable and harder to find. At great risk to themselves, our Elderlings dug this well bigger and deeper, and built a kiosk to shelter the well. As the Silver receded, it became more and more difficult to bring Silver to the surface, but they found ways to manage it. Wells were made deeper, this one in particular. The Silver from this well seemed to ebb and flow with the seasons, sometimes shallow, sometimes flowing. Other, lesser Silver wells in this area eventually went dry. But this one remained, always, and so it became our treasure."

Mercor paused. Thymara heard only the breathing of dragons and Elderlings and the distant whispering of the river. He spoke again. "We were not the only dragons then. There were others, but without the pure Silver, they were not clear minded as we were. Sometimes, they were little better than the lions and bears they hunted in their own lands. When we encountered them, in mating flights or migrations to the warm lands, they could smell the Silver on us. They wanted it. And sometimes they followed us back here, to the source, but we stood them off. They came, sometimes in droves, but always we prevailed against them and sent them back to their own regions.

"As Kelsingra prospered, we made many Elderlings, to tend the wells for us and to make places of warmth and comfort for us in the winter season. And to help us guard this, the best source of Silver in the world. And so our city grew around it. The Elderlings quarried stone that had threads of silver running through it, and they found many uses for it for themselves. We used Silver to change our Elderlings, and in turn, they used what they learned from us to change this part of the world. The Silver remains here, in threads in the stones, and it speaks to us of those days. But dragons cannot drink stone. And if this well has failed, and we have found no more seeps . . ."

"Why do dragons need Silver?" Sylve spoke her quiet question.

Her dragon swung his large head to look at her. Black on black, his eyes spun in the torchlight. Thymara felt that he spoke with reluctance. "It extends our lives, just as we extend the lives of our Elderlings. It is a part of us, in our blood and in our venom and in the cases we weave as serpents for our transformation. That was why Cassarick was so important. The clay banks there have Silver in the sand. It cannot be drunk, but in our thread spinning, it holds memories for us, in much the same way as the stones held memories for the Elderlings. It helps us to recall our ancestral memories as we pass from serpent to dragon. If the Silver is gone from the world, much of what dragons are will be gone also. We will continue, but I think our wealth of memories may be greatly shortened. Our minds will dim. And our life spans dwindle." He lowered his voice and added, "As will our ability to shape Elderlings."

The great golden dragon turned to look down on Malta and Reyn. As always, Malta carried her bundled baby against her chest as if she were a child and he her dearest doll. Even in the cold of night, she would not part from him.

Did she think he could not die if she held him close? Mercor spoke words that drove all color from her face. "If Tintaglia ever returns, she will need Silver to change your child to a creature that can survive. All our lives depend on Silver, in one way or another."

"No. Noooo!" Malta drew out the word in a low cry and then turned to her husband, folding herself into his arms and sheltering the child between them.

Anxiety rippled Sylve's brow and she reached a sympathetic hand to touch her dragon's face. "Mercor, if there is any Silver to be had in any way, I will get it for you."

"I know," the dragon responded calmly. "That is what Elderlings do. But I will warn you that it is at peril of your life that you touch Silver. Dragons may drink of it, but any touch of it on human skin is a precursor to a slow death. Only some of the Elderlings mastered it. At a cost." He fell silent for a time, musing, and no one ventured to speak.

Malta lifted her bowed head. Tears tinged pink with blood showed on her face. "But you said I had been touched with Silver. If that is so, how is it that I am not dead?"

The dragon shook his great golden head slowly. "Elderlings found a way, but I do not recall the details of it. They could touch it and wear it on their hands to work their magic. It gave intent to stone, and it spoke to wood and pottery and metal, bidding it be a certain shape or react in a given way. And those things did as the Elderlings bade them. They made doorways from it, entries of stone that they used to travel to their other cities. They created buildings that stayed warm in the winter. They made roads that always remembered they were roads and did not allow plants to break them. The most powerful of them sometimes used Silver to transform themselves at death, going into the statues they made to preserve a strange sort of life for themselves.

"Sometimes they used Silver to heal, to recall for the body how it should be and help it to make itself right. Their own skill with the uses of Silver contributed to their long life spans. If an Elderling still existed with such a great level of skill with the Silver, he might even be able to heal your child. Magical creatures those ancient beings were. But perhaps their time is past, not to come again. And perhaps so it is with dragons."

"Don't say that!" Sylve cried and flung herself against his flank. She was not the only keeper to stand with brimming eyes. Had they come so far to fail?

Reyn gathered Malta and his child close to him and spoke a promise to her. "If there is Silver to be had, I will get it for Phron."

TINTAGLIA WAS WEAKER than she had thought. The blows she had dealt to their tiller had splintered it but not shorn it from the ship as she had intended. She snaked her head in and seized the wood in her teeth, clamping her jaws on it and tearing at it, intending to pull it free of the vessel. Instead, the ship gave way to her pulling, throwing her off balance. She reflexively opened her wings to brace herself, and the unthinkable happened.

It was a lucky cast of the spear. Even the man who threw it gave a wild shout of surprise when it struck and went in. Tintaglia screamed. In the darkness, the cast had unerringly found her weakest spot, striking the swollen site where the buried spearhead still festered. She felt a hot stab of unbearable pain, and then the soft infected tissue gave way and the spear tore free. Blood and fluid poured from her into the cold river water. Pain surrounded a terrible relief of pressure as the wound drained. The world spun around her, distant stars and light glinting on the river's face. She struggled to get away from the ship.

The first blow from the pole hit the side of her head. Suddenly there were men at the railings of both ships, raining blows down on her with oars and poles. Arrows shot at close range thudded painfully against her even if they did not pierce her scaling. In her confusion, she had trapped herself between the two vessels instead of evading them. Someone flung an empty cask; it struck the back of her head and for an instant, she was stunned, her head sinking beneath the water.

She lifted her head to the wild cheers of both crews. They were killing her and she knew it. Fury washed through her

that puny humans should be able to treat a dragon so. Heedless of how she exposed her underbelly, she reared onto her
hind legs and battered at the ships with her front legs. At the
same time, she threw back her head in a wild trumpeting of
anger and despair.

*They kill me! The men of Chalced have stabbed and
bludgeoned me. I die! Dragonkind, if any of you yet live,
avenge me! Icefyre, if you can hear me, know that our
young die unhatched! Avenge them!*

CARSON SPOKE GRUFFLY. He sounded almost apologetic,
as if he had told Malta the child must die. "I said the well
was sanded in. Not dry. There are ways to dredge out a well
and open it again. Drinking-water wells in the Rain Wilds
mud in often enough. I just wonder why this well isn't full of
water, as close as we are to the river. Tomorrow, when there
is more light to work by, we will hook onto that pot and all
lend our backs to drawing it up. And then we will be able
to see more clearly how deep the Silver is. But for now, it's
getting colder, and I suspect we will have rain again before
morning. Let's get back to shelter for the night, now. All will
look better on the morrow."

The keepers were nodding, and some of them were
taking up torches from their makeshift holders. Hennesey
offered his arm to Tillamon and she accepted it readily.
Skelly was saying a private farewell to Alum behind the
stack of timber. The dragons were turning to begin their
slow promenade through the streets toward the sand beds or
the hot-water baths as keepers and crewmen gathered tools
from the work site. Spit followed last, head down, hissing a
dribble of venom that sizzled as it hit the paved streets.

"They need Silver to live?" Tats said quietly beside Thymara.

"To live long. And to pass on their memories to their offspring, I think," Thymara replied. Reluctantly, she added,
"As we will need it. I suspect the old Elderlings extended
their own lives by repairing their bodies as they aged."

They had both heard Mercor's words. It simply made it
more believable to discuss it with each other. Neither men-

tioned what had been said about Malta's baby, nor what it might mean to future children born in Kelsingra. In her heart, Thymara believed the child was doomed. He needed a dragon that had not been seen in years, and a magical element that had not flowed in decades. She felt sorry for the family but held her heart back from feeling too much. Privately, she was grateful she had not risked a pregnancy. She had no desire to feel what Malta was feeling.

Rapskal was suddenly beside them. "Tomorrow, I think that some of us should find the smaller wells that Mercor spoke of, and see if they are still dry. It seems to me that if a well goes dry because of an earthquake, perhaps another one might open it again."

"Good plan," Tats said, and in his voice she heard his worry for his green dragon. She tried to decide how she felt about this possible threat and sensed an echo from Sintara as she said, "I will wait to see how we fare with this well before I become too fearful. It may be that the well is shallow but refills fast. Some Silver at least we can draw from it, once the final blockage is cleared."

"There is that!" Rapskal exclaimed hopefully. "And my Heeby will need . . ." His words trailed away. His eyes widened as he drew a deep breath and then held it.

"Rapskal?" Thymara ventured.

He turned his head sharply, and his eyes suddenly focused on her. "Treachery most foul! Dragons are set on by men! We must fly to her aid, now, tonight!"

His words were nearly drowned in the wild trumpeting as the dragons took up his call. A moment later, the meaning of it all permeated her brain. Somewhere, a dragon was dying, killed by humans. A queen dragon. Tintaglia! Tintaglia, she who had guided them all up the river as serpents, Tintaglia was falling to human treachery! She summoned them to avenge her!

"Tintaglia, Tintaglia!" Malta's anguished shriek was a higher note among the dragons' trumpeting. "If you and your offspring die, so do mine! Blue queen, wonder of the skies, do not die! Do not allow yourself to be taken!" She turned suddenly and spoke to the other keepers. She stood tall in the night and the force of her plea was something they all felt. "Elderlings, rise! Go to her aid, I beg you! For the sake of my child, yes, but for the sake of all our dragons! For if you let this happen to sapphire Tintaglia, what safety is there for any of you?"

Malta gleamed in the yellow light of the torches and lanterns, and with a strange thrill, Thymara recognized the queen of the Elderlings. No wonder all of Jamaillia had seen her so, commanding with words as compelling as the glamour of the dragon. Thymara was suddenly certain that if Tintaglia could feel Malta's words, she would take heart from them.

"We fly!" Rapskal roared in response. His voice had gone husky and wild. His eyes glared with fury, and the set of his mouth made him a stranger to Thymara. He paced among the churning Elderlings and dragons, seeming suddenly taller. "My armor! My spear!" he cried aloud. "Where are my servants? Send them for my armor. We must fly tonight. We cannot wait for light, for by then she may have gone into eternal darkness. Rise up and seize your arms. Ready the dragon baskets! Bring forth the battle harnesses!"

Thymara stared at him, openmouthed. She felt caught alone in a vortex of whirling times. Tellator. Tellator spoke in that tone of command, Tellator strode like that. All around her, dragons were rearing and trumpeting furiously. Keepers darted among them, some imploring their dragons to stay safely here, to not try to fly in darkness, while some of the keepers had moved clear of a horde of dragons shaking out their wings and snapping their necks to fill their poison glands. Rapskal's peculiar behavior seemed to have gone unnoticed.

He strode toward her, a clenched-teeth smile on his face. She froze as he took her in his arms and held her to his heart. "Have no fear, my darling. A hundred times have I gone into battle, and always I have returned to you, have I not? This time will be no exception! Have faith in me, Amarinda. I will safely return to you, both honor and life intact. We will turn back any that dare to enter our territory uninvited!"

"Rapskal!" She shouted his name and broke free of his

embrace. Seizing him by the shoulders, she shook him as hard as she could. "You are Rapskal and I am Thymara. And you are not a warrior!"

He stared at her oddly as he drew himself up taller. "Maybe not, Thymara, but someone must fight, and I am the only one who has a dragon willing to carry me. I have to go. Those cruel murderers have attacked a queen dragon, seeking to butcher her like a cow! It cannot be tolerated."

The voice was Rapskal's and his very earnest stare, but the cadence of his voice and the words he used were Tellator's. She tried again. "Rapskal, you are not him. And I am not Amarinda. I am Thymara."

His eyes seemed to focus on her again. "Of course you are Thymara. And I know who I am. But I also bear Tellator's memories. The price of his memories is a small one, and that is to honor the life of the man who gave them to me. To continue his duties and work." He leaned closer to her and peered into her eyes as if looking for something. "As you should honor Amarinda's memories by continuing her tasks. Someone must, Thymara, and that someone is you."

She looked at him and shook her head. She became dimly aware of Tats standing beside them, watching them both intently. She could take no time for him now, regardless of what he thought. She held tight to Rapskal and spoke earnestly. "Rapskal, I don't want you to be Tellator. I don't want to be Amarinda. I want us to be us, and whatever we do, I want it to be our own decision, not some continuation of someone else's life."

He gave a small sigh and shifted his gaze to Tats. "Watch over her, my friend. And if I do not return, think well of me." His eyes met Thymara's again. "Someday you will understand. And sooner, I think, would be better than later. For the sake of my honor and my word. Heeby! Heeby, to me!"

He turned away from her. Some other woman from another time exclaimed, "Your sword! Your armor!" She very nearly ran after him.

But Tats was at her side, holding firmly to her arm. He spoke by her ear in the milling chaos of dragons and keepers.

"He has neither, and never has had them. Thymara. Come back to me. You cannot stop him. You know that."

"I know." She wondered if Tats spoke of Rapskal charging off to fight a battle weaponless, or of his assumption of another man's life and duties. She looked at the man beside her. Tears welled painfully in her eyes. "We're losing him. We're losing our friend."

"I fear you may be right." He pulled her into his arms and held her head against his chest to shield her as all around them, dragons trumpeted and then leaped from the ground to take flight. The wind of their beating wings battered them, and their war cries buffeted her ears. In moments, they were high above them.

Thymara lifted her eyes to watch them go, but the over-cast sky had swallowed them all, and only rain fell on her uplifted face.

✦ ✦ ✦

Day the 6th of the Plough Moon

Year the 7th of the Independent Alliance of Traders
From Kim, Keeper of the Birds, Cassarick
To Trader Finbok of the Bingtown Traders,
Bingtown

Dear Trader Finbok,

I am in possession of a message from you that, I must admit, confuses me greatly. Either you have sent this message to me in error and are unaware of the great damage such a missive could do to my reputation, or you are a villain and a scoundrel who deliberately seeks to disgrace me. Perhaps you are deceived by some evil person who has slandered my name by pretending to be me. I choose to hope that you are not truly the malicious sort of person who would risk both our reputations.

The letter I received claims that I have not only been sending you information stolen from other Traders' messages but also shows that you have been paying me a great deal of money for such information. And it declares that unless I surrender certain information about your son, of whom I assure you I have never heard, you will betray me to the Guild masters in Bingtown!

I am astonished and shocked to receive such a letter. It has occurred to me that perhaps it is actually from an enemy of yours who seeks to cause you financial and social disaster! For surely if I took this to the Guild masters, protesting my innocence, they would present it to the Bingtown Traders' Council, and leave it to them to determine if you have been a party to the theft of secrets of other Traders and profited by such knowledge.

Please immediately reply to this missive so that we may clear up this whole matter.

CHAPTER THIRTEEN

FINAL CHANCES

D ead things float."

The Chalcedean spoke the words firmly, as if ordering someone or something to comply with them. The weary men gathered on the deck shuffled their feet, but no one replied. It was all too obvious to them that perhaps dead dragons did not float. In last night's uproarious battle, they had slain the blue monster and seen her sink beneath the water. Many of the men had cried out in dismay as the lifeless hulk had sunk. The others had counseled them to wait: she would rise.

The sun had passed its zenith. No carcass had bobbed to the surface yet. No one had slept. All hands had kept watch on the water, fearing at first that the dragon was not dead and might venture another attack. Then, as the night wore on and she did not rise, they watched, fearing that their long-sought prize, the foundation of all their dreams, was on the bottom of the river, forever out of their reach.

They had probed the area between the moored ships with their longest poles and felt only water or river bottom. One hapless oar slave, secured by a rope about his ankle, had been thrown overboard and commanded to dive as deep as he could and see what he might see. He had not wished to go; he had cried out in protest as his fellows had obediently lifted him and then flung him over the side. No swimmer he; he had sunk, risen to the surface to splash and beg for help. The shouted commands for him to dive and look for the dragon carcass had not, in Hest's opinion, moved him.

Rather, his own ineptitude had sunk him again. The second time, they had dragged him from the water by the line about his ankle. He had lain on the deck like a dead thing, his skin kissed red by the river, puffing air into his lungs, his eyes filmed with gray from the acid water. They shouted at him, demanding to know what he had seen. "Nothing! I saw nothing, I see nothing!" The man's terror at being blind had robbed him of his fear of his master.

The Chalcedean had kicked him disdainfully, proclaimed him useless, and would have discarded him over the side if one of the others had not insisted that a blind man on an oar was better than an empty bench. Hest had noted that none of the Chalcedeans had volunteered to dive overboard.

Now as the rising sun granted them enough light that they could see under the trees, they scanned the nearby banks to see if the dragon's carcass had washed ashore. There was nothing. Then the Chalcedean had announced that perhaps the current had carried their prize downstream. His haggard men stared at him with sick doubt in their eyes. The dragon was gone and they knew it.

Their leader did not share their gloom. "Oh, come!" Lord Dargen cajoled them. "Will you rest now and let our fortune slip away from us? The current has carried our prize downstream. We will seek her there, and know that every stroke of the oar carries us closer to home as well as closer to a golden future!"

It sounded like chicanery to Hest, a mother's lie to make

a child open his mouth for the bitter medicine. But the crews accepted it and began to make ready for a day's travel. What choice did they have? Odd, how living as a slave was showing him how little choice most men had in their lives. His existence had always been shaped by his father's authority. Last night when his stolen rags and chill hold had begun to seem like a cozy refuge from standing on the deck holding a lantern aloft for the searchers, he had reconsidered Sedric's fantasy of the two of them running off to a distant country. Sedric had voiced it only once, toward the end of their time together in Bingtown. Hest had scoffed at it back then and forbidden him to speak again of his idiotic dream.

Hest had recalled the quarrel in detail as he had stood on the darkened deck, spending hours of his life functioning as a lamp stand as he held the lantern high. It was Sedric's fault he had come to this, he had decided. His lover had dreamed of gaining a fortune and moving far from Bingtown, to dwell together in luxury where they did not have to hide their relationship from Hest's wife or Bingtown society. Hest had told him not to be ridiculous, that they were fine as they were. Hest had had no wish to gamble his comfortable life. But, whether he willed it or not, Sedric had cast the dice for them. And instead of a fortune and a life of freedom in some exotic location, he had won slavery for Hest and whatever peculiar exile Sedric now endured.

He had heard the dreams of the Chalcedean dragon hunters. Sedric had not imagined the vast value of dragon parts. For the first time, he wondered if Sedric had gained his ambition, had harvested blood or scales, sold them, and gone off to live alone the dream that Hest had mocked. No. He had not. For if Sedric had taken such plunder to the Duke of Chalced or to any of the trade contacts they knew, these others would have known of it. Perhaps they would even have been able to go home, knowing that someone else had finished their terrible quest for them. And if Sedric had acquired a fortune, he would have come back to Hest and pleaded with him to go with him. Of that Hest was certain. Sedric would always come back to him.

So. What had become of Sedric and Alise? He did not

much care why his frumpy little wife had not returned
to him, but what had kept Sedric from his side? Being so
deeply infatuated with Hest in his juvenile and romantic
way, surely if Sedric could have come home, he would have,
with or without dragon's blood to trade. And Captain Leftrin
had claimed that both Alise and Sedric were alive. So much
he had gleaned during his time in Trehaug and Cassarick.

"What is that?" A man's cry, full of wonder and perhaps
fear, sent everyone scrambling to the rails to peer over the
side. Had the dragon returned? But a glance at the lookout
showed him pointing, not at the river but at the sky.

"Parrots," someone exclaimed in disgust. "Just a flock of
blue and green parrots."

"And gold and silver and scarlet and blue," another man
cried.

"They're a bit big for parrots . . ."

It was not a flock of birds startled from their canopy
home. These creatures came on swift, wide wings, more
batlike in motion than birdlike. They flew in formation like
geese, and even the powerful downstrokes of their wings
were orchestrated, as if someone called cadence for them.
Hest stared with the others and felt blood drain from his
face. His hands and feet tingled, and he could not voice
what someone finally shouted, his voice still tinged with
disbelief.

"Dragons! A flock of dragons!"

"Fortune favors us! Ready your bows!" Lord Dargen
shouted joyously. "Attack as they fly over us. Let us bring
down one or two of them, and return home with our holds
full of dragon parts!"

For the first time, Hest realized that the man was mad.
Insane with fear for his family, believing that somehow he
could get the magical items that would bring them safely to
him when he returned home. Hest suddenly knew with terrible certainty that they were no longer alive, that they had
died terribly, probably months ago, possibly screaming the
Chalcedean's name as they perished.

This quest was all the man had left. It was only a fantasy.
Even if he filled the ship with chunks of bloody meat and

kegs of blood, there was no grand life for him to reclaim. To fulfill his mad goal would be as disastrous for him as to fail. But this was his life now, and he was trapped in it as surely as he had imprisoned Hest in his madman's mission. Whatever doom he had brought upon himself, Hest would share. Weaponless he stood and watched them come. Creatures of legend, glittering like gemstones against the endless gray sky, in the distance they looked more like adornments to a lady's elegant music box than vengeful flying predators. All around him on the decks of both ships, men were running and shouting, stringing bows, demanding arrows of their fellows, limbering their arms with their throwing spears. *They have no idea,* Hest thought to himself. He had seen the blue dragon of Bingtown, Tintaglia, once. It had been in the distance, as he returned to Bingtown after she had driven off the Chalcedean warriors. He had thought her pretty then.

But on his return to the city, he had seen what a dragon's wrath could do. She had not intended to pock paving stone with acid holes, nor fill the harbor basin with sunken ships. That damage had been incidental. He had seen the harm that one dragon, fighting on behalf of a city, could do.

He stood on the deck and tried to count the oncoming dragons. He stopped at ten. Ten times dead was very dead indeed. The slaves chained to their oars were praying. He was tempted to join them.

THE DRAGONS HAD flown through the night, ignoring cold and fitful rainfall. Sintara had expected to be exhausted by dawn, but they were not. They had flown on, as the sun rose, and on as it climbed into the sky. They had flown as if they had but one mind, reverting to the animals that perhaps dragons once had been. Mercor led their formation, and Sintara had been proud to fly to his right. Blue-black Kalo had taken his left, and then Sestican and Baliper. Those three, she knew somehow, had been a long time with the golden dragon, perhaps swimming with him as serpents once. Quarrel they might among themselves, but now there was a common enemy to fight and vanquish. All differences among them were gone. Even their thirst for Silver had been suppressed. Fifteen strong, they had risen to Tintaglia's cry for vengeance.

Silver Spit lumbered along at the tail of the line. Copper Relpda flew strongly, her early awkwardness scarcely a memory for her now. And ridiculous red Heeby flew wherever she would, now part of the formation, now trailing it, now flying to one side. Her slender scarlet rider sang as they flew, a song of anger and vengeance, but also one that praised the beauty of angry dragons in flight and painted a glorious victory for them. Ridiculous, and ridiculous that she and the others enjoyed it so. Thymara had complained more than once about how freely the dragons used their glamour to compel their keepers to tend them. Yet not once had she ever admitted the power that human flattery and praise in song could exert over dragons. She was not the only dragon who flew with her mind full of Rapskal's glorious images of exotically beautiful dragons triumphing over every obstacle.

They had flown straight, not following the river's meandering course. Dawn had come earlier for them than it had for the ships on the river's surface. The tall trees that surrounded this section of the Rain Wild River also blocked the earliest rays of the sun. The dragons had flown over the treetops, feeling the warmth of the sun limber their weary wings, and then, as the trees gave way to the open space of the river, they had seen their enemies in the distance.

"Vengeance, my beautiful ones, jewels of the day! We will visit death on them, a death so glorious they will die praising you!"

"Destroy them all! Sink their ships!" Kalo's trumpet call of fury rang against the dead gray sky.

Rapskal laughed aloud. "Oh, no, my mighty one! There is no need to destroy such useful vessels. Only the killers must die. Leave enough crew to row our prizes home! Some we may allow to live, as servants, to tend our kine and flocks for us. Others we may ransom! But for now, blaze terror into their hearts!"

The young Elderling glittered scarlet in the morning

light, his garments of blue and gold like a battle banner in the wind. He broke into a deep-throated song in an ancient tongue, and Sintara discovered she recalled it of old. When Rapskal paused at the end of a stanza to draw breath, the dragons trumpeted in unison. Her hearts swelled with fury and joy at her own mightiness. They neared the hapless boats and swept low over them.

THE SHIPS ROCKED in the wild wind of their passage. Those few crew members who remembered to release their arrows saw their puny missiles wobble and spin in the dragon tempest. Leaves and twigs from the nearby trees showered down with a *shushing* sound and even the river surged up in wavelets. The force sent Hest staggering to the wall of the ship's house.

"We're going to die here!" he shouted, for he suddenly saw it all clearly. The dragons would circle back and fly over them even lower. But no wind need they fear, for the danger of the acid they would spew down on them would make the wind seem like a friendly pat. Even a falling drop of the stuff would kill a man, eating through clothes and flesh and bone until it emerged from a stumbling corpse and buried itself in the earth. If the dragons breathed it out as a blanketing mist, only sodden wreckage and sizzling bones would remain of them.

Hest screamed wordlessly as the images fully penetrated his mind.

"Get off the ships! Hide in the trees!" Someone shouted the order, and a wave of men scrambled to obey. From beneath the closed hatches, screams of terror rose, but there was no time for Hest to think of anyone except himself. *Get off the ship.* It was his only possible chance to survive. He rushed to the railing and jumped amid a fountaining wave of other men doing likewise. He was fortunate that his ship was closest to the bank. The water, cold and stinging, closed over his head. He had shut his eyes tightly as he jumped and as he came up he floundered blindly, scarcely daring to open his eyes until he felt the slimy river bottom under his boots. Then he blinked rapidly, feeling the river water sting and haze his eyes for a moment before he scrabbled out onto the muddy, reed-choked bank.

He was one of the first ashore. Behind him, all was chaos on the boat and in the waters between them. Men had jumped haphazardly, some on the river side of the vessels, to be swept away in the stronger current there. Others were trapped between the ships, half blinded and stunned by cold water and terror. They yammered and shrieked as the dragons swept back over them. The wind of their passage rocked the vessels, and the cries of the drowning men were submerged by the earsplitting roars of the dragons as they passed. Hest was stunned by the sound, staggering and covering his ears. A full knowledge of the majesty and power of dragons suddenly filled him, and he fell to his knees, weeping to think that he had dared defy such magnificent creatures. All around him, men were doing the same, begging for forgiveness and promising lifelong servitude if only they were spared. They knelt or prostrated themselves in the mud. Hest himself stood, his arms uplifted to the sky, and suddenly realized he was shouting praise to their beauty. In the distance, the dragons were beginning a wheeling turn. He knew two things with certainty: this time they returned to kill, and then, with an even greater clarity, he knew that the thoughts and feelings of the past few moments were not his own. *It's like a dream,* he told himself. *A dream in which I do and say things I would never do or say in my waking life. This is not me; this is not of my own will.* Then, as the dragons approached, all rational thought fled.

———◆———

EVERY HUMAN WHO could flee the ships had. Sintara was vaguely aware of men wailing in trapped dismay. Some were jumping about, heedless of how they damaged themselves as they fought chains that secured them to rowing benches. Humans evidently confined humans. Why, she could not guess and did not find it intriguing enough to puzzle about. It did not please her when Mercor led them to land in the shallows of the river and then wade ashore, but she sensed his purpose. The humans were now cut off from their ships. A few, she knew, fled mindlessly into the forest. They would die there, tonight or tomorrow. Humans were not able to live without shelter and food.

But others crouched in the grasses or hid behind trees or simply prostrated themselves, sick with terror. Not one had been killed by tooth or claw or dragon's breath. Those who had perished had wrought their own deaths, their little minds unable to stand before the terrible glamour of a dragon's wrath and majesty. As the dragons waded out of the river, some of their captives wailed in terror. Then Heeby spoiled their grand procession out of the water by skidding to a halt on the mud bank, sending muck up in a spattering spray over the cowering humans. Sintara snorted in disdain.

She noticed that Rapskal did not leap down from the scarlet dragon's back until she had moved to a less marshy site. Then he hopped down, his gay Elderling cloak aflutter about his shoulders. Those few invaders who were capable of a response other than terror gasped in awe at the sight of him. Grudgingly, she had to admit that he looked far grander than the squat humans in their murky clothes. Tall and slender, he was a fitting companion to the dragons. He looked about, a grim smile on his face, and then flung his cloak back over one shoulder. She felt almost proud of him as he strode forward and ordered the humans, "Stand up! Come forward! It is time to be judged by those you have wronged."

They obeyed. Even as the dragons eased the glamour that held them, the humans obeyed. Pulverized by terror, they had already been defeated. Wet and shaking with cold, they came forward to stand in a huddle. They were a motley assortment. Some were in rags, thin and scarred. Others were attired as bowmen, with leather on their wrists and close-fitting shirts, and there were those in the finery of noblemen. Of old, dragons had known all these sorts of men and found that, stripped of their fabrics, they were all soft-skinned shrieking monkeys.

HEST FOUND HIMSELF obeying the command to come forward for judgment. He had found a small corner of his mind
to call his own, so even as he stepped forward to join the
others in a kneeling row, he recognized that the awe and
terror he felt were not entirely rational. He dared a quick
glance at the faces of his fellow captives. Some looked as
blank as sheep facing slaughter, but in others, he saw the
struggle in their eyes. He knew a moment of consternation
that some of the Chalcedean's rowing slaves were more cog-
nizant of their own minds than the nobles who had commanded them. Then there was no time to think of anything,
for a tall scarlet warrior was striding toward the line. Hest
had never seen such bright garments as he wore. He walked
with a fighter's stride, but wore no armor nor carried any
weapon. Perhaps he needed none.

He stopped a short distance from them. A red dragon had
followed him to his inspection, but it was the great golden
dragon that towered over both of them that held Hest's gaze.
The creature's eyes were large and liquid, black over blackness. They seemed to swirl as he gazed into them, radiat-
ing calm. The largest dragon of all, a blue-black mountain,
towered over the others. Light seemed to sink into him and
vanish into his shimmering anger. His silver eyes reflected
nothing. Someone spoke, the red man or the dragon, Hest
did not know. "Have you offered harm to a dragon?"

"No," he said, for he had not. He had never shot an arrow
or jabbed with a spear. He found himself standing and stepping back. Others were doing the same, slaves and crewmen
and even one of the Chalcedean bowmen. Some remained
kneeling, and Hest had an ominous sensation of doom.

"Judgment is done," the scarlet man proclaimed. "You
who have dared to raise hands against the glory of a dragon
will spend the rest of your lives in servitude to them. That is
the mercy of Mercor the Wise. A workman's village awaits
you, where you can become useful. If you fail to serve willingly and well, you will be eaten. One way or another, your

lives are forfeit for what you have done. You others have been part of a most evil expedition. You are not without guilt. But your families can buy you back, if they are inclined. If not, you can find useful labor among us. That will be discussed later, after we reach Kelsingra. For now, those who are evil will be transported in constraints." He narrowed his eyes for a moment, and then pointed at two slaves and a crewman. "You three will see to that. Confine them. Then organize a crew. The rest of you will bring the ships to Kelsingra. Those we claim as rightful booty, for you have invaded out territory without our permission and forfeit all that you have brought with you."

He turned away from them and the shocked murmur that was arising. "That is as much mercy as can be offered to you," he concluded without regret and walked back to the waiting red dragon. She lowered her huge head and sniffed him. He stroked her face, his own expression becoming silly with affection for the beast.

Hest knew a moment of utter disbelief. "But . . ." he began to protest, and then fell silent as the Chalcedean leaped to his feet. He shook his head like a man who stands in a swarm of midges and then raised a shout. "No! I will never be a slave. I am Lord Dargen of Chalced and I will sooner die than bow my head to the yoke!"

His hands were just as fast as Hest remembered them. The little knives were snatched from hiding and took flight as if they had wills of their own. They did not miss. They rattled like hailstones off the hulking blue-black dragon's thick scales. One stuck for a moment at the corner of one of the great creature's silvery eyes. He shook his head and the dagger fell free. An oily drop of scarlet dragon blood welled from the wound and began a slow slide down the dragon's face.

The Chalcedean gave a shout of triumph. It rang oddly in the absolute silence that had framed his act. Then a smaller silver dragon gave a shrill trumpet of outrage. But the blue-black one made no sound as he took one step forward. All around the Chalcedean, his fellows crouched or cowered as the dragon stretched his head toward the man. He did not hiss or roar as he opened his jaws. As a man might snap an offending branch from a wayside path, the dragon bit the Chalcedean in half. In one head-snapping gulp he swallowed his head and torso. A moment later, he picked up the man's hips and legs and likewise downed them. Then he turned and stalked off. One of Lord Dargen's hands and part of a forearm had been sheared off in the dragon's first bite. It remained where it had fallen, palm up on the muddy earth as if offering a final plea. One of the other Chalcedeans turned aside and vomited noisily.

The scarlet man seemed unsurprised and untroubled. "He has had his wish. He will not bow his head." He turned back to his dragon and vaulted lightly onto her shoulder and then settled himself just forward of her wings. She snapped her wings wide. All around them, the other dragons were crouching and then leaping skyward. Wave after wave of wind, heavy with the smell of dragon, washed over Hest, until only the red dragon and her scarlet rider remained. The warrior looked over them with hard eyes.

"Do not be slow. If you need guidance, look to the sky. There will always be a dragon over you, making sure that you do not pause until you reach Kelsingra."

Then, to Hest's astonishment, the red dragon made a trundling run down the muddy strip of riverbank before leaping into the air. She flapped her wings frantically and ungracefully until she was airborne. In another time and place, he might have laughed at her ridiculous launch. Today, he knew only a moment of great relief that the dragons were gone.

A ringing in his ears that he had not noticed faded. He blinked. The day seemed dimmer, the smells of the swampy riverbank less intense. Around him, other men were shifting, looking at one another, shaking their heads and rubbing their eyes.

"They made us accuse ourselves!" one of the Chalcedeans shouted in fury.

A slave next to Hest stared at the man, and then a sneer crossed his face. "Is that what it takes to make a Chalcedean tell the truth? A dragon standing over you?"

The man lifted his fists and advanced on the slave, who stood his ground to meet him.

Someone screamed. A silver dragon swept in low over them, and the slave stood alone. Hest had a glimpse of a body dangling from the dragon's jaws before it flew over the trees and out of sight. He turned and ran for the ships. He was not the first to get there.

THERE WAS AN interruption in the light. And another. A gust of wind rattled the tall rushes all around her. Tintaglia managed to open one eye a slit. She was still dreaming. A female green dragon looked down on her. *Too late.*

I fear you are right.

She had not seen the golden dragon. He had landed behind her. It was only now as his head came into view that she knew he was there. He sniffed her, his black eyes roiling with sorrow. *The infections are too far advanced. She will not fly again.* He lifted his head. *A shameful way for us to lose her. Killed by humans. No dragon should die so.*

Other dragons were alighting nearby. A blue queen, a silver drake, a lavender drake. Dragons. Real dragons, dragons that could fly and hunt.

Dragons have avenged you, Tintaglia, the golden one told her, as if he could sense her next thought. *The humans have been judged and punished. Never again will any of them lift a hand against dragons.* The golden dragon glanced skyward. *You were long coming back to us. Perhaps you had given up on us just as we had given up on you. But we will not abandon you here. Your flesh will not rot, nor be food for rats and ants. Kalo will gather your memories, blue queen. And all of us here will bear our recollections ever forward through time. Your name and deeds will not be forgotten among dragonkind.*

A scarlet Elderling stepped forward. She had not seen him, had not known that Elderlings had returned to the world. She thought of the three she had begun and knew a moment of sorrow. Incomplete, and without her continued presence in their lives, doomed to die. The scarlet Elderling was speaking. " . . . and a statue to your glory shall be raised in the center of the new Kelsingra. Savior of dragonkind, first queen of the new generation, Serpent-Helper, you will never be forgotten so long as Elderlings and dragons still breathe in this world."

His praise warmed her, but only faintly. He was not a singer such as Selden had been. She thought of her little dragon singer, only a boy when she had claimed him, and knew a moment of nostalgia for him. Dying, she sent a thought winging to him. *Sing for me, Selden. For whatever time remains to you before my death ends you, sing of your dragon and your love for her.*

Somewhere in the distance, she thought she felt a response from him, the sympathetic thrumming of a far string in tune with her own heart chords. She closed her eyes. It was good to know that a drake would circle over her and watch her death, good to know that no small animals would chew at her as she lay dying, that her memories would not be feed for maggots and ants. All she had learned in this life, all she had known would go on in some form. It would have been better if she had been able to lay her eggs, if she had died knowing that one hot day her serpent offspring would wriggle free of their shells and slither down the beaches to begin their sojourn as sea serpents. It would have been better, but this, at least, was as good a death as any dragon might have.

THE KEEPERS HAD awakened to a city bereft of dragons. None strolled out from the baths, gleaming in the spring dawn. None alighted in the square with a rush of wing and wind. In the absence of the dragons, the city became vast and empty and far too large for humans.

Tats had been startled when Thymara tapped on his door to waken him. If she hadn't come, it was likely he would have slept longer. But he rose and went down with her to enjoy a hot cup of fragrant tea and a round of ship's biscuit with jam. Odd, how such simple foods seemed so good after a time without them. Midway through breakfast, Thymara had set down her cup and tilted her head. "Do you hear anything from Fente?"

Tats closed his eyes and reached out toward his feisty little queen. He'd opened them again almost immediately. "Still flying, I think. I wonder how far they are going. Whatever she's doing, she's intent on it and wants no distractions." He cocked his head at her. "Has Sintara spoken to you?"

"Not directly. She seldom does when she's away. But I felt something, a thrill of excitement. I wish I knew what was happening."

"I'm almost afraid to know," Tats admitted. "The way they rushed out of here was frightening. So much anger in the air."

"And Rapskal became so strange," Thymara added shyly.

Tats gave her a look. "He's my friend still," he said. "Don't think you can't speak of him to me. I think he has spent more time in the memory stone than any of us, and it's beginning to show. When he returns, I think it's time we sat him down and talked with him about it."

"I fear it may be too late for that. He's so sincere in his belief that this is how Elderlings are meant to live, immersed in the memories of those who have gone before us."

"Perhaps he is." Tats had drained the last of his tea and looked reluctantly at the few uncoiled leaves in the bottom of his cup. "But I won't give him up without trying."

"Nor I," she admitted, and she'd smiled at him. "Tats," she had added frankly, "you are just a good person. My father once told me that about you. 'Solid to the core,' he said. I see what he meant."

Her words flustered him more than any declaration of love could have done. He felt his face heat with a rare blush. "Come. Let's get down to the well and see what is to be done there."

He had not been too surprised to see that Leftrin and Carson were already at the well site and discussing methods of reaching the silver. Carson had been pragmatic. "It doesn't look like there's much left blocking the way. Send someone down with an axe, and a hook and line. If the blockage won't come up, chop at it until it goes down."

"Send who?" Leftrin had demanded, as if no one would be foolish enough to go. "That's deeper than any of the previous jams. It's going to be cold down there and pitch-black."

"I'd never go down into that black hole," Thymara had muttered. She'd shuddered.

And Tats was almost certain that was the reason why he'd stepped forward, saying, "I can do it."

They had sent him down with a hatchet and a line and a ship's lantern. Leftrin himself had fastened the harness they rigged for him, and the captain hadn't said a word of protest when Hennesey had checked all his knots. "Better once too often than once not enough," he muttered, and Tats had felt his belly go cold. The descent had taken an eternity; allowing his body to dangle freely from the line had been the hardest part. He'd listened to the sounds of the heavy timber and the pulley rigged to it as they took his weight and he began his creaking descent. They lowered him slowly, and the lantern in his left hand showed him almost smooth black walls; the worked stone that composed it fit almost seamlessly together. His right hand gripped the line that held him, and he could not seem to let go, even though he knew it was securely fastened to his harness.

The voices of his friends receded to anxious birdcalls in the distance. The circle of light overhead became smaller, and the sounds of the straining line louder. The harness dug into him. And down and yet down he went.

When he came to the wedged timbers, the circle of light overhead had become a well of stars. It made no sense to him. He shouted up at them that he had reached the blockage. He gave his weight to it, standing on the heavy plank, and felt the line that held him go loose, and then abruptly tighten again. He felt like a puppet, suspended weightlessly on the plank. "A little slack!" he shouted up at them, and heard their distant voices arguing. Then they complied and he stood, balancing on the blockage. He lowered his lantern to rest it on the plank.

They'd sent him down with an extra piece of line tied to his harness. His first task was to unfasten it. It was surprisingly difficult to do, for his hands quickly chilled. Once he had it freed, it took a surprising amount of courage before he could bring himself to kneel and then reach down to wrap the line around the timber he stood on. It was a hefty piece of wood, as big around as his waist and just slightly longer than the well shaft was wide. He knotted the line with the knot that Hennesey had insisted he use, and then tested it, pulling with all this strength. It held.

Then he moved on his knees to the higher end of the timber, took out the hatchet looped to his hip, and began to chop. The vibration traveled, at first just an interesting phenomenon, and then an annoying buzz in his knees. The wood was dry and hard and lodged as tightly as a cork in a bottle neck. He wished he had a heavier tool with a longer handle, even as he realized the hazards of trying to stand and chop something under his feet. He spent a good part of the morning chopping away the final barrier in the well. He had to pause to warm his hands under his arms and rub the numbness from his knees. Only his Elderling tunic kept the cold at bay. The tips of his ears and his nose burned with cold.

Eventually, the timber under his feet began to give small groans. Even though he had known the harness stood ready to take his weight, he had roared in terror when the beam suddenly gave way beneath his feet. The short end of it fell away into the darkness. The larger piece fell and swung wildly, the knotted line singing with its weight. He dangled next to it and only slightly above it. He clung to the lines with both hands, knowing a moment of shame when he realized he had dropped his hatchet in his terror. A heartbeat later he was being hauled up so swiftly that he could not even brace his feet on the wall to steady himself.

He was dragged over the lip of the well so enthusiastically that it took the skin off his shins. Big Eider picked him up in a rib-crushing hug of pure relief that he was safe. But Thymara was the next to seize him in an embrace, and he counted his moment of terror a fair price for feeling her hold him so close and hearing her whisper, "Sweet Sa, thanks be. Oh, Tats, I thought you were gone forever when I heard you shout!"

"No. Just startled, that's all." He spoke over her head, his arms still around her. She was so warm under his chilled hands. "The way is cleared once we haul up that last piece of timber. We can go after the Silver now."

Hennesey and Tillamon had just arrived to trade shifts with Big Eider. It startled Tats to realize that a full shift had passed since Hennesey had sent him down the shaft. The mate dropped easily to his knees and peered down the well. "That's even deeper than I thought it was. First thing is to haul up that old beam and then get the bucket out of the way." He got up slowly with a wry grin. "Time to go fishing, boys."

LEFTRIN TOOK THE first fruitless turn at the "fishing." It was arm-wearying, shoulder-wrenching work. Hennesey had rigged a line through the same pulley that had supported Tats. On the end of it was not only a heavy hook, but a necklace made of flame jewels. Malta had brought it and all but begged them to use it to light their way to the well's bottom. Wrapped a few feet above the hook, the gleaming metal and sparkling stones gave off their own light as he attempted to guide the hook down. The illumination did not spread far. Leftrin lay on his belly, one hand on the line, and tried to guide the hook toward what they guessed was the handle of the bucket as he peered down into the well. It was far deeper than Tats had descended. Too deep, Leftrin had decided, to risk sending a person down.

When his back began to ache unbearably and his eyes to water and blur, he gave the task over to Nortel and stood up slowly. His gaze traveled around the circle of watchers. The keepers and some of his crew watched anxiously. At a distance behind them, as if their misery were too great to bear any company, were the king and the queen of the Elderlings.

Malta sat on a crate that Reyn had carried there for her, her baby in her arms. Her eyes were fixed on the crumbled wall that surrounded the well. Her Elderling robes gleamed in the sun, and a golden scarf swathed her head. Spring sunlight glittered on the fine scaling of her perfect features. *Dignity,* he thought as he looked at her. Dignity, no matter what. Reyn stood beside her, tall and grave, and the three together were like a sculpture of royalty.

Or misery, when one looked at their faces. The child was crying, a thin breathless wailing that made Leftrin want to cover his ears or run away. Neither parent seemed to hear it anymore. Malta did not rock Phron or murmur comforting words. She endured, as did her mate. They waited in a silence beyond words, their desperate hope as thin and sharp as a knife blade. The well would yield Silver and somehow one of the dragons could tell them how to use it to heal the baby. The child wailed on and on, a sound that peeled calm from Leftrin's mind. *Soon it will stop. It will be exhausted,* he thought to himself. *Or dead* was the darker thought that came to him. The child was so emaciated now that Leftrin did not want to look at him. Scales were slipping from his grayish skin; his small tuft of pale hair was dry and bristly on his head. The captain knew that if the well yielded Silver, the parents would risk touching Phron with it. They had no other course. For a long moment, he tried to imagine what they must feel, but he could not. Or perhaps dared not.

"Leftrin."

She spoke his name breathlessly, and the weakness in her voice jerked his eyes to her. Alise appeared at the bend of a narrow street, walking slowly toward them as if the weight of her Elderling cloak were almost too heavy to bear. "What is wrong with her?" Tats muttered, and Harrikin quietly replied, "She looks drunk. Or drugged."

Leftrin spared a moment to shoot them a warning look, and then hastened toward Alise.

"She looks very sick," Sylve suggested.

Leftrin broke into a run with Sedric and Sylve not far behind him. Up close, Alise looked more haggard than Leftrin had ever seen her. Her face was slack and heavy, and his heart sank as he gathered her into his embrace. She sagged against him.

"I found nothing." She spoke the words loud and clear, but there was little life in her voice. She leaned into him and looked past his shoulder at Malta. Her voice had the quaver of an old, old woman. "My dear, I tried and I tried.

Everywhere. I have spent the night listening to stone, touching anywhere that I thought they might have stored it. I feel I have lived a hundred lives since last I spoke to you. Many things I have learned, but of how pure Silver might be used to heal, of how to touch Silver and not die, I have found nothing."

Alise swayed in Leftrin's arms, and he tightened his embrace to keep her from falling. "Alise, I thought you had gone apart to take some rest! How could you risk yourself so? We are not Elderlings, to fearlessly touch the stones!"

"How could I not?" she asked him faintly. "How could I not?" She laughed brokenly. "The music, Leftrin. There was music, in one place, and dancing. I wanted to forget what I came for and just dance. Then I thought of you and I wished you were with me . . ." Her voice trailed away.

He tipped her face up to look into her eyes. "Alise?" he begged. "Alise?" Her gaze shifted to meet his. She was still there. A bit of life came back into her face. Sedric hovered nearby, with Sylve at his side. He knew they wanted to help, but he could not surrender her to them. He suddenly saw them as Elderlings, impossibly different from himself and the woman he held in his arms. He spoke hoarsely by her ear. "Why did you do it? It's dangerous. You know it is! Regardless of what Rapskal may say or the others do, we know what memory stone can do to us. Many of the Rain Wild folk have drowned in memories. Perhaps Elderlings can use such stones without threat, but *we* cannot. I know you wish to know all about the city, but touching the stone is something you must leave to the others. What could make you do such a foolish thing?"

"It wasn't for the city," she said. He felt her pull herself together. She stood on her own now, but chose not to leave the circle of his arms. "Leftrin. It's about the baby, little Phron. And Bellin's babies, never born. About—" She paused and took a long breath, then plunged into it. "About your baby that I would want to bear someday. You heard what Mercor has told us. If we live near the dragons and the Elderlings, then we will change also. Skelly will change. Our children will continue to be born changed, and for those of us not

Elderlings with dragons, they will die young. As we will. If there is another way, we have to discover it, my dear. No matter the cost."

Her words drenched and drowned him like a flash flood. He hugged her close to him, his mind whirling with possibilities that had never seemed quite real to him before. "I'll clear the well," he promised her. "I'll get that bucket up and out of the way. It's as much as I can say for certain, but I'll do it."

"It's the missing piece," she said into his chest. "Of that I am certain. Silver is what is needed. You will be restoring full magic to the Elderlings."

Now there was a frightening thought. He looked around at the keepers, marking how they had drawn near to hear her words. *All these youngsters with magic. What would they do with it? Use it wisely?* He shook his head at such a foolish hope.

Malta had stood, and Reyn had trailed her as she approached them. Her lips were chewed and chapped, her hair like straw. The babe in her arms mewed endlessly. "Thank you," she said. "For all the ways you have tried to help us, thank you." Leftrin did not doubt her sincerity, but pure weariness and unadulterated sorrow sucked the heart from her words. She might have been thanking Alise for a cup of tea instead of thanking her for risking her sanity.

Leftrin stepped back, holding Alise by the shoulders. "Bellin!" he barked suddenly. "Take her down to the ship. Get a hot meal into her and see that she goes to sleep in my stateroom. I want her out of the city for a night at least." As Bellin approached, he looked at the well with new eyes. "I'll clear it," he promised her again.

Alise muttered a protest, but she did not resist as the deckhand took her arm and led her away. As they walked away from him, Leftrin heard Bellin's husky words. "Oh, Alise. If only it can be. If only it can be."

THE "FISHING" CONSUMED the rest of the day. The line was long and the ghost light of the jewelry barely enough to see anything by. Sedric took a fruitless turn at the effort. A hundred times, a thousand times, the hook slid past the bucket's handle without catching on it. Keeper and crewmen, all took turns. All failed. When Sylve finally hooked it, she gave a single whoop of excitement.

"Keep it taut!" Carson barked at her, but he grinned as he said it. Everyone gathered in a circle around her held their breaths. The Elderling girl grasped the line firmly, holding the tension while Carson slowly took up the slack on the other side of the pulley. "Got it," he told her, and very slowly she let go of the rope. She backed away from the well's edge and then stood up, arching her back. Lecter came without asking to take up the line behind Carson. "Slow and steady," Carson told him, and he nodded.

All saw the strain as the two men pulled. The rope creaked, and Leftrin came to add his strength. "Stuck in the dried muck," Carson guessed breathlessly and Leftrin grunted in agreement. The rope creaked more loudly, and then Sylve gave a small shriek as all three men abruptly stumbled back.

"You've lost it!" she cried. But she was wrong. The line swung slowly as it took the weight of the bucket in full.

"Keep the tension on it." Carson advised them. "Go slow. We don't know how strong the bail is on the bucket. Try not to let the bucket touch the wall; it might jar it loose. Then we'd have it all to do over again." Sedric watched the keepers trade their grips, hand over hand, as the ancient bucket slowly rose toward the surface.

The sun was toward the horizon when the flame jewels finally emerged and the handle of the bucket was seized with eager hands. "It's plain damn luck that line held," Leftrin exclaimed as they lifted it over the lip and onto the ground. The keepers crowded round. It was, as Rapskal had speculated, large enough for a dragon to drink from, lovingly crafted from dark wood lined with beaten metal.

"Silver!" Tats had gasped.

Sedric stared at it, unable to speak. Carson came to rest a hand on his shoulder and stare with the others.

It was obvious the bucket had long rested at an angle at the bottom of the well. There was a slope of packed silt in the bottom of the bucket. Draining away from it and gathering itself into an uneven puddle on the bottom was Silver. Sedric stared at it, his breath caught in his chest. Yes. He understood now what Mercor had said about the stuff, that it was in the blood of dragons. For that was where he had seen it before.

The unwelcome memory burst into his mind. He had crouched in the darkness, full of greed and hope, and cut the dragon's neck and caught the running blood. She had not been Relpda then, his gleaming copper queen. She had been a muddy brown animal dying on the riverbank, and his only thought had been that if he took her blood and sold it, he could buy himself a new life in a distant land with Hest. He had trapped her blood in a bottle and left her to her fate. But he remembered now how the dragon's blood had swirled and drifted in the glass bottle, scarlet on silvery red, always moving before his eyes.

Yes. There was Silver in dragon's blood, for he watched it now as it stirred and moved like a live thing seeking an escape. Such a shallow puddle to evoke such awe in all of them! It drew itself together in a perfect circle and stood up from the bottom of the old bucket like a bubble of oil on water. There it remained in stillness, and yet silver in every variant of that color moved and swirled through it. "It's beautiful," Thymara breathed. She stretched out a hand, and Tats caught her by the wrist.

Malta and Reyn stood side by side. The babe fell suddenly silent.

"It's deadly," Tats reminded them all. The young keeper looked around at the circle of faces that hemmed the bucket and its contents. "What do we do with it?"

"For now? Nothing," Leftrin declared sternly. He met Malta's stare with one of his own. "We brought it up. There's Silver down there, though this is scarce enough to wet a dragon's tongue. What little we have here, we save until the dragons' return, in hopes they can use it to save the baby. Do any disagree?" His eyes roved the assembled keepers.

Sylve looked shocked as she said, "What else would we do with it? All of us want the young prince to live!"

Sedric concealed his surprise. Prince. So they thought of the sickly child, and so they had risked all for him. Leftrin cleared his throat. "Well then. I say we take no more risks this evening, but set this aside and all of us go take some rest."

SHE COULD FEEL the light fading from the day. Her last day? Probably. Pain lived in her, a fire that did not warm her. Some little scavenger, braver than most, tugged at her foot. Tintaglia twitched, a reflex that hurt now, and it scampered off into the rushes to wait. *Not for long,* she thought. *Not for long.*

She felt him land not far from her. The thud of a grown drake vibrated the mud beneath her, and the wind of his wings washed over her. She smelled his musk and the fresh blood of his latest kill. It stirred hunger in her, but suddenly even that sensation took too much effort. Her body released her from that need. Nothing left to do but stop.

She felt him coming closer.

Not yet. It was hard to focus the thought at him. *I've had enough of pain. Let me die before you take my memories.*

Kalo came closer and she felt him stand over her. She braced herself. He would finish her with one bite to the back of her neck, at the narrowest part, where her skull joined her spine. It would hurt, but it would be quick. Better than feeling the ants that were already investigating her wounds.

Blood from his jaws dripped down, falling on her face and on the side of her mouth where her jaw hung ajar. She tasted it with the edge of her tongue. She drew a sharper breath. Sweet torture. Her eyes flickered open.

The big drake stood over her. Light touched him, gleaming him black and then blue. A riverpig hung limp from his jaws. The blood dripping onto the side of her mouth was warm. He had brought his kill here to devour while he waited for her to die. The smell of it was intoxicating. She moved her tongue in her mouth, tasting life one last time.

He dropped the pig right in front of her.

Eat that.

Her incredulous response had no words.

*Eat that. If you eat, you might live. If you live, I might
find a mate worthy of my size.* Kalo wheeled away from her.
I will make a kill for myself. I will be back.

She felt the sodden earth under her shudder as he bounded
into flight. Stupid male. She was too far gone for this. It was
of no use. She opened her jaws slightly and the fresh blood
ran over her tongue. She shuddered. The dead pig was so
close to her, reeking of warm blood. She could not lift her
head. But she could snake it along the ground on the length
of her neck and open her jaws wide enough to close them
around its water-gleaming hindquarters. As she closed her
jaws, her teeth sank in and blood flowed into her mouth. She
swallowed it, and her hunger woke like a banked fire does to
wind. She lunged, snapped, and tipped her head up to swallow. A short time passed, and she lifted her head. She had
dragged the pig closer with her first assault on it, and now
she could scissor off chunks and gulp them down. Blood
and life flowed back into her.

Pain came with vitality. When the pig was gone, she
shuddered all over. Small creatures that had crept closer
under cover of darkness suddenly scattered back into the
rushes. She rolled onto her belly and then gave a roar of
pain as she lurched to her feet. She walked to the river's
edge and then out into the icy water. Ants and beetles that
had come to feast on her wounds were washed away in the
water's chill rush. She felt the acid's hard kiss and hoped it
would sear some of the lesser wounds closed. She groomed
awkwardly, too swollen and stiff to reach some of her injuries. And the worst one that still held part of the damned
Chalcedean arrow forced her wing out at an odd angle.
There was less pressure from it since the second piercing,
and it seemed to be draining still. She forced herself to
move the wing and felt a rush of liquid down her side. She
screamed her fury at the pain to the night, and night birds
lifted from the trees and a passing troop of monkeys fled
shrieking from the river's edge. Good to know that something still trembled in fear of her. She staggered from the
water and found a less trampled place among the tall rushes
and fern fronds and lay down to sleep. *Not to die. To sleep.*

That's good to know. His thought touched her before she felt the wind of his wings sweep past her. He landed heavily, and the gelid earth quaked beneath him. She smelled fresh blood on him; so he had made another kill and fed himself.

Tomorrow morning, I will hunt meat for you again. He stretched out his body casually beside hers and she knew a moment's unease. This was not the way of dragons. No dragon brought down prey for another, nor did they sleep in proximity to each other. But his eyes were closed and the stentorian breath of his sleep was regular. It was very strange to have him so close to her. *Strange, but comforting,* she thought to herself, and closed her eyes.

✦ ✦ ✦

Day the 6th of the Plough Moon

Year the 7th of the Independent Alliance of Traders
**From Erek Dunwarrow, former Keeper of
the Birds, Bingtown, presently residing in
Trehaug
To Kerig Sweetwater, Master of the Bird
Keepers' Guild, Bingtown**

*Master Sweetwater, I send this sealed missive by a bird
released from my wife's own hand from her coop here in
Trehaug. I write of a matter of great concern to all of us.*

*I trust you to remember that I was your apprentice
once, and that from you I learned my standards of
honesty and integrity. I am now married to Detozi
Dunwarrow, long known as an excellent and honorable
bird keeper here in Trehaug.*

*This day as I approached Detozi's coop to deliver
her noon meal, I heard and then saw a bird in distress,
a messenger bird tangled and hanging by his foot. I
climbed out into the smaller branches of the pathway
and was able to cut him free. Imagine my surprise to
recognize a bird I had myself raised in Bingtown, one
that was subsequently sent as an unmated male to the
coops in Cassarick. Although he was unbanded, I assure
you that I recognize this bird. In my care, he was known
as Two-Toes and was unusual for hatching with a
missing toe. Even more shocking was when I confirmed
what I recalled from the red lice plague. This bird
had been listed as one of those who had perished in the
Cassarick coops.*

*The message fastened to his leg was not in a Guild
tube, the bird was badly fed and in poor health, and the*

careless manner of the fastening for the message tube was responsible for his becoming entangled.

I believe he was sent from Cassarick to Trehaug clandestinely, and only by happenstance have I intercepted him. Please do not suspect me of ill doing; I have concealed the bird in my home until I can bring him back to full health. He deserves that at least. I have preserved the illegal message packet unopened. I beg you to tell me to whom I can entrust it here, for I fear to hand it over to the very villain who has constructed this deceit.

If you find fault at all with how I have handled this, I beg that all blame fall upon me and not Detozi. This is none of her doing, but only mine.

Erek Dunwarrow

CHAPTER FOURTEEN

BLOOD PRICE

Selden jerked awake to the pounding on the door. Shaking with alertness, he rolled from the divan to the floor and then, surprising himself, to his feet. He had no time to wonder if he was getting better or if his fear was overriding the weakness of his body. He heard the key turning in the lock.

"Lady Chassim, we must enter, on the Duke's orders. He wishes the dragon man brought to him immediately!" A man shouted harshly as the door swung open.

The lady herself strode from her bedchamber, an unfastened robe hastily thrown over her nightdress and a stone vase balanced over her head in her two hands. The set of her mouth said she would battle first and then find out why. Selden had taken to sleeping with a stick of kindling on the divan beside him. His was a feebler weapon than hers, but he gripped it tightly, intending to defend her to the death this time.

The two guardsmen fell back at the sight of her fury. "Lady, please, we are sorry to disturb you. Our orders are absolute. We must take the dragon man to the Duke. His need is dire and he cannot wait longer."

Dizziness swooped through Selden's brain at those words, and the stick of wood tumbled from his nerveless hand. Here was death, barging in the door in the middle of the night. "I am not ready," he said, to himself rather than the guardsmen.

"He is not!" Chassim snapped out her agreement. "Look at him. He coughs and spits gobs of yellow mucus. He has a fever, and his piss is the color of old tea. He is thin as an old horse, and he shakes when he tries to stand. You will take this to the Duke? Sick as he is, you will take this diseased creature into his presence? Woe betide you when you are his death!"

The younger of the two guardsmen blanched at her words, but the grizzled older guard only shook his head. He looked haggard, as if sleep had long abandoned him. "Lady, you know well we are dead if we return without him. Disobeying the Duke's order will only ensure that we are tortured to death along with our families. Stand back, Lady Chassim. I have no desire to handle you roughly, but I will take the dragon man now."

Vase in hand, she stepped boldly between Selden and his abductors. She set her feet and he knew she would fight them. He staggered in a wobbly circle around her and into their arms before she realized what he was about. "Let us go quickly," he told them. They seized him by the arms, and as they hastened him out the door, he called over his shoulder, "For a few days of respite, may Sa bless you."

"Sa, the god that fucks itself," the younger guardsman sneered.

The heavy vase landed with a crash on the floor just behind them. "You didn't lock her in?" the older man exclaimed in horror, but there came the sound of a slamming door. "Run back and lock it," the guard told his junior in disgust. He kept his grip on Selden's upper arm and half dragged him until the youngster caught up with them to seize Selden's other arm.

"You sick like she said you were? Are we going to catch your disease?"

The younger guard huffed as he spoke, hurrying to keep up with the older one. His grip was not as tight as the older man's; plainly he didn't even want to touch Selden's scaled arm. In response, Selden went off into one of his coughing fits. Over and over, the air was squeezed from his lungs, and he struggled to take in each shallow breath. *Be calm,* he told himself. *Be calm.* He had discovered it was the only way to recover his breathing. He closed his eyes, went limp, and made them drag him as he put all his focus into trying to get breath back into his body. *Why?* he asked himself. *Why not die on the way and thwart the Duke?*

But breathe he did, if shallowly, on the long haul that continued down several flights of stairs and then through an endless dim corridor. Lanterns in alcoves burned with low flames, and a short train of servants bearing armloads of bloodied sheets and basins met them and streamed past them in a nightmarish parade.

"How can he lose so much blood and still live?" the younger guard asked.

"Shut up! Someone hears you, that can be called treason," the other barked.

They marched on in silence. At the end of that hall, they handed Selden off to two servants in spotless white robes. They escorted him, just as ungently, through grandly carved doors into an antechamber where two servants garbed in pale green seized him without comment. Another set of impressive doors and he entered the Duke's lavish bedchamber.

A death chamber, he thought, for the smell of death permeated the room. The heavy drapes of the bed had been roped back and lamps burned everywhere. Incense burned as well, and Selden lowered his face, trying not to breathe the smoke that would choke him. The basket of bloody cloths by the grand bed smelled of rot, the red stains streaked with brown and black. The circle of healers around his bed looked terrified, as did the guards who stood watch behind them. At the end of the bed, his hands clasped behind him, stood Chancellor Ellik. He was elaborately and carefully attired as if he had readied himself for a special occasion. Did he hope to proclaim the Duke's death tonight?

The Duke himself sprawled on his back, his head thrown back, his mouth open wide. He pulled in breaths and pushed them out with a sound like a bellows. Selden thought him unconscious until the bony head on the ropy neck turned toward him. The man's pale blue eyes were framed in pools of red. "Laggards!" he croaked. His withered lips trembled as if he wished to utter a thousand curses. Then they firmed, and he said only, "The blood!"

They dragged Selden forward and one healer brought out a gleaming knife while others set a small table, a white cloth, and a polished silver basin ready. He fell to his knees, but they paid no more attention to him than if he were a chicken being prepared for the pot. His left hand was seized and drawn forward, and when his wrist was over the basin, the healer cut him with a deft and practiced flick of his knife. His blood, thin and bright red, ran freely. Selden watched dully as his life poured out of his body and into the bowl. It fell in spatters and then a tiny stream. The gathered healers watched it puddle and then pool in the basin.

"Enough!" one cried suddenly, and with an expert wrap and a tight twist, a white cloth bound his wrist. An assistant darted forward to seize his hand and hold it up over his head. Selden sagged helplessly in their grip. He longed to be taken away, to not witness any of this, but they held him there. Through stunned eyes he watched them pour his blood into a crystal goblet. No less than four healers assisted in the lifting of the Duke's head, while two held the goblet to his lips. Another one bade him, "Sip slowly, my lord."

Breathe it in and choke on it, Selden thought. But he did not. The Duke sipped his blood and then, gaining strength, lifted his own head and drank it. In horror, Selden watched color come back into the man's face. His tongue, grayish, lapped at the last scarlet drops in the glass. He drew in a deeper breath. Then he tried to sit up. He could not manage it, but there was unmistakably new strength in his voice as he commanded, "Bring him here! Directly to me!"

They dragged Selden to the bedside on his knees. One of the attendants forcibly bent his head down before the Duke while another snatched the cloth from his wrist. His face was pressed hard against the bedding. Selden struggled to draw breath, but no one cared. Someone grasped his arm firmly and twisted his wrist toward the Duke.

He felt the cracked lips brush his wrist in an obscene caress. The Duke's tongue was warm and wet as it probed for his wound, leaving chill slime as its track on his arm. Selden gave a low moan of disgust as the old man's mouth latched onto his wrist and suckled at his blood.

After a short time, he felt the Duke's clawlike hands fasten their own grip on his arm. The sucking grew stronger and an ache extended from his wrist to the inside of his elbow and then up his arm. When it reached his armpit, he thought he would faint with the pain. The world was spinning, and the distant cries of amazement and joy that reached his ears mocked his death.

ELLIK WATCHED IN repugnance as the Duke suckled at the freak's arm. *Coward. What battle could not do, disease has done. It has made him a coward, and he will perform any act, no matter how demeaning, to hold death at bay.* Long practice kept his thoughts hidden. To any onlooker, he watched with concerned eyes as his beloved duke tried once more to snatch life from the jaws of death.

The Duke breathed through his nose as he sucked the blood, a panting breath that took on the same rhythm as coitus. The chancellor looked aside from the revolting display, expecting that at any moment the Duke would breathe his last. But as the slow moments dragged by and the breathing became stronger, he looked back at the man. Horror blossomed in him. Thin he still was, but there was a faint flush on his cheeks now. His eyes were half opened as if in pleasure, and they were brighter than Ellik had seen them in months.

"My lord. My lord, may it not displease you that I speak, but if you wish to preserve this creature's life so that you may have a later treatment of his blood, you must stop now."

The healer who gripped the dragon man's wrist spoke in a timorous voice. His thumb was on the creature's pulse. The Duke paid no heed. The healer shot a frightened glance at the older man who grasped the dragon man's forearm. Now Ellik noticed that he, too, kept a monitoring thumb on the pulse point inside the creature's elbow. He met the younger man's stare, gave his head a tiny shake, and pressed down. The Duke sucked harder for three breaths and then abruptly lifted his head. His voice was stronger, thick with his drink as he demanded, "Has he died? The blood has stopped!"

"No, my duke, he is not dead, but he flutters close to it." The healer spoke in a gentle voice full of deference. "Would you finish him now, or send him back to be fed up again for a later treatment?"

Greed and caution warred in the Duke's face. Abruptly, he pushed the thin wrist away from his mouth. "Take him away. Bid my daughter feed my fine blue cow fat again. Whatever Lady Chassim desires for him, she may have! See that she does all she can to bring him to where he can be bled again. Tell her this is my most ardent wish for her, if she would retain the goodwill of her duke."

"My lord," the healers chorused. Ellik saw concern in how quickly they bandaged the creature's wrist. Before they wrapped it, he glimpsed the deep purple bruising all around the wound. The Duke's teeth had left deep dents in the flesh.

"I will eat now," the Duke declared.

As he leaned back into his pillows with a deep sigh of contentment, the room around him erupted into a frantic bustle of activity. A basket of clean cloths appeared as the used cloths were whisked way. Fresh bedclothes appeared, and the servants deftly folded away the soiled ones as the new ones were spread over him so that not even for a moment was he chilled. An array of musicians bearing their instruments trooped in and stood ready against the wall in case he should bid them to play. A narrow table was carried into the room, followed by an ant stream of servants bearing trays of

all manner of food and drink. Water beaded on the outside
of pitchers of iced wine while other pots steamed fragrantly
with hot, mulled drinks. Covered platters stood shoulder to
shoulder with steaming tureens. The array would have done
credit to a banquet, and once again Ellik wondered where
the hardy warrior he had once followed had gone.

The chancellor cleared his throat, and the Duke's eyes
turned to him. He waited, watching the Duke count and
measure the words he would give him, and Ellik knew he
was on the cusp of losing all he had gained. "Your gift has
pleased me," the old man said at last.

Ellik waited ten heartbeats. The Duke said no more, and
in that quiet, the chancellor read that he would not keep his
promise to him. When a man hopes to live, he does not prepare a stronger man to take his place. It would be more important to him now that he coddle his daughter so that she
might keep his blood cow alive. "Lady Chassim," he had
called her. He could not recall the Duke ever granting her
both honorific and name when he had spoken of her before.
Her status had changed in his mind. He would not again
offer his daughter to Ellik. But the chancellor replied only,
"Then I am very well pleased, my lord." He lowered his
eyes, so that no one might see how his mind seethed with
fresh plans to take the reward he had earned.

FOR THE FIRST time in months, he had ordered his servants to open the heavy draperies that sealed all light from
his chambers. From his bed, he had watched the pale gray
light of dawn venture across his carpets and then the linens
on his bed. He had opened his hand to that light, light he
had believed would not touch him again, and smiled as it
became the full gold of daylight. He was alive this morning.
Still. And as he resolved that he would live, he'd issued his
orders. The chief of his healers looked aghast.

"My lord, favored of the gods, beloved of the people, I
fear you attempt too much too soon. Your recovery has been

swift, but so quick an improvement, if followed by too much activity, may lead to a relapse and—"

"Be quiet or die." The Duke kept his response short. He knew the wisdom of not taxing himself just as he was starting to recover. But to no one else could he entrust this errand. "Carry me to her chambers, set down the chaise, and leave. Stand ready outside the door until I summon you. Do not otherwise disturb us."

Last night, after the dragon man's blood, he had eaten and drunk wine with pleasure for the first time in months. When he awoke, he could sit up in bed, and could control his bowels once more. He had not soiled himself, nor spat blood today. He knew it was soon to demand to be conveyed to his daughter's presence, but it was a risk he had weighed well. Beneath the light coverlet, he grasped a knife in each hand. If she saw fit to show her vicious side, he would kill the bitch regardless of the consequences. But if she could be reasoned with at all, there might be great benefit for both of them. He intended to show her that.

He had sent a messenger ahead, to inform her of the visit. He had no wish to have a vase flung at him. Something almost a smile hovered at the corners of his withered lips. She got her spirit from her father. Briefly, he considered ordering that all heavy objects be removed from her rooms. No. That was not how to begin with her. She must not think that he feared her, or know, completely, just how much power she held. This would be a delicate negotiation, one only he could perform.

The locks were unfastened. "Knock!" he ordered the guard who had begun to open the door. The startled man hesitated as if questioning his order. Then he hastily rapped on the heavy panel of the wooden door and called out, "Lady Chassim, you are honored with a visit from the Duke!"

A moment of silence stretched almost long enough to be insolence. Just short of defying him, she called, "Enter and honor me, then."

His guards looked uncertain. Had she mocked the Duke? Were they required to kill her? It was almost amusing, and he nodded for them to obey.

They carried him into a sunny room with thick carpets on the floor. There was a cage of songbirds in one corner and a table with a silver bowl of fresh fruit from his hothouse. Evidently courtiers had already begun to send her favors. How quickly word spread in his court! He narrowed his eyes and decided to put a stop to it. Nothing must enter this room save that he sent it. To him she must come for any little favor she sought. She must depend on him for every single thing, even a glass of water or a husk of bread. For he knew his life now depended on her.

"A pleasant room," he reminded her as they lowered his chair to a spot before her hearth. A slight motion of his head dismissed his guards and bearers. He did not deign to watch them leave. He would not take his eyes off her. Witches were best watched closely. She had muffled herself most peculiarly, covered her entire body in drapery from head to foot. All he could see was her face, but at the same time he took in the details of the room. He listened to the door close behind them as he met his daughter's gaze.

A divan in the corner held his dragon man. He was very still, but the sheet that swathed him rose and fell. By the divan were a tray bearing partially consumed food and a glass with the dregs of wine in it. So, she had fed him and the creature had eaten. Good. "Plenty of sunlight," he added to her lack of response.

"There would be more were there not bars on the window."

"That is true. Would you like me to have the bars removed? Or move you to larger quarters that do not have bars on the windows?"

That unbalanced her. The flicker of uncertainty in her eyes warmed him more than her fire did.

She drew a breath, hesitated, then bravely countered, "I would wish to go back to my own quarters among your women, free to walk the gardens and use the baths as I once did."

"Impossible, I am afraid, for it would scarcely do for my dragon man to be quartered among my women. I do not trust them as I do my only daughter."

The uncertainty was consternation now, and she could not mask it. Wariness swam behind her eyes. "What do you want?" she asked bluntly. "Why have you come to see me after years of banning me from your presence?"

He stared at her for a time, and she held his regard. *She looks,* he thought, *more like me than her mother. I should have seen that years ago. There is more of me in her than in any of the sons who failed me. I have battled my dilemma, and the solution was before me the whole time.* A rush of inspiration filled him. He kept his voice low. "I know what you've done. And I know your ambition."

A shadow of fear flickered across her face, but she did not speak.

"You sought to stir insurrection against me. Rebellion. Your exhortations were skilled, for a woman. But you sought your alliances in the wrong places. To build a throne, you must build on stone, not flowers. I am stone."

"I don't understand."

He hadn't intended that she should. He needed to draw her into the conversation, to make her think she negotiated for what he would offer her. "You should have come to me with your ambitions for power. Am I not your father? As much of my blood flows through you as through any son I sired. Did you think I would find your craving for power reprehensible rather than true proof you are worthy to be my daughter? To be my heir." He dropped his voice on the last words and was gratified to see her lean forward to catch them.

She swayed slightly; the offer had dizzied her. But she recovered quickly. "Mother of your heir, perhaps. Ellik told me the terms of your agreement when he . . . visited me here. I will be the cow that drops a calf for both of you."

That explained the fading shadow of bruise on her face. Ellik had been quick to take him up on his offer. The Duke rather hoped she was not pregnant. He did not want her mawkish with maternity, not until his own health was fully restored. And that, he was convinced, rested on her keeping his dragon man alive and well.

"I will not allow him to 'visit' you again, if that is what

you wish. I will move you to better, larger quarters where your ward can have a chamber of his own, and there are no bars on the windows." He thought of a set of rooms in a tower not far from his own. Windows set so high in a sheer wall had no need of bars on them. She was staring at him. Recklessly, he enlarged the offer. "And you, not El-lik's child, shall be written as my heir. With the power to choose your own consort, when the time for that is right." He paused. What other female silliness might please her?

"Why do you come offering me these things?" She did not even pretend to be anything other than astounded. And cautious.

"Because you have proven yourself worthy," he told her grandiosely. "I do not think you really sought to overthrow me," he lied. "Even you must have seen that you could not come to power in a land torn by civil war. Every warlord beneath me would have risen, seeking to claim my throne, with you the swiftest path to legitimacy. No matter how many women you could rally to your cause, they would swiftly be subdued by their own husbands and fathers and sons. No. You cannot rest your throne on frail flowers, my dear. You must build it on the stone of your father's strength."

He lifted a hand and gestured casually at the dragon man. "I gave you a task, thinking that I would test where your loyalty lay. Would you obey my request, or purposely kill the valuable creature put into your keeping? You knew that I wished him restored to health. And, my Chassim, you have passed my test of you. Last night when he was brought to me, I found his health much improved. And by that I knew that your wishes aligned with mine."

"He was swooning when they returned him to me, his wrist chewed as if an animal had been at him."

She spoke the accusation in a low voice. He felt a muscle twitch and thought of killing her. How dare she? Instead, he smiled affably. "Another small test. And again, you have passed it. I see that you have made him comfortable, have persuaded him to eat and drink. I do not doubt that soon you will have restored him even more completely than he was last night. You have done well, daughter. And that is why I have come to see you, and to offer you your earned reward. Continue as you have begun. This very day, you and your charge will be moved to better quarters. If there is food or drink you wish, music or books or flowers, make your desire known to the servants I will give you. And it shall be done."

"Freedom to come and go as I please?"

He smiled again, but he was wearying of her. "In time, perhaps. For now, I think you will be too busy taking care of our special guest. Occupy your time and thoughts with tending to him. As you can see, my health is improving. Soon I will begin instructing you in the ways of power. Before I can formally declare you my heir, I must show you well groomed for the position. It has been long since a woman has come to power in Chalced. The way must be prepared for you, my dear."

He took a breath. Tired. Time to return to his bed, to sleep. Tired, yes, but not sickened with weariness. Only tired as any man would be after having to deal with a witch. She opened her mouth to speak. He lifted a cautioning finger. "Later," he said. "After you have had time to think well, and have shown me, yet again, that you can employ your skills for love of me." He nodded toward the supine dragon man. Then he lifted his voice. "Guards! I wish to return to my rooms."

They entered with alacrity. Had they feared for his safety? Good. To his daughter he said, "You see. They respect your abilities as I do." As they lifted his chair, he leaned back on his cushions. Let her ponder what he meant by that.

"YOU ARE AWAKE."

He opened his eyes. The room seemed very bright, and he quickly lidded them again. He felt her hands on him. They were light and cool as she felt his brow and then slipped her fingers down to his throat to touch his pulse.

"Don't go back to sleep. Not until you've eaten and drunk."

"To make me strong." He could manage no more than a hoarse whisper. "So your father can bleed me again."

She didn't deny it. "I knew you were awake and listening.

And yes, for now, that is what we must do, to buy time for ourselves."

"I must live, waiting for him to want to use me again? That is why I should get better?" He did not have the strength to put the full outrage he felt into his voice.

"Not so different from what I have had to do, and more than once," she hissed back at him. "Do you think that to be kept in a pen and fed like a fattened bullock is so different from being confined until you are bred like a cow for the calf you may drop? Yes. It will be hard for you. It has been hard for me. But we are both still alive. And that is what it will take for both of us to remain alive long enough for us to make a different plan."

"What plan?" He hated that her words made sense to him. He wanted her to be wrong, wanted to be offered a future that did not include the ghastly old man's withered lips sucking at his wrist.

"If I knew already, we would not have to make it. Here. Let me help you to sit up a little. I want you to drink some wine and eat something. It seems you can have whatever you wish to eat or drink now. Is there anything you would fancy? Anything that would tempt your appetite?"

"Meat. Fresh meat," he demanded. He spoke the words without thinking and then fell suddenly silent. He looked up to find her staring at him quizzically.

"Just a touch of the dragon speaking," he said, meaning it as a jest. But he wondered.

✦ ✦ ✦

Day the 12th of the Plough Moon

Year the 7th of the Independent Alliance of Traders
From Sealia Finbok, of the Bingtown Traders
To Hest Finbok, of the Bingtown Traders

To be held at the Cassarick Traders' Hall.

My dearest son, how can you leave us in such suspense? All matter of strange tidings have my friends received from the Rain Wilds, and yet not a word from you! My dear, it is humiliating that I must hear tales of dragons sighted, and the mysterious and sudden departure, upriver, of the very impervious ship that you were on! I am told that it set off without a word to anyone, and that several very important Traders appear to have departed with it! If you know anything of this delicious bit of gossip, I implore you, send me tidings by bird at your earliest possible opportunity! All my friends are boiling with curiosity. Some are saying it was an incredible trading opportunity that led the boat to depart immediately, and others that it has to do with the other ship that followed the Tarman upriver.

My friends are speculating that you have dashed off on a mad adventure to find your missing Alise. They imagine all sorts of romantic reunions and rescues, but I will tell you again, I have always found her an unsuitable match for you. I do hope you will not put yourself into any danger or great inconvenience for her sake.

I am trusting that you will contact me almost immediately, by the swiftest messenger bird that can be hired!

Your loving mother

✦ ✦ ✦

CHAPTER FIFTEEN

HOSTAGES

W e're wasting our time, Cap," Skelly said.
She stood squarely before Captain Leftrin as she spoke.
"It's too dark down there, the drop is too long, and the
Silver too shallow. We'll never bail up any Silver dropping that bucket. It lands wrong every time. Weight it to
tip on its side, and it's going to stay tipped on its side,
spilling out any Silver it might take in as we haul it back
up."

She paused to draw breath. All around the well mouth,
the few keepers who had gathered remained silent. Three
fruitless days of fishing for Silver had brought them only
discouragement. Carson had insisted today that regular
work be resumed. So some had gone to the hunt to add meat
to their stores while most of Tarman's crew was back at the
docks, tending Tarman or working on reinforcing the dock.

Thymara and Tats had returned to the well to see if any progress had been made.

"You saying we should give this up?" Leftrin scowled down at her.

"No, sir. I'm saying, it's going to take hands. You have to let me try. I'm the smallest and lightest of the crew. And you need someone with some muscle in her arm for the climbing part. It has to be me. Sir."

Tats lowered his eyes, and beside him, Thymara was silent. She knew they both agreed with the deckhand. Skelly was the one for the job. At the same time, she suppressed a shudder. She could not imagine trusting her life to a length of rope, let alone descending so deep into a cold, lightless hole in the ground. Just the thought of it made her queasy. The job might need hands, but they wouldn't be hers.

"I'm not going to trust your life to a piece of line that long." Captain Leftrin was blunt. "Your rigging skills won't be much use to you if your hands are numb from cold. If the rope breaks, you die from touching the Silver. We heard that from Mercor himself. So. That's not going to happen."

"Then *you're* saying we're giving up?" She was so astounded that she forgot the "sir."

"Not giving up. Just not doing it your way. We've got a lot of salvaged chain. In pieces. I don't know what broke it into lengths, but whatever did it is a lot stronger than a man with a hammer. I had Big Eider working on some last night, trying to see if he could open some links and hammer it back together. No luck so far. But once we get it mended, if we can make it long enough, then I might trust it to take someone down that hole. Not you, but someone."

"Sir, I—"

Her offended protest was cut short. Distant trumpets were sounding. Everyone froze, and then the meaning dawned on them.

"The dragons are coming back!" Lecter shouted. "Sestican! Sestican!"

"Fente will want a hot soak and a grooming." Tats sounded almost apologetic.

"As will Sintara." Thymara knew what it meant. Until the

dragons were bathed and groomed, their lives would not be their own. And as Sintara did not enjoy the company of any of the other queens, chances were that she would not see Tats for that time. She felt a pang that surprised her. Had she so quickly become accustomed to spending her days with him? It had been simpler without Rapskal and her feelings for him complicating her life. And with that thought came another on its heels. She would have to deal with Rapskal again and what he was becoming. A shiver of dread went through her. Each time she saw him, he was stranger. And more of a stranger.

"Are you coming?"

The others, keepers and ship's crew, had already begun hurrying back toward the Square of the Dragons. Tats had paused to wait for her. "I'm coming," she replied, and she hurried to catch hands with him before they ran together.

BY TWOS AND threes, the dragons arrived. The boasting and trumpeting and the cries for attention from the keepers made it nearly impossible to get a coherent account of what had happened. Fente was disgusted that she had had to land in the river and walk about on the mud. She had made several kills on the journey home, all in the muddy margins of the river, and insisted that she was filthy even though, to Tats's eyes, she was her green gleaming self.

Her account of how the dragons had flown into battle, cowing the evil humans into submission by virtue of their glittering beauty, seemed far-fetched to him. "So you captured them all without shedding a drop of blood?" he asked as he inspected her claws after her long soak in the hot water.

She stretched her toes languorously. He found a bit of grit caught between two of them and diligently brushed it away.

Some died. One demanded to be eaten, so Spit ate him. Some jumped in the river and drowned. Some ran off in the forest, and so we left them. Then they had a fight among themselves on the way here, and some of them were injured. Stupid humans.

"I see," Tats said quietly. "And Tintaglia, who you went to rescue?"

"Dead by now. We were too late. All we could do was avenge her. Kalo remained behind with her, to eat her memories when she was gone."

Tats looked away from her. Tears stung his eyes. So the firstborn child of the king and queen of the Elderlings must perish as well. "That will be hard for Malta to hear."

"She is deaf now?" Fente asked, her curiosity idle. Tats shook his head and gave it up. From the way she dismissed the events, he knew there was no use in asking for details. She would be far more interested in telling him what she killed and exactly how it tasted than in explaining to him how a battle had been won and two ships captured.

Or so they claimed. Not all the dragons had returned yet. Of the ships and Rapskal and Heeby there was no sign, nor of Kalo, Mercor, and Baliper. *They are coming, very slowly,* she had explained to him. And then she demanded that he clean very carefully around her eyes, for she feared she had picked up water ticks from hunting in the river.

He had just finished that task when he heard more trumpeting from the river. *The others have returned,* she told him. He followed Fente out to the square where she launched into the air without a word of farewell. She was off to the hunt. She had no interest in ships or homecomings, not while her stomach was empty. He watched her depart and then followed the other keepers down toward the city docks.

That area had changed substantially since Tarman's return. Leftrin and his crew had turned to, making a dozen small changes to Carson's handiwork and expanding it in other ways. Tarman was now tied securely within a slip, his lines run to stout shore anchors as well as to an anchor set in the river to keep him from being driven against the shore. It looked to Tats as if the ship could not possibly be torn free, but Leftrin insisted that two hands be aboard him at all times, and none of the crew seemed to think that odd.

When the dragons had arrived and told them that they could expect two more vessels to dock soon, the first reaction had been disbelief. It had been followed by activity that reminded Tats of a stirred-up wasps' nest as keepers and crew frantically tried to make space for two more boats at their ramshackle dock while dealing with the demands of the dragons.

Mercor had been the first of the dragons to land. He came in gracefully, landing against the river's current and sending a plume of water rooster-tailing behind him. He had calculated his speed precisely and emerged quickly from the water to Sylve's shouts of admiration.

But his first words had not been a greeting but a query. "Have you found Silver yet? Is the well cleared?"As the other dragons landed and made their way to shore, he listened gravely as he was told that only a small quantity of the precious stuff had been pulled up from the well, and that efforts to reach the bottom of the well had been suspended by news of the dragons returning with two ships.

"And the Silver you did find?" he asked avidly.

The small quantity of the precious stuff had been carefully poured into an Elderling flask made of heavy glass and placed in the center of the table where the keepers dined. There it sat and shimmered, casting an unearthly glow of its own into the room. Tats had been certain that Malta and Reyn would try to apply it directly to the child, but they had not. Perhaps Kase's small mishap had persuaded them of its danger. In the transfer from the large bucket to the much smaller flask, a single drop of Silver had fallen onto the back of his forearm. He had exclaimed in fear, and then as the others drew near, he bent his head over his arm and stared at the Silver as it shimmered.

"Wipe it off!" Tats had exclaimed, tossing him a rag.

He had dabbed at it, to no effect. "It doesn't hurt," he had told them. "But it feels very wrong, all the same." They had all watched in silent fear as the Silver spread on his skin, outlining the scales on his arm and then almost disappearing.

"Nothing happened," Sylve said hopefully.

Kase had shaken his head. "Something's happening there. It doesn't hurt, but something is happening." He'd swallowed uneasily and then added, "I hope Dortean comes back soon. He'll know what to do about this." In the day since then, he had shed all his scaling where the Silver touched him, and the skin beneath it looked raw and angry. And remained a dull, silvery gray.

Mercor had listened attentively to their tale. "Yes. Dortean will be able to deal with that much Silver, if Kase goes to his dragon promptly." The golden dragon's eyes had whirled slowly. "And that was all the Silver you were able to bring up?" he asked again.

"I'm sorry," Sylve had told him, and her dragon had wheeled away from her in silent disappointment.

The other dragons soon knew the full tale and had unhappily conceded that until all the dragons had returned, the vial of Silver would remain untouched. They had accepted the news that the well was all but dry and that the Elderlings would have to work on a device that would lower one of them down to harvest what little Silver there might be. They had not seemed very excited at the news and he guessed the reason. The well was already incredibly deep. They surmised, as he did, that the Silver was all gone.

"Tats!" Thymara called, and he glanced back to see her running toward him. The back of her Elderling tunic stirred as her wings struggled to open. She had confided to him that sometimes that happened when she hurried, as if some part of her thought she should take flight. Now as she came toward him, smiling, the wind lifting her hair, he saw how much the wings were changing her. She carried them, a weight on her back, and even folded, their angles projected up higher than her ears. Lovely as they were, he suddenly wished she did not have them, for they forced him to recognize that all of them were changed as much as she was, just as far from the humans they had been. And all were just as much at risk from the lack of Silver as the dragons were. He thought of Greft, dying of his changes on the journey to Kelsingra. Did such an end await all of them?

"You look so solemn," Thymara said as she caught up with him.

"I'm a bit worried about Rapskal," he said, and it was not a lie even if it was not the immediate truth.

They crested the last hill and looked down at the docks.

Sintara and Baliper were wheeling overhead, and Spit had flown up to join them. Rapskal circled them on his scarlet dragon. His shouted victory song reached them as a thin whisper on the wind.

Oars powered the two ships that were coming in to dock. They were long and lean, low to the water. Their masts were stripped of sail and folded down to the deck. The oars rose and fell in an uncertain rhythm that spoke either of weariness or of clumsy oarsmen. "Catch a line!" Big Eider's cry rang out as he threw a coiled line to them, and the men who scrambled to catch it were certainly not sailors. They caught it, and then stood staring at it until one of the oarsmen jumped up to take it from their hands.

The rest of the docking proceeded with similar awkwardness. Some of the men on the ships were doing nothing to help, only standing and shouting that they were innocent men, honest Traders from Bingtown, and that they had done nothing to hurt a dragon or to deserve to have their ship stolen from them. Tats and Thymara halted where they stood to watch the spectacle. As the second ship ran into the first, tangling oars and breaking several, the shouts and curses rose in a storm. Other lines were thrown, and a man stood on the raised deck of one of the ships screaming orders that either his crew ignored or did not know how to obey. On the other, a reasonably competent crew ran about frantically trying to protect their vessel.

"This is bad," Tats said in a low voice. "Fente told me the dragons conquered evil warriors. They don't look like warriors. They look like merchants."

"Trouble will come of this," Thymara agreed.

Slowly they moved down the hill to see what the river had brought them.

"LIKE A COURTING bird," Big Eider said, and Leftrin growled in agreement. It had driven him nearly mad to see ships handled so. They might not be alive, but they were gracious, well-built craft and they did not deserved to be run into pilings or each other in the course of a simple docking. As they were finally being secured to the dock that he

did not completely trust for one ship, let alone three, Heeby
landed Rapskal nearby. The young Elderling slid down from
the scarlet dragon's shoulder, patted her, and suggested she
"go take a long soak, my lovely, and I'll be along to scrub
you down soon." As his darling lumbered off, Rapskal
promenaded down to the tethered ships. He stood, looking
at his prizes and nodding to himself, prompting Big Eider's
remark.

As Rapskal's fellow keepers began to close in around
him, he lifted up his hands and his voice. "Hostages! Disembark and show yourselves."

"Hostages?" Skelly asked in disbelief.

"That's what he said," Leftrin growled at her, and then
went forward to be certain the captured ships were not
left completely unmanned. Hennesey had followed him,
and with a shrug and a jerk of her head, Skelly had motioned to Big Eider. They trailed their captain while Swarge
looked on from Tarman's deck, smoking a pipe and shaking his head in disapproval. Leftrin glanced back once at
his own vessel. Alise, still looking pale, had come out of
their stateroom and onto the deck. She was freshly attired
in a long, pale-green tunic over leggings and boots of darker
green. Her long red hair, freshly plaited, hung in loops to
her shoulder and was secured with rows of bright pins. He
knew that style. He had seen it portrayed in mosaics in the
city. It worried him that she had unthinkingly adopted it,
as did the preoccupied look on her face. He wished she had
stayed in bed. Since her excursion into the memory stones
of Kelsingra, she had seemed distracted and weary. He had
begged her to stay out of the city for a few days, to rest on
Tarman and be away from the stone. She had complied, but
even so, she didn't seem quite herself yet.

"All of you! Right now!" Rapskal's shouted order rang in
the air. Leftrin was astounded to see how quickly his captives scrambled to obey him. He had heard scattered talk of
the "battle," and most of it had seemed rather incredible to
him. He had resolved to hear from a human exactly what
had happened, but as he watched Rapskal, he wondered if
his account would be any more coherent than those of the

dragons had been. The youngster stood, fists on his hips, watching the men disembark. Leftrin mentally sorted them. Here were two merchants, from Bingtown or beyond, and there was a fellow he recognized from Trehaug. Tattooed faces and ragged clothes and their limping gaits proclaimed those bewildered men as slaves, and there, to Leftrin's astonishment, was Trader Candral from the Cassarick Traders' Council. He looked a bit the worse for wear, and the bruises on his face appeared to be recently acquired.

The Chalcedeans came ashore in a group, eyes wary and backs straight. They moved with discipline, and he spotted their leader easily as he chivvied them into a tight formation. They might be captives, but they had not fully surrendered. Leftrin watched them grimly, knowing well why they had come to the Rain Wilds. Wondering what was to be done with them, he glanced back to see the last of the men leaving the ship. A few lingered behind the rest, checking tie-up lines, and he wagered that the last man walking down the gangplank with slumped shoulders was one of the erstwhile captains. "What would it be like to have someone take your ship from you by force?" he wondered aloud.

"A wooden ship or a liveship? Because I don't think anyone could take our liveship from us." Skelly denied the possibility of ever losing Tarman.

"It's been done a time or two, sailor, as you should know. But it's not a thing I like to think about." Leftrin didn't look at her as he spoke. He was watching Rapskal's captives as they left the dock and crowded together on the shore. The other keepers were gathering, expressions of anger and curiosity on their faces. Reyn and Malta were there as well, with Malta clutching her rag doll of a child to her chest. The captives stared wide-eyed at the keepers, as astonished by them as they were by the dragons. What Leftrin noticed was that most of the keepers were staring at Rapskal rather than the strangers he had brought among them. They watched him as if he were the novelty, something they had never seen before. Perhaps he was.

Rapskal strode up and down before his captives, bidding them line up with their fellows. Even so, the Chalcedeans kept to themselves. When it was done to his satisfaction, Rapskal finally turned to the other keepers. "Here they be!" he announced in a ringing voice. "Here be the ones who dared come into our territory to shed dragon blood, to slaughter dragons like cattle, for foreign gold. The dragons have defeated them and judged them. Those judged blameless of aggression against dragons shall be ransomed back to their own people. Those who are not ransomed will labor for us, in the village across the river. Those who have risen up against dragons, who have shed dragon blood or shown aggression to dragons, shall be executed by those they have offended."

A gasp rose from the assembled keepers and cries of outrage and fear from the prisoners. Leftrin was transfixed with horror. Executions?

Several of the prisoners were shouting that he had told them they could live in service to the dragons. One man fell to his knees weeping and crying out that he had been forced and had had no choice. Leftrin strode forward and then broke into a run as Rapskal crossed his arms on his chest and set his mouth in a flat line. "The truth is not owed to our enemies! I said what I said so that you would labor willingly to bring our captured vessels here. But a man who has lifted a hand against a dragon is not fit to live, let alone live among us. So you will die."

"No! NO!" Leftrin roared the word, and a silence swept through the gathering as if borne on the wind. His crew came at his heels, to stand with him.

The keepers were clutching at one another, wide-eyed with shock. Thymara, her face white beneath her blue scaling, stepped forward stiffly, walking like a puppet. Leftrin held up a forbidding hand and she halted, agony in her eyes.

"This is not the Trader way!" Leftrin shouted. Rapskal transferred his gaze to the captain, and his eyes blazed with outrage at the interruption. Leftrin advanced on the Elderling anyway, his burly hands knotting into fists. "Rapskal, how can you speak so? Never have we executed anyone! Leave that for Chalced, or corrupt Jamaillia. Never have we condoned slavery, nor have we killed as punishment for wrongdoing. If they did wrong, punish them. Judge a cost, make them labor until it is paid. Exile we have used, and indenturement. But not death! Whence come these terrible ideas? Who allows dragons to be the sole judges of the fates of people?"

Emotions flickered over Rapskal's face. The set of his mouth wavered, and for a moment, a startled boy looked out at Leftrin. "But it has always been so, has it not? Death the punishment for attacking a dragon?" he asked in honest confusion, all the eloquent elocution gone from his voice.

"Rapskal! Stay, stay with us, don't go!" Thymara dashed forward suddenly and seized him in her arms. "Don't go. Look at me, speak to me. You are Rapskal! Remember yourself!"

Tats joined her, putting a hand on Rapskal's shoulder. Sylve stepped forward and tall Harrikin, each putting a hand on him. In another breath, Rapskal was surrounded by all the keepers, all straining to touch him.

Leftrin watched in confusion. "Don't go?" he muttered to himself.

"You were right to warn him, my dear, all those weeks ago." He turned, startled, to find Alise beside him. Her gaze met his, her gray eyes true. "Elderling or not, he has spent too much time in the memory stone. It is not that he has drowned, but that the memories of someone else's lifetime have overshadowed his own. I know the man who lives again in Rapskal. Tellator. He was a leader among the Elderlings during a time of war with their neighbors. He was passionate in all things, and bloody minded in his hatred of those who fought against them." She shook her head slowly. "We would like to believe the Elderlings were always wise and kind, but their roots were human. They had their failings."

"I have to protect the dragons," Rapskal was saying now. He looked around at the worried faces of his fellows and added, "What else are we to do with such villains? Let them live among us? Let them go, to plot further against us? I, I don't like to kill, Thymara. You know I am not even a good hunter. But in this, what else are we to do?"

The bunched prisoners sensed the division in those they

faced. Some howled for mercy; others shouted that they
were Traders and only the Council could judge them. Three
men made a break for freedom, only to have Heeby trumpet
a warning at them that stopped them in their tracks. The red
dragon half opened her wings and advanced on the men, her
jaws wide. They retreated into the huddle of prisoners. The
Chalcedeans had formed up, back to back. Weaponless, they
would still fight. Leftrin shook his head. "What *are* we to
do?" he asked no one quietly.

THE WORLD HAD gone mad.

Hest stood in the center of the captives, his head bowed,
the hood of his cloak up. On the final leg of the journey
up the river he had asserted his rights to his stateroom and
his possessions, such as they remained. Most of the Chalcedeans had gone onto the other ship, and no one else had
the will to challenge him. It had been a relief to don different clothing and throw his worn-out rags over the side.
The foods and wine Redding had brought aboard for them
had largely been consumed by their Chalcedean captors, but
the bed and bedding had seemed an exotic luxury after his
days of sleeping in the hold. He had still had to help work
the deck and labor in the galley, but he had managed not
to have to take an oar. Between what remained of his own
clothing and Redding's, he was warmly and almost stylishly
attired again, and he had found time enough to shave and to
trim his own hair. He had not known what to expect when
they docked in Kelsingra but had fallen back on one of his
father's old axioms: a man who bears himself with authority will often have authority ceded to him. And so he had
locked himself in his room and readied himself for the city
and all it might hold, emerging only when he knew docking
was under way and thus avoiding most of the work. And
when the order had come to disembark, he had taken care
to blend with the others until he knew what sort of welcome
awaited them.

Yet he had not been prepared for the reality he confronted. He had expected a muddy excavation, or vine-
draped ruins. When they had come around the final bend in

the city and seen Kelsingra spilled out across the hillsides, he had been just as shocked as the rest. To see a city flung wide across low rolling hills, a city that reached to distant foothills and cliffs, had been astonishing. How could such a place have ever existed, let alone withstood the ravages of time, weather, and nature?

And how much treasure did it hold?

However Kelsingra had survived, here it was. Yes, the docks were gone, replaced by makeshift planks, logs, and crude pilings, but they functioned. And when a small committee of Elderlings had come down to meet the ships, he had decided they were the ones he must impress with his importance. Shock and horror had numbed him when the scarlet man condemned some to death and others to slavery. It was only now, as the denizens of the place squabbled with one another and shouted over the top of one another that he pieced together the puzzle. They were not truly Elderlings. These were the banished changed ones, sent off with the dragons. They had dressed themselves in Elderling finery, and for a time he had been deceived. There was the old *Tarman,* the ugliest liveship ever built, as evidence. So if this was where the ship had ended its voyage and these were the survivors . . . He lifted his head but kept the hood of his cloak pulled well forward as he surveyed the gathered "Elderlings."

After seeing the ferocity of the dragons and enduring his own journey up the river, he had doubted if either Alise or Sedric had survived. Both of them lacked his adventurous nature, and Alise especially was a creature of drawing rooms and tea shops. If he found himself a widower, as Alise's heir he would—

And then he recognized her. The incongruity of her gleaming garments with her plain features almost broke a guffaw of laughter from him. Her freckles were more obvious than ever, and if possible, the red of her hair was redder. Contrasted with the slender and youthful Elderlings in their bright garb, she looked short and stout. Her hair hung in ropes, and the snug trousers she wore showed every curve of her calves. Scandalous attire for any Bingtown woman, it was even more shocking on a woman of her years. She chose to stand with the rough-cut ship's crew; did she think their crude company made her look superior? If so, she was mistaken; the contrast was even more laughable.

Then, as he watched in abhorrence, the weathered ship's captain who had first dared to countermand the execution order put an arm around Alise and pulled her to his side. Did she struggle? No. She leaned into his familiarity, letting her head drop onto his shoulder. It was when she set her open hand to his chest that he realized with affront that she was intimate with the man. A common riverman, coarse and ignorant, was bedding the wife of one of Bingtown's most eminent Traders? The insult was unthinkable, to him and to his family. He could not, would not take her back into his home and bed. Dirtied as she was, how could she bear him an heir worthy of the Finbok name? He would disown her and dissolve the marriage!

But *not* before he had asserted his right to half of her claim to the city. As his eyes roved over Kelsingra, the magnitude of that fortune stunned him. He almost laughed over his earlier fears. There were his "captors," probably less than two dozen people. Why, their captives outnumbered them! He tried quickly to count the clustered keepers, to work out Alise's approximate percentage of claim to the city, but they were milling and clustering tightly around the scarlet man who had condemned the Chalcedeans. One of them shouted something about judging the "foreigners." Ridiculous. They had no authority! Tall they might be, but their scaled faces were still young, almost childish!

Even so, he had nothing to fear from their judgment. He had not done any physical harm to a dragon, nor could anyone ever prove he had intended to. As a Bingtown Trader, only the Bingtown Council could sit in judgment on him. These people might be dressed in Elderling clothing, but if they presumed to judge him, they'd soon have the Council and every Trader in Bingtown on their backs. Masquerade as they might, they were still citizens of the Rain Wilds and subject to its laws. They might detain him, might even demand ransom of his family, but eventually they would find that their little gaggle of misfits could not stand before the combined economic might of the Rain Wild and Bingtown Councils. If they thought they could ship treasure from here and live by their own rules, they'd be sadly surprised when they found the sole navigable waterway held against them. Young as they were and foolish, they probably had no idea of how things had always worked. Neither Bingtown nor Trehaug or Cassarick would suffer their grip on the Elderling artifact trade to be loosened.

With every passing moment, Hest gained more confidence in his position. He was just on the point of stepping forth and demanding that his rights as a Bingtown Trader be recognized when four of the Chalcedeans attempted to escape. The response of the red dragon sent them scurrying back, and Hest quickly moved as far away from the culprits as he could. If the dragon decided to dispatch one or more of them, he did not want to be confused with them.

The tumult among the Kelsingra Elderlings was subsiding. A woman was weeping and holding on to the scarlet man while a stouter fellow had draped an arm across his shoulders. Some crisis had passed, it appeared, though he had no idea what it meant. In avoiding the Chalcedeans, he had moved to the outer fringe of the huddled captives. Most of them had fallen silent, though a few still wept or cursed quietly. The slaves had squatted down to passively await whatever fate would befall them now. Clearly this was not the first time that the course of their lives had changed without their consent.

His fears calmed, Hest coldly assessed his position. So his "wife" had turned sailor's whore. There was a lever he could use. If she had any sense of shame left at all he might be able to persuade her to pretend she was dead and let him inherit all her share in return for his keeping silent about her sluttish behavior. She could not possibly return to Bingtown after what she had done, not if she cared for her family at all. So Alise was not a problem. He'd have all he wanted from her and be able to return unencumbered by her.

He could see that others among the captives were likewise evaluating their positions. The two Jamaillian merchants were talking fast and low to each other, surely discussing what trade terms they could offer, and who would not only ransom them but send enough coin that they could buy priceless Elderling relics to take home with them. He saw them look over at the keepers who had been joined by the ship's crew and were in earnest discussion. Only the dragon was watching the captives now, but one dragon was an ample guard for all of them. What were the Jamaillians trying to discern? Probably the same thing that Trader Candral was puzzling about. Who was truly in charge here? Who would not only decide his fate, but be the person who would negotiate their future?

Hest ran his eyes over them, dismissing the sailors in their rough clothes, considering only those masquerading as Elderlings. His eyes snagged on one tall fellow, standing at the edge of the crowd. He was watching the street behind him, waiting for someone, and ignoring the lively discussion among the dragon keepers. Hest read him carefully. Of all the Elderlings, he best maintained his bearing. Carefully attired in garments that complemented one another as well as his own coloring and in gleaming black boots, he had a born gentility to his posture. The wind tossed his cloak gently and moved his hair on his shoulders. A handsome fellow, lean and tall and well muscled, his scaling was coppery-brown over his own tanned skin. Hest felt a stirring of interest in him and smiled to himself. It would be a novelty to run his hands over smoothly scaled flesh. The tall man turned and said something to one of the others. From the depths of his hood, Hest stared at the copper Elderling.

Sedric.

But it could not be. The man would easily be of a height with Hest. Sedric had always been willowy and slight, forever boyish. This fellow was unmistakably a man, his shoulders wide and his chest deep. Then as a smile broke out on his face, he was unmistakably and forever Sedric, but a Sedric transformed by magic into an exotic and magnificent creature. Hest gazed at him, entranced. All Sedric's flaws had been burned away. Hest evaluated him, studying how he stood, watching and waiting. The almost-childish softness that had become an irritant to Hest over the last few years had been chiseled away, perhaps by hardship. However it had happened, it was gone, replaced by muscle and firmness. Here was someone who would yield to Hest, but not as easily as the old Sedric had. His pulse quickened at the thought. Sedric had become worthy again of his attention. And when Hest took him back to Bingtown, what a sensation he would be in their circle!

With a dizzying lurch, Hest suddenly realized that Sedric had fulfilled his dream. Dragon parts or no, the share of the city that Hest could claim through his trollop wife and his employee was a staggering amount. His eyes roamed over the city above the docks, and his heart suddenly leaped to new ambitions and ideas. Any one of those mansions could be claimed as his. Here, truly, he could live however he wanted to live, away from the condemnation of Bingtown and family. Did he need to return to Bingtown and take up his life there, under his father's watchful and disapproving eye? With the wealth he could rightfully claim, he could establish himself here, his friends could join him, and once trade was launched with other cities, he could travel wherever he wished. And Sedric had done it! He'd done it for both of them!

Sedric. He had been a half-schooled youngster when Hest had plucked the unsophisticated and naive lad out of his dull and stunted life. Everything about Hest had left Sedric wide-eyed with wonder. Hest had educated him in the ways that a young Trader's son should live, taught him how to dress and ride and dine, to choose a wine or critique a play. And he supposed that along the way, he'd wakened his appetites and his ambition for a finer life than that for which his humble family had prepared him. Hest shook his head in wonder, not just at Sedric but at himself. They'd laugh about all this someday, how Hest had inadvertently set Sedric's feet on the path that had won him a fortune. He looked at him with fondness and some pride. *So many misunderstandings along the way, Sedric. So many missteps on your part. But nonetheless, here we are, and fortune smiles on me through you.*

Hest took a moment to straighten his collar. He would step out from among the captives, stand proud as he threw his hood back and called Sedric's name. He paused a moment to savor the amazement and joy he would kindle in Sedric's eyes. Not to mention the awe and envy of the prisoners as he alone was greeted and welcomed by the gleaming bronze man.

He had stepped free of the others and lifted his hands to his hood when he heard someone call Sedric's name. And there, coming down the street, a bow slung across his shoulder, was the man Sedric had been watching for. There was a youngster at his side carrying several dead birds. Hunters returning with their kills? He saw how the smile widened on Sedric's face, a look of both welcome and relief. Sedric strode hastily to meet them as Hest watched in consternation. What could he possibly have to say to such a rough man?

He lost all interest in his own fate as he watched Sedric greet the two newcomers. He took a moment to speak to the youngster who displayed his grisly trophies with evident pride. Hest was shocked when Sedric actually took hold of one bird and hefted it approvingly before returning it to the lad. But then, as Sedric began explaining with obvious excitement all that was going on, the tall hunter put his arm around him and pulled him close. Sedric leaned on him for an instant in obvious affection. Then, in an open display of warmth, the tall hunter kept his arm around Sedric as they walked toward the others. It was impossible to miss the bond between the two of them. A wash of numbness spread up from Hest's belly. Sedric had replaced him? Had forgotten him and set him aside for a handsome savage? The insult scored him with a thousand claws. Jealousy and hate roiled through him, followed by cold.

Sedric would regret his faithlessness. There were many ways to hurt a man like him.

✧ ✧ ✧

Day the 12th of the Plough Moon

Year the 7th of the Independent Alliance of Traders
From Reyall, Keeper of the Birds, Bingtown
To Detozi, Keeper of the Birds, Trehaug, and
Erek

Dear Aunt Detozi and Uncle Erek,

I think perhaps you have been expecting to receive this letter for a long time, perhaps for as long as I have been hoping to send it. I know that initially you both had reservations about me courting a Three Ships girl. But I thank Erek for not only taking the time to get to know Karlin, but speaking well of her and of our desire to become engaged. I know that my parents have expressed trepidations about how an "outsider" will react to a Rain Wild youth with quite a bit more than "minor" scaling. Neither she nor her family have ever made an issue of it!

And now, I will remind you all quite cheerfully of what Erek told me when he was instructing me in managing the breeding records of the birds given into my care: "It is always healthy to introduce new blood of a good quality into an established line."

And such is our intention!

Her parents are, of course, just as conservative as mine in this matter. They have told us that we must wait a full year, but they are allowing us to announce our intentions publicly at last!

So, enclosed, the public announcement of our engagement! Please post it prominently so all may share my pride and joy! One scroll on every tree in the Rain Wilds still could not express it!

Reyall—a Very Happy Man

✧ ✧ ✧

CHAPTER SIXTEEN

EXPECTATIONS

I wish we could take this discussion somewhere warm and speak of it calmly," Alise said quietly. She was sheltered in the angle of Leftrin's arm, his cloak around her as well as her own. She knew her body was not cold, but the rising cold that she felt inside her was making her feel ill. She was still tired from her time in the stones; even with Leftrin holding her, she felt the lure of them tugging at her like small children begging for her attention. Too much was happening too fast. She felt shamed by the misery and uncertainty in the eyes of the captives, and the abject resignation of the thin, scarred slaves filled her with horror. Alone, that would have been bad enough, but the keepers were quarreling as if they were still the youngsters they had been when they left Trehaug. Kase, Boxter, and Jerd were in favor of letting the dragons do whatever they wished with all the captives. They were the extreme. All the others had taken up varying opinions as to what fate the slaves deserved, the Jamaillian traders, the Chalcedean dragon hunters, and the others. Rapskal had calmed somewhat. His earlier martial attitude had been completely at odds with all Alise knew of the young keeper. Thymara's attitude toward Rapskal's transformation had mirrored her own. She and Tats flanked him now, Tats with an arm across his shoulder and Thymara clasping his arm, as if their physical touch could keep him in this world and time.

Perhaps it could. She knew that she only slept deeply now when she could anchor her body to Leftrin's warm back, only felt solidly in this world when, as now, she held his hand in both of hers. She regretted her sojourn among the memory stones even as she knew that it had been necessary, and that she would one day attempt it again. The knowledge she sought was too important to all of them. She tightened her grip on Leftrin and struggled to keep her thoughts in this world and time.

She glanced away and her eyes met Carson's. He shook his head slowly at her, mirroring her dismay. He had arrived late on the scene, come back from hunting with Davvie and his catch. She knew from Leftrin that he had been taking more time with his foster nephew lately. Davvie and Lecter quarreled often of late, and Carson had been blunt with them both, telling them that he thought they were choosing each other by default rather than based on a true attraction. She did not think his bald stating of the situation was very helpful to either of them, even if she secretly agreed with it.

Carson lifted his voice in a shout that silenced half a dozen angry and worried arguments among the keepers and stilled the anxious shouts of the prisoners. "Let's round them up and take them to the baths. No matter how guilty they may be, they are still human, and even the dragons have said there are innocent men among them. So let us act as befits who we are, rather than who we think they might be. Take them to the baths, let them be clean and warm, and let us be comfortable as well while we discuss this."

He had a way, Alise thought. Harrikin backed him with,

"Carson's right. They may be brutes, but we are not." Kase and Boxter were already in motion as if they were sheep-dogs given a command. The cousins moved in unison, flanking the prisoners and shouting at them to get up, follow the Elderling in forest green, they were being taken to a judgment place. That was a bit more harsh than she would have phrased it, but it did get them up and moving.

Leftrin tugged at her arm. "Come, my love. Let's get you a hot cup of tea and something to eat. I'll wager you haven't eaten yet today."

"I haven't," she admitted. It was strange to sit down with him to their simple foods and humble settings when her mind still reeled with memories of elegant meals in elaborately staged venues. Scarlet wine would not fountain from a carved flower to fall into a chilled crystal goblet for her. Just hot tea with Leftrin. That was as she preferred it. Surely not all the Elderlings had lived that way, but the ones who considered themselves worthy of preserving their complete memories seemed to have pursued lives of utter luxury. Perhaps, she mused, she had been seeking information from the wrong stratum of society. Where, then, should she have looked?

"Alise!"

Startled, she turned her head to see who had shouted her name. The voice was hoarse. She looked at her friends but found that the Elderlings around her were staring back over their shoulders at the weary prisoners who were trailing them. As she stared in consternation, a tall man flung back the hood of his cloak. "Alise!" he cried, and his voice trem-bled with warmth now. "My darling, is it truly you? After all the days and all the hardship, I've found you at last! I've come to take you home!"

She stared. Then she began to shake, not a trembling, but a shuddering. Her knees buckled, and she would have fallen if Leftrin had not tightened his arm around her. She felt every muscle in his body tighten and his chest swell with anger. "Hest," she breathed in a choked whisper, confirming what Leftrin had already guessed.

"If he tries to touch you, I'll kill him," he promised her heartily.

"No, please," she gasped. "No scenes, not in public. Not like this." Most of the keepers guessed or knew that she had left a husband behind in Bingtown. Only a few knew how he had deceived her and hurt her, and even fewer knew the extent of Sedric's role in it. She and Sedric had protected each other, leaving those griefs and deceptions behind as they both built new lives in Kelsingra. But now Hest had come to tar them with shame, and everyone here would change their opinions of her. She had come among them as the dragon expert, the learned woman who had helped them believe in the existence of Kelsingra. They had seen her as a bit eccentric, but most of them admired her for her toughness and resourcefulness. She had survived Rapskal's thoughtless comment that she was not one of them, proving that even if she was not an Elderling, she was still essential to the colony.

Hest would take all that from her now, revealing her as a foolish woman who had been mastered by a man who cared nothing for her. All would know her past shame, and she would have to carry it forward into the future.

The thoughts flashed through her mind like a bolt of lightning that burned an image into her eyes. Without thinking, she turned her gaze to Sedric. His face was as white as hers. He had taken two steps out of Carson's sheltering arm to stare in disbelief at what fate had washed up on their shores. The hunter's face had gone still and stoic, as if he waited in the eye of a storm for the cold winds and rain to return. But Hest's charade of affection was for her alone.

"Alise, my dearest one, don't you know me? I know, hardship has changed both of us, but it's me, your husband, Hest Finbok. You'll be safe now. I've come to take you home."

The entire procession had halted to watch their interchange. Prisoners were exchanging confused looks. The keepers were parting to open a way between Alise and the man who had called her name. Hest moved toward her confidently, advancing from the gaggle of prisoners to walk through the ranks of the stunned keepers and up to Alise. They watched him curiously as he passed. He was, Alise thought, as dapper as ever. If he had endured hardship, it showed only in that he was leaner than she recalled him and perhaps a bit more muscled. The skin of his face was weathered, but it only made him more handsome. His fine black boots were scuffed, his tailored trousers a bit worn, as was the ruffled shirt he wore, but as always, the cut and colors of his clothing drew every eye to him. He pushed back his cloak from his shoulders. The wind stirred his dark hair, and a smile lit his face and eyes as he advanced on her, his arms open as if to embrace her.

"Who is that?" Davvie demanded in awe. He looked dazzled.

Carson replied with a terse, "Shut up."

Reyn startled everyone when he stepped into Hest's path. "Who are you? Go back with the others until you are judged." He met Hest's stare eye to eye.

Hest responded with wide-eyed shock. "But . . . but I'm Hest Finbok! I've come all this way to find my wife, Alise! I hired passage on the newest and swiftest ships I could find to come in search of her. When treachery by the captain let it fall to Chalcedean pirates, I thought all was lost. But here I am! Sweet Sa, your miracles never cease! I am here, and alive, and so is my darling wife! Alise, don't you know me? Has your mind been turned by this harsh place? I am here now, and you need no other protector than your loving husband."

His words, she thought, danced all through the truth, never touching it. Reyn, startled, stayed as he was as Hest stepped around him.

"No." It was the only word she could manage. Her throat was dry, her heart pounding. She could not find breath to say more than that, but she clung to Leftrin's arm as if it were her only lifeline in a wild sea storm. And he did not let go of her. He stood firm at her side.

Leftrin spoke in a low growl. "The lady says no."

"Take your hands off my wife!" Hest ignored Reyn's challenge of him as he stepped around the Elderling to glare menacingly at Leftrin. "She is obviously not right in her mind! Look how she stares! She does not recognize me, poor thing! And you, scoundrel, have taken advantage of her! Oh, my Alise, my darling, what has he done to you? How can you not recognize your own loving husband?"

She felt a low rumbling from Leftrin as if he snarled like a beast. His arm in her clutch had become hard as iron. He would protect her, he would save her. All she had to do was let him.

"No," she said again, this time to Leftrin. She squeezed his arm reassuringly and then stepped out of his shelter. She stood free of him, and the wind off the river blew past her. Her unbound hair lifted in wild red snakes, and she knew a moment of dismay as she wondered how ridiculous she looked, her skin weathered, her woman's body garbed in the bright colors of an Elderling as if she did not know her age or her place in the world.

Her place in the world.

She squared her shoulders. As she walked forward, Reyn stepped toward her as if to offer her his arm and support. She waved him off without meeting his eyes. She advanced on Hest, hoping to see some flicker of doubt in his eyes. Instead his smile only widened as if he were truly welcoming her. He actually believed that she would resume that role, would pretend to be his loving, dutiful wife. That thought touched fire in her soul. She halted before him and looked up at him.

"Oh, my dear! How harshly the world has treated you!" he exclaimed. He tried to put his arms around her. She set both hands to his chest and pushed him firmly away. As he staggered backward, it pleased her that he had not expected her to be so strong.

"You are not my husband," she said in a low voice.

He teetered a moment, then caught his balance. He tried to recover his aplomb. But she had seen the sparks of anger flare in his dark eyes. He tipped his head, solicitous, his voice stricken. "My dear, you are so confused!" he began.

She lifted her voice, pitched it for all to hear. "I am NOT confused. You are NOT my husband. You broke the terms of our marriage contract, rendering it void. From the earliest days of our marriage, you were unfaithful to me. You entered into the contract with no intent of keeping yourself to me. You have deceived me and made me an object of mockery. You are not my husband, and by the terms of our marriage contract, all that is mine comes back to me. You are not my husband, and I am not your wife. You are *nothing* to me."

It was gratifying to see the surprise on his face. This was not what he had expected. He had thought to take control of her just as easily as he once had. But it was frightening, too, to watch the expression in his eyes shift. How quickly he reassessed the situation; how swiftly he found a new tactic and a new balance.

"Unfaithful? Me?" He stood taller. "How dare you! Would an unfaithful man have risked all to come this far to rescue you from this place? You! Traders of Bingtown and Trehaug, I call you to witness!" He spun back on the dumb-founded prisoners who were taking in the scene as if it were a puppet play. "This is my wife, Alise Finbok! I sent her, at her most earnest wish, to visit the Rain Wilds. How she became caught up in this expedition, I do not know, though I know that some of you were there when she embarked on it. I *do* know she is rightfully married to me, and if this beast has alienated her affection for me, then he must answer for it! Annul our marriage agreement she can, if that is truly her own heartfelt desire. I will set her free! But I have not violated our contract, and I will not be denied my rightful claim on properties she has acquired during our marriage!" He spun back and pointed a finger at Leftrin. "And you, scoundrel, do not think you will go unpunished for your part in this! You have stolen my wife's affection and alienated her from me. The Council shall sit in judgment on you. Prepare to forfeit every greasy coin, every bit of property, even that stinking barge you own for this grievous insult to me and my family."

Alise cursed the weakness that made her legs shake. "You were unfaithful!" she cried out again, and she could not control the waver of her voice.

"My dear, you are not yourself!" he cried again, heartbreak in his voice. "Come back to me. Forgiveness is still possible. I will take care of you, restore you to a safe life where you are free to pursue your studies in quiet and calm. Say but the word, and I will see that no word of this scandal ever touches your family or your name." He looked earnestly into her eyes, the picture of a wronged but forgiving man.

But she clearly read his threat, couched as an offer of forgiveness. Her family. Her reputation in Bingtown. Did she care for such things anymore? She thought of her mother, of her younger, unwed siblings. Her family had no wealth, only their status as honorable Bingtown Traders, folk who always kept their bargains. The scandal he threatened could destroy them. She hesitated, duty to her family's name shredding her heart.

"You were unfaithful. From the very first night you made her your bride. I will testify to that."

She scarcely recognized Sedric's voice. It thrummed with deep passion. He pushed his way past the staring keepers to stand beside her, where he lifted her hand and tucked it into the crook of his arm. She clutched at him and felt his unseen trembling as they confronted together the man who had dragged them both through so much misery.

Hest drew himself up straight, and sparks of scorn danced in his eyes. "Ah. My valet. My runaway servant. Do you think I don't know of your private bargains? Your disgusting dealings with Chalcedean merchants to sell them dragon parts? Do your friends know of that? Now that they do, will they believe you? A man who lies once will lie often."

Sedric went even whiter, but his voice was steady. "My friends know all, Hest. My dragon knows all. And she has forgiven me."

That rattled Hest. Alise's thoughts scattered as one part of her mind rejoiced. *You never saw that he might have a dragon, did you, Hest? You saw his changes, but you could not truly imagine how much he had changed.*

But Hest had not changed. He recovered as neatly as a tumbling acrobat who comes to his feet again. Only those who knew him well recognized the tiny pause of uncertainty before he spoke. He still played to the crowd as he disbelievingly asked, "And knowing of your treacherous nature, you think they will believe whatever foul thing you say? *You* will testify against me? You, Sedric Meldar, a lowly servant? Then do so now, before all of us. Tell us then, give us one instance of my unfaithfulness to my wife. Just one will do." His gaze was sharper than a knife. Alise saw victory dancing in his dark eyes.

Sedric drew a breath. The trembling she had felt as she gripped his arm stilled. He spoke clearly, his voice pitched to carry to everyone there. "I shared your bed for years, before you took Alise as your wife, and for years afterward. You spent your wedding night with me. And in the years that followed, you made her a laughingstock among our fellows. In that circle, all knew that you disdained the company of women for that of men. I was your lover, Hest Finbok. I helped you deceive her, and I did not speak up when you mocked her.

"And if need be, I will stand before all of Trehaug and all of Bingtown and attest to that. You were an unfaithful husband to her, and I, I was a treacherous friend."

Alise stared at Sedric as he committed social suicide. But he turned and met her gaze and said, "And again, Alise, I am so sorry. Would that I could take back those years of your life and give them to you unscathed."

Her eyes brimmed with tears. Sedric had just destroyed all chance that he could ever return to Bingtown and resume his life. Even if he remained in Kelsingra forever, if even one Trader returned to Bingtown, all would know not only what he had done to her, but what he was. "I forgave you, Sedric. I told you that a long time ago."

"I know that," he said very quietly. His hand covered hers as he added, "But I did not deserve your forgiveness then. Perhaps I can say I have earned it now?"

"You have," she said quietly. "And more. But Sedric, what have you done? All will know that you . . ."

"That I am what I am," he said calmly. "I do not apologize for that. Ever."

She sensed someone behind them and turned slightly, thinking it might be Leftrin. It was not. Carson was grin-

ning, but as he stepped forward, a single tear tracked down
his sunburned cheek. He folded Sedric into an embrace
from behind that lifted the smaller man off his feet. "Proud
of you, Bingtown boy," he said huskily. He set him down
on his feet and leaned down to kiss him. The kiss did not
end quickly, and Sedric's hands came up to cradle Carson's
bearded face to his own. Several of the keepers favored the
couple with knowing whoops that drowned out the incredulous muttering from the watching prisoners. Alise found
herself smiling, as much for joy for them as for the stunned
expression on Hest's face.

She felt a nudge and turned to see Leftrin. He stuck out
the crook of his elbow, and she took his arm in his ragged
coat sleeve. "I think we were going to get some tea?" he
asked her conversationally. She nodded, and instantly forgave him the triumphant look he shot over her head at Hest.
She walked a dozen steps with Leftrin before she glanced
back. Hest was standing alone, staring after them.

"How IS HE?" Reyn asked as he took a seat beside his wife.
He spoke quietly, not to interrupt the conversation going
on in the central part of the gathering room of the baths.
A strange site selection, he thought, but at least it offered
ample space. Every keeper and the full crew of the *Tarman,*
except for Big Eider and Bellin, sat in rapt attendance. Reyn
wondered if the chaotic discussion was similar to how the
earliest Rain Wild Council had begun. Every keeper had an
opinion and seemed intent on airing it. Leftrin and his crew
seemed likewise focused on having a say.

Several of the dragons, still steaming gently from their
baths, had remained as well. Reyn wondered if they were
really interested in how the humans settled things, or simply
hoping for an easy meal if executions were indeed the final
decision. Spit had stretched out alongside the captives, who
were seated in a group on the floor. From time to time he
extended his neck and took a deep snuffling breath as if sa-
voring the aroma of their fear. Mercor, gold and dignified,
made up for the smaller dragon's lack of gravitas. Baliper
was present as well, eyeing the captives thoughtfully. The

presence of the dragons threw the room into its rightful perspective. Humans and even Elderlings seemed small and
transient in the massive gathering space.

Malta looked down on the quiet bundle in her arms. "He
nursed for a short time. He's not asleep. He seems too tired
to eat or to cry right now."

"The quiet is a relief," Reyn said honestly and then wished
he could bite the words back. She gave him a stricken look,
and he read her thought: *Soon enough, it would always be
quiet.* "Let me hold him for a time," he said, to soothe the
hurt, and she gave the baby over so readily that he knew she
had already forgiven his thoughtless words. The bundled
child was lighter than he had been the week before. He was
losing flesh, and his dark eyes were dull. Reyn began the
methodical rocking that holding the child seemed to trigger
in him, and Malta smiled faintly.

"Have they made any progress over there?"

He nodded. "Most of the talking now is just the keepers
agreeing with themselves and saying why they think they've
reached the right decisions. But that's an important step for
them, too. Sometimes I forget how young most of them are.
There was some hot talk at the beginning. It almost made me
smile. Some of them seemed to echo what their dragons were
saying. Leftrin said, several times, that people should decide
the fates of humans, not dragons. I don't think that that sentiment was completely accepted, but it cooled things down.
They'll take a final vote soon. But I think the slaves will be
freed and allowed to determine what they want to do. Leftrin
has said that the next time Tarman goes down to Trehaug, the
slaves can ride for free. From there, it would be up to them
what they did. Some spoke of families, long lost to them.
Others seemed dazed at their sudden freedom. They were offered the chance to stay in the village across the river. Not sure
if they completely understood what they were being offered.
My Chalcedean is rudimentary at best, and pretty rusty."

Malta nodded. "Mine is the same. Selden was the only
one of us who ever learned our father's language. I think he
did it to impress him. But it didn't." Her eyes had gone far
as she thought of her vanished brother. Reyn waited. After

a moment, she stirred herself. "Selden is gone, along with Tintaglia. I suppose that's fitting, somehow." She sighed, dragging herself back to the present. "And the other prisoners?" she asked.

"That was harder. Leftrin accused Trader Candral to his face of being part of a conspiracy to slaughter dragons and sell the flesh to Chalced. Evidently there was a woman, Trader Sverdin, who was also involved. The Chalcedeans threw her overboard before they even left Cassarick. She probably drowned. Some of the keepers were for letting the dragons eat Candral, but Leftrin talked long and hard that Candral needed to be taken back to Cassarick and put before the Council there. He told them that unless they did so, the Council would never confront the corruption within their own ranks. Candral begged for his life and promised he would this very night write out who was involved and how. Evidently he had a hand in the hiring of some hunter who was part of the *Tarman* expedition and had made a try to kill Relpda."

She nodded at his words, and he wondered if she was really hearing them. He spoke on anyway. "The Chalcedeans are claiming they were forced to come here, that their families are hostage back in Chalced. I find that believable, but the dragons are finding it hard to understand that perhaps that means they deserve mercy. They drew dragon blood. There is no denying that. Then there are the crewmen from the ships. Some say that they were only obeying their captains' orders. Well and good, I suppose, but at least one of their captains was a traitor to the Traders.

"There are two merchants from Jamaillia who seem to have just got caught up in the whole mess, as well as several investors from Bingtown who thought they were making a maiden run on their wonderful new vessel. The keepers won't compromise that they are keeping the ships; they do seem to be impervious to the water from what Swarge told us after a look at their hulls. I'm not sure it's fair for them to seize the ships, but I suspect that before all is done, some deals and bargains will be negotiated. The Jamaillians already asked about future trading treaties. And that led to the Bingtown Traders interrupting and saying that only a true council could negotiate such things. And then several keepers asserted that neither Bingtown nor either of the Rain Wild Councils had any authority over them. That led to some very interesting discussion."

Malta nodded and her smile touched her eyes. "I heard. You didn't even ask me if I wanted to be queen before you told them all that wasn't why we had come here."

Reyn lifted a hand from their child to caress her golden hair. It was coarse under his touch, but his memory told him it was spun gold. "That was because I was sure you would say yes." He smiled at her. "And they would have let us simply walk in and take charge of all this." He took a deep breath. "I never want to be the one to say 'this man lives and that man dies.' I am glad they think so highly of us, and I am glad that they listened to me when I pleaded for clemency for the prisoners. But I am even gladder that they are talking and reaching the same conclusions on their own."

"Negotiation. It's the Trader way of solving things," she said, and he smiled.

"I haven't forgotten all you did for Bingtown when you faced down the Satrap of Jamaillia and the Pirate King."

She returned his smile faintly. "That seems a very long time ago. Where did I get that energy?" She shook her head. "Trader Finbok?"

"Claims to have simply been on his way to look for Alise and Sedric before he was abducted with the other passengers. Some of the others dispute that; Candral says that a note from Finbok lured him down to the vessel. Hest denies it. Right now, there's no hard evidence and no reason to charge him with anything."

"It doesn't quite add up somehow. But I'm too tired to put my mind to work on it." Malta frowned. "Candral must go back. Someone must pay for what those horrid men did to me the night Phron was born." She looked down at her baby. "If I must go back to stand before the Council and speak about what I did that night, I will."

"I've no desire to put you through that. Sooner or later, the truth will out," Reyn told her.

She nodded slowly. All spirit had gone out of her since she had heard of Tintaglia's death. The dragons had not wished to discuss it, other than to say that Kalo had stayed behind to eat her memories. He had not returned with the others; Reyn privately suspected that devouring a dragon the size of Tintaglia would take even Kalo several days. He was surprised at the depth of loss he felt at her death. Tintaglia had abandoned the other dragons to their fates years ago. She had left without a word of farewell to either Malta or him. Not even Selden, her beloved poet, had she warned before she vanished. For a short time, they had heard reports of her, including one that she had found a mate in the far north. What she had been doing for all those absent years they would never know, nor why she had decided to come back to the Rain Wilds. It sounded as if she had died but a day's flight from Kelsingra.

He thought of her as he had last seen the dragon. Tintaglia had been arrogant and full of vitality, a queen in every sense of the word. She had left her mark plainly on himself and Malta and Selden. And, he now realized, on their children. Malta had miscarried several times. He tried to imagine himself as he could have been, a father surrounded by children, if only the dragon had been there to change the babes in Malta's womb so they could survive. It was a useless fantasy.

"Tintaglia," Malta said suddenly.

He nodded. "I was just thinking of her, too. She was not so bad, for a dragon."

Malta sat up straighter. "No. I feel her. Reyn, she's not dead. She's coming here."

Reyn stared at her, his heart breaking. When they had first received the news that Tintaglia was dead, Malta had screamed like a madwoman. He had gathered her up and taken her away from all the others, even Tillamon. They had sat together with their doomed child, sat and rocked and wept and ranted behind closed doors. And when it was done, a strange calm had fallen over her. He thought perhaps it was a woman's way, to come out of such a storm of emotion and pain as if she were a ship emerging onto calm seas. She had seemed, not at peace, but emptied of

sorrow. As if she had run out of that particular emotion and
no other one arose to take its place. She had tended Ephron
with gentleness, even during the long hours when his shrill
keening nearly drove Reyn mad. She had seemed to be ab-
sorbing every sound, every scent, every sight of her child
back into herself, as if she were a stone taking his memories into her.

It had frightened him, but this was worse.

"She's dead, Malta," he said gently. "Tintaglia's dead.
The dragons told us so."

"The dragons were wrong!" she insisted fiercely. "Listen,
Reyn! Reach out to her. She's coming, she's coming here!
She's in a lot of pain, she's hurt, but she's alive and coming
here." She reached for the baby and whisked him out of
Reyn's arms, standing suddenly. "There's a chance, just a
chance she can save him. I'm going to meet her."

He watched her stride away from him. Then he glanced
back at the others gathered at the other end of the hall. They
were still deep in their discussion. None of them seemed
aware of anything unusual. But Malta had seemed so certain. He stood still and let his eyes close. He reached out,
opening himself, trying to still all his own thoughts.

Tintaglia?

Nothing. He sensed nothing. Nothing except the pain of
looming death. His pain or a dragon's pain?

He threw the thought aside and, catching up the cloak
Malta had left behind, hurried after his wife and son. In
the distance, he heard a dragon trumpet. Another replied,
and another, and suddenly a chorus of dragon cries were re-
sounding. As he stepped out into the early evening, the city
seemed to light itself more brightly. Dragon cries came from
every direction. Malta was a thin figure hurrying toward the
center of the Square of the Dragons, her baby a tiny bundle
in her arms. The wind whipped her hair. He looked up to see
dragons against the reddening sky of evening, flying in like
a murder of crows summoned by the caws of one.

Not much farther.
  Hurts too much.

Look. Look there, that haze on the horizon. Those are the lights of Kelsingra, welcoming you home. Think of nothing else, Tintaglia queen. Get there and you will find hot water and Elderlings to tend you, and Silver. They were descending into the well to repair it when last I was there.

Silver. There was a thought she could hold to. Silver could do marvels when administered by a skilled Elderling. She had ancestral memories of a drake struck by lightning. He had crashed to earth, his wing a scorched framework of bone and little more. It had taken over a year, but he had flown again. They had healed his burns with a spray of Silver. An Elderling artisan had built him a wing of Silver, light, thin panels that articulated on tiny gears. It had not been his own wing, but he had flown again.

Just fly. I will summon them to meet you. Then Kalo trumpeted an alarm cry such as she had never heard. She heard it taken up in the distance, by dragons hunting on the wing, by dragons roused from sated slumber, and by dragons that were on the ground within the city. She thought she heard it echo from the distant hills and then knew that it was no echo. The dragons were continuing the calls as they began to gather. More dragons than ever she had seen in her life were welcoming her.

"Down there!" Kalo trumpeted it to her. "You see it now, don't you? You remember it?"

"Of course." If she had not been in so much pain, his query would have annoyed her. She had been here before, even in this lifetime. She'd found it dead and deserted and had left it in anger. Now it was warm with light and welcoming sounds.

"Go there. They will help you. I go to hunt."

She already knew of his hunger. She wondered why he chose to tell her obvious things and decided it had to do with his daily exposure to humans. They were always speaking the obvious to one another, as if they had to agree a thing was so before they could act on it. Below her, she saw the open square. Two Elderlings stood in the center of it, pointing up at her. "Tintaglia! Tintaglia!" They were shouting her name in voices full of joy. Others were just starting to pour out the doorway of . . . of the baths. Yes. The baths had been there. Hot water and soaking. The thought almost made her woozy, and then flapping her injured wing just became something she could no longer do. She was falling, trying to swing her body's weight toward her good wing, trying to spiral down to land gently. Then she realized who it was standing to meet her. The relief that washed through her slacked all her muscles.

My Elderlings. Silver. Heal me. She threw the command at them with all her strength, too breathless to trumpet the words as she plummeted the last bit of distance to the ground. Her once-powerful hind legs folded under her as she struck, and then she fell to her side on the ground before them. Pain and blackness swallowed her whole.

"SHE HAS DOZENS of small wounds. Lots of nasty parasites in them. But if that was all that was wrong with her, I'd say we could clean them up, feed her good, and she'd be fine. It's the infection and that big injury just under her wing. That's foul, and it has eaten right into her. I can see bone in there." Carson rubbed his weary eyes. "I'm not any kind of a healer. I know more about taking animals apart than I do about curing one. I'll tell you one thing, though. If that was game I'd brought down, I'd leave it lie. She smells to me like bad meat, through and through."

Leftrin scratched his whiskery chin. It was venturing toward morning of a day too filled with events. He was tired and worried about Alise and heartsick about Malta's child. He had felt a wild thrill of hope when some of the keepers had begun shouting that Tintaglia had returned. But this was worse than the news of her death had been. The dragon lay there in the grand open square, soon to be dead. Malta sat on the ground beside her, huddled in her cloak, her child in her arms.

"The Silver!" she had cried out into the stunned silence that followed Tintaglia's fall. "Bring me all the Silver we have!"

Leftrin had expected that someone would object, that some other dragon would wish to claim a share. To his surprise, no one had challenged her. All the keepers seemed to think it an appropriate use. Only one of the dragons had lingered to watch what would happen. Night was chill and dark; dragons preferred the warmth of the baths or the sand wallows for sleeping. They were not humans, to keep a vigil by a dying creature. Only golden Mercor had remained with her. "I do not know why Kalo kept her alive, nor why he brought her here to die," he had commented. "But doubtless, he will return for her memories. When he does, I caution you to be well out of his way." When the others dragons had wandered away from the dying creature as if Tintaglia's fate shamed them, he had remained, standing and watching.

Sylve had run to fetch the flask of Silver and brought it out to the plaza. She carried the flask two-handed, and the Silver inside it whirled and swam as if alive and seeking escape.

"What do you do with it?" she asked as Malta gave the child to Reyn and took it from her hands. Such trust there had been in her voice, such belief that the queen of the Elderlings would know what to do for the fallen dragon.

But Malta had shaken her head. "I don't know. Do I pour it on her wound? Does she drink it?" All were silent.

Malta followed Tintaglia's outstretched neck to her great head. The dragon's large eyes were closed. "Tintaglia! Wake! Wake and drink of the Silver and be healed! Be healed and save my child!" Malta's voice quavered on her final plea.

The dragon might have drawn a slightly deeper breath. Other than that, she did not stir. In her opalescent robe that brushed the tops of her feet and clutching the flask of gleaming silver liquid, Malta looked like a figure from a legend, but her voice was entirely human as she begged, "Does no one know? What should I do? How do I save her?"

Sylve spoke quietly. "Mercor told me the dragons drank it. Should you pour it into her mouth?"

"Will she choke?" Harrikin ventured a cautious question.

"Tintaglia? Tintaglia, please," Reyn ventured.

"Should I pour it in her mouth?" Malta asked the golden dragon directly.

"There is not enough there to save her," Mercor said. "No matter what you do with it." Then he had turned and walked away from them, up the wide steps and into the baths. Sylve looked shocked.

The words seemed not to register with Malta. "I can scarcely feel her," Malta said, and Leftrin knew she did not refer to the hand she laid lightly on the dragon's face. "She has grown so much since I last saw her," she added, and for a moment, she sounded almost like a doting parent. She stroked Tintaglia's face, and then pushed at the dragon's lip. Leftrin drew closer to watch, as did the gathered Elderlings. The lifted lip bared reciprocating rows of pointed teeth, neatly meshed together.

"There is room between them, I think, if I pour it slowly," Malta said. She spoke very quietly as if she and the dragon were the only creatures in the whole world. She tipped the flask and the silver spiraled out in a slender, gleaming thread. It did not flow swiftly, as water would have, but cautiously, as if it lowered itself to the dragon's mouth. It touched her teeth, pooled briefly along her gum and then seemed to find the entry it sought. It vanished between her teeth. No last drop fell from the flask; it had poured like a spooled thread unwinding and so it vanished, too.

The night seemed darker with the Silver gone from sight. The ghost light of the Elderling city gleamed softly all around them. The keepers stood, waiting and listening. After a long, chill time, murmurs began. "I expected a miracle."

"I think she is too far gone."

"She should have poured it on the wound, perhaps."

"Mercor warned us there wasn't enough," Sylve said miserably, and she hid her face in her hands.

Reyn had been crouching beside Malta, their child in his arms. He stood up slowly and lifted his voice. "We would be alone with our dragon and our child, if you do not mind," he said. He did not speak loudly, but his words seemed to carry. Finished, he sank back down to the cobblestones beside his wife.

In ones and twos, the keepers drifted away. Sedric tugged gently at Carson's arm. "We should go," he said softly.

Leftrin glanced over at them. "You should," he agreed gently. "There's nothing else any of us can do here. And death is a private thing."

Carson had nodded, plainly reluctant to leave. Sedric had stepped forward. He unfastened the catch of his cloak, lifted it, and swirled it around Malta, Reyn, and their child. "Sa grant you strength," he said, and then stepped quickly away, shaking his head.

Leftrin looked around the square. He was the last. He stepped forward, thinking to ask them if they were sure, if there was anything he might bring or do for them. Then he thought better of it. He turned and walked slowly away from the dragon. Away from the Elderlings and their dying child. He felt as if loneliness filled in the space he left behind him. Loneliness and heartbreak.

He pulled his old coat tighter around himself. It was not a time to be alone. The city whispered all around him, but he didn't want to hear it. Long ago, the city had died, and now he suspected he knew why. A cataclysm might have shattered it and sent some of the Elderlings fleeing. But when the Silver had run out, then the end had been inevitable.

He thought of the youngsters he had brought up the river. He had not meant to come to care about them. Just fulfill a contract, have a bit of an adventure in the process, maybe draw a chart that would carry his name into history. And then return to running freight on the river on his beloved liveship. He hadn't wanted his life to change this much.

Alise.

Well, perhaps he had. He sighed, feeling selfish that while others paid a serious price, he had gained a woman who loved him. A woman who was giving up everything to be with him. Hest had made it real for him today. So tall and grand a man, dressed so fine, speaking so genteelly. He had begged her to come back to him.

And she had turned her back on all that, for him.

She was waiting for him now, back on his liveship. He walked faster.

✦ ✦ ✦

Day the 14th of the Plough Moon

Year the 7th of the Independent Alliance of Traders
From Erek, of Trehaug
To Kerig Sweetwater, Master of the Bird
Keepers' Guild, Bingtown

Kerig, it is with great relief that I have received your message. Detozi has also felt great anxiety and fear that our actions would be interpreted as disloyal to the Guild or perhaps even indicative of being traitors to the Guild.

I am glad to say that Two-Toes has gained weight and that the color to his hackle and bib has brightened. His foot was badly cut from hanging, but he has recovered warmth and movement in his toes. If he does not recover sufficiently to carry messages, I suggest that he is still of great breeding value and should be retained in that capacity. As you suggest, I will ask permission to continue to care for him until his recovery is complete. In any case, a live bird that was listed as dead is definitely a part of a much larger mystery!

Detozi and I will together take the sealed message, along with your letter, to Master Godon and ask that he present it unopened to the full circle of master bird handlers here in Trehaug for them to open and study.

I am extremely grateful to have this serious business taken out of my hands.

Your former apprentice,
Erek Dunwarrow

✦ ✦ ✦

CHAPTER SEVENTEEN

THE WELL

P lease. I can't sleep. Go walking with me. Please."
Thymara blinked her eyes. Rapskal's gaze was pale blue
in the dimly lit room. In a bed on the other side of the room,
Tats was snoring softly. Without speaking of it, she and Tats
had resolved that they would not leave Rapskal on his own.
Not tonight. Tats had claimed one of the larger rooms in
the dormitory above the dragon baths, one with multiple
beds in it. Carson had given them the nod for that. Some
of the other keepers had drawn lots for guard duty for their
"guests." They had been confined for the night to the dining
room. They'd been allowed to bathe and given bedding, and
most of them seemed to have accepted their fates. A few
had complained, and one Jamaillian merchant had wailed
and ranted about being treated like a "criminal and forced
to lie down alongside 'filth.'" Carson had drawn a lot for the

first watch, and Sedric had stayed with him, with Relpda to keep them company. Privately, she doubted that any of their "guests" would attempt to leave with a dragon snoring across the entryway.

She and Tats had herded Rapskal away and up to one of the unoccupied sleeping rooms. Weary as they were, there had been much to discuss. There they had sat, listening to Rapskal unwind his story of the dragon attack on the ships. The longer he talked, the less he sounded like Tellator and the more like his old self.

Rapskal had always been a talker, always the one who could go on and on about any topic. Tats had dozed off before she had. She had listened to Rapskal tell his story, listened to him brag of how brave Heeby had been and how glorious the dragons had looked in flight. She had waited in vain for him to say that he was horrified at how many men had died. The old Rapskal would have done so. Instead, he simply seemed to accept it as how a battle went. When she mentioned it, he asked her incredulously, "Would you rather that more dragons had died? Poor Tintaglia lies in the Square of the Dragons! By morning, all that will be left of her is her memories and her flesh. The eggs inside her that should have become serpents, our next generation of dragons, die with her tonight! Have you thought of that, Thymara? I must look at that and wonder how I would feel if it were my Heeby lying there. What if it were Sintara?"

"Sintara," she said quietly, and wondered how she would feel. A spark of anger in her heart surprised her. In a distant corner of her mind, her dragon spoke softly. *You would be devastated. And furious. Just as they are.*

I would, she admitted. She pulled her mind free of the dragon's. But what would she do if something befell her dragon? What happened to an Elderling when her dragon died?

They die, too. Not right away, but sooner than if the dragon had lived.

She pushed Sintara from her mind again. She didn't want to think about that. Didn't want to think about what would become of Malta and Reyn and their baby. "Our dragons are back in Kelsingra now, alive and well. It's over, Rapskal."

"It's not over," he insisted, and she heard a tinge of Tellator's stubbornness in his voice.

"It is," she replied. "Our dragons are here in Kelsingra and safe. They never need leave here again. The man who led the attackers here, that Chalcedean noble, is dead. And that corrupt Trader promised he would reveal everyone who plotted against the dragons. They will be punished. So. It's over."

Rapskal shook his head. They were both sitting on his bed. Tats had dozed off on the bed across from them. Thymara leaned back on the wall. She was ready to fall asleep but wanted Rapskal to sleep before she did. She could outlast him. She hoped.

Rapskal crossed his arms on his chest. "The dragons can't and won't stay here forever. It's not in their nature, and you, as a hunter, must know that they can't. They need to move seasonally, to find new prey and give these populations a chance to rebuild. Even if we had the herds and flocks here that they need, they were never content to be resident here year-round. And they must leave when it's time to go lay their eggs."

Those words were not Rapskal's. She'd never heard him choose such words. She stared at him and he mistook it for avid interest. He smiled at her.

"Thymara, it won't be over until the man who sent them is stopped. Think about it. Those men today, those Chalcedeans, they said they were forced against their will to come. I listened to what they said. If they go home without dragon flesh, they and their families will die. Horribly, slowly. If they stay here much longer, sending no messages promising success, their families will be tortured. And when they are all dead, the Duke of Chalced will find others to send. He's not going to give up."

"He'll die soon. He's old and diseased, and he'll die soon. And then it will be over." She just wanted to go to sleep. He was making her think of all sorts of things she didn't want to consider just now.

He turned his head and looked at her sadly. "You're right about one thing, Amarinda. When he dies, it will be over. And while he lives, it isn't over."

"That's not my name," she said, and she couldn't tell if she were more chilled by his comments or how he called her "Amarinda."

He smiled at her tolerantly. "You still haven't come to understand the city completely. Or what it truly means to be an Elderling, bonded to a dragon. But you will, and so I won't argue with you about it. Time is on my side. You'll grow into the concept that you can lead more than one life, be more than one person."

"No." She said it flatly.

He sighed. And she had closed her eyes for just a moment. She must have dozed off because she woke to him tugging at her hand, asking to go walking. She sighed wearily. "It's night, Rapskal. Chill and dark."

"It's not that cold out, and the city will light our way. Please, Thymara. Just a walk, to help me relax. That's all. A quiet stroll alone through the city."

He had always been good at nagging her into whatever he wanted. She didn't wake Tats. He could sleep now and take the next watch with Rapskal if the walk didn't wear him out. She swirled her cloak around her shoulders, fastened it, and followed him out of the room and down the hall. He led her to the side entrance, away from the Square of the Dragons and the death watch there. She did not object.

Outside, the chill wind kissed her face roughly.

Rapskal lifted his face. "Smells like spring," he said.

She opened her senses to the night. Yes, there was something in the wind, something more wet than freezing. It wasn't warm, but all threat of frost had fled.

He took her hand, and she was grateful for his warm clasp. He ran his thumb over the fine scaling on the back of her hand. "You can't deny the changes," he said, and before she could reply, he added, "Tomorrow, if you look up at the hills behind the city, you will see the birches and willows flushed with pink. On the taller slopes behind them, the snows are almost gone. Very soon, Leftrin will have to make a run to Trehaug to see if the seeds and livestock he ordered have come in." He turned and smiled at her. "This will be the year we reawaken all Kelsingra. Years from now, it will be hard to remember that there was a time when cattle and sheep didn't graze in the pastures outside the city, a time when only fifteen keepers lived in the city."

The fullness of his vision astounded her. She let him lead her as they walked through the dimly lit streets. As always, he filled the silence with his talk. "Once this city never slept. Once it was so populated that people walked through it by night and by day. There are whole sections of the city that we haven't explored yet. All manner of wonders awaiting rediscovery by the new Elderlings. Places where artists wrought miracles and craftsmen plied their trades."

She thought of the dry Silver well and how it would limit their future. But this was not a night to talk of that. Let him talk himself out, and when his words ran down, she'd take him back to the baths and let him sleep. She thought of the morrow and all it must bring. She dreaded wondering how long Tintaglia would linger between death and life, and the child with her. She thought of Kalo devouring the dead dragon in the square and felt squeamish. She did not want to think of the arguments that would continue tomorrow over the fate of the Chalcedean warriors who had come here to kill dragons. She thought of the days before Tarman had returned, days filled with the simple work of hunting and trying to rebuild the docks and exploring the city. They had seemed so tedious, and now she longed to have that comforting boredom back.

She had suspected that Rapskal would try to take her back to the house Tellator and Amarinda had shared. She was relieved when he didn't. They walked through other streets, and he spoke of what he knew of them. A poet had lived in that house and written epics on the walls and ceilings. This bakery had been renowned for its sweet berry pastries. Here was a street where weavers had made the sort of garments that they both wore now. She knew he spoke Tellator's memories aloud as if they were his own, but she was too tired to rebuke him. Let him talk them out, and then perhaps Rapskal would come back to her.

He took her down a side street, and she found herself in a humbler part of town. "A tinsmith had that shop," he told her. "The pans he made needed no oven to cook the food put into them. And over there? The woman who owned that store hammered out wind chimes that played a thousand melodies when the wind stirred them."

"They worked in Silver," she guessed, and he nodded.

"Silver was the great secret treasure of the Elderlings and the tonic that made both Elderlings and dragons what they became." He halted at a door hole. "Lack of it will kill us all," he said conversationally, and he stepped inside the empty door frame of the shop. She followed him reluctantly.

"It's dark in here," she complained and felt his assent.

"They did not use the Silver everywhere. Even then, it was a precious commodity. Where many might gather, they used it for light and for warmth. For art that all shared. But in the small personal spaces, they used far less of it." He reached into his pouch and drew forth light. He held something out to her, shaking it free. A necklace with a moon-face charm on it. It brightened as he shook it, filling the room with a thin silvery light. It looked oddly familiar.

"Put it on," he urged her, and when she did not, he stepped closer to push back her hood and loop it around her neck. The gleaming moon rested on her bosom and she looked around the shop. Little remained of the humble wooden furnishings, but there were things among the rubble that she recognized. An anvil of a kind she had never seen, yet she knew it for what it was. A stone table with grooves and drains in the surface: for working Silver. Reflexively, she lifted her eyes to where tools had once hung on a rack. The rack was gone, the tools a jumble on the floor where they had hung. A battered ladle tangled with a pair of shears. A sudden urge to pick them up, to tidy her workspace came to her.

"Let's go outside," she said abruptly.

"We could," he agreed. "But it wouldn't help. You can't run away from it. I don't want to force you, but time is running out. For all of us."

Cold filled her. She turned to look at Rapskal, and the reflected light from the moon charm made his eyes silver. "What do you mean?"

"You *know*," he coaxed her gently. "I've been waiting for you to admit it. You do know." He paused and looked at her accusingly. "Amarinda knew. And so you know."

You know, Sintara echoed his words. *And it is time for you to stop being stubborn.*

"I don't know," she insisted to both of them. It hurt her feelings that they would close ranks against her and force her to this. Whatever "this" was. She spoke frankly to the man with the gleaming silver eyes. "You are scaring me. Tellator, go away. I want my friend Rapskal back."

He sighed and spoke reluctantly. "The need is great. I love you. Then, and now, I love you. You know that. I have waited as long as I can, as long as any of us can. But we are Elderlings, and ultimately, we serve the dragons. Will you let Tintaglia die? Will you let Malta and Reyn and their baby die because you want to cling so strongly to who you were born? Thymara, I know you are frightened by this. I have tried to let you go as slowly as ever you wished. But tonight is our last chance. Please. Choose this. Choose this for me, for Rapskal. Because I would not force you. But Tellator would."

She was shaking, fighting a battle inside herself as well as withstanding the crushing fear he woke in her. Memories were stirring, ones she did not want to acknowledge. She looked around her. "This was her little shop. She made things here."

He nodded. "Not a shop, really. She sold the things she made, but she gave as many away. This was where she created her art. This was where you worked Silver with your hands."

"I don't remember it." She spoke flatly.

"Not easily, no. Silver was too precious. The memories of working it were not saved in stone. Some secrets are too precious to be entrusted to anyone except the heir to your trade. Those secrets were passed only from master to apprentice. The locations of the wells could not be kept completely secret, not when the dragons came to drink from them. How the wells were managed, season to season, that was a guild secret."

He took her arm suddenly, and she almost pulled away from him. But he was walking her to the door and she was too grateful to be leaving the building. Amarinda had worked there. She knew it now, recalled the busy little street of artisans as it had been. Not from memory stone; it had not been used in this part of the city, but from the residue of memories that her time as Amarinda had left in her mind.

"Ramose had his studio there. The sculptor. Remember?" His voice had gone colder.

She glanced at the empty sockets of windows in the wall. "I remember," she admitted grudgingly. Something else popped into her mind. "You were jealous of him."

Rapskal nodded. "He had been your lover before I was. We had a fight once. Foolish of me, not to know that a man who wields a hammer and chisel all day builds up an arm."

She shied away from those memories. *Too close,* she thought, *too close to something.* And then they turned a corner, and she was in a familiar place. There was the well plaza, just as they had left it, beams stacked to one side, broken mechanisms to another, tools in a third. The ship's crew had put some hours in on the chain. There was a mended length of it by the well's lip, the end fastened to the stub of one ancient post that had once supported the well's cover. Heeby was there, too, standing quietly in the darkness. A sense of dread rose in Thymara.

"Why did we come here?" she asked breathlessly.

"So you could get the Silver. So Tintaglia can live. So all the dragons can become all they were meant to be, and their Elderlings as well." The light from the locket she wore did not reach his eyes here in the open. They were the lambent blue they had always been, but the silvery sheen the jewelry gave turned his face to a ghost mask. She did not know him.

He spoke softly but firmly. "Amarinda, you have to go down the well. You are the only one who knows how to bring back the Silver."

"My love?"

Reyn spoke the words softly as if he thought she could be asleep. She wasn't. Couldn't be, wouldn't be, and might never sleep again. She huddled by her dragon's face, her baby on her lap. Her hand rested by Tintaglia's nostril where she could feel the slow sigh as the dragon continued to breathe. "I'm here," she told Reyn.

He hitched closer to her. "I'm trying to make sense of what I'm feeling. When I was a boy and Tintaglia was a shadowy presence underground, trapped in her wizardwood case, I was fascinated with her. Then she all but enslaved me, and I hated her. I loved her when she helped me recover you. And then, off she went, and for years we heard nothing, felt nothing from her."

"I was as angry with her as you were. To leave us the care of the young dragons, to go off without a word. To send Selden off to Sa knows where, never to return to us." She caressed the dragon's snout. She sighed. "Do you think he's dead, Reyn? My little brother?"

Reyn shook his head wordlessly.

The night had turned clear, the clouds blown aside, yet it was not as cold as it had been. Spring was in the air. Above them, the moon sailed on and the stars shone, heedless of mortals below. Their Elderling cloaks kept them warm. The stones were hard beneath them. Malta had her husband and his firstborn son at her side and the dragon who had shaped all their lives. Life and death merged at this spot, an untidy tangle of endings. The dragon's breath flowed over their son. The smell of her infected wounds hung in the damp air.

"She is still so incredibly beautiful," Malta said. She willed her voice not to choke in her tight throat. "Look at these scales, every one a tiny work of art. It's even more a wonder when you realize she determined their decoration, every one of them. Look at these, around her eyes." Her fingers walked to them, traced the intricate pattern of white, silver, and black that framed the dragon's closed eyes. "No dragon will ever be as glorious as she was. The young queen Sintara flaunts herself, but she will never be as blue as our Tintaglia. Fente and Veras are plain as tree snakes compared to her. My conceited beauty, you had every right to be vain."

"She did," Reyn conceded. "I hate that she dies like this, broken and flawed. Such a waste to lose her. I could feel the hope in the other dragons surge when she appeared in the skies. They need her; they need what she remembers."

"We all do," Malta said quietly. "Especially Phron."

The baby stirred in her lap, perhaps at the mention of his name. Malta lifted the corner of her cloak that covered him. He still slept. She bent close to study his face in the moonlight. "Look," she said to her husband. "I never realized it before. The tiny scales on his brows? They are the same pattern as hers. Even without her presence, he carries her marks on him. Her artistry would have lived on in him. If he were to live." The baby stirred at her touch as she traced his face, and he whimpered more strongly. "Hush, my little one." She lifted him from her lap. His thin arm and scrawny hand sprawled from his wrappings. She put the little hand on the dragon's brows, held it there between Tintaglia's scales and her still soft, still human palm. "She would have been your dragon, too, my darling. Touch her once, before you both go. Imagine how beautiful you would have been if she could have guided you." She guided the baby's hand down the dragon's scaling in a caress. "Tintaglia, if you must go, give him something of yourself first. Give him a memory of flight, give him a thought of your beauty to carry into the dark."

"I DON'T KNOW anything about Silver or about this well. I'm not Amarinda and I don't know. And I'm not going down that well. Not now, not ever. I hate places like that, dark and small. Go down there in the night, alone? That's crazy." Her heart was pounding at the mere thought of it. She crossed her arms, hugging herself. Tats. Why hadn't she wakened Tats and made him come too? No one knew they'd gone out walking.

He insisted relentlessly, in such a gentle voice. "Tintaglia is dying. Now is all we have. Thymara or Amarinda, it doesn't matter. You have to go down the well. I'll go with you. You won't be alone."

She tried to fight her way back to her own reality. He was just Rapskal, just strange Rapskal, and she didn't have to let him bully her. "I won't! I'm tired of this, Rapskal. And I'm tired of trying to help you. I'm going back to the hall and get some sleep. You are being too strange even for me."

She turned to go, but he seized her arm in a grip of iron. "You have to go down the well. Tonight."

She slapped at his hands and tried to twist free of his grip. Could not. When had he become so strong? He did not even appear to be making an effort to hold her as she fought his hold on her. She could not bear the gaze of the stranger looking out of his eyes at her. "Let me go!"

Wings flapped, and a gust of air washed over her. The paving stones of the square shook as the dragon's claws met them and skidded to a halt. Sintara! Thymara knew her scent as well as she knew her mind's touch on hers. *Be calm, Thymara. I am here. All will be fine.*

Relief washed through her, bringing icy anger with it. She met Tellator's stare coldly and stopped struggling. "Let go of me now." She suggested it calmly. "Or my dragon may do you harm."

Heeby had advanced on them as she spoke, the spikes on her neck rising at the perceived threat to Rapskal. Thymara caught her breath. This could be bad. She had no desire to see the two dragons fight each other, especially not with her in the middle of it.

Neither did he. His hand dropped away from her arm. "You're right. It's better this way." He turned away from both of them.

Hurt choked her voice as she rubbed her bruised arm. "Rapskal. I loved you. Now I don't think I ever want to see you again. You're not my friend anymore. I don't know who or what you are now, but I don't like it."

She turned to go.

"Thymara," Sintara said gently. "It will be all right. We have not always trusted each other. But now you must."

Thymara walked slowly to the well's mouth and looked down. An unnamable dread rose in her, a horror of confined dark places. She shuddered. Rapskal had followed her. He did not try to touch her but knelt on the other side of the well. He seized the fastened chain, pulled a length free, and dropped it in the hole. It clanked against the side. He pushed another loop after it, and then another, and suddenly the links were rattling over the stone lip as the chain paid out and down into the darkness. It stopped, taut against the pole, and Rapskal said to himself, "Not long enough." He stood up and walked off into the darkness.

Thymara remained by the well, staring down into it. An eternity of blackness. And she would go down into it.

She lifted her eyes to her dragon. "Don't," she pleaded. "Don't."

Sintara only looked at her. Thymara felt the compulsion building in her. But this was not the dragon pushing her to go hunting when she wanted to sleep, or encouraging her to groom every single scale on her face. This was different.

"If you force me, it will never be the same between us," she warned the dragon.

"No," Sintara agreed. "It won't. Just as I haven't been the same since you left me hungry, with no choice but to face my fear and try to fly."

"That was different!" Thymara protested.

"Only from your point of view," the dragon replied. "Thymara. Go down the well."

She shook her head. "I can't." But she walked stiffly around to the other side of the well and knelt by the chain. She put a hand on it. It was cold. The links of it were big, big enough to slip a hand into. Or the toe of her boot.

"I'll go first." Did Tellator or Rapskal make that offer? He stood next to her, a coil of line over his shoulder.

"You can do no good down there," Sintara objected, and Heeby whiffled nervously.

"I won't send her alone," he said. He looked at Thymara,

his eyes unreadable. "Like this. It won't be easy, but you're strong." He cocked his head at her, and for an instant he was Rapskal again, telling her that one day she would fly. "You can do it. Just follow me."

She moved out of his way as he knelt beside her. He clambered over the lip of the well, his hands snugged tight to the chain. She saw him grope with his feet, find a toehold in the chain for one and then reach for another. He gave her a strained smile. "I'm scared, too," he admitted. He moved his hands and slowly he walked down the chain and away from her. She watched until his upturned face had vanished in the darkness.

She glanced at her dragon and made a final plea. "Don't make me."

"You have to go down there. You are the only one who might be able to find the Silver. You knew how the well worked, you knew how to touch Silver and not die. It has to be you, Thymara-Amarinda."

She wet her lips, felt them dry and then crack in the chill. She could hear the chain working against the lip of the well. He was still going down. She was furious with Tellator and possibly hated him, but she would not let Rapskal go alone. "I'll do it," she conceded. "But let me be the one to do it. Please."

"Do you think you can make yourself?"

"I can make myself do it," she said.

She felt Sintara lift the glamour from her mind. It peeled away, making her skin stand up in goose bumps and leaving the night darker around her. She blinked her eyes, becoming accustomed to her lesser human vision and then the gleam of the locket she wore. She did not speak and did not let herself think. She inserted her hands into the links of the chain and positioned herself on the edge of the well. The chain vibrated with Rapskal's weight. He was still moving down it.

She closed her eyes and remembered her childhood days in the treetops of Trehaug. Climbing had been far more familiar to her than running. She took a breath and stripped her Elderling boots from her feet. She levered her body around and groped for the links of the chain. Her clawed toes found them. She began her descent.

Darkness swallowed her as she went down, and then the gleam of the moon medallion seemed to grow stronger. Her eyes adjusted. The walls of the well were not as blank as they appeared from up above. When the gleam of the medallion met the black, there were markings engraved into the smooth face. There were not many, and it took time for her to realize they were dates and levels. The Elderling system of measuring time meant nothing to her. But Amarinda recalled that the Silver had risen and fallen, sometimes seasonally and also over the years. Sometimes the Silver was scant; sometimes it flowed so strong that the well must be capped, lest Silver flow through the streets. She passed a notation scribed by Amarinda's hand, for those who could work the Silver tended the wells also.

And regulated them.

The deeper she went, the less she felt like Thymara. She was no stranger to the inside of this well, though climbing a chain down was not how she usually descended. There had been levers and chains and gears. A carefully fitted platform with a hatch once traveled up and down in the shaft, just for visits such as this. She could recall the tediously slow process of turning the crank to travel down or up the shaft, and the loud clanking of the chain as it had moved through the mechanism.

She stopped. It was getting colder as she descended. Amarinda had never liked coming here, had never shrugged off as routine the task of managing the Silver. It was not the danger of the volatile stuff. The Silver was always dangerous whether confined to a vial on her workbench or flowing in threads down the street. Casual contact with Silver was always eventually deadly for everyone. Amarinda knew the dangers of the Silver and chose to work with it anyway. Slowly she began descending again. But she had never liked the confinement of this shaft. Nor the dark. Nor the cold.

She stepped on his hand. Tellator cursed, the language foreign to her ears.

"Wait!" He commanded her. "I'm at the end of the chain. I'm trying to tie the line to the last few links so we can get down the rest of the way. It's not easy."

She didn't respond. She clung to the cold chain in the dark, felt it vibrate with his motions. It swung slightly with their weight. No different from holding tight to a skinny tree, she told herself, and waited.

"There. I heard the rope hit the bottom when I dropped it. It's hand over hand from here on down."

"If you step down into live Silver . . ." She left the thought dangling.

"I saw debris down there when they fished for the bucket. I'll stand on it."

She felt him moving again. He was working harder now, and his weight jerked the chain back and forth. Her hands were cramping from their grip on the cold metal, and the links bit into her feet. She freed one hand to lift the necklace over her head. Rapskal was too far below her to hand it to him. She gritted her teeth and then dropped it, letting light fall away from her. "Look where you step," she warned him, and she realized that she was back to it being her and Rapskal doing something foolhardy together. She was still angry at being compelled to be here, but she was not sure Rapskal was the one to blame for it.

The jerking continued for some time. Bereft of the jewelry's shimmer, the blackness closed in on her. She closed her eyes and willed herself to remember that the shaft was not, truly, that narrow. Deep, yes, very deep. So far from light and moving air. She began to tremble and not with the cold. She hated this. Hated it and feared it. Darkness was a thing to her, not just the absence of light, but a choking thing that could cover her over like a smothering hand.

"Come down," he whispered. "I'll catch you. But be careful."

She did not want to go down to him, but her hands were losing their strength. She moved down to the end of the chain, and then onto the rope. Her numbed hands slipped, refused her weight, and she slid, shrieking, the rope burning through her hands. He caught her hard and swung her to his side. "Open your eyes!" he demanded of her, and only then did she realize they were clenched shut.

She held tight to him and opened her eyes slowly. He wore the moon necklace now. The light it cast was faint and yet bright in contrast to such utter darkness. She looked away from it, trying to let her eyes adjust.

They stood together in the bottom of the shaft. Looking up, she was startled to see distant pinpricks of light. Stars. The walls of the shaft were almost smooth, the seams of the stonework fine and straight. They stood on rubble of metal and pieces of ancient wood preserved by the cold. "Stoop down," she requested in a whisper. When he did, he brought the light with him as she bent beside him. Squatting, she touched the long-broken platform beneath their feet. Here was a piece of a gear. "This is the part that went up and down in the shaft. It must have broken and fallen a long time ago."

The necklace moved slightly with his nod. "It did," he said. "In the quake. The last big one." There was a clutter of smaller sticks that crunched as she stepped on them. Something gleamed among them. Silver?

He caught his breath as she pushed the sticks aside with her bare hands and then peered more closely. "It's a ring," she said. She picked it up, and her touch woke it. Elderling-made. A flame jewel lit with a pale yellow gleam in a jidzin setting. Jidzin. She knew it for what it was now, Silver trapped in iron. She held it between two fingers, using it as a tiny lamp. "All kinds of stuff on the ground down here. But no Silver. Just earth." She peered closer.

"Rapskal, look here, where we can see past the broken platform. The bottom of the shaft is paved with stones! That makes no sense for a well! Think how we lined our drinking-water holes on the way here. We wanted the water to seep up from the bottom and in from the sides. We filtered it, but we didn't block it. Why would they make a shaft this deep and close it off on all sides from the Silver? It makes no sense."

"I don't know." His voice was shaking. "This is the first time I've ever been down here. I wanted to come down here, but I couldn't." He swallowed.

"Well, we're both here now." She recalled Carson's frequent words. "Everything the Elderlings did, they did for a reason." She turned in a half circle. Her boot snagged on something: a piece of dirty fabric. "Someone's old tunic is down here. Did they throw garbage down here when the well went dry?"

"No," he whispered. "No."

She tugged at the dirt-caked folds. "Look. Here's a glove. No. It's a gauntlet." She picked it up by a fingertip, shook it free of dirt and sticks and studied it.

"There's the other one," he said, but he made no move to touch it. He crouched with his back braced against the wall, watching her. She found the mate and tugged it from under a stone that had trapped it. The stone rolled slightly and tapped against the wall with a hollow sound. She turned to look at it.

"Amarinda," he said, and his voice choked on the word. She leaned closer. It was not a stone she had dislodged. It was a skull, brown and cracked. She stared, feeling the pressure of a scream build inside her. Then it died away to nothing. She took a long careful breath.

"These were her gloves. For working the Silver."

He nodded. She heard him gulp back tears before he gasped, "After the quake. I couldn't find her. I was desperate. I even went to Ramose. I threatened him, and he finally told me that she might have gone down the well when it hit. To make it safe somehow. Everyone was running, trying to get on the boats, pushing toward the pillars, trying to be anywhere except in Kelsingra. In the distance, the mountain was smoking. They feared mudslides and floods. It had never happened here, but other Elderling towns had been buried that way. So many people were fleeing, but I couldn't go without you. I came here, but the mechanism was broken, half of it fallen down the shaft and no one answered my shouts. My shoulder was broken. I tried to move the debris but I couldn't. I shouted myself hoarse, but no one answered. Then the second quake hit." He cradled his arm, his face creased with a memory of old pain. "I wanted to get down here somehow, to be sure. But I couldn't. I went back to our home, hoping to find you. Someone told me they had seen you, leaving through one of the pillars. I knew it was a lie, knew you wouldn't leave without me, but I hoped it wasn't. I left you a message in my column by our door. And I went with the others." He shook his head slowly. "We all meant to come back. We knew the streets would mend themselves and that the walls would heal if we gave them time. The Silver in them told them what they must be."

His voice died away. He looked around the well shaft blindly.

"I must have died before I ever returned. Where or how, I'll never know. After the message I left for you, no other memories are stored in the pillars. Nothing from me. Nothing from you."

Thymara straightened slowly. She shook the gauntlets, and the last stick that fell from them was a finger bone. The broken sticks under her feet, thin ribs preserved by the cold. "Is this why you made me come down here? To see this, to prove she died here?"

He shook his head. Her eyes had adjusted to the pale light the jewelry made, but there was no color to his features, only planes and shadows. "I wanted you to be her. That's true. I still want that. We always dreamed that we would live again in another Elderling couple. That we would walk and dance and dine together. Make love in our garden again. That was why we made the columns as we did." He drew a deep breath and sighed it out. "But that's not why I brought you here. I brought you here for the dragons. And for Malta and Reyn and their child. For Tintaglia. For all of us. We need the Silver, Thymara. A bit of dragon blood or a scale can start the changes. But to sustain them, to move them in directions that let us live, that will let our children live? That will take Silver."

She knew that. It didn't change the facts. "There's no Silver down here, Rapskal. Only bones."

She found she had slipped the ring on her finger. It hung loose against her knuckle. Not her ring. The jidzin against her skin whispered secrets she didn't want to hear.

"You used to tend this well. You and some of the other artisans. You spoke of managing it. I thought . . ."

"I don't remember any of this, Rapskal." She slapped the gauntlets against her thigh, and tried to push them through the loop in her gear belt. She wasn't wearing one.

"Don't you?" he asked her quietly.

She looked at him without speaking. She stared around at the faintly gleaming walls of the small space. "I remember it was dangerous to come down here. We always carried lights. We were always supposed to have a partner."

"Ramose," he said quietly.

She smiled bitterly. "Never trust a jealous man," she said, and she wondered what she meant by it. A silence built and she did not fight it. She studied the smooth black walls, waiting for a memory to push into her mind. Nothing came. She looked down at the bones and tried to feel something about a woman who had died here a long time ago.

A stray thought came to her. "I've always been afraid of this well, since I saw it. But I couldn't have known that Amarinda died here. She couldn't go back and put this memory in the stone."

"No. You couldn't have known. But I did. Even back then, when I left a message for her and then left the city, I think I knew. And my memories tinged yours."

"But you still brought me here."

"It was a last chance. For all of us."

She thought about that for a time. A last chance. She had warned him that if he forced her down the well, it would never be the same between them. Well, she had come of her own free will. But she still suspected that everything she felt for him had changed.

"My hands are cold," she said, to say something. Then she added, "It's useless to stay down here, Rapskal. There's nothing for us here. I don't remember anything. We'd best get back up there while we can still climb."

He nodded, defeated, and she gestured for him to go first. She had always been a better climber than Rapskal. She boosted him high and then held the line tight for him and waited until she heard him say, "I'm on the chain now!" before she started to follow him.

She realized she had put on the gauntlets only when her claws pressed against the ends of the fingers. "Huh," she said, only to herself. The gloves had closed off the light from her ring. *It doesn't matter,* she told herself. *I'll soon be up and out of here.* She took a wrap of the line around her hand and set her bare foot to the wall. Cold. She reached over her head with her free hand, gripped the rope, and began her ascent in the dark. Going up was much harder than the burning slide down had been. She had no one to hold the rope tight for her; it swung and whipped below her as she climbed, and the claws of her feet skittered on the smooth wall.

Below the chain she paused. The gauntlets had saved her rope-burned hands, but they'd be a hazard on the slick chain. She moved her weight onto the chain, then looped the rope around herself, braced her feet on the wall, dragged off one gauntlet . . . and found herself staring at a small tracery of Silver on the black stone before her. Had it been here when she climbed down? She was certain she would have seen it. Unless the gleam of the moon locket had hidden it from her.

She stuffed the gauntlet down the front of her tunic. She gripped the chain afresh and leaned closer. Writing. She put a fingertip to the letters, traced their almost familiar curves. It said . . . something. Something important. Almost of its own accord, her hand reached the end of the line of letters and then tapped a glyph there. Twice.

Below her, the grind of stone on stone startled her. She wanted to flee up the chain, but sharpest curiosity made her back slowly down the rope instead. There it was. A large block of stone in the wall was retreating, sliding smoothly away, leaving an opening behind it. "The seam valve," she heard herself say out loud.

And then the memory came, of her first trip down the shaft with the older Silver worker. He'd shown it to her, halting the platform on its slow descent. "Can you believe," he'd asked her, "that sometimes the Silver pressure was so high, it came into the reservoir at this level? Sometimes, we'd have to come down here and open the drains to let it out. There were pipes that would carry it out into the river and away from the city. And when the Silver seams were really producing, we'd have to shut down some of them, to keep it from welling out the top and running through the streets." The oldster had coughed and wiped his mouth on the back of his hand. "This seam has been dry for decades," he continued sourly. "And if the Silver pressure keeps dropping, we probably never will open it again. Well, start cranking, girl. It's a long way down to where the Silver comes in now. We need to measure the level of standing Silver and log it. That's your job now, once every seventeen days. Can't ration it if we don't know how much the seams are producing."

Thymara blinked, abruptly surprised to find herself alone and hanging on a rope in a well shaft. "Reservoir shaft," she corrected herself quietly. Reflexively, she reached over and tapped the glyph again. She heard the grinding halt, and then resume with a different note. She moved down the line and set her hand to the wall until she felt the brick moved back into alignment. Relief slowed her thundering heart. Best to leave things as they had been until someone like Carson could help her understand what little she remembered.

As she lifted her hand from the block, it seemed to tremble under her fingers. Then it suddenly shot out, past her hand, to land with a clatter at the bottom of the shaft. A square of liquid Silver followed it, pushing out thickly, at first keeping its shape and then turning into a fat worm wriggling down the wall. She stared at it, trying to make sense of what she saw. The seam had replenished itself. And the old valve had given way. Stone grated as two adjacent blocks swung out unevenly from the wall as the heavy Silver forced its way out and into the shaft. A slow bulge began around the leak. She heard a pop and heard another brick fly out of the wall. It hit the opposite side of the shaft with force, and a gout of Silver surged after it. She stared aghast, then shrieked, "Rapskal! Something broke down here!"

"What?"

"Climb!" she shouted up the shaft. "Climb fast!" She

went up the rope like a frightened monkey, gained the chain and did not pause. The one gauntlet was a hindrance on the slick chain; there was no time to strip it off. She raced a zigzagging crack in the wall that paralleled her progress. It shone silver as the long-suffering stones gave way to the pressure behind them. They opened with sharp pops that hurt her ears.

Rapskal had paid attention to her cry. He was waiting for her at the top of the well, grabbing her by the shoulders of her tunic and jerking her to safety. "Do we run?" he asked her, and his eyes were his own again, wide in a scared face.

"Uphill!" she confirmed, and they retreated to the edge of the plaza. Dimly she recalled a tale of a time when the silver had overflowed the well and run down the streets to the river. People, fish, and birds had died from its touch.

Overpowering curiosity made them pause at the edge of the square to look back. The dragons had not fled. They stood by the well mouth, visibly shivering with excitement. They both had their heads lowered inside the shaft. As they watched, Sintara dropped to her front knees and stretched her neck down farther. She looked ridiculous, hunkered down. Her ribs worked as she crouched there, and abruptly Heeby followed her example. Were they drinking?

Thymara gasped for breath, her gauntleted hand on Rapskal's shoulder. Dawn was starting to gray the sky at the eastern edge of the horizon. The dragons still drank. No Silver reached the top and brimmed over. Then Heeby uttered a squeal of protest and lifted her gleaming dripping muzzle. She stared at Rapskal indignantly. His voice was his own as he said, "She's furious. Sintara's neck is longer and she can still reach the Silver, but Heeby can't." He lifted his voice. "Don't you worry, pretty girl. I'll fill buckets and buckets for you. I promise."

Thymara's mind began to work again. "The buckets Tats and the other keepers used to haul rubble away from the well. We need to fill them with Silver and get them to Tintaglia. I'll lower them down and haul them up. You don't touch them unless I say it's safe."

He nodded and turned to look at the gloved hand that

gripped his shoulder. He scowled. "What is that made from?" he demanded.

Thymara didn't look at him or it as she put the second gauntlet on. Heeby lay as much on her belly as a dragon could, her head down the well, struggling to reach the stuff. She watched her own dragon gulping down the Silver as if her life depended on it. It did. She understood a little of what Sintara had told her about hating dependence of any kind. Dependence forced one to make compromises, ones they would rather not recall. She looked at the glove on her hand, heavy leather with the scale beds still visible.

"Dragon hide," she said. "The only thing impervious to Silver." She felt a shadow wash over her and looked up. Dragons were circling, and a moment later, their wild trumpeting filled the air. "We'd better get those buckets filled now if we're going to get any," she told him, and he nodded.

THE BABY WAS squalling, a lusty angry cry. Malta was laughing and crying as she fumbled at the front of her tunic. When she freed her breast, Ephron seized it indignantly; his cries stopped so suddenly that Reyn laughed aloud. Their son was thin, his eyes sunken and his little hand a claw on her breast, but he was alive and fighting to remain so. He suckled so hard that Malta winced, and then laughed again.

"She heard me," she told Reyn. "At the last, she heard us. She changed him." Tears ran down her face and followed the curves of her smile. She leaned forward to touch her dragon. The breath from her nostrils barely stirred the fine hair on Ephron's head. "He's going to live, Tintaglia. He's going to live, and I will see he remembers all I know about you."

In another part of the city, a wild trumpeting of dragons suddenly arose. Malta turned to Reyn. "I think they know. And soon Kalo will be here to take what is left of her."

Reyn asked the dreadful question they had both wondered. "Will that make him of her lineage, if he takes her memories? Will he know how to help Ephron again if he needs it? Or if we have other children?"

"I don't know," she replied. *Other children.* A foolish dream, perhaps. They had one, one to cherish, one whose eyes were closed now, his little round belly tight and full. Had they a right to hope for anything more than that?

"That's Kalo coming. He's flying fast. My dear, we have to leave her now. Come. Up and out of the way." Reyn stood stiffly and bent to help Malta stand.

Kalo was coming in fast, and he pushed them with a wild command. *Out of the way!*

Malta shot to her feet and scrambled back, clutching the baby that now wailed at being awakened. There were other dragons coming in behind him, gold Mercor and nasty little Veras. "I don't want to watch it," Malta wailed, turning her face into Reyn. "She's not even dead yet! How can they?"

"It's their way, my dear. It's their way." His arms closed around her and the child. Despite the horror she felt, she turned back to watch the dragons land around the fallen queen.

Kalo flung back his head and then snapped it forward. He darted his head in, jaws wide, and despite herself, Malta screamed.

A thick silvery mist emerged from his mouth. He leaned closer to Tintaglia, breathing it out on her. Then he whipped his head again, and again spewed a fog of Silver onto her. Mercor landed beside him. Kalo trumpeted territorially, but the smaller male ignored him. He copied him, misting Tintaglia with drifting Silver as Veras waited her turn. It settled on the supine dragon, coating her in Silver.

The slight morning breeze was carrying the stuff. "Get back!" Reyn shouted as sleepy keepers began to emerge from the bath hall. They stumbled back, but the mist was heavy. Malta flung her cloak over her baby. They turned and ran, fleeing up the steps of a nearby building. The Silver made a sizzling sound as it settled on the paving stones. Malta looked back. For an instant, tiny silver balls seemed to rattle and dance on the pavement before they darted into the cracks and vanished.

"Look at her!" Reyn gasped, and Malta turned her eyes back to her dragon.

Tintaglia was shrouded with moving Silver. It slid over her skin as if caressing her. She saw it boiling in the dragon's wounds and cried out in low horror at the sound and the smell it made. It sank into the dragon where it coated her, vanishing like ink absorbed into a cloth. Like ink, the color remained on her, a silver haze over her blue scales, like fog on a window. Malta held her breath.

Malta stared at a slash on Tintaglia's shoulder. It bubbled at the edges. Slime and bits of dead flesh rose and dribbled down the dragon's skin. In their wake the gash was closing, filling in with sound flesh and a coating of paler, smaller scales.

Tintaglia made a low rumbling sound, perhaps an expression of discomfort. Malta's sense of the dragon grew stronger; she shared both her distress at the unfamiliar sensations racing through her and her discomfort as her torn flesh was so quickly rebuilt. Her breath came louder, faster, and then the dragon was panting as if she were flying hard. The thundering of her hearts as her blood raced through her healing body became an audible thumping. Her eyes opened, wide and staring, and she opened her mouth to gasp in deep breaths of air.

"It's killing her!" Reyn voiced their fear.

No. Mercor's thought was reassuring. *We think she is strong enough to endure this. And if she is not, well, we have done no harm.*

The dragons that had sprayed Tintaglia stood at a respectful distance, watching. Briefly, Malta was more aware of them. They radiated vitality now. The glamour of their beauty was effortless. So magnificent were they. She could not doubt the wisdom of what they had done to Tintaglia. They were dragons; what right had she to question them in anything?

Hungry. The thought was strong enough to send every keeper staggering back. Tintaglia closed her eyes. When she opened them again, she once more looked out from them. "I need to hunt," she said. She came slowly to her feet, as if every motion had to be remembered before she could perform it. She was emaciated still, but her scales shimmered with light. She lifted her wings, stretched them, and then refolded them. As she did so, a small metal object fell to the paving stones. She looked down at the ejected arrowhead, and then thrust it away with her foot. "They will pay for that," she vowed. And then, "I go to hunt."

Tintaglia, blue queen, crouched and then sprang into the air. The wind of her wing beats staggered Malta and stung her eyes. "She flies!" she cried aloud. Pride filled her heart. "The most beautiful of all queens flies!"

I am that, Tintaglia agreed, and winged toward the hunting grounds of the foothills.

✧ ✧ ✧

Day the 15th of the Plough Moon

Year the 7th of the Independent Alliance of Traders
**From Master Godon of the Trehaug Bird
Keepers' Guild and with the consent of the
full circle of masters in Trehaug**

Sent in a triply sealed message cylinder and to be
opened only before a full convening of the Guild masters in Bingtown, with Master Kerig Sweetwater in
attendance to explain the circumstances, and in completely discreet circumstances.

*Please allow Master Kerig to explain the circumstances
of how we have come into possession of this document. He
and we are of the considered opinion that it is genuine
and that the Guild should extend thanks to Detozi and
Erek Dunwarrow for the discreet manner in which they
have handled an extremely difficult situation.*

*The message we have intercepted appears to be
from Master Kim, Keeper of the Birds, Cassarick, to
a Chalcedean merchant in Bingtown. The message
is water damaged and written in Chalcedean, but its
existence, regardless of content, is sufficient cause to
suspend Keeper Kim and make a complete and intensive
inspection of his coops and records.*

✧ ✧ ✧

CHAPTER EIGHTEEN

SEDUCTIONS

I have broken no laws. I am the son of a Bingtown Trader. I did not come here to kill dragons. I should be free to walk about the city."

"Don't think so, my fine friend."

Hest scowled, making the sailor grin as he added. "See, it's our city, so we get to make the rules. And we decided that none of you are going to go walking about on your own. So. Here you'll stay, unless one of us thinks it's a good idea to take you for a stroll. Somehow I doubt that will happen. So relax. You're not suffering. You're warm, you got food. You can go take another bath if you want. That's fine. You can go up to the tower and look out of the window. That's allowed. But you're not leaving this building alone until we load you up on the boat to take you downriver. That's one thing everyone agreed on." He shrugged. "Find someone willing to trust you, and you can take a walk outside with him. Some of the others have. But you don't get to go anywhere alone."

"You're not an Elderling. What right do you have to the city? What right do you have to a vote on what becomes of us?" Hest raised his voice, hoping that some of the others might take up his cause. No one did. The Jamaillian merchants had begged paper and ink from Alise and were attempting to draw up some sort of a trade agreement, as if they could just bypass Bingtown's and Trehaug's Traders' Councils. Fools. Trader Candral continued to stare morosely into the distance. He'd already written his confession and handed it over to the river captain. He was probably imagining what would become of him when he returned to Cassarick. His face was still bruised from the drubbing the sailors and Traders had given him on the journey here. The rowing slaves seemed to be enjoying idleness, warmth, and food. The Chalcedeans were watching the altercation but seemed unwilling to be associated with his cause. *Cowards. No allies there at all.*

"Some might say I've no right to a vote here," the sailor conceded. "Except that everyone else from the expedition agreed that I did. So I cast my vote along with the others. You might be a bit nicer to me. I voted that we shouldn't let the dragons eat any of you. Might start a real bad habit, was my thought. Though when I'm dead, I've decided, it's fine with me if they eat me and remember everything I've ever seen or done. Spit's the one I'd choose to eat me. That mean little devil is full of spite and vinegar. I'm betting he'll outlive all those other bigger dragons."

Hest shook his head in disgust and turned away. There were two doors out of the gathering hall, and they'd put a guard on each of them. Earlier today, one had been a skinny girl with pink scaling and blond hair. He'd tried to charm her into letting him take a stroll around the square, just to stretch his legs. She looked at him and replied not a word. When he'd tried to just walk past her, she hadn't blocked him. She'd only said, "My dragon is the large gold one sleeping in the sun on the steps." Hest hadn't challenged her after that.

"Glad to see you. Boring way to waste the first nice day we've had!" The sailor's words weren't for him. The youngster who came to take the sailor's place nodded. "Wind off the hills today, Hennesey. You can smell spring in the air." His words were cheery, but his tone was dispirited. The sailor slapped him on the shoulder as he walked by him.

"Davvie, lad, it will all come right. Sometimes you just have to wait a while for the right one to come along." He did a ridiculous little sideways skip and added blithely, "Finally happened for me!"

"Right," the lad said, and he sat down on the bench the sailor had just vacated. The new guard heaved a sigh, and his shoulders settled into a slump. He was not as heavily scaled as the others. Cobalt outlined his brows and went in a stripe down his nose. His Elderling cloak was scarlet, as were his boots. His tunic and close-fitting leggings were black. The weave was so fine it was imperceptible. Hest had never seen the like. This mere lad wore a fortune on his back. Did he know it? Would he part with any of it?

Hest studied him for a moment, and then he looked at the other new guard at the far door. There were two of them, actually, sitting on a bench together with the ease of long familiarity. Both were orange-scaled Elderlings, dressed all in gleaming black. One took a dice cup and dice from his pocket. The other one nodded. The game began.

Hest ventured closer to his morose jailer. "Nice day outside?"

Davvie looked at Hest suspiciously for a moment, and then responded. "Nice enough. Weather's changing. Lots of good news for us."

Hest cocked his head at the young man and ventured a sympathetic smile. "You don't look as if the good news did much for you."

"It's not going to help me with my problem," he said. He looked away from Hest.

"Too bad." Hest seated himself on the other end of the guard's bench. The boy turned and glared at him. *Yes, boy,* he decided, though it was hard to read age through his scaling.

"I know who you are." He stated it flatly.

"Do you really?" This was intriguing.

"Yes. Carson and my dad were like brothers. He's raised me and talks straight to me. So I know who you are. And I don't think much of you."

"Really. Why is that?" *Who is Carson?*

"Sedric's been pretty honest with Carson. Well, not at first maybe, but now it's all in the open between them. I know you treated Sedric real bad. And he's happier now, living simple with Carson, than he ever was in your fancy house with your rich friends. He told me that."

"Did he?" Hest turned away from the boy and looked at the floor. "There are two sides to every story," he said huskily. He glanced up to find Davvie watching him intently and lowered his gaze again lest the boy read his eyes too well. "Two people can love each other and still hurt each other. Still make mistakes, big mistakes." He shook his head slowly. "I know I can't win Sedric back. I see that perhaps he's better off here. That doesn't mean I have to be happy about going back alone. Doesn't mean it won't leave a big hole in my life."

The scaled youngster was silent, full of listening. Hest shot him an earnest look. "You're lucky to be out here. I see how things are in this place. Oh, maybe it's a thin, bare life here, but you can love who you want, and no one shames you. I've never had that. Never. Maybe if Sedric and I had been able to be open with everyone around us, maybe . . ." He let his voice die away and shook his head regretfully. The boy leaned closer. *Such an easy target. Young and still inexperienced, his heart freshly broken.* Hest wanted to smile. *Could he take a better vengeance on Sedric and his damned Carson than seducing this boy?* He looked at Davvie with wounded eyes. "I tried to give him a good life with me, as much as I could manage. We traveled a great deal together. And when we were in town, there were many evenings with our friends. Fine wine, good food, wonderful fellowship." He shook his head sadly. "I thought it would be enough for him. I shared with Sedric all I had, introduced him to a life he had never known. We would go to the theater together.

Or go out riding. Or simply to a tavern to drink ale and listen to music. Every night we were together, experiencing all that a city has to offer young men." He broke off to look at the boy more closely. "Have you ever been to Bingtown? Or any large city?"

Davvie shook his head. "Carson was teaching me to be a hunter and a trapper. Now that I got a dragon of my own, I'm a keeper. I wanted to be a keeper mostly so I could stay with Lecter. But now that he's thrown me over, and my dragon is all busy with other things, I've wound up with nothing." He lifted a hand and touched his own cheek. "Don't think I'll ever visit Bingtown or any other city looking like I do. I'd be a freak there now."

"A freak?" Hest laughed heartily. A few heads turned his way, and he quieted. Attention from anyone other than Davvie was not what he wanted. "No, my young friend. Not a freak. An Elderling. Rarest of the rare and honored wherever you might go. Why, everyone knows the names of Malta and Reyn Khuprus! They stayed for a time at the Satrap's court in Jamaillia and were honored with balls and feasts every day they were there. Showered with gifts and attention! I have no idea why they chose to go back to the Rain Wilds."

"The dragons needed them," the young man said, surprised that Hest didn't know such things.

"Ah, of course. They did. But your dragon, you say, does not? So are you not free to go where you will?" Hest pushed a hand through his dark hair, tousling it slightly. He tapped his fingertip on his lips, drawing the boy's eyes to his face. "You're a handsome fellow, and wealthy. You could travel to the city. Or anywhere. See more of the world. The right companion could show you off, teach you everything you'd need to know to fit in there. Introduce you to people who would appreciate you. After all, you can't mean to spend the whole of your life here, can you? You're much too young and too wealthy to settle in one spot."

Davvie gave a snort of laughter. "Wealthy? Me? I've the clothes on my back. A knife. My own bow. Little enough beside that."

Hest was astonished. "Young man, wealth is all around you here. Surely you are entitled to a share of it? There is so much in this city that, presented to the proper buyer, would bring you a fortune. I see others wearing Elderling jewelry; why do you not?" He touched the back of the boy's ringless hand, drew his finger slowly away. "I'll tell you this; a single Elderling bracelet would buy you a year of carousing in Bingtown. Easily."

"I've never worn jewelry."

Hest feigned astonishment. "Never? Ah, but you should! A sapphire ring to match the scaling on your hand. Or—" He lifted his hand and playfully tapped the boy's ear, and then spoke as Davvie drew back at his touch, Hest using the motion as a way to trace his jawline with his forefinger, "Dangling earrings. Silver. Or rich gold to draw the eye to your face."

"I FEEL DRAINED," Selden said, and he managed a feeble smile at his joke.

"This looks infected," Chassim replied tartly, glaring at his swollen wrist. The Duke's teeth had broken his skin in the most recent session, and the flesh around it was hot and red.

Selden had not felt that bite as a separate pain. He'd lost consciousness early in the act and only recovered his awareness here in the tower room. Each time the Duke bled him, his stamina dropped. He did not look at his arm as she put a hot, wet cloth on it. A strong aroma of garlic rose from the poultice, and he turned his head to avoid it.

"Is it a pretty day out there?" he asked inanely. Chassim had opened the shutters, and a soft wind was blowing through the heavy curtains. Beyond their fluttering he glimpsed the stone balustrade of the balcony. Their new quarters were spacious and airy, with a wide view of the city and the surrounding countryside. Spring was coming, he thought and smiled weakly. Spring was coming and he was going.

"Nice enough. Do you want your curtains opened? It's clear but not very warm out there."

"Please. What's the worst that can happen? I catch my death of cold?"

"The infection will kill you first," she said bluntly.

"I know how bad it is," he admitted. "It hurts, and the healers told your father that next time he must take blood from my other arm, lest the infection spread to him. I'm not looking forward to that." His fingers twitched against his bedding as he thought of it. Bad enough to have the Duke break open the cut on his arm every few days. Adding another one was a whole new horror. "I'm dying," he said, trying the words aloud. "His drinking my blood is killing me."

"And every time he takes your blood, he seems to get stronger. He is so triumphant about it. It's disgusting." She pushed the heavy curtains aside and tied them back. The sky was blue with puffs of white clouds in the distance. No mountains in this direction. The horizon stretched on to forever. The wind wandered into the room.

"Maybe when I die, he will start to fail again."

"Maybe. I won't live to find out. If you die, then I die, too." She came back to sit on a stool by his bed.

"I'm sorry."

She made a strangled noise. "Scarcely your fault that my father is killing you. Nor mine. I was born into this disaster. I'm sorry that you fell into it." She looked out of the window. "I've been thinking that if you die, I won't wait for him to discover it and punish me for it." She nodded toward the balcony. "I may jump from there."

"Sweet Sa!" Selden exclaimed in horror. He tried to sit up, but he was not quite strong enough.

"Not in despair, my friend. Just to make it harder for him to pretend I died a natural death. If I leap from here, it may be that some will see me fall. There are people who have pledged to avenge me if I die at my father's hands."

Selden felt far colder than he had before. "And your leaping will launch a wave of vengeance?"

"No," she continued to look at the sky. "I hope to avert it. There was a time when I wanted people to know what he had done to me; I dreamed they would all rise up and avenge my death. Now I think about it like ripples ringing out from a dropped stone. Do I want my death to result in misery and death for others? Or would I rather slip away at a time of my choosing?" She reached over and took his good hand without looking at him. "I don't really want to die at all," she confided to him in a whisper. "But if I have to, I'm not going to let him be the one to make me die. I'm not going to wait here alone, wondering if he will torture me first." She finally made eye contact with him and tried for a faint smile. "So, when you go, I'll go, too."

He looked at the tray on the low table beside him. The cream soup still steamed slightly. Slices of mushroom interrupted that calm sea. A brown loaf of bread was beside it and a shallow dish of pale yellow butter. Stewed Chalcedean peppers, purple, yellow, and green, surrounded a slab of steamed white fish. All so prettily arranged. They wanted him to eat well. He knew why. Earlier, he had defiantly refused the food. It had seemed pointless to eat, merely an exercise in extending his life as a blood source for the Duke. Now it seemed a way to extend Chassim's life. "While there's life, there's hope," he said.

"So they say," she conceded.

He reached for the napkin and shook it out.

"I'LL GIVE THEM another three or four days of my work here, to shore up those pilings. Then we have to load up and head downriver. Reyn sent a bird back to that fellow at Cassarick, asking if our seed and stock had come in from Bingtown. No bird has come back yet, so I guess we'll have to go back there and find out for ourselves. I think it flew off in the wrong direction myself. Anyway. We've got a lot to straighten out in Cassarick. I still haven't been paid. And I'm not letting the Council get away with that."

"What about the other boats? Will they go with us?"

Leftrin shook his head. He was seated across from Alise at the little galley table. Thick white mugs of brown tea steamed on the scarred board between them. An empty platter held only crumbs of the bread and cheese they had shared. They were the only ones aboard, but the boat wasn't quiet. As always, Tarman and the river had their own conversation as the current tugged at him and his lines restrained them. Good sounds, Alise thought. Here on Tarman, she was immune to the whispering lure of the memory stone. When she and Leftrin planned their future, as they did now, the only voices she heard were their own.

"Those boats might be 'impervious,' but they were handled rough. There's dragon scorch and broken oars and all sorts of repair they need. The hold of one of them is disgustingly filthy. And we don't have enough real sailors for a proper crew. Those slaves didn't know much more than how to pull an oar and had no reason to try to learn more. None of them started out wanting to be sailors, either. It's going to take time for them to get used to being free men. They all seem a bit stunned yet. So there's a lot to be done before we worry about whether they want to work a deck or not. Teaching the keepers to operate their own boats is going to be a task for milder days, when the river runs quieter."

Leftrin chewed his lower lip thoughtfully and then pushed his mug of tea to one side. "You know how Tillamon told Reyn she knew at least a dozen young women who wouldn't mind leaving Trehaug and Cassarick behind for a chance to walk in the summer breeze without a veil? She got permission from the other keepers to invite them here. Well, I'm thinking I know a few able deckhands who might be persuaded to come this way, at least for a time. It's easier to teach a young captain his business if he's worked the deck himself. But, lacking that, I'd like to find experienced crew for them to learn with."

"So much to think about," Alise murmured. New settlers for Kelsingra. Farm animals and seeds for crops. Did anyone here know how to care for them? She did not ask him if anyone had asked him to teach the new captains their business. She was sure he had just assumed it. She smiled as she asked him, "Which of the keepers will step up to captain the boats?"

"Not sure. Rapskal might. He's looking for something lately, and that would be better than some of the wild talk I've heard from him."

She shook her head sadly. "I think that's wishful thinking. Not that he couldn't rise to that if he wanted to. But the stone memories have changed him. All he speaks of now is the need to put an end to the threat against the dragons. A permanent end. I don't think he understands how far away Chalced is, or what sort of resistance he and Heeby would face."

"Wouldn't be only him and Heeby. Kalo's hot to take vengeance on them. Fente wants to go, as does Baliper, Sestican, and Dortean. Ranculos, too. And Tintaglia, of course. She says that once she's fed up a bit, she's taking her wrath to them."

"Mercor?" she asked faintly. She suspected that if the golden went, all the others would follow.

"He's keeping his own counsel, so far. I don't know what he thinks. But Rapskal keeps stirring up the keepers. You know about that armory they found?"

"I do." Not even to Leftrin had she mentioned that she had discovered it a long time ago but never mentioned it to Rapskal. Her discovery of it had further changed her image of Elderlings. And dragons. The battle gear for the dragons had been mostly decorative, with rings where perhaps riders had once secured themselves. Sintara's assertion that dragons had never been ridden by humans had seemed disproven to Alise, but the blue queen had insisted that carrying an Elderling into battle was not the same as being ridden like a donkey. The thought she had conveyed was that, in that instance, the dragon was using the Elderling as a sort of auxiliary weapon rather than serving him as a charger.

There had been armor for Elderlings hung neatly on hooks on the stone walls. It mimicked the scaling of dragons in how the fine plates overlapped one another as well as in colors. The wooden shafts of the spears were long gone, bows and quivers of arrows faint outlines of dust on the floor. But the arrow points and spearheads had survived. There were other devices there, of green-coated brass and iron infused with Silver, ones she did not recognize even as she guessed their martial uses.

"Those young men tried on that armor and helms like

Jerd trying on jewelry," Leftrin complained. "They have no idea of what it means. But if Rapskal and Kalo and Tintaglia keep urging them on, I think they'll soon find out."

She shied away from thinking about it. "So. If you were choosing captains for those two ships, who would you train?"

"Harrikin, I'm thinking. He's steady. Maybe Alum. Lad seems capable and smart."

She lowered her face to hide a grin at that. She suspected he could not imagine Skelly with a man who didn't know how to run a boat. His next words surprised her. "But it might not be a keeper who steps up, you know. Dragons keep them pretty tied up. Could be Hennesey stepping up to take a command. Or Skelly, when she's a bit more seasoned."

"So many changes," she mused. "There will have to be regular freight runs until Kelsingra can support itself. And after that, maybe we'll be selling meat and grain to the Rain Wilds. New settlers coming to Kelsingra. They'll have to understand what they're risking, of course, but I think Tillamon is right. There will be people who are willing to come and start fresh here. And we'll need what they know. Farmers and smiths, bakers and potters and carpenters . . . but they'll come. It's not often that people are offered the chance to just begin anew."

"Not often," he agreed. He was silent, mulling something. Then, "Be my wife," he said suddenly.

She stared at him, startled by the sudden change in topic. "I can't, Leftrin. Until my marriage contract is formally annulled, I'm still marri—"

"Don't say you're married to him! Please don't. I hate to hear those words come from your mouth." He reached across the table and set his fingertips on her lips. He looked at her with earnest gray eyes. "I don't care what they say in Bingtown or anywhere else in the world. He broke his contract a long time ago. He never even meant to honor it, so how could you ever have been his wife? Be mine, Alise. I'm already yours. I want to call myself your husband. Marry me here, in Kelsingra. Start a new life with me here. Forget Bingtown and its rules and contracts."

She tilted her head. "You don't want a marriage contract?"

"I don't need one. If you want one, you can draw up anything you want and I'll sign it. I won't bother reading it because anything you want to say about how it is going to be will be fine with me. I don't need a paper or a contract or any of that. Just you."

"What brought all this on?" Alise felt flustered.

He shook his head. "I knew Hest existed. I knew you'd been his. There were times when I felt like a thief. There was a day when Sedric took me on about it, saying that I was going to ruin your whole life by loving you. Made me feel selfish and low for wanting you."

"It seems a lifetime ago." She smiled at him. "We used to worry about such peculiar things."

"It doesn't bother you now? What Hest might say when he goes back to Bingtown?"

"After Sedric spoke up? No. I think he will say as little as he possibly can and hope others do the same. Before he leaves, I will speak to him and ask him to give me my nullification. We can draw it up, and there are plenty of possible witnesses. It will happen quietly here. I will send my explanations to my family, and he will have to deal with his." She took a breath and met his gaze with clear eyes. "I've finished with him, Leftrin. Did you doubt it?"

He dropped his gaze. "Worst thing I ever heard in my life was him calling you 'my darling.' I wanted to rip the tongue out of his mouth. Wanted to tear him into pieces with my hands and feed the bits to Spit."

He spoke with a low vehemence she had never heard before from him. "My dear!" she exclaimed, torn between shock and laughter.

"He was frightening you. I could see that; I could feel it. I wanted to destroy anything that could scare you like that."

"I was scaring myself. Giving him power he didn't really have. Just like I used to do." She smiled almost sadly. "It's done, Leftrin. All done." She stood up and walked around the galley table to stand behind him. She leaned forward to embrace him and spoke by his ear. "I'm looking forward to sailing away with you."

"Won't be much privacy aboard for a time until we off-load all those intruders in Trehaug." He shook his head. "I'll be glad to give over the judging on the Chalcedeans to someone else. Poor bastards, caught between the mortar and the pestle. Doubt there's anything left for them to go home to. But I'm not looking forward to having a whole boatload of them all the way to Trehaug."

She gave him a quick kiss, and as he pulled her closer, she said, "So perhaps we should use this quiet time well, now."

"I CAN'T BE gone long. I'm off watch now, but my uncle will have more work for me. As always."

"Keeps you busy, does he?" Hest was amused. "Probably thinks you are too young to manage your own life. That's often the case with men who take on the care of young boys. They don't see when they've become young men, ready to take wing on their own."

Davvie's eyes flickered to Hest's, neither confirming nor denying that he resented Carson's control of him. He cleared his throat. "I'm surprised you haven't gone up the tower yourself to take a look around. It's allowed to any of you. We decided that at the meeting."

"Indeed," Hest agreed. "But looking around from a tower isn't the same as having someone explain the layout of the city." He was letting the lad do most of the talking, and he was talking himself into far more than Hest had thought he could persuade him to. Today, a visit to the tower together. Tomorrow, perhaps, a brief stroll outside. The boy preceded him up the stairs, and Hest had a fine view of the lad's hips and legs. He was young, younger even than Sedric had been, and even more green to the ways of the world. He'd break easily, Hest decided. Entice him with elegant and sophisticated pleasures he had never even imagined. Tempt his young hunger for adventure and worldliness. Make him see that only Hest could introduce him to that wonderful world.

"Let me catch my breath, Davvie. An old man like me doesn't take these stairs as easily as you do."

The young Elderling halted obediently on the next landing. "There's a fine view from here if the steps are taxing you," he offered. "You needn't climb the whole way to the tower top."

Hest stepped to the window and looked out over the city silently. He had expected the boy quickly to refute the notion that he was an old man. It pricked his vanity that he had not. *Don't let it show.* He looked out of the window to feign interest, but as his eyes took in the full extent of the city, even his worldly soul was amazed. The view from the river was no way to comprehend the vastness of Kelsingra. From this vantage, the city spread out in every direction. He saw a few collapsed buildings and scattered areas of damage, but for the most part, the city seemed intact and unplundered. He could not begin to imagine the riches of the place. His eye marked half a dozen statues presiding over empty fountains. He knew a collector in Jamaillia who would beggar himself to add even one of them to his collection. He ran his fingers along the tiles that framed the windows. Each featured a dragon in a different posture. The lad saw him admiring them.

"Oh, those are great fun. Watch!"

The boy ran his hand along the line of dragons, and they cavorted at his touch. When he stopped, they froze as they were.

"Amazing!" Hest exclaimed. "May I try?"

"Of course." Davvie had become the guide now, tolerant and amused by Hest's amazement. Excellent. Hest assayed a clumsy attempt to activate the dragons as the boy had. He missed half of them. He tried again, with as little success. He drew his hand back in disgust. "I haven't the knack for it," he exclaimed in disappointment.

"It's easy. Like this." Davvie took Hest's hand in his own and ran it over the dragons. This time they leaped and pranced for him.

"One more time," Hest suggested and set his free hand to Davvie's shoulder to allow the boy to control his hand more surely. Davvie was intent on his dragon play. As he drew Hest's hand once again over the tiles, the man leaned forward and kissed him warmly on the side of his neck.

Davvie sprang back with an exclamation of shock, but Hest managed to maintain his touch on the boy's shoulder. "You are so handsome," he said throatily. "So exotic. How could you think your scaling ugly?" He breathed out through his mouth, a sigh of desire, and then caught his breath raggedly. Davvie was staring at him, his mouth slightly ajar. Hest imagined sealing those lips with his own, and his feigned passion was suddenly real. He moved toward the Elderling, and when Davvie backed into the wall, Hest pressed his body against him.

"This is not . . . I don't . . ." Davvie stuttered. Searing curiosity and fear battled in his dark eyes.

Excellent. Hest risked that he was the sort aroused by danger and the forbidden. He pressed himself against the youngster and spoke by his ear. "Sedric broke my heart. I'm alone. You've been discarded. What harm do we do anyone if, for a short time, we forget those pains?" He leaned his weight hard on the youth, and the hands that he put on him were purposeful and demanding. "There is so much I can teach you. Ask me to teach you." One hand suddenly moved, to grip Davvie's throat. "Say 'please,'" Hest suggested pleasantly.

———◦◦◦◦———

"I'M NOT GOING to wait on him forever," Carson said over his shoulder. "He said he wanted to go hunting, and I waited for his guard shift to be over." Sedric was trailing Carson as he strode into the baths. The hunter opened the doors to the soaking room and a cloud of humid air engulfed them. Kalo, his eyes closed to slits in pleasure, was dozing in the water. "Davvie?" he called, but there was no response. Sylve looked up from scrubbing Mercor and shook her head.

They were halfway to the dining hall when they heard a commotion from the stairwell. There was a wordless yell, anger mixed with outrage, followed by a muffled stream of words.

"That's Davvie!" Carson exclaimed and spun toward the steps. The hunter went up them at a run and Sedric followed, his heart in his mouth. Davvie and Lecter had been quarreling lately. Both had been sullen and unpredictable, but as far as he knew, they hadn't come to blows. Yet the unmistakable sounds of a physical struggle were in progress.

Sedric reached the landing a half step behind Carson and halted in shock. Hest was there. He had not seen him since he had faced him down in the street; had not wanted to see him, ever again. Yet there he stood, a hand to his cheek as a rumpled-looking Davvie tugged his tunic straight. At the sight of Carson and Sedric, Davvie flushed a deep scarlet. Hest only smiled knowingly. He leaned back against the wall and crossed his arms on his chest.

Carson's eyes darted from Hest to Davvie and back again. Breath shuddered in and out of him, and possibly Hest did not know how furious he was as he asked Davvie, "What's going on here?"

"Nothing," he declared sullenly, and Sedric saw Carson's shoulders swell. "Whatever it was, it's my business. I'm old enough to take care of myself," the boy added defiantly.

Carson seemed barely able to contain himself as he looked from Hest to Davvie. "Looks like you're doing a fine job of that," he growled. Fury put sparks in his eyes as he added, "Boy, you go from one bad decision to another! How could you be so stupid as to take up—" He strangled on his anger.

Davvie's eyes went wild. "You never even give me a chance to explain! And I don't need you trying to protect me."

He spun back to Hest when the Bingtowner snickered. Davvie's fists were clenched as he gritted out, "I don't play your sort of games, old man. I don't need to pretend I'm being forced. I've chosen to be who I am."

Sedric barely managed to dodge out of his way as Davvie stamped away down the stairs.

"Well. A misunderstanding, on all parts, I see." Hest

seemed completely unruffled. He smoothed the hair back from his brow and smiled at them both. "You shouldn't blame your boy, Carson." He smiled at Sedric as he added, "He's not the first youngster to find me attractive. Though I did misjudge how ready he was for me. Moved a bit fast for him, I suppppose." He tugged his cuffs straight.

For the first time, Sedric noted the red spot on Hest's left cheekbone. So. The boy had landed one on him.

Hest seemed to feel his gaze. He lifted his eyes to meet Sedric's and added, "Not like Sedric. He needed the game. And he was very, very ready for me."

Sedric found his voice. His words were soft. "You're right, Hest. I was ready. Ready for you, or any other predator. Just as naive as Davvie."

"Predator?" Hest lifted one sculpted brow. He transferred his gaze to Carson. "Is this his new pretense, perhaps for you? Nothing was his decision, I 'preyed' on him? Ridiculous. He was only too enthused to put himself into my control. He relished every moment of it, and he was a very apt student. I trust you've enjoyed all I taught him?"

Carson made a small sound. Sedric shot his hand out to rest on the hunter's chest. He felt oddly calm as he said, "Davvie was right about one thing, Carson. You didn't need to protect him. And you don't have to protect me, either."

The hunter looked at him with unreadable eyes. "Please go," Sedric added quietly.

Consternation and then hurt showed in his dark eyes. "I need to do this," Sedric said even more softly. "Trust me."

Carson's gaze searched Sedric's soul. Then he gave one slow nod and moved stoically away down the stairs.

"Well, well." Hest turned away from Sedric. He ran his hand along the tiles and set the dragons to dancing. He didn't turn to look at him. "Are you ready to come to your senses and return to Bingtown with me?"

"No."

"Oh, come. You've made your point. You left me, and I will tell you that I quickly discovered just how hard it was to replace you. I shouldn't have mocked your plan for us. I still think trafficking in dragon parts was a foolish venture, and I think events have proven me right. Am I correct in guessing that your current friend knows nothing of what your original intent was?"

Sedric found his heart thumping against his ribs. Why? Why was this so hard? He cleared his throat. "I doubt there is anything you could tell him that he doesn't already know about me. He's not like you, Hest. He listens when I talk."

"I should have listened, I'll admit that." Hest turned to look at him. The damn boy had landed two good blows to his ribs. They still hurt, but the epitaph "old man" that he had thrown had hurt even more. At least Sedric seemed to be coming to his senses. He'd sent his forest man away. Hest sensed what he wanted. Just enough sentiment to allow him to come back to Hest. And a touch of the old mastery to remind him how much he'd enjoyed it. Had he felt a moment of jealousy when he came upon Hest and the flustered boy? Hest thought so. He'd noticed how Sedric's eyes had lingered on his face.

"It's not too late for us," Hest said. He let his voice go deep on the words and was secretly delighted with the look of incredulity that blossomed on Sedric's face. He liked the scaling, he decided. Showing off Sedric's changed appearance in Bingtown would definitely add a fillip of triumph to his return. He was fairly confident that if he returned with Sedric's share of the wealth of Kelsingra to set at his father's feet, the old man would forgive the absence of his wife. His mother would certainly understand that Alise had become completely unsuitable to share their name. He'd tell her what he'd seen, and then beg her mercy and discretion in letting him quietly annul his marriage to Alise. He wouldn't marry again. Let his father name who he wanted as his heir. With Sedric's share of Kelsingra, he wouldn't need the family money to live very well indeed.

It could all be managed. All of it. Beginning with Sedric. "You were right. I admit it, and I apologize for doubting you. You gambled yourself and won us a fortune. I can't even calculate the value of what you've won for us. It isn't just in what we can take out of the city. People will want to come here, to visit. To have country homes, perhaps. Everything you dreamed for us can come true. Here, we can live openly, in luxury, as we wish. And when we go back to Bingtown, we can enjoy the best of everything the civilized world has to offer. Sedric, my boy, you've done it."

"I'm not your 'boy,' Hest." The words were spoken so quietly.

Hest shifted his tactics slightly. "How well I know that. Ah, well, we've both changed, haven't we? Sweet Sa, if you knew the half of what I've gone through to find you and bring you home! Well, someday we'll share that tale with the fellows, won't we? And have a good laugh about your sojourn in the wilderness. I'll wager you're more than ready for a comfortable home and a glass of good wine. And an evening alone with me." He smiled at him, an inviting smile that Sedric would well recall. He licked his lips.

Sedric was meeting his gaze steadily. His mouth was flat, unsmiling, his eyes unreadable. "No, Hest. No to all of it."

"No?" His grin grew wider. "Ah, you've always begun by saying no to me, haven't you? Sedric, you want me to make you change your mind, don't you? Well, I don't mind that. I don't mind that at all."

HEST SWAYED SLIGHTLY as he advanced. Sedric watched him come, preoccupied with trying to decide what it reminded him of. And then he knew. A snake. A snake after a mouse.

Except that he wasn't a mouse anymore. As Hest reached for him, Sedric shot his fist out, pivoting to put his weight into it. He felt it connect solidly, saw the other man stumble back against the wall. "No," he said again as Hest lifted both hands to his bleeding mouth. "No to all of it."

He turned and went down the stairs. He didn't look back. He went out of the baths and spotted Carson at the bottom of the steps, deep in conversation with Davvie. He was listening while Davvie gesticulated and then threw a punch at the air. Then the youngster looked up at his uncle earnestly. Sedric couldn't hear what was said, but at the end of it, he saw the hunter nod gravely. He reached out to tousle the boy's hair. In midreach, he suddenly changed the gesture to a clap on the shoulder. Davvie gave him a nod and a half smile before turning away from him. So. It wasn't all right, not completely, but in time, it would be.

Sedric increased the length of his stride and caught up with Carson as he started to walk away. He linked arms with him and then flinched when Carson covered his hand with his own.

Carson looked down and then glanced up at him in surprise. "Your knuckles are bleeding."

"Are they?" Sedric held his hand up for his own inspection. "No." He wiped the blood off on his cloak. "They're just bruised."

"Let me see." He took Sedric's hand, studied the puffing knuckles, then lifted it to his mouth. He kissed them gently, gravely. "All better," he told him.

Sedric bit his lower lip to keep it from trembling, but he didn't try to hide the tears that rose in his eyes at Carson's tenderness. "I think you're right," he agreed huskily.

They both startled as dragons trumpeted, a peculiar note in their cries. The sound was passed from one creature to the next, until it filled the sky over the city and echoed back from the hills. "What are they going on about?" Sedric wondered.

"It's an alarm. A stranger approaches." Carson was already studying the air above them.

Sedric lifted his eyes to the sky. He didn't ask Carson how he knew these things. The hunter just did. After a scan, he pointed. "There. Right at the horizon, very low. Black dragon. Kalo?"

Carson squeezed his shoulder. "You've a good eye, Bingtown boy. But that's not Kalo. He's bigger than Kalo. And Kalo was soaking in the baths." He squinted. "No. That's not one of our dragons."

The dragons shrieked again, more urgently, and began to converge, coming from all corners of the world to spiral above Kelsingra.

"Icefyre." Sedric spoke the name aloud. "It has to be the drake that Tintaglia spoke of. But why does he come here?"

DAMN, BUT IT hurt. Hest took his hand away from his

384 ROBIN HOBB

mouth, looked at the blood running down his wrist and grimaced. This sort of play had rules, as he had so clearly established with Sedric years ago! What was Sedric learning among these brutes? There was a limit, and Sedric had just found it. Play was play, but marring Hest's face was never on the menu. He'd pay for it now.

His fingers found the split in his lower lip. The taste of blood was all through his mouth; his own teeth had cut into his cheek. He blotted his lip on his cuff and scowled at the spreading stain as he walked to the top of the steps. "Sedric!" he barked, and then winced at the pain of shouting. "You've gone too far, Sedric! You know that."

He knew Sedric, knew him better than he knew himself. He always had, and that had been why he'd always been able to manage him. Sedric would be waiting at the bottom of the flight of steps, already repentant, already frightened by his own defiance. Perhaps weeping and desiring forgiveness and comfort. He dabbed at his split lip again, and his tongue found a loosened tooth. Damn him!

Forgiveness and comfort? He would get neither until he had apologized and atoned. And demonstrated his contrition. He waited. Don't break the discipline. Make Sedric come back to him. *Don't let him think I'm going to come running after him. Let him worry for a bit. Let him see I truly don't need him anymore.* It was always important to establish who was in charge early.

Hest jumped and then cowered at the first blast of dragon trumpets. When the racket continued, he straightened slowly. It wasn't an attack. They wouldn't attack their own city. Probably nothing more serious than dogs barking at one another, or howling at the moon. His mouth hurt, his ribs ached, and he decided he had waited long enough. Let Sedric think he had won this round. Give him a tiny triumph so he didn't feel totally beaten. It would make their next encounter even more interesting when Hest brought him back to his knees. He started down the stairs.

He reached the next landing, but Sedric wasn't there. Nor on the next. "Sedric!" He put a sharper note into his voice. He was wearying of this game. The youngster had bruised him; Sedric had cut his mouth and now this foolish chase. Not amusing. None of it.

He reached the main floor and scanned the foyer. No sign of Sedric. The door to the plaza was ajar, and a chorus of dragon noises and people's raised voices washed in. A young man's voice was suddenly raised, the higher pitch cutting through the noise. "It's as I told you! It's not revenge. It's self-preservation. They've given us no choice!"

No. Sedric would not seek out that sort of conflict, not right now. Sedric had no interest in politics. And he would have only one thing on his mind. He would want to be alone when Hest found him. The baths? It hurt his mouth to smile. Of course. What better site for reconciliation and reunion?

He pushed open the huge door to the room. It moved easily for such a large slab. Designed for the dragons who shared it, of course. He found it a rather disgusting concept but had no objection to bathing there when no dragons were about.

But one was. The immense creature, so dark blue as to be almost black, had just emerged from the water. The liquid was sheeting off his gleaming hide, running in rivulets onto the floor. It was obviously trying to leave via the door Hest had just entered. Hest halted where he stood and eyed the wet animal disdainfully. He crabbed a few steps sideways to try and see past him. "Sedric!" he called.

Not here.

The dragon's voice was a low rumble, the force of his thought against Hest's mind almost stunning. Others had claimed to hear the dragons speaking to them, but he had dismissed those claims as the product of susceptible minds. But there was no mistaking this. The dragon had spoken to him and he had understood it. Fascinating. He halted and stared at him, Sedric forgotten for the moment.

The dragon clamor outside grew louder.

Move out of my way.

This close, he suddenly realized how magnificent a creature a dragon might be. Like a prize stud horse. Only much larger. As with a horse, he knew the key was to dominate it. "My name is Hest." He kept his words simple and spoke clearly. "Do you have a name, dragon? What does your owner call you?"

The animal cocked his immense head like a puzzled dog. Then he yawned, showing some extremely large teeth and the interior of his mouth patterned in scarlet and yellow. He exhaled strongly, a foul blast of meat-scented moisture. *You are standing where I am going to walk. The others call to me.*

Hest stood firm. "Dragon, come here." He extended his hand and pointed to a spot directly in front of him.

When Hest didn't move, the dragon came a step nearer. Good. Obedience seemed to come to it easily. It spoke again. *Davvie serves me.* The dragon's eyes seemed to whirl slowly, thoughtfully. *Davvie does not like you. But I think I might.*

Hest stood his ground, his mind spinning with new thoughts, as the creature came closer to him. The dragon obeyed him, and he could understand what it said. The dragon might prefer him to Davvie. Better and better. Let the boy think on that when Hest took his dragon. Yes, and let Carson and Sedric mull it over, too. He imagined himself returning to Bingtown as an Elderling astride his own dragon. If he took the dragon, if he became an Elderling, would not he be able to claim his own place in Kelsingra, regardless of what Alise or Sedric thought of him?

It was perfect. Vengeance, beauty, long life, and wealth were all within his reach. All he had to do was master the dragon and transfer its loyalty from Davvie to himself.

The dragon had come very close now. He was quite a stunning creature, really. Extraordinary. What was it like to own a dragon? Sedric had one, as did his primitive friend. Even the little pink girl with the gold scaling had a dragon. How hard could it be to master one if someone like Sedric had done it?

The dragon's eyes spun like whirlpools, gleaming swirls of deepest blue mixed with black. Hest imagined himself dressed in black and silver, astride the creature. A black saddle and bridle, trimmed in silver and blue. They would alight in the center of the main market in Bingtown, mid-

morning when the trade was thickest. He imagined how
people would point and shout as they looked up at him on
his circling dragon. They would scatter before him as they
swooped down. "All eyes will be on me," Hest murmured,
entranced by his vision. He reached out to touch the dragon's muzzle.

It swung its head aside from his touch. That wouldn't
do. "Dragon, stand still when I reach for you." *Dragon?*
That wouldn't do. Evidently Davvie had neglected to give
his animal a name to answer to. Hest would correct that
right now. "I will give you a name now, a special name to
show you are mine." Easy enough. No harder than naming
a horse or dog. "Your name is Blue Glory now. Blue Glory.
Do you understand, dragon? You're mine now, not Davvie's,
and you have to learn to obey me. So when I call you Blue
Glory, you should come to me. And stand still when I reach
to touch you." Hest spoke simply and firmly, dominating the
animal with his stance and stare. He radiated confidence
and command as he reached out a hand to rest it on the dragon's muzzle.

The animal's eyes were spinning more rapidly. Deep gold
sparks seemed to ride the whirlpool of blue and black.

"That's better, Blue Glory. The sooner we understand
each other, the easier this will be."

Just as his fingertips brushed the animal's scaling, the
dragon swung his head aside, lifting his head high and looking down on Hest. "I understand you, human. And I think
I will give you a special name, too." The words rode a low
rumble of sound from the beast.

Extraordinary. But an excellent sign of how swiftly they
were bonding. Hest smiled at his dragon. "Shall I help you,
Blue Glory? You could call me Glory's Master. Or Silver
Rider."

The dragon still looked down on him, considering each
name carefully. His eyes spun faster and faster. "No. I think
not," he said, and amusement shimmered in the rumbling
voice. "I think I will name you 'Meat.'"

Then the creature turned his head sideways, his jaws
opened wide, and the gleaming teeth and brilliantly colored

maw came at Hest, swift as a serpent's strike. Hest jumped back, shouting in anger and fear, but the trumpeting of dragons outside swelled loud. Hest spun and dived for the steaming bath. The dragon snapped after him, and he felt a sharp tug at his leg before he fell free into the water. It had barely missed him.

The water was hot, almost scalding. Hest fought his way to the surface, sputtering and shuddering. He shook water from his eyes, snorted it out of his nose, and looked up to see the dragon standing at the edge of the pool. "I do like you," the creature said, and there was no mistaking the amusement in its voice. "You're delicious."

Hest drew a deep breath and prepared to dive beneath the steaming water. In one awful moment he glimpsed the red swirls in the water around him and grasped their significance. The dragon had not missed him. His leg was bleeding badly.

No.

His leg was gone.

He screamed then in the full horror of what had befallen him. Hest with one leg? Hest a pathetic cripple whom others would mock? "NO!" he shouted.

"Yes," rumbled Blue Glory.

The open jaws closed on him, and his last scream was engulfed in the scarlet and yellow cavern of the dragon's maw.

✦ ✦ ✦

Day the 16th of the Plough Moon

Year the 7th of the Independent Alliance of Traders
**From Erek Dunwarrow and Detozi, Keeper
of the Birds, Trehaug
To Reyall, Keeper of the Birds, Bingtown**

*Reyall, it may soon be that the Masters of the Birds
in Bingtown will request you to bring to them all
my breeding records, including my side notes and
nicknames for the birds, for an intense inspection and
review. Please do not be alarmed. I wish you to be
completely forthcoming with them and have complete
confidence that I do not have anything I wish to hide.*

*We wish we could tell you more at this time, but we
cannot. This note will be delivered to you by one or more
masters of the Guild. Please take no alarm from this.*

*Truly, all is well, and will soon, we hope, be even
better as a cloud of doubt that has hung over the Bird
Keepers' Guild is dispelled.*

Have faith in us.
Erek

✦ ✦ ✦

CHAPTER NINETEEN

ICEFYRE

Thymara peered at the black dragon, trying to discern what was wrong with him. She took a half step forward, and Tats seized her upper arm and drew her back. "He's mad with pain," Tats said apologetically. "He isn't one of ours, Thym. He might do anything."

The battered black dragon threw back his head and roared again. The insides of his mouth and throat were bright green with red streaks. When he dropped his head, a red froth dripped from his mouth to sizzle on the paving stones. He stared around at all the gathered folk, his eyes swirling madly. Thymara could not tell if the sounds he was making indicated pain or whether he was threatening anyone who came near. He had not uttered a word that she understood. His half-folded wings were ragged and rent. Some of the tears looked old, but there were recent ones as well. He looked both healthy and yet battered. He lifted his head and roared again. Then he curled his head in and down and swung his head from side to side.

"Can't we help him?" Thymara spoke the words but didn't step forward again. When the dragons sounded the alarm, their keepers had come running from all directions. Thymara had thought Mercor and the other drakes would drive the black intruder away, but they had let him land.

"Icefyre." Sintara had confirmed his name for her when she had reached toward her queen. "Stay clear of him. I think he's mad."

All the keepers had gathered to stare at the oldest dragon in the world, but they had halted at a sensible distance. Mercor, Sestican, and Sintara were on the ground. Even they had not approached within striking distance of the black. The others circled overhead in a whirlwind of colors and wings. The keepers exchanged looks, but no one approached him.

And into the midst of the chaos came Heeby and Rapskal, dropping through the circling dragons like a dumpling falling into soup. The red dragon landed ungracefully, and her rider slid from her shoulder.

Tats gave a distressed groan.

"What is he thinking?" Thymara demanded of no one. Since their night in the well she'd kept Rapskal at arm's length. There had been moments, during a meal or a shared task, when he'd seemed to be his old self, and her heart had yearned for them to be friends as they'd once been. But then there were the moments when he seemed completely foreign to her, calling for death by dragon for the prisoners. Or, as now, dropping down into their midst in extravagant and fanciful dress. Rapskal had put a heavy shaft to one of the spearheads he'd found in the old armory, and he brandished it aloft as he walked in a slow circle around the black dragon. The scale armor he wore over his Elderling tunic and trousers shifted as he walked, and it seemed to Thymara that he deliberately rocked his hips as he walked to encourage the movement. It was effective. The sunlight caught and bounced off it, making him gleam black and gold. Heeby wore a matching harness. A water skin hung from it, and something that was perhaps a horn. Thymara could not identify the rest of the items that dangled from it. The red dragon jingled as she pranced to follow Rapskal, well pleased with herself.

He circled the growling and groaning dragon once before stopping directly in front of it.

"Now what?" Tats demanded.

"Rapskal, no!" Thymara cried, but he did not react to that name and she would not call him Tellator.

Rapskal walked fearlessly up to the roaring black, dropped to one knee before him, and bowed his head. At the sight of him, the black dragon's groans suddenly stilled. Rapskal lifted his head and his voice rang out clearly. "Kelsingra welcomes you, Glorious One! How may we serve you?" He swept a wide arm to indicate the outer circle of keepers and ship's crew. "I am Rapskal, Elderling to Heeby, the wondrous scarlet queen. I and all my fellow Elderlings would be honored to guide you to the Silver well and watch you drink. The baths await you, and attendants who would swoon with joy to groom every one of your glorious scales! As the dragons of Kelsingra have permitted you to come here, the Elderlings of Kelsingra stand ready to serve you. Tell us your need, O Eldest of Dragons, and we will rush to meet it."

Silence flowed in to follow his words. The black dragon regarded him intently. Rapskal continued his obeisance, his face lifted fearlessly. At last the creature spoke. "Icefyre am I called by humans. At least one here recalls the old courtesies of your kind!" His gaze swept over them all, dragons and humans. "By treachery, I am poisoned. Humans have done this to me, luring me with fat cattle filled with death. If you have Silver, then lead me there. But I did not come here seeking Elderling praises or even Silver, though I welcome both. I came to see if any dragons still lived who are worthy of that name, if any would rise to avenge me against the ones who seek to kill dragons for their flesh."

Rapskal stood and lifted his spear high. "If no other rises to serve in that glorious cause, I will go. Fearless Heeby and

I will take to the skies and slay any who have dared to lift a hand against dragons."

Mercor spoke. "I will lead you to the Silver and you may drink your fill. Then we *dragons* will speak of vengeance, when you are rested and all are gathered." The golden drake's gaze swept over the gathered Elderlings and came to rest on Rapskal. "Do not speak for dragons, Rapskal. Not even Heeby." His tone was severe. "Dragons alone can judge the gravity of the offense, and dragons alone will determine if it is an uprising against dragonkind, or foolish herdsmen seeking to claim grazing beasts as theirs alone."

Instead of calming the black dragon, Mercor's words seemed to focus his anger. He lifted his head high, eyes whirling as he stared at the golden dragon. "Humans knew where I hunted and deliberately put out poisoned cattle. When I ate, I slept, and awoke sickened and weak. Then they came out with nets to snare me, and spears to let my blood flow and basins to catch it. They did not seek to kill me because I had eaten cattle. They put out cattle in the hopes that a dragon might become prey for them! But I was not as weakened as they thought. Many I killed! And many more will I kill!"

"Only if you live," Mercor pointed out calmly. "First, we must give you strength against the poison. This way to the Silver."

Mercor wheeled and walked away. Icefyre let his gaze wander balefully over the gathered humans, Elderlings, and dragons. Then he turned to follow Mercor. The other dragons fell in behind them, and the keepers parted to let the procession through. Heeby looked at Rapskal and then trailed after the others. Rapskal remained standing where he was. He looked mildly stunned.

The vortex of circling dragons shifted, and Thymara suspected they would land near the Silver reservoir and hold their council there. The keepers were left standing, looking at one another uneasily. Into the silence and stillness, Tintaglia descended. The blue queen had recovered most of her strength, but she still lacked flesh. As she landed, Malta hurried to meet her. Like her dragon, the Elderling queen was still recovering, but Thymara had to smile at her impeccable grooming. She wore not a tunic and trousers as most of the keepers did but a flowing gown with draped sleeves. Her face was still thin, but her hair had been dressed in meticulous curls heaped high on her head and framing her scarlet crest. Her face shone with welcome for the dragon who had saved her child.

Tintaglia accepted the welcome as her due. She looked after Icefyre's vanishing procession. "He made no cry for vengeance when I was the one who was dying," she observed sourly to her Elderling. "Yet let them succeed in giving him a bellyache, and he will melt all their cities with venom." She snorted in disgust, and added, "Vain as he is, he is right. And so I will tell the rest of them. The time has come. The city of Chalced must be destroyed." She looked at her Elderling and added, "You should stay here. Dragons alone will decide what we will do next." Malta halted, startled, and Tintaglia strode away from her.

"We have to take action!" Rapskal was undeterred in his effort to rally them. "We must begin to ready ourselves to ride to war now!"

Thymara sighed, and Tats took her hand. Harrikin lifted his voice. "We know nothing of war. Is this our vengeance to take?"

Rapskal shook his head as he turned to confront him. "It's as I told you! It's not revenge. It's self-preservation. They've given us no choice!"

"I'm afraid he's right." Thymara was shocked to hear calm, sensible Alise taking that stand. The Bingtown woman's face was grave rather than fired with enthusiasm for war as she added, "You heard what he said. This wasn't about a dragon preying on herds and cattle owners becoming angry. This is humans hunting dragons for meat, scales, and blood. We have all heard Malta's tale. We have seen Tintaglia's suffering. The Chalcedeans we hold have admitted it is why they came, and now that they have failed, others will be sent. It cannot be ignored any longer." She was not speaking in a loud voice, but her words were clear, and the keepers had begun to gather in a circle around her. Thymara thought that Leftrin looked as surprised as she herself felt, but he did not interrupt or contradict her. "I cannot speak for the dragons and what they will do, but at the least, humans should speak out against it."

"They will not respond to people speaking. When has Chalced ever listened to us asking them to respect our boundaries and to stop preying on our ships?" Hennesey stood with his arms crossed on his chest.

"So it's war! Who goes with me?" Rapskal asked. He looked around at them all. Did anyone breathe? Thymara knew she did not.

He pulled something from his pouch, shook it out, and dragged it on over his head. A head covering. A helmet that shaped to his head, making him appear far less human as it capped his skull with overlapping scales. He gave his head a shake and a crest like a parrot's stood up on the helm. Thymara was torn between a desire to laugh or to gasp in horror as he became even more foreign to her. "All you who desire to be warriors must follow me to the armory, to see what weapons we can repair and what armor will fit you all. Some of your dragons will accept harnesses and be willing to bear you."

"And others won't," Tats predicted sourly. He stepped forward. "Rapskal, we are not warriors. I am good at hunting, and if a man lifts a hand to me, then I will stand up to him. But you are speaking of attacking a city, days and days away from here. A city full of people who have never even thought of coming here to prey on dragons. It's a completely insane idea. And the dragons have not yet said that they wish to go to battle. They told us, clearly, that it was their decision."

Rapskal cocked his head. He appeared to listen for a time, then took a breath and looked around with confidence. "Icefyre has finished drinking. He believes he will soon be fully recovered. And the others have decided to take Tintaglia's advice. Strike at their main city, where their duke rules. Remind them that dragons are not riverpigs to be slaughtered as they wish, but the lords of the Three Realms, Earth, Sea and Sky." He looked at Tats and said in a voice that was more Rapskal's than Tellator's, "Tats, will you ride beside me?"

Tats hesitated, looked at Thymara, and clasped her hand tightly for a moment before he let go of it. "I can't let you go alone, my friend. I'll go with you."

The dragon doors to the baths swung open, and Kalo sauntered out. He looked fresh from the baths, but a strand of gut still dangled from the side of his mouth. Thymara reflected that for all their superior claims, not one of the dragons could groom well without a keeper's aid.

"Davvie!" the immense blue-black dragon bellowed. "Davvie, fetch a harness for me. We fly tomorrow at dawn."

Davvie stepped forward, eluding Carson's reaching hand. His eyes were wide, but he did not seem altogether unwilling as he objected, "Kalo, we cannot be ready that fast. There are weapons to repair, and so much to learn."

The dragon snorted disdainfully. "Begin now, and you will be ready when I summon you. Those who come with us will learn on the way. Icefyre has drunk from the Silver. He is recovering swiftly. Once he has hunted and eaten, we will take vengeance to the Duke of Chalced. I fly with Icefyre. Ready yourself or do not, as you please. This is dragons' business. We fly at dawn."

Davvie stared at him. "I thought you were going hunting after you bathed . . ." he objected weakly.

"I am fed well enough for now. To the armory and quickly. I wish to be first to make a choice of the colors there." With a fine disregard for his keeper, Kalo strode away.

Sintara watched the others as Icefyre drank from the Silver well. Tintaglia eyed the black dragon speculatively, as if measuring him against the other males. He was definitely larger than the others, but she knew that was not the best criteria in selecting a mate. She lifted her eyes and looked back toward the baths; watching for Kalo? Sintara copied the older female and compared him to Sestican and then looked at Mercor. High summer was the time for mating, but it was never too soon to assess one's choices.

Icefyre lifted his head at last. His muzzle dripped silver in languid drops. He stepped away from the well, stretched, and then sprawled out on the paving stones. He curled his head and his tail toward the center of his body and was abruptly asleep. Mercor advanced a step toward him and sniffed the air around him. "He was sickened but he will recover, and quickly," the golden dragon announced.

He looked around at the others. Sintara tried to remember the last time they had all gathered in a group. Even when they had been on the other side of the river, they had seldom convened. *Cassarick,* she thought. *Back in the days before we were true dragons. When we were caught at the edge of the river, living in mud, fed on carrion.* Then Mercor had rallied them, and together they had concocted the plan that would persuade the humans to help them find Kelsingra. They had thought they were lying when they hinted of a storehouse of Elderling wealth in Kelsingra. Little had they realized that, to humans, the whole city was a vast treasure.

She thought of the days and distance they had traveled, the changes they had undergone. They had made their keepers into Elderlings and learned to feed themselves, to fly and to hunt. They had become dragons. And tomorrow?

"We go to battle against humans," Mercor said gravely. "Truly, there is no choice." He looked at Tintaglia. "You have done this before?"

She gazed at him oddly. "I have, and in my own life. But dragons have all done this before and more than once. You have no memories of this?"

Sintara kept silent. She possessed no such memories. Mercor was thoughtful for a time, his eyes whirling as if he spun his way back through years and lives. "A few," he conceded. "But our memories are incomplete. We were too short a time in our cases, and you were but one dragon spread among many serpents when you helped us to spin them. You did what you could, but we are not dragons as you and Icefyre are. And our Elderlings are not as you recall them. They are newly made, and still discovering the memories of those who went before them. They will not know how to fight, or how to aid us in fighting." He looked at her gravely and asked, "How dangerous is it to make war on humans? To ourselves and to our keepers?"

The large blue queen looked astonished that he would ask such a question. "We cannot worry about that!" she snapped. "Humans have risen against us. You saw my wounds! I nearly died of them. Icefyre was poisoned, but even before that, humans had attacked him, with nets and spears. They do not fear us as they should, and while they do not fear, they do not respect us. I have traveled far and had much to do with humans. Some cannot understand us at all when we try to speak to them; they think us dumb beasts, no different from a lion or a wolf. Or a cow, awaiting slaughter. Others are so overwhelmed at the sight of us that they are idiotic in their worship. You have been fortunate in the ones they chose to send with you when you left Cassarick. The changes they had already undergone seem to have readied them to be fit companions to you.

"But of the humans you will encounter where we must go? They are nothing like the humans you have known. They will try to kill you. They will not greet you or speak to you first. They will feel no wonder, but only the awe that is based on terror. Fear will motivate them, and killing you is all they will think of. And you *can* be killed by them. Do not think of them as puny or stupid. They are sly and treacherous, and they will kill you if they can." Her gaze raked over the assembled dragons as if they opposed her. Her own words were inflaming her anger.

"You can stay here and hide from them. But the longer you wait before you make them recall their proper place in the world, the more resistance they will give you when you find you must defend yourselves. They will discover the places that we must use, the nesting beach, and the clay banks that we must use to spin our cases to change from serpent to dragon. They will find them, and they will fortify them against us. Do you want to wait until you have to fight for them? Wait until they come in and devastate our nests and the unhatched young?" Her colors had brightened, and Sintara could see her poison glands working.

Mercor spoke his question calmly. "Our keepers. Our Elderlings. If we take them into battle with us, the other humans will try to kill them, also?"

Tintaglia looked amazed at the stupidity of Mercor's question. "Of course they will! And they will most likely shoot first at them. Your Elderlings will be more vulnerable to their weapons, too, as well as to our own venom. Our attack must be coordinated. One dragon attacking a city can do as it pleases. But when we fly to war together, then we must consider the wind, and what targets we wish to destroy, and how to keep venom from drifting onto another dragon or his Elderling. So. If you bear your keepers into battle, you must have a care for them, if you wish them to survive." She paused as if thinking. "But they are useful to have in a battle. If you are caught on the ground, they will fight alongside us. When your eyes are fixed on one enemy, they can spy another one behind you and give warning. They can slay only one at a time, but they are useful." She paused and then added, "Sometimes it is kinder to take them with you than to leave them alone. If you do not return, they will mourn and then die anyway." She walked forward to the Silver well. As she bent her head to drink, she added, "It is a decision every dragon must make for herself."

"THEY FLY AT dawn," Leftrin told her. He and Alise were leaning on Tarman's rail, drinking tea and looking across the ever restless river. "And I think we should leave tomorrow too."

She looked at him in astonishment. "Tomorrow?"

He nodded. "My dear, Reyn has sent his last bird, but news such as this cannot depend on those little wings. Nor do I think it was well trained, for when he set it free, it seemed to fly off randomly. No. When the dragons take flight, Tarman must leave as well. The dragons all say it is dragon business, but Chalced may very well view it as a strike by Bingtown and the Rain Wilds. We need to get to Cassarick and warn them, so they can send on word from there. The Traders must be given the chance to prepare for whatever may come."

The sun was setting on a day that had shaken Alise's world to its foundations. Yesterday, her life had had a routine. She had Leftrin in her arms again at night, a fascinating city to study, and a lifetime of useful tasks before her. Then Icefyre had arrived, a dragon such as dragons had once been. His accusations of human treachery and his call for vengeance had fallen on fertile soil. She had been willing to admit that something must be done, but she was horrified at how quickly the dragons had decided to destroy Chalced. For that was their avowed ambition. Alise and Leftrin both suspected that Tintaglia had already been preaching the necessity of war to the other dragons, just as Rapskal had been trying to stir the keepers. And the keepers! How willingly the youngsters had leaped at the chance to ride off to war. They had raced one another to the armory, selecting armor and battle colors, working earnestly to repair ancient weapons. Sylve had come to her, begging her to come and help them make sense of the dragon harnesses and armor. And so she had gone, taking her sketchbook of all the ancient murals, and using her drawings as examples of how dragons were once garbed for battle. She had been torn between fascination at making her sketches come to life, and dismay that she would help the young Elderlings ride off to risk their own lives.

And to kill.

It made no sense to her. When had the keepers become capable of killing? Did they not understand what they were going into? Her own memories of the Chalcedeans invading Bingtown flooded back into her mind. She smelled again the stink of the burned-out warehouses in the days that had followed the raids and looting. Her mother's sister and her entire family had perished in the first attack, slain in their nightrobes, even the youngest girl, a child of three. Alise had gone with her mother, to find the bodies and take them to their house on a cart and wash them for burial . . .

"Alise? Do you agree we must leave tomorrow?" Leftrin took her hand and tugged at it gently to turn her gaze to meet his. She had been silent and thoughtful for too long. He would be fearing she was wandering in her stone memories again. She would not tell him she had been somewhere far darker.

"The dragons are right. The old saying is true. 'Sooner or later, there is always war with Chalced.' It is all they know there. And better that we take war to them than that they bring it to us again. Leaving tomorrow isn't a problem, my dear. I have little enough to pack. I've spent so much time on Tarman lately that most of my things are already in your cabin."

"Our cabin," he said, and grinned. "Our home now. I wish I could offer you a more pleasant voyage than what is before us. The crew will rig shelters on the deck, and more than half of the slaves have decided to build new lives here. The other slaves want to be taken back to Trehaug. But even leaving some behind, the galley will always be crowded. I'm glad the weather has turned milder. Half our passengers are going to have to sleep out on the decks."

"I'm sure I will be fine. As long as I can retreat to the cabin and have a bit of time alone with you, I can manage. And I'm looking forward to journeying with Tarman again. He will show these 'impervious' sailors how a true liveship runs the river." She ran her hand along Tarman's railing in a caress, as if she stroked a dragon. Leftrin shook his head in wonder as he felt his ship give a shiver of pleasure. Her hand stilled as she added in a lower voice, "But I'm not looking forward to being around Hest. I know I must see him, and so must you. Pledge to me now that you will not let him provoke you to violence."

"Me? With my mild temper?"

She seized his shirtsleeve and shook it lightly. "I'm not teasing you, Leftrin. The man's arrogance knows no bounds. No matter what anyone says or does to him, he sees the world only as it relates to him and what he wants. You haven't truly seen how he is. Any situation, he always finds a way to turn to his advantage. He will find some sort of profit from this. Some advantage for himself. Nothing else has ever mattered to him."

"Well . . ." Leftrin hesitated, and Alise felt dread rising in her soul. He met her gaze, wet his lips, and added, "Transporting Hest may be a problem that we don't actually have."

"The keepers haven't offered him asylum here, have they? Who did he talk to? They should be warned! That man can make any lie believable! Does Sedric know Hest will be staying here?" She felt sick with dread.

"No. Nothing like that, my dear. Actually, I've been wondering how to tell you this. Harrikin has been in charge of those keeping watch on the captives. He always had at least two guards on the doors at all times. He allowed a few of the captives to go out for walks, well chaperoned, but the Chalcedean hunters and Trader Candral, he kept on a tight leash."

She was nodding, her brow furrowed. "And Hest?"

Leftrin licked his lips, clearly uncomfortable with the news he had to share. "Hest is missing." He blurted the announcement and added hastily, "When they took a count tonight, there was no sign of him. Davvie was the last guard to see him. He let him go up the tower and look out of the windows. Sedric and Carson both vouch that they last saw him there, on the second landing. They admit there was a quarrel and it got physical, but they left him there and walked out right in the middle of Icefyre coming down. The guards didn't leave their posts, but they were distracted. Hest could have come down the steps, gone into the baths, hidden, and then escaped when everyone was caught up in Rapskal's speech making. However it happened, Hest is gone."

Alise felt sick. Hest. Hest loose in her city, looking for treasure. Hest where she might round a corner on one of her rambles and suddenly confront him. She knew an instant of chilling dread. Then she reconsidered and smiled at Leftrin. "He'll have gone treasure hunting, to try to fill his pockets with whatever he can carry. But soon enough, he'll discover that we have the only food supplies in the city. And if he knows somehow that this boat is leaving tomorrow, he'll want to be on it. I doubt he wants to stay in Kelsingra any longer than he has to." She took a breath and squared her shoulders. "Eventually, I'll sit down with him and get what I need from him. But until then, I'm not going to worry about him."

"Then neither shall I," he promised, and he drew her closer. Then he looked at the sun and sighed. "Go gather your things. I have to stay here. The crew is loading supplies for tonight. They'll bring our passengers down in the morning."

THE MOMENT SHE opened the door to her chamber, she was aware of him. Rapskal was sitting on the edge of her bed, waiting for her. She halted where she was, the light from the long hall spilling into the room. Wariness rose in her, and she felt a surge of hatred for the circumstances that made her so wary of him.

As she moved into the room, the light strengthened. "Shouldn't you be sleeping?" she asked him, her voice tight.

"I wanted to see you before I left tomorrow. I don't know how long I'll be gone. Or if I'll come back. I thought we might have a last night together. Not a commitment from you, just a last night."

Thymara stared at him. He looked very fine. His long hair had been brushed until it gleamed and was fastened back from his face. It bared his features and made him look older than she knew he was. But his face had changed from the boyish Rapskal who had embarked on the expedition with her. His jaw was stronger, the planes of his face flatter. Heeby had scaled him red to match her, but his scales were as fine and supple as those on a tiny fish. The tunic he wore was gold and brown, and the breadth of his shoulders filled it. He was muscled differently from the other keepers, his body deliberately built rather than showing the strengths of his work. His eyes gleamed blue at her.

She realized she was staring at him. A smile very slowly came to his face. He lifted a hand, crooked a finger at her.

"No," she said. "I want you out of my room, Tellator."

"Thymara, please. I know I was harsh that night. It was necessary. Think of what would have happened if I hadn't insisted you go down the well. It was much more than you finding the Silver for us. You found yourself. You discovered anew who you were meant to be, how strong you were . . ."

"Stop it." She walked swiftly to a bag on the vanity table, opened it, and drew out the moon-faced pendant. It glowed at her touch. "You should take this with you."

"It's yours."

"It's not mine; it was never mine, and I don't want it. I'm not Amarinda, and I don't want to be Amarinda."

He hadn't moved. "You don't have to be Amarinda for me. In this life, I loved Thymara long before I knew that I had loved Amarinda."

She crossed the room, and when he made no move to take the pendant, she dropped it in his lap. He caught her wrist. She didn't struggle against his grip, but only said, "If you don't let go now, I'm going to hit you as hard as I can in the face."

He gave a snort of amusement. "You might try, but it would never land on me." He let go of her wrist, and she stepped away.

"You're not Rapskal," she said unevenly, hating that her voice caught in her throat. "Rapskal wouldn't act like this. He wouldn't talk to me this way. Rapskal was strange and silly, but he was also honest and honorable. And yes, I loved him. I don't love you."

His eyes followed her as she moved away from him. "I'm Rapskal. I've always been Rapskal."

"You were Rapskal. You're someone else now. Rapskal would never talk to me this way, would never resort to trickery or pry at me with emotions—"

"Everyone changes," he said, cutting off her words.

She looked at him. Tears threatened, but she would not weep in front of Tellator. Rapskal would have known that she wept for loss. Tellator would see it as feminine weakness. With a sickening lurch of her heart, she realized that there was enough of Amarinda in her to know exactly how he would react to her tears. "Not everyone changes as you have. Rapskal let you in and you became him. But if he had never touched the stone, he would never have become you. He would have grown and changed but—"

"You're being ridiculous!" He laughed. "Are you saying I should have grown and changed only exactly as you wanted me to? Am I a plant, to be snipped and pruned and kept in a pot? Is that what you want? Someone you can completely control, someone that you dictate exactly who and what he is? How is that fair? What sort of a love did you have for me, that demands that I must always remain the same? If you had never groomed a dragon, you would not be the woman you are now. Does that mean your changes are wrong? Can you go back and be the Thymara you were the day we left Cassarick?"

"No," she admitted. She took a ragged breath. His words were like a shower of stones. He spoke so quickly, built his logic so fast that by the time she'd seen the fault of his reasoning in one thought, he was ten thoughts away from it. His voice was low and reasonable, but she felt battered by his words. She spoke quickly. "I'd give anything to speak to the Rapskal who journeyed here with me. He is the one I wish I could embrace one last time. Because I now know that I will never see him again, regardless of whether you come back or not."

He opened his arms. "I'm here, Thymara. I'm here right now, and always have been. You're the one who has refused to grow and change. You want to stay the girl who scampered through the treetops and accepted her father's rules. Your parents made all your decisions for you, and now that you're on your own, you still can't step away and decide things for yourself. You want nothing to change, Thymara. But things that don't change die. And even after death, change happens. You are asking the impossible. And if you keep requiring the impossible of your friends, they are going to grow and change and leave you behind. There you are right now, always standing apart and alone. Is that what you want? To be alone the rest of your life? Is that how you are choosing to grow? You used to be so indignant at how Jerd regarded you, but truly, what did you expect? She was growing into this new life. And you were not."

The hateful, painful tears spilled. She knew that he twisted the facts, that what he said was not true, but the words wounded her all the same. She gave up trying to talk to him. Gave up trying to defend herself from Tellator. "You drowned him," she said in a low savage voice. "You pulled him down and drowned him."

He shook his head at her, and his eyes went hard. "You want me to be silly and boyish, don't you? To chatter like a brainless squirrel, to hold your hand and run beside you and never think of you as a woman or of myself as a man. Why would I want that? The other keepers are beginning to respect me and my dragon. Listen to what you are saying! To win your love, I must remain the laughable idiot Rapskal, keeper of foolish, tubby Heeby. Is that what you are saying?"

His words trampled her. "That's not what I'm saying," she protested. "You're twisting everything."

"No. I'm just making you look at things as they are. Do you want to love a lackwit boy, a bumbler, the butt of the jokes? Or do you want to love a man, a competent fellow who can protect you and provide for you?"

She shook her head, helpless before the onslaught of his words. "Stop talking about Rapskal like that," and it was as if she pleaded with a stranger to stop mocking her friend. She just wanted it all to stop. She wanted him to go away, but also wanted to never have the memory of this horrid, useless quarrel. The realization came to her, as clear as water. "You're not trying to talk to me anymore. You're not trying to talk me into being Amarinda; you're not even trying to get me to spread my legs for you tonight. You're just trying to hurt me now. To say anything that will hurt me because I won't let you rule me. The Rapskal I loved would never do this to me. Or to anyone."

His face changed. It was only for a moment. Then the lines of his jaws and eyes firmed again, and she had to wonder if it was a trick, a deception, that for a moment she had glimpsed her old friend. The man stood abruptly. The moon pendant fell unheeded to the floor.

"I came here to say farewell," he said harshly. "If all I wanted was a woman to spread her legs, well, Jerd would doubtless oblige. I wanted you to become all you should be, Thymara. To grow into being the sort of woman that is suited to a man like me. And you've changed our farewell into a stupid, childish argument about who I am. So. Have it your way. I'm leaving. I'm leaving this room, and you, and tomorrow I'm leaving the city. And if I never return, well, I'm sure you won't regret that you turned your last chance to bid me good-bye into another one of your silly plays. I can't waste any more time on you. Tomorrow I fly, to lead the dragons in their vengeance against Chalced. To put an end to people hunting dragons. That doesn't seem to be something you much care about."

The cold river of his words tumbled and bruised her on the rocks, drowning her in his acid criticism. She pointed wordlessly at the door. Tears streamed down her cheeks, and she fought the sobs that tried to rise and choke her. He stalked to the door and she followed, two paces behind, out of reach. *I fear him,* she thought, and she knew by that admission that the love she had felt for wild, silly, gentle, thoughtful Rapskal was only a memory.

He turned in the hallway, his eyes hard and glittering as jewels. "One more thing," he said coldly.

She shut the door in his face. She crossed the room and sat down on the small chair in front of the mirrored vanity. She looked at herself, at the winged Elderling Thymara.

And then she let her tears take her.

"Dawn," Thymara scoffed. "I think the dragons meant, 'After we wake up and when we feel like it.'"

"They need the sun." Tats excused their late arrival. "And it is important for them to have the Silver, as much as they can drink. They will fly faster and longer."

"And their venom will be all the more potent," Thymara added. "Sintara told me so. She said that Tintaglia had counseled them all to drink deeply before they departed."

The small group fell silent. The force was finally massing in the middle of the Square of the Dragons as the sun approached noon. All the dragons were going. Some, like Heeby and Kalo and Sestican, had chosen elaborate harnesses. Others had submitted grudgingly to a simple strap that secured a perch for a rider. A few, like Sintara, had refused any harness and even the idea of carrying a rider into battle. Sintara had dismissed Thymara's offer to go with her with a brusque "You'd be in my way." Fente had listened to Tats's ardent pleas to accompany her with great pleasure, but in the end she, too, had dismissed him. He now watched the others with undisguised envy. Davvie was already perched high on Kalo, staring around him as if he had never seen Kelsingra or his fellow keepers before. A half smile came and went on his face. Thymara watched him and wondered why all the boys were so eager to go to war.

Reyn was going too. Tintaglia was resplendent in a jeweled harness, the metallic plates fastened together with wires. She had chosen gold and a pale sky blue that set off her own indigo scaling. Next to her, Reyn wore a helm of pale blue and an Elderling tunic of the same color. There had been no armor that fit him. He had dismissed it with, "It would have been too hot and heavy anyway. And at least this time, when I travel with Tintaglia, she will not squeeze me in half with her claws as she nearly did the last time I flew with her."

His attempt to make light of his departure with the dragon failed with his wife. Malta was not pleased to let him go and not only because she feared for him. No, *she* had wanted to be the one to ride the queen into battle. Her anger at what had been done to her dragon had only grown as the full tale became known. And she had old reasons of her own to wish revenge upon Chalced, as well as her more recent injuries at their hands. "The vengeance should be mine! I have never forgotten my days aboard a Chalcedean ship, and at their mercy. Nor will I ever forgive that they tried to kill my child!" Only her baby's needs had kept her in the city and on the ground.

Jerd had not wanted to go, but Veras had insisted. Thymara pitied her. Her face was pale and strange with all her hair tucked away under a helm. She gripped one of their old bows, and her quiver was full of hunting arrows. She sat on the ground near her queen and looked as if she might be sick. Sylve stood beside her, looking more insubstantial than ever in the sleek-fitting armor. Harrikin stood staring at her, his heart in his eyes. His dragon had refused him. He had begged Veras to take him instead of Jerd, but the queen had refused, and Ranculos had been livid with jealousy at the idea. "You will stay here," he had told his keeper, and Harrikin was left with no other choice. Nortel was going and looked almost as pleased as Rapskal about it.

On the steps of the baths, seven former slaves sat watching the chaos and pageantry as if it were a puppet show. Long servitude had left harsh marks on all of them, minds as well as bodies. Thymara wondered if they fully grasped that the *Tarman* had truly departed, leaving them here to begin new lives. Only a few had adopted the Elderling garb they had been offered. The others had washed and mended their tattered clothes and seemed to be grateful that they were allowed time to do that. They still kept to themselves and spoke mostly Chalcedean to one another.

Rapskal was everywhere, striding about, directing keepers to tighten or loosen a harness strap, asking each keeper if he or she had filled a water bag and packed rations. He had a practiced air to his motions and questions that near broke Thymara's heart. She knew it was Tellator who was seeing to his soldiers as she watched. She watched him sternly assist Jerd to mount and stand by her as she settled into place on Veras. The other keepers imitated her.

Spit had insisted that he would carry no one, not even Carson. They had quarreled about it, and when the hunter had attempted to put a harness on the silver dragon, Spit had hissed at him. Mercor had intervened. "This is something a dragon decides for himself," he had warned Carson gravely. The hunter stood beside Relpda and looked up at Sedric perched on her back. Tightly packed gear bags hung from the rings on her bell-studded harness. Thymara thought to herself that Carson had packed everything he could possibly imagine Sedric needing. The men regarded each other gravely. Carson reached out to touch Sedric's boot, nodded tightly, and then turned away. She saw Sedric swallow and lift his face to stare into the distance. Thymara shook her head sadly for them.

"Kase and Boxter?" she asked Tats.

"Going. Alum isn't. You know how Arbuc loves to show off when he flies. He didn't want to worry about spilling Alum off if he did a back loop." He sighed and shook his head. "It's going to be very strange to be such a small group here in the city. Especially with Tarman and most of the captives gone."

She touched his hand. "At least we'll be together," she reminded him.

He didn't look at her. His eyes were following Fente. She had chosen a bright yellow harness, and once Tats had adjusted it for her, his dragon had dismissed him. "I wish we were both going with them."

Malta drifted over to stand with them. In silence, they watched Rapskal climb up the straps that dangled from Heeby's harness and take his place in a high-backed saddle almost between her wings. Once settled, he lifted his horn to his lips and blew out a precise ascension of notes. "Tellator." Thymara growled the name to herself and looked away from the Elderling who had stolen the boy she had known. Heeby gathered herself under him and instead of her familiar trundling takeoff, vaulted into the air, bearing him up with her.

In the next moment, Thymara and Tats were blasted with wind as the rest of the dragons launched into flight. The beating of their wings battered her ears and blew her hair across her face. The rank smell of dragon musk assailed her and then, just as abruptly, they were standing in the silent square, looking up as the dragons grew smaller above them. She blinked dust from her eyes.

Malta spoke into the silence. "Tintaglia's gone, and Reyn with her." The baby she held hiccupped, and she patted him absently. "I never imagined how hard it would be to watch them both leave us." She folded the child closer to her.

Thymara heard her unvoiced thought. How many of them would return and when?

"Oh, Fente, be careful," Tats murmured, his eyes fixed on his diminishing green dragon. He turned to Malta. "I don't even know how far Chalced is from here, or how long it will take them to get there."

Malta shook her head. "No one knows how long it takes a dragon to fly anywhere. They have clear weather, at least for starting the journey. The dragons will have to take time to hunt each day, and they will sleep at night when it's dark. But they will travel straight this time rather than following the river. So I have no idea at all." She gave a sigh. "Tarman left this morning with a full load of passengers, Tillamon among them."

"Why didn't you go?" Tats asked her curiously.

She looked startled. "This is my home now," she said. "Kelsingra is the city of Elderlings. I may go back to visit Trehaug or Bingtown someday. Or perhaps my family will come here. But Ephron will grow up here, among his own kind. He will never go veiled. Kelsingra is where we belong. This is our home now."

"Mine, too," Tats admitted, and Thymara nodded.

Spring sunlight glittered on the dragons in the distance. Alum drifted over to join them. It was a small, disconsolate group that stood in the plaza and watched the dragons wing away into the distance. Carson cleared his throat. "Well. There's work to do. From what Thymara has told us, there's a danger from that well if we can't find a way to cap it in times of high Silver. And the dock isn't going to build itself. Nor those boats get cleaned up." He looked up at the sky. "No sense standing around wasting daylight. The sooner we start, the sooner we're finished. And work keeps the mind busy."

"There's always work where Carson is involved," Tats muttered, and Thymara smiled her agreement.

✧ ✧ ✧

Day the 21st of the Plough Moon

Year the 7th of the Independent Alliance of Traders
From the Masters of the Bird Keepers' Guild, Trehaug
To the Masters of the Bird Keepers' Guild, Bingtown

To our fellows, greetings.

As was suggested by Master Kerig Sweetwater, we have proceeded with great circumspection and attention to detail in the matter of Kim, formerly Master of the Birds, Cassarick, and the grave allegations that have been made against him.

Close scrutiny of the birds coming and going from his coops, an accounting of revenues collected, and the judicious interception and inspection of messages passing through his hands have revealed too many irregularities to be ignored. At best, they indicate a complete disregard for Guild standards, and at worst, treachery to the Guild and treason to the Independent Alliance of Traders. The full extent of his wrongdoing has not yet been established.

For now, he has been stripped of all authority, his birds confiscated, his apprentices reassigned for retraining in correct procedures, and his journeymen rebuked for not reporting irregularities that they must have witnessed. Some may eventually be dismissed from the Guild or required to spend additional years as journeymen.

There are indications that the corruption was not confined only to Cassarick. As the connections become clear, other bird keepers may face charges of broken contracts or dismissal from the Guild. A painful time is before us, but at least we have flown through the worst of this storm and may soon emerge into better weather.

CHAPTER TWENTY

DRAGON DECISIONS

Thymara felt strangely shy as she took them out of
the pouch where she had stored them. "They don't really fit
me. My claws stick out too far." By daylight, the gauntlets
were green. No trace of Silver clung to them. "They're very
supple, and I think perhaps they were made especially for
her. Amarinda."

"Where did they get the dragon hide?" Harrikin wondered aloud.

Thymara shook her head wordlessly. Tats hazarded
a guess. "It would have been a special gift from a dying
dragon, maybe. Or maybe from a dragon who had the duty
of devouring a dead dragon."

"I don't know. Maybe the answer will be found in one
of the memory stones one day." A darker thought came to
Thymara. "Or it might have been taken from a fallen enemy.

A dragon who came and tried to raid the well and was defeated."

"Did you look for it in Amarinda's pillars?" Carson asked her.

She found she was blushing. "No. I didn't find anything about working Silver in her pillars."

Those who had stayed behind were gathered around the Silver well, former slaves as well as keepers. The slaves still kept their own company, but they were beginning to take an interest in the keepers' daily tasks. Carson had been trying to convey to them that if they wanted to share the keepers' food, then they had to share the work as well. Thymara was not completely certain that they understood that. But all of them had begun to look less haggard and cowed. When asked to help, they did, but so far none of them had volunteered. The keepers had debated keeping the Silver and the gauntlets secret from them, but in the end they had decided to not worry about it. To whom could the slaves tell the secrets of Kelsingra? "If we knew what the secrets really were," Carson had added dourly.

In the absence of the dragons, Carson had declared that they had to devise an effective cap for the Silver reservoir. He and Harrikin had hunted the hills for downed trees and had the good fortune to find the trunk of a substantial oak. All had labored to cut and shape the slabs of timber that they had fashioned into a well cover. It was rough, little more than a rectangle of wood that fit over the well mouth. As it was, it might keep anyone from falling into the well, but it would do little more than that. It was Carson's hope that Thymara might be able to shape it into a securely fitting cap.

A bucket of Silver, drawn from the well, waited on the paving stones before her. "I suppose I just put on the gauntlets, dip my hands into the Silver, and then . . ." She looked all around at the others. "Has anyone ever found a memory of anyone working Silver? Seen them at work?"

"I've seen people wearing Silver gloves, still gleaming. But I didn't really see what they were doing. They were crouched down by a statue, looking at the base of it and talking as I walked by. In the memory," Alum added, as if to explain.

Thymara slowly began to draw on a gauntlet.

"What if it leaks?" Tats demanded wildly. "What if it soaks through? What if there's something about this that we don't understand, something that hurts her or kills her?"

She spoke patiently. "I tested them earlier. In water. Not a drop got in."

"But that's not water in that bucket!"

"I know." She had both gauntlets on now. She flexed her hands and felt the pull of the supple leather against them. For only a moment, she considered that she was wearing someone else's skin on her hands. A dragon's, certainly, but had not he or she thought and spoken just as clearly as a human? How would she feel about someone else wearing her skin as gloves? She stared at her green-gloved hands for a moment and then shook her head. "I'm going to try it," she said, as if any of them had doubted it.

The Silver in the wooden bucket swirled sluggishly. No one had jostled it. It had not ceased its restless motion since Carson had slowly lowered the bucket into the stuff, poked it with a long stick to make it tip, and then gingerly hauled it up again. He had held it by a length of dry rope to allow every droplet of Silver to drip back into the well before setting it beside the well mouth on the paving stones. They had all gathered around it, to watch the slow undulation of the liquid within.

"Is it possible it's actually alive?" Tats had asked.

No one had tried to answer. And no one had touched the bucket since, but still the stuff moved, coiling within itself, silver, white, gray, a fine thread of black, moving like liquid snakes tangled with one another.

Slowly, being very careful not to splash, Thymara pushed her right hand into the bucket of Silver. She went no more than fingertip deep and then drew her hands out. For a moment, the Silver clung smoothly. Then it began to pull away from the glove in droplets. She held her hand over the bucket and there was silence as they watched the silver droplets fall.

"Do you feel anything?" Tats asked tensely.

"Just heaviness. Like a wet glove."

She moved her fingers, flexing them slowly, and the droplets ceased falling and spread evenly over the gauntlet. Thymara caught her breath as they began to spread upward, toward the cuff, but they stopped at the wrist, forming a perfectly straight line there.

"Umh." Carson had squatted down beside her to stare at her hand over the bucket. "Wonder how they made it do that? Stop instead of spreading all the way up to your arm."

"Enough experiment for one day?" Tats suggested.

Thymara shook her head slowly. "Stand back. I'm going to move over and touch the wood."

As she slowly straightened and then took the two steps toward the completed well cover, the gathered observers moved in a circle around her. She turned her hand slowly as she went, palm up, then back down, then palm up, keeping the Silver evenly spread.

"Is that something you remember to do?" Carson asked her, and she replied tightly, "I don't know. It just feels like the way to do it. To keep it from dripping off."

She squatted by the well cap and set her laden glove on it. "What do I do?" she wondered aloud. Then, before anyone could reply, she drew her hand along the wood, stroking the rough plank with the grain. "I'm pressing on it, trying to make it smooth," she said.

All were silent, watching. As she trailed her fingers on the board, the Silver drained from the glove onto the wood until her hand was gloved only in green dragon leather. The Silver was smooth on the wood in the wake of her hand, but only for a moment. Then it began to gather itself up into tiny balls on top of the plank.

"I knew it couldn't be that easy," Tats muttered.

Thymara scowled at it. She ran her glove over it again, and again the Silver coated the wood obediently. She stopped and watched it gather itself up into tiny balls like droplets of dew. "Why does it do that?"

"No one told it not to," Alum observed.

Thymara gave him a sharp look. She ran her fingertips across the Silver and wood again. "Be flat, be smooth."

The Silver scattered before her touch, ran in erratic circles behind it. For a moment, it smoothed itself into an even sheen over the wood, and then bubbled up again. Harrikin crouched down beside her. "May I try?" he asked hoarsely. "With the other glove?"

"You remember something?" Carson asked him, almost sharply.

"Maybe it's like the dragons. Maybe you don't tell it what to do. Maybe it needs to be persuaded."

Thymara held out her free hand, and he carefully drew the glove from it and slid it onto his hand. It fit badly on his larger hand, and the fingertips were empty and flopping. Thymara lifted her hand away and his took its place. He glanced at the others self-consciously, then visibly focused himself. "Be smooth and lovely. Bring your beauty to the wood. Shine and gleam. Be as strong and smooth as the face of a placid lake, be strong as polished metal."

Unevenly, his fingers trailed along the wood, and unevenly did the Silver obey him. Narrow streaks of gleaming silver-polished wood followed his touch. Where he had not touched it, the Silver darted about, formed itself into balls and danced nervously, uncertainly on the surface of the rough plank.

"Try it again," Carson suggested, his voice barely a whisper.

Alum looked up at him and then back at the wood. "Look how narrow the stripes are. It would take forever to . . ."

"Don't say it!" Carson interrupted him hoarsely. "Don't suggest anything we don't want it to do." He stared at the beaded dancing Silver as if it were game he were stalking.

"Add your beauty to the wood; give it your gleaming strength." Harrikin had gone a bit pink on his cheeks, but he spoke on. "Like a shimmering, gleaming pond of shimmering, gleaming beautiful still water. Please be like that. Let me see how you can make your beauty part of the lovely, pretty, smooth wood." He looked up suddenly at the others, his eyes desperate. A thin line of polished wood was following his awkward touch.

"You are like the moon's shimmering path on a still pond," Thymara suggested. Harrikin nodded tersely.

"Let your beauty on the wood be like the moon's shimmering path on a still pond." Harrikin spoke to the Silver, and another narrow streak of gleam joined the first.

"The glorious strength of molten iron running in a steaming stream," Carson muttered.

Harrikin nodded and spoke again to the Silver. "Add to this wood your glorious strength, like the smooth running of molten iron in a steaming stream."

"I've got one!" Alum said softly. "The beauty of a woman's hair, unbound and falling down her bare back before her lover's eyes."

"Lucky for you that Leftrin's not here," Carson muttered. Alum flushed pink under his pale green scaling.

Thread by thread, compliment after compliment, the Silver was persuaded to merge with the wood. When the final dancing drop was stilled, Harrikin rocked back on his heels. He heaved a sigh. He drew the glove off slowly and offered it back to Thymara. She took it slowly. He stood, flexing his back and shaking his head. "Alum was right. Look how long it took to persuade one gloveful of Silver to bond with the wood. There it is, a stripe that's barely a finger wide. It's going to take days to finish that well cap!"

"Seems likely," Carson replied thoughtfully.

"And it seems likely that if we do it, it may last a hundred years," Tats added.

Thymara was gazing around at the city. "How did they do it? How did they raise it all?"

"Very slowly," Carson replied. "And not with magic alone." He seemed to be thinking something through and then he added, "I don't think they used it because magic made it easier or quicker. I think they used it to do things that otherwise couldn't be done. Then the effort would be worth it." He scratched his chin thoughtfully. "Obviously, we've a lot left to learn."

MALTA LOOKED UP from perusing the empty beds of soil. Through the glass panels overhead, she could see the sun venturing toward the horizon. Another day gone, and no word from the dragons or any of the keepers. How many times a day did she stop whatever she was doing and scan the skies? The rooftop hothouse offered her a view in every direction, but the skies remained stubbornly empty of dragons.

"I'm sorry," Alum said as he shut the glass door behind him. "Am I disturbing you?"

"Not really," Malta said. "As long as we speak softly. Phron is sleeping." She nodded toward him. She had spread an Elderling robe out on one of the hothouse benches and put him down there. He looked like a different child. He was still not the chubby pink infant she had dreamed of cradling, but she suspected that, for an Elderling's child, he was very healthy. Tintaglia's influence was more obvious on him than it was on her or Reyn. His scaling was a decided blue, as were his eyes. His body shape was more lithe than rounded. She did not care. His eyes were bright; he slept deeply, ate eagerly, and stared at her with wide trusting eyes while he nursed. Every day he grew, and every day she wished his father were there to see it.

The tall youth advanced hesitantly and then perched on the edge of a bed. "I thought we didn't have any seeds to plant?" Alum studied the soil Malta had loosened in one of the long, narrow beds. She realized that, with Skelly gone with Tarman, he was probably as lost as she was.

"We don't," she admitted. "But it's something we used to do in our gardens back in Bingtown in springtime. We loosened the soil in the beds and renewed it before the seeds were planted or the young plants set out."

Alum tilted his head at her. "But you were a Trader's daughter. Surely you had servants for that sort of work?"

"We did," she admitted easily. "But my grandmother spent time in her own hothouses when I was very small. And by the time I was older, we no longer had servants, and we were growing not flowers but vegetables for the table. I admit I did as little of the dirty work as I could; I had a horror of ruining my hands then and I could not understand the pleasure my grandmother took in nurturing growing things. Now, I think, I understand her better. And so I ready seedbeds even when we don't have seeds yet."

Alum idly stirred the soil with a long-fingered, silvery green hand. "I thought all Trader-born were wealthy."

"Some are. Others, less so. But wealth doesn't mean idleness. Look at Leftrin. Or Skelly." She suspected she knew why he had sought her out. She'd lead him right to it, then.

"Oh, yes," he agreed. "She works, and she works hard. For years now, she's been working toward a dream. Taking over the family liveship when Leftrin . . . when he was finished with it."

"When he died," Malta said easily. "When he goes, he'll die on the deck of his ship, Alum. And everything he was and all he knows of the river and the ways of Tarman will go back into the liveship. It's how it's done. And it's important that there is someone there who is ready and willing to take over the captaining of the ship."

"I know," he replied quietly. "We've talked about it." He fell silent.

Malta waited. It was coming.

"This time, when she's in Trehaug, she promised she'd talk to her family, with or without Leftrin. She's going to tell them that Leftrin and Alise want to get married and maybe have a child and so she wouldn't be his heir anymore. To see if she can break her engagement to that Rof fellow that her family promised her to. She thinks that he won't want to marry her if it's not certain that she'll inherit."

"And then what?" Malta prodded him gently when he fell silent.

"She'd come back here, to me." He sounded confident of that part.

"And then?"

"That's the hard part. I'm an Elderling. Ranculos says I'm going to live a long, long time. Hundreds of years, perhaps."

"And she isn't," Malta said ruthlessly.

"No. Not unless Arbuc will turn her into an Elderling, too. It must be possible! Tintaglia has you and Reyn and now Phron. So, if he wanted to, he could make her an Elderling, too. Then we both could have a long life. Together."

"I suppose he could. I still don't understand everything about it. But I know that he would have to want to do it." She watched Alum's face and added, "And she would have to desire it, also."

"She says she'd feel disloyal to Tarman. That in some ways, the liveship is her dragon."

She knew what he would next ask her. She wasn't surprised when he said, "You came from a liveship family. You chose Reyn over your family ship. Reyn and Tintaglia. Could you talk to her for me? Tell her there's nothing wrong with choosing her own happiness?"

He was so earnest. His eyes were fixed so hopefully on her that she hated to disappoint him. But "It wasn't that simple, Alum. I did not have a close bond with my family's ship. Truth to tell, I had little interest in Vivacia. I thought my aunt or my brother would inherit her—"

"But Selden became Tintaglia's as well. And Skelly told me that Althea chose Paragon, not her own family ship. So it doesn't always happen that a liveship trader stays with her own liveship!"

Malta sighed. "It was very complicated, Alum. And some of us did not have as much of a say in what we 'chose' as you might think. Tintaglia never asked me or Reyn if we wanted to be her Elderlings. She took us. Nor did my elder brother, Wintrow, want to be bonded to a liveship. Yet he is, and content with it now, I imagine."

Her heart sank as she thought of her brothers. Wintrow long gone to the Pirate Isles and seldom even visiting Bingtown these days. And Selden, gone Sa knew where. Her mother alone in Bingtown. And all at the whim of dragons and liveships. How little of her life path had been determined by what she thought she had wanted. And now, once more, she and Reyn were separated by a dragon's decision.

She swung her gaze back to Alum and spoke her truth. "There can be much more to a decision than you can know at this stage of your life. Wise or foolish, well thought or on the impulse of a moment, Alum, the decision must belong to Skelly."

He dragged his hand again through the soil and then admitted, "She still dreams of captaining Tarman. She loves the ship and she said that if Leftrin doesn't have a child, or if he dies before his child is ready to captain the ship, she would want to step in." He squirmed uncomfortably. "I asked her if she couldn't be an Elderling *and* a liveship captain, and she said—"

"Tarman would hate it. As would Arbuc." To his unwilling nod, Malta added, "Dragons in any form are jealous creatures, Alum. You have given your life over to one, and with it, you have surrendered many choices . . ."

"Arbuc is worth it!" he declared before she could say more.

"I am sure he is, to you," Malta went on implacably. "And Skelly might say the same about Tarman. Would you leave Arbuc to follow Skelly to a life on the river with her liveship?"

The look on his face confirmed for her that he had never even considered such a choice. "Don't rush her," Malta suggested quietly. "As you have said, you have scores of years before you. Possibly hundreds. You have more time to wait than she does to decide. If she waits ten years to decide, will you no longer want her? And if that is true, if she became an Elderling for you, would you still want her in ten years? Do not be too hasty to cut her off from what she has in favor of what you think you could make of her."

His mouth had gone flat, and there was a resentful sadness in his eyes that had not been there before. Malta tried not to regret that she had put it there.

"I know you are right, Elderling Queen," he said huskily. "I was afraid to consult you, without knowing why. Well, now I do. I was going to ask you if I should request this of my dragon when he returned. I was going to ask if you had ever resented sharing Tintaglia." He shook his head at himself. "It's not my choice, is it?"

Malta shook her head slowly.

He stood up and then bowed to her gravely. She thought of telling him she was not queen of anything, and then decided that, for now, perhaps it hurt nothing if he thought of her that way. He turned to go, and then suddenly halted. He reached into a pouch at his hip.

"Carson and I hiked up into the hills. It's spring up there. It's like nothing I've ever seen. The ground is dry and you can walk over it, and plants cover it everywhere. I thought I understood dry land after being here most of winter, but . . ." He shook his head in wonder at it. "Carson found these and gathered them. He said we should give them to you since you were spending so much time in the hothouses."

From his pouch, he took a small prickly branch. Shriveled brown husks clung to the end of it. "Rose hips. From wild roses."

"Yes! That's what he said, too. He said you might want to try planting them."

She took them from him and looked at them in her palm. Three shriveled rose hips. She turned and looked back at the scores of empty gardening beds. "It's a start," and smiled at him.

"A start," he agreed.

IT HAD BECOME almost a ritual for her. Every evening before the sun went down, Thymara climbed the map tower and looked out.

It was a different place compared to the first time she had seen it. She had spent a day helping Alise clean all the windows, inside and out. Alise had been very unhappy with the crude cover of scraped leather that covered the broken pane, but Carson had apologetically assured her it was the best he could do. It kept out the wind and rain.

The table he had devised to support the ancient map that had fallen to the floor was likewise rough, but at least it raised it out of danger from errant feet. The long-ago fall had cracked it and parts of it had crumbled, but it was correctly oriented to the city, and it had been useful to the keepers any number of times. Carson never seemed to tire of studying it, and he repeatedly insisted that it was capable of telling them far more than they were capable of asking of it. Thymara had dismissed that possibility. She climbed the endless stairs, not for the map but for the view.

She stared out over the ever-changing terrain. The sere grasses of the wild meadows beyond the city had gone green. The forested hills had taken on new colors as trees leafed out. Even the color of the river seemed different; it was certainly not the chalky gray of the Rain Wild River that she had known. Here it appeared a silvery brown between verdant banks.

But it was the sky she scanned, looking for signs of returning dragons each evening.

She heard the scuff of feet on the stone steps and turned to see Tats emerge from the stair. "See anything?" he greeted her.

"Only sky. Coming here is a bit silly, I know. Why would they be coming home at sunset rather than any other time?" She shook her head at herself. "And even if they were, likely I'd see them from the ground almost as soon. Sometimes it seems like worrying is something I feel like I have to do, that maybe worrying about them actually keeps them alive and real."

Tats gave her an odd look. "Girls think strangely," he observed without malice, and then stepped to the windows to scan the world outside. "No dragons," he confirmed needlessly. "I wonder if they've reached Chalced yet." His eyes wandered to the panels between the window frames. They, too, were decorated to be a continuation of the map on the wall. He studied them idly. "They built this room for a reason."

"Probably a lot of reasons. But it's like Carson says. It can't give us answers until we know what questions to ask."

Tats nodded. He gazed out over the river as he asked her, "You miss him a lot, don't you?"

She tried to think of how to answer. "Rapskal? Yes. Tellator? Not at all." She lifted a hand to her chest. Anxiety squeezed her heart. It was becoming too familiar a sensation. "Tats. Which of them do you think will come back to us? Rapskal or Tellator?"

He didn't turn to look at her. "I don't think there's any separating them anymore, Thymara. I think that it's useless to think of him that way."

"I know you are right," she said unwillingly. She told herself it wasn't true, that she would never think of Rapskal and Tellator as one and the same. Then she recognized it for what it was. Like her worrying, a useless belief that by thinking a certain way, she could make it so. Tats said something in a gruff, low voice.

"What?"

He cleared his throat and took a deep breath. "I said, I thought you loved Tellator. That he was the love of Amarinda's life. Lovers never to part in that life or this one." He hesitated, refusing to meet her shocked stare, and then muttered, "Or so Rapskal explained it to me."

She bit down on her anger, refusing to give it voice. After a long, tight pause, she said unevenly, "Rapskal? Or Tellator?"

"Does it matter?" The misery in his voice was plain.

"It does." Her voice came out more strongly. "Because Tellator is a bully. And perfectly capable of deceiving anyone to get what he wants." She walked away from Tats to look out a different window. "The night he asked me to go for a walk and then took me to the Silver well . . . that's not something Rapskal would have done. I even think he knew that if Rapskal went down the well, I'd follow him." She had not spoken of her last encounter with Rapskal to anyone. Did not ever intend to.

"Thymara, they're the same person now."

"You're probably right. But even if Amarinda loved Tellator, *I* don't. I am not Amarinda, Tats. I went down that well for Rapskal, not Tellator."

He didn't respond. When she looked over her shoulder, he was silently nodding as he stared out the window. "For Rapskal," he said, as if that confirmed something.

She reached a decision. "Would you come for a walk with me?"

Tats stared at her. The daylight was fading, and the city itself did not gleam yet. He squinted at her through the gathering dimness in the tower, his own face an unknowable landscape of lines and shadows. She thought he would ask her where or why. He didn't. "Let's go, then," was all he said.

The coming of evening seemed always to stir the ghosts

of the city. As they descended, they walked through three
errand boys running up the steps, yellow robes hiked up
around their knees. Thymara strode through them, and only
afterward thought how strange it was that it was no longer
strange.

The twilight outside was partly of the sky and partly of
the city itself. Daylight gave way to stone light. The insubstantial throngs that milled in the city became less transparent, their music stronger, the smells of their food more
alluring. "I wonder if this city will ever again swarm with so
many Elderlings."

"I wonder if it ever did," Tats countered.

"What?" His words almost startled her out of her determination.

"Just something I speculate about. All these people . . .
are we passing through one night of Elderling time here, or
the overlay of years?"

She pondered his question and some time later realized
that they were walking in silence. She led him away from
the heart of the city, into a district of fine homes. The streets
grew quieter, with less public memory stone, and only a few
private monuments to haunt them. There an elderly dragon
slept near a fountain while a woman played upon a flute
nearby. The music followed them and then faded as they
reached the cul-de-sac at the top of the hill. She halted for
a moment. Thin moonlight poured down. The double row
of pillars marched to the front door, one line marked with
shining suns, the others with the round-faced moon.

"I know this place," Tats said. A chill had come into his
voice.

"How?"

He didn't reply, and she sighed. She didn't want to hear
him say that he had once followed her and Rapskal here.
Had he watched them touch the pillars, hands joined, observed as they sank into sensual dreams of another time,
other lives? He had halted as if turned to stone.

"I'm going inside," she told him.

"Why? Why bring me here?" There was pain in his
voice.

"Not to rub salt in a wound. Only to have someone with me. While I finish something. I won't be long. Will you wait here for me?" She didn't want to come out alone to the black stone pillars veined with Silver. Even as she stood there, the memories tugged at her mind, beckoning her. She dreaded walking inside alone.

"What are you going to do?"

"I just . . . I've never been inside their house."

"Never?"

"No." She couldn't explain it and she wouldn't try. Perhaps it had been that while she didn't walk where they had lived, she could pretend that their lives were still real, still existing in some "now" that was just around the corner.

"Why now? Why with me?"

Time for honesty. "Because I have to. And to give me courage." She turned from him and started the long walk between the pillars. The Silver was strong here, the stone of the finest quality. Only the best for Amarinda the Silverworker. As Thymara passed each pillar, the memories tugged and snagged at her. By night she glimpsed them, over and over. Tellator in evening dress, leaning on one of his pillars, an insouciant smile on his perfect face. Amarinda, wearing a summer dress of white and yellow. Flowers studded her flowing hair, and a breeze that Thymara could not feel stirred her dress. Tellator, grave of mien, standing bold in armor, gripping a scroll of paper. Amarinda in a casual robe, perched on a stool, barefoot and playing a small stringed instrument. Thymara passed incarnation after incarnation of the two lovers until she came to their door.

Her hand found wood softened with age to the consistency of a sponge; her memory told her it was dark, polished panels embellished with suns and moons. She pushed it open; it scraped over the floor and she stepped inside. After a few steps into the room, the house roused to her and lit unevenly. She glanced around, her memory imposing order on the room's chaos.

Time had not treated their love nest kindly. All the furniture was long gone, collapsed into wood dust, and the draperies that had graced the wall were now only threadbare shadows. She more felt than saw that Tats had followed her. *Don't hesitate now,* she told herself. The archway in the wall led to a hall. She walked hastily, denying the ghosts that plucked at her. That darkened room would have been a bath, that one the bedchamber they had shared. This door at the end of the hall was the one she wanted. The broken slab hung unevenly. She did not think Rapskal had ever come here. She pulled the pieces of wood down and stepped through.

It took a moment to adjust to the reality. The ancient quake had tumbled the back wall of the room into her little garden. Her fountain with the statue of the three dancers was buried under rubble. The ceiling hung in jagged teeth against the sky. Winter storms had rained into her wardrobe, and summer sun had baked the wreckage. Next to nothing had survived in this room. But in her mind's eye, she could still see it as it had been. There had been expensive paintings and rich hangings on the walls. A little vanity table, the surface cluttered with pots of cosmetics had been there. An enameled shelf had held her collection of spun-glass sculptures.

All gone. She reminded herself that none of it was hers, and she could not miss what she had never owned.

She turned her back to the gaping hole in the wall. Her fingers walked over the chill stone of the interior wall. There was the indentation, and when she pressed with three fingers, she heard the familiar click. As the concealed compartment swung open, light blossomed from it. Gleams of yellow and blue reflected on the dusty wall. She leaned forward and looked in. Oh, yes. She recalled it now. Flame jewels awoke after lifetimes of slumber. She heard Tats gasp, heard him step forward to glimpse the treasure.

Thymara allowed her eyes to linger on it. The significance of each piece swelled forth. The lavender circlet Tellator had given her on their anniversary, the earrings of topaz that he had brought her when he returned after nearly a year's absence . . . She pushed back at the memories, reached into her pouch, and took out the softly shining moon pendant. A last time she looked at it. Tellator had worn a matching one, a gleaming golden sun. She had seen it often against his naked chest, felt its press against her breast when they made love.

No. *She* had never felt that.

Thymara lowered the pendant into the hidden compartment, let the fine silver chain slither in after it. A moment longer she stared at the mementos of another woman's passion. Another woman's life. Amarinda's. Not hers. Gently, she pushed the drawer back into alignment with the rest of the wall and heard it latch.

She turned back to Tats. "I've finished," she said quietly.

Puzzlement showed on his face. "What were you doing? Is that where you keep your—"

She shook her head and turned away from it. As she led the way back through the hallway she said, "No. As I told you, I've never been here before. I don't keep anything there. I was just returning something that wasn't mine. Not ever."

In the dimness she reached out to find his hand waiting for hers. Together, they walked out into the night.

"It's a different world," Alise said.

"It's my world," Leftrin asserted quietly. "The world I know best."

She looked up at the small houses perched in the branches overhead. In a few more minutes, they'd be at the docks of Cassarick. She had resolved that once they tied up she would disembark and confront her old life. She'd go with Leftrin to the Traders' Hall, not just to confirm his stories that dragons had left Kelsingra to attack Chalced, but to stand before the Council and demand her wages. She would go with Leftrin when he informed them that he had Chalcedean captives to transfer to their custody, be with him when he handed both Trader Candral and his written confession over to Trader Polsk, head of the Council.

Several hours ago, the small fishing boats that plied the river had discovered Tarman. Some had shouted greetings and questions, while others had stopped their fishing and now trailed behind them. At least two of them had raced ahead of them to spread the word that the *Tarman* was returning. Leftrin had responded to each of them in an identical manner: a smile, a wave, and a toss of his head toward Cassarick. Alise knew their curiosity would be boiling over. There would be questions and interest in every detail.

With every passing tree trunk, she held tighter to her resolution to face it all squarely. It was time to stop running away, time to prove she had begun a new life on her own terms. As she looked up at the more numerous houses they passed, folk were coming out to point and shout to one another. She had expected their arrival to stir interest, but not on this scale.

"I'm not sure I belong here anymore," Alise said quietly.

Tillamon came out on deck and advanced to stand by the railing next to her. Alise glanced over at her. She had gathered her hair back from her face, and then pinned it to the top of her head. Every scale on her brow, every wattle along her jawline was bared. She wore an Elderling gown that was patterned in gold and green. Matching slippers shod her feet. Earrings dangled beside her pebbled neck. She answered Alise's smile with "Hennesey and I are going with Big Eider to visit his mother. Then I'm taking Hennesey to Trehaug to meet my mother and little sister."

"And your older brother?" Alise asked her teasingly.

Tillamon only smiled wider. "Bendir will, I think, be pleased for me. At first. When he and Mother discover that I've decided to live in Kelsingra when I'm not traveling on Tarman, they'll fuss. But once I tell them that Reyn has gone off to Chalced on a dragon to destroy the city, they'll probably forget all about me." She smiled as she said it, and added, "For years, Bendir has used our younger brother to distract Mother from his ventures. Now it's my turn."

Leftrin grinned, but her words had turned Alise's mind to the dragons and their mission.

"I wonder if they're there yet," Alise ventured.

Leftrin took her arm. "There's no point in worrying. We won't know anything until they come back. For now, all we can do is take care of our own business here. And we've plenty of that."

"What do you think will become of them?" Tillamon

nodded toward the Chalcedean captives. They sat on the deck, glumly watching Cassarick draw closer. A length of anchor chain was coiled in a circle, and each man's ankle was manacled to it. Alise had not witnessed the "incident" that had led to that drastic solution. She had awakened in the dark of night as Leftrin sprang out of bed and raced out of the door. An instant later, she heard shouts and impacts, flesh on flesh and bodies on wood. By the time she had flung on clothes and followed the noise, it had all subsided. A furious Skelly was helping Swarge drag out chains while Big Eider sat at the galley table, head bowed and barely conscious, with a cold wet cloth on the back of his head. Bellin stood, feet spread wide, with a fish club in her hand, glowering at the Chalcedean captives. Several of them showed the marks of her club, while Hennesey, with blood running over his chin, sported a brass fid for mending lines. The former slaves had stood alongside the crew, one of them holding an obviously damaged fist to his chest. The looks of satisfaction on his face made little of his pain.

"We had a little mutiny," Leftrin had explained to her as he guided her back to their cabin. "They thought they could take over Tarman and make the ship their own. Ignorant fools. I can't believe they thought they could get away with that on a liveship."

The Chalcedeans had traveled in chains on the deck since then, wearing the slave manacles that Hennesey had quietly transferred to Tarman before they departed Kelsingra. It horrified Alise, but she was more horrified by the injury to Big Eider, who had been dazed for several days afterward. Several of the former galley slaves had stepped forward to help man the ship during his convalescence. The crew had hesitantly accepted their aid at first; now they almost seemed to belong on Tarman's deck.

Leftrin looked over at the captives and shook his head. "Traders don't execute anyone," he said. "They'll be condemned to work off their crime, possibly in the excavations. Cold, hard work that grinds a man down. Or maybe they'll be ransomed back to Chalced, with extra penalties for being spies."

Alise looked away from them. *Not executions but death sentences,* she thought to herself. It wasn't fair, not for men forced by threats to do as they had done.

"Looks like they have room for us at the end," Hennesey called back to them. He was standing ready with a mooring line as Swarge guided Tarman in. Alise craned her neck and saw substantial sections of the old dock had been replaced with new planks.

"Let's tie up," Leftrin grumbled, and then he left her side, and she and Tillamon moved up onto the roof of the deckhouse to be out of the way of the crew working the deck. The two Jamaillian Traders were already up there, as well as the other merchants. The remaining members of the impervious boats' crews had been pressed into service for the journey down, and they worked alongside the Tarman's crew and the former slaves. Alise was well aware that the liveship needed little help from humans when traveling with the current, but as Leftrin had observed, "A busy sailor has less time to get into mischief. And there isn't a man among them who hasn't dreamed of working on a liveship. Maybe we'll find a lively one or two to take back to Kelsingra with us, to crew the keepers' vessels."

Trader Candral was there, too, looking pale with dark-circled eyes. He had been an especially unpleasant passenger, weeping or complaining how he had been tricked into his treachery and once trying to bribe Leftrin with promises of later riches if he would just let him off the ship without "betraying" him. Alise found it hard even to look at him. It had been a crowded journey, and Alise was looking forward to having them all off Tarman's decks.

A sizable crowd had gathered to meet them. Alise recognized Trader Polsk, and perhaps a few others from the Traders' Council. Several were dressed formally in their Trader robes; all watched them approach gravely. Others seemed to be just gawkers and bystanders, drawn down to the dock for whatever spectacle the *Tarman* might offer.

Skelly jumped from the boat to the docks with the first mooring line and quickly made Tarman fast. She caught the second line that Hennesey tossed, and in moments the liveship was secured. The Council members surged forward to meet them, and at once the Jamaillian merchants began shouting that they had been kidnapped and held against their will and their investment, a lovely impervious ship, had been stolen from them. Trader Candral joined his voice to theirs, exhorting them not to believe a word of what Leftrin or anyone else said of him: he had been forced to pen a false confession.

In the midst of the general cacophony, Alise saw the Chalcedean prisoners come to their feet, lift the length of anchor chain that joined them, and begin their dull shuffle to the gangplank. Their heads were bowed. One man was muttering something in a low voice, perhaps a prayer. As they neared the gangplank, one at the end of the line began shouting frantically and trying to pull away. The other men looked at him, grim faced, and then two of his fellows seized him and dragged him along.

"Sit down. Not ready for you yet," Hennesey told them irritably. His lower lip was still bruised and swollen, and his tone plainly conveyed his dislike for his charges. But if they understood that he spoke to them, they gave no indication. If anything, they stepped up their pace. Trader Candral was now shrieking almost hysterically that it was all a lie, he had never betrayed the Rain Wilds, while the Jamaillians were trying to outshout him with their badly accented accusations of piracy and kidnapping.

Alise divined their intention a moment too late. "Don't let them!" she shouted, even as the first four Chalcedean captives stepped up on to the gangplank. And then off, into the river.

Connected by their chains, the others followed them, some willingly, others not. Hennesey and Skelly caught hold of the last two, but the weight of the chained men and the pull of the current snatched them out of their hands and into the water. The gray river closed over the last man's scream, cutting it off as if it had never been.

Silence cloaked the dock.

Skelly stared, stricken, at her empty hands and scratched wrists. The last man had not wanted to go into the river.

"No one could have stopped that," Hennesey told her. "And it was probably a better death than they would have faced back in Chalced." A muttering began from the shore. Before it could rise any louder, Leftrin stepped to his ship's railing. "Dragons are on their way to attack Chalced, to punish them for hunting dragons! Send word to Bingtown that they must be braced for retaliation."

A breathless quiet followed his words.

Tillamon shocked everyone when she lifted her voice. "And perhaps Cassarick and Trehaug may wish to consider well what happens to cities that harbor dragon killers!"

✧ ✧ ✧

Day the 21st of the Plough Moon

Year the 7th of the Independent Alliance of Traders
From Kerig Sweetwater, Master of the Birds,
Bingtown
To Erek Dunwarrow of Trehaug

Erek, old friend, this is not an official notification. It will take the Guild masters here a month of dithering before they can decide to take the action, but I am sure it will be approved. Your name is almost the only one that has come up to fill the recently vacated post of Bird Master at Cassarick. Kim had risen to control his own coop and oversee those of his journeymen. There will be fewer birds and journeymen under your supervision than in your Bingtown post, but I feel it will be every bit as difficult a task. It is a large responsibility and to be honest, you will be stepping into a shambles of dirty coops, unhealthy birds, poorly kept records, and undisciplined apprentices.

So, of course, I consider you precisely the man for the job!

But if, by any chance, this is not something you would take on, please notify me immediately via a Dunwarrow carrier, and I shall withdraw my advocacy of you.

Not likely, say I!

With pride in my former apprentice,
Kerig

✧ ✧ ✧

CHAPTER TWENTY-ONE

CHALCED

Reyn felt slightly queasy. He took a deep breath,
then reached for his water skin and took a sip. It helped.
A little. This mode of traveling by dragon was, as he had
hoped, much different from when Tintaglia had once carried him clutched in her claws. Back then, his fear and
worry that Malta was already dead and the clench of the
dragon's powerful feet on his ribs had distracted him from
the actual flight. This time he rode high, between her wings,
the wind in his face; and always aware of how high above
the ground he was and how much his seat swayed with the
motions of her flight. His back ached and his stomach was
very unhappy.

He tried not to think of how old was this contraption in
which he sat. Tried not to wonder how strong those peculiar straps and buckles were, and if it had been built more

for show than strength. It was too late to worry about such things, and still too early to worry about the war they were bringing to Chalced. Far below him, the world was spread out like a lumpy carpet. The first day they had flown over rolling meadows and forested hills. Then they had crossed a region of swamps full of fronds and reeds and sloughs with still brown water and dead trees jutting from them. There had been a river they'd crossed, running shallow over its rocky bed, its face broken by white plumes of spray. Beyond the narrow river there had been a range of flatlands and broken hills, with trees and rushing streams in gullies. He knew by the rising of the sun that at least twice the dragons had made sharp course corrections. They were not flying directly to Chalced, but following some incomprehensible dragon route, probably one that maximized hunting opportunities and places for landing and resting. It made sense. It would have made more sense if the dragons had deigned to discuss it with the humans. Since their council of war, they'd been remarkably uncommunicative with the humans, with the possible exception of Rapskal.

Or perhaps it was only Heeby who made no barrier between herself and her keeper. Whatever the reason, Rapskal had started to irritate Reyn with his martial airs. Late last night, he had put his finger on the source of his annoyance. It was that Rapskal spoke and carried himself as if he were a man older and more experienced than Reyn. Some of the keepers seemed to have accepted him in that role. Nortel seemed to have attached himself to Rapskal as his lieutenant, passing on his tolerantly received orders about how camp was to be set up and nightly weapons drill. Of the other keepers, Reyn felt that only Kase and Boxter had fully fallen in with Rapskal's insistence that they must now begin to conduct themselves as dragon warriors. The four of them spent much time of an evening sharpening knives and polishing armor and checking dragon harnesses.

Today, Reyn looked down on a harsh rolling brown land with upthrusts of rock and random patches of dusty green brush. He'd never imagined such a place and knew that it appeared on no map he had ever studied. Chalced might claim to rule the lands right up to the edge of the Rain Wild River, but these regions, he would wager, had seen little of men in the last hundred years.

To either side of him, in front of him and behind him, dragons flew, some with riders and harnesses, some bare of any adornment. Despite Rapskal's posturing in Kelsingra, he and Heeby did not lead the way. Ranculos was out in front most often, though sometimes it was Mercor, and for a time it had been Tintaglia. All the dragons seemed to know whence they were bound, whether from ancient memories or from shared thoughts, he did not know. Reyn had thought that Icefyre as the eldest dragon and the one hottest for vengeance would lead the dragons. Instead, he was uncomfortably aware that both Icefyre and Kalo constantly vied for a spot just behind and above Tintaglia. He suspected he knew the significance of that, for several times Tintaglia had caused him to roar with terror as she folded her wings to drop down and then come up behind both of them, or suddenly put on a surge of wing beats that carried him up so high he felt he could not breathe. He knew from conversations with Davvie at night that the drakes' open rivalry for that position terrified him.

"Icefyre knows he scares me. He overflies us so close that I can scarcely draw a breath in the wind of his wings. Or he goes very high, and then sweeps in right in front of Kalo, so that he must either dodge or collide with the old bastard. And if I get frightened and beg Kalo to let him fly where he wishes, Kalo becomes annoyed with me."

"I could ask Sestican if you might ride with me," Lecter offered, but Davvie had shaken his head.

"No. That will just make Kalo angrier with me. He wants me to shout insults at Icefyre. He says he will not dare to attack us, but how can he know?" After a moment, he added quietly, "Thank you all the same."

Their camps at night often seemed oddly festive to Reyn. He felt the old man among such youthful Elderlings. They quickly fell back into the routine they had obviously shared before. Every day, as afternoon began to approach evening, the dragons descended, demanding to be rid of riders and harnesses so they might hunt. Once dismounted and the dragons launched, the keepers commenced gathering firewood and setting up a camp. The dragons gave little thought to the comfort of the humans they were abandoning for the hunt. The keepers might find themselves in a hillside meadow one afternoon and on a rocky mountain ridge the next. Reyn watched in admiration as they quickly arranged their bedrolls and set out to look for water and meat. Sometimes they found neither, but as often as not, one of them would bring down a rabbit or a wild goat to share. They all carried hardtack, tea, and dried fish, so even when the hunting was scarce, they did not go hungry. Spring was upon the land, and at one stopping point, Sedric amazed them all by teaching them to gather dandelion greens and watercress from a stream. So they shared food and a fire and conversation every evening.

The first two nights there were jests and songs and some mock swordfights as some of the keepers experimented with their Elderling weapons. Rapskal tried to give them advice on stance and grip for their weapons, but soon gave up when it turned into good-natured roughhousing. Reyn watched the younger men measure themselves against one another and was relieved when a shout that food was ready broke up their exercises.

Shared hot meat and cold water seemed to content all of them. They told him stories of their journey up the river, and he recounted how Tintaglia had carried him in her claws to search for Malta and dropped him into the sea when they found her. Pirates and rescued slaves and a Chalcedean fleet opposed by liveships seemed only a wonder tale to them, and he feared that his small effort to convey the terror and horror of that war only made it seem a glorious adventure.

Sometimes Rapskal told stories too. He spoke with a strange cadence, and sometimes he groped for words, as if the language of his birth did not allow for names of weapons and maneuvers. He spoke of dragon wars, when Kelsingra had had to defend itself against raiding parties of dragons seeking to make a claim on the silver seeps in the river. Reyn was heartsick to hear him speak of Elderlings battling one another on the ground as their dragons fought savagely in the air. Even worse was to know that the dragons' and Elderlings' enmity with Chalced reached back, not decades, but possibly centuries. The keepers sat in rapt silence when Tellator recounted stories of Elderlings captured and tortured by Chalcedeans, and the vengeance taken on their captors. There were times when Reyn thought that perhaps Elderlings were not so different from humans after all.

And times when he decided they emphatically were.

None of the keepers seemed to think it odd when Jerd chose a partner for the evening and they retired from the others, not even when she chose a different partner the second night. Davvie and Sylve shared blankets and a long night conversation that kept Reyn awake with their confidential murmuring. The lack of sexuality in their obviously intimate friendship puzzled him almost as much as Jerd's casual promiscuity. He and Carson and Malta had had several long and philosophical conversations about how these new Elderlings might form their society. This was his first unveiled look at it, and he tried to conceal his surprise and dismay. He suddenly felt a stranger to their culture, as provincial as when he and Malta had been shocked by the hedonism of old Jamaillia. He lay awake both nights, wondering if this was the world that Phron would grow up in, and how the influx of other changed Rain Wilders that Tillamon would bring with her would view these new Elderlings. Those thoughts were almost more disturbing than pondering about the war that lay before them.

By the third night, he had accepted it as how things were among the keepers. That was the first night that Rapskal had all but bullied them into weapons practice after their meal. Reyn had thought it a bad time for it. They were all weary, and as soon as he had eaten, all he wanted to do was sleep. But he knew a bit of swordsmanship, more than any of the keepers, he thought, and he agreed with Rapskal that if they were going to carry such weapons, they should have some idea how to use them. In the evenings that followed, he tried not to let his discouragement show. Some of the keepers, such as Nortel and Boxter, were enthusiastic about learning and probably more dangerous. Davvie and Kase tried but were easily discouraged. Both Sylve and Jerd had brought bows, and both were fair but unexceptional shots with them. Rapskal was the one who surprised him. He easily matched Reyn's level of skill, and in some areas he surpassed him. Even so, Reyn tried not to wonder how well any of their talents would hold up in battle conditions. He'd seen men fighting one another and dying on the decks of ships and had hoped never to witness it again. It was one thing to swing a blade in practice; it was another thing entirely to drive a knife into another man's body.

Down below them, the late afternoon shadows stretched longer from the bushes, revealing to him that they were taller than he had thought they were. He did not look forward to spending a night in such a barren place but kept his mouth closed. It was useless to voice an opinion on where they landed. That would be determined by the dragons, and right now they were led by Skrim and Dortean. Their riders sat low in their saddles, leaning forward or dangerously far to the side and shouting comments to one another. Kase and Boxter were as alike as their orange dragons, and they had even chosen matching harnesses and tunics for themselves. He watched them and wondered if he had ever seemed as youthful and carefree as they did. They rode to war on dragons and seemed to accept it as just another day in their lives.

Behind him, he heard a wild shout and looked back to see that Icefyre had just made another pass at Kalo and his rider. He had only a glimpse of Davvie's white face and open mouth before Tintaglia tipped sharply to one side. He seized the low arms of his dragon saddle and held tight as his body was thrown heavily against the side of it. They fell away from the formation. Distantly he heard Davvie shouting something about "you torn-up old umbrella!" His effort to insult the black dragon would have made Reyn laugh if he hadn't been in fear for his own life.

He fought to draw a breath against the wind slashing past his face. His fingers hurt from holding on so tightly, and still they fell. He felt blood start to pound in his face and then it dripped warmly from his nose. He could not form his thoughts into words to beg mercy from the dragon; instead he simply pressed his terror toward her mind and held on as tightly as he could as the sere brown earth rushed up at him.

Then the world shifted and he closed his eyes and gripped until his fingers were numb as his body was slammed in the other direction. When he opened his eyes, the wind against his face pressed out tears that ran along the sides of his face. Tintaglia was moving in a long swift glide over the face of the hard earth. Ahead of them, a herd of deerlike creatures were bounding along in high leaps. He feared he knew what was about to happen. "No!" he pleaded, and then the impact came.

Reyn was flung against his chest strap so hard that it drove the breath from his body. He felt something furry hit him hard and then bounce away. For a moment or perhaps longer, he lost awareness. When he came back to himself, dusty air filled his nostrils and the shrill bleating of injured animals. He opened his eyes, wiped at them, and blinked. He tried to climb out of his seat before he remembered that a strap across his chest secured him. He unbuckled it with sore fingers, stood up, and tumbled to the earth. He collapsed there, delighting in how still it was, how firm under his hands. Then he felt the dragon move and he got up, first to his knees and then barely upright as he made a shambling run away from her. He passed two bleating deer, their shattered bones sticking out of them like bloody sticks. A third was lying still, and the fourth had its head bent at an improbable angle. He threw himself down on top of it.

He waited for his heart to calm. His hearing came back more strongly and he could breathe again. He wanted water but didn't want to go back to the dragon saddle to get it. He could wait. Never bother a dragon in the first few moments of a kill, he counseled himself.

He heard shouts and dragon roars and then felt the blast of hot air against him as other dragons landed. Riders were hitting the ground, pulling straps free, and then standing back as the unburdened dragons took flight again. He sat up slowly, taking care to retain possession of the deer. If nothing else, he intended to have a decent meal out of Tintaglia's rough treatment of him.

Sylve, her blond hair a mat of permanent tangles after days of windy flight, came to stand over him. "Are you all right?" she asked him timidly. Her fingertips touched her own lips and chin lightly, and she worried, "That's a lot of blood."

He swiped his arm across his face. "Just a bloody nose," he assured her. Staggering to his feet, he seized one of the deer's hind legs. "Let's carry this off before the dragons take it away from us," he suggested.

She seized the other hind leg and they began dragging it over the desiccated earth. The air was hot and dry. The other keepers were already gathering in the dappled shade of one of the taller trees. Most of the other dragons had already left. Tintaglia was still crouched over her kills. He noticed that no dragon had been bold enough to claim any part of it. And that her harness had been removed. "Who unsaddled her?" he asked.

"Rapskal." Sylve looked back at Tintaglia. The dragon was tearing a deer carcass in half, one foot bracing it on the ground. "Sometimes I think he's fearless. Other times, I think he's just stupid."

"Sometimes they go together," Reyn observed. His head suddenly spun, and he had to stand still. He dropped the deer leg and held his hands over his eyes for a moment. "She gave no thought to me at all when she dived on that herd," he muttered. "No thought at all."

"They never do," Sylve agreed with him. "Oh, Mercor is better than most at considering what might happen to me. But even he dismisses my well-being when it comes to 'dragon business.' Otherwise, I wouldn't be here at all."

Rapskal, having approached them, overheard the last of their conversation. He stooped, gathered the deer's front and back legs in each hand, slung the carcass over his back, and stood up easily under the burden. Reyn's estimate of his strength abruptly changed.

"We cannot expect dragons to consider us: it is our duty to consider them. I think we will reach Chalced tomorrow and see the capital city soon after. We will be flying into battle immediately; there is no point in letting them prepare to meet us."

They followed him, and now they reached the other keepers. Rapskal shrugged the deer off his shoulders, and it fell with a thud to the earth. He went down on one knee beside it, drawing his belt knife as he did so. Jerd came to stand at his shoulder and watch him. "We cannot expect them to think of us tomorrow during the battle. It will up to each of us to be sure we are securely fastened to our dragons. While we are mounted, our tasks are to watch for risks that our dragons may not notice. Of old, that would have meant that we had to watch for enemy dragons diving down on us or coming up behind us. That is not the case now, luckily.

"But the city of Chalced has long been fortified against its enemies. Of old, the fortified portion of the city of Chalced was upon a hilltop. I expect that will be the Duke's residence. In any case, it is what we must first destroy. The ballista there will be set to rain missiles down on an army approaching from below. But if some clever commander keeps his head and thinks clearly enough, he may be able to adjust his machinery to fling large stones upward at us. And bowmen with powerful bows on top of towers may be able to speed shafts toward us. Even a small arrow driving deep into tender flesh can do great damage to a dragon, as Tintaglia has shown us. So it is the task of every keeper to watch for dangers to his dragon. That, above all else, must concern you."

As he spoke, he began gutting the deer. He watched his hands, but spoke loudly and clearly, obviously intending to reach all the keepers. Once he had opened it, Sylve crouched opposite him and began skinning it, pulling the hide toward herself as she slashed it efficiently free of the meat below. Nortel came with a long stick, to spear the heart on a spit. Kase and Boxter were already busy with tinder and broken tree limbs. A thin spiral of pale smoke began climbing skyward.

Rapskal rocked back onto his knees, the liver a dark mass in his hands. His arms were blood-smeared to the elbow. He lectured on. "If your dragon lands, you are at his command. He may tell you to go into a building to drive the enemy out to him. If he is injured and unable to fly, it is your task to defend him to the death if need be. He may choose to leave you on the ground so that he can fight unencumbered. It is his choice." He flipped the liver to Nortel, who caught it adroitly.

"Do any of us actually like deer liver?" Nortel asked rhetorically, earning a scowl from Rapskal.

The red-scaled Elderling's knife moved surely, disjointing the deer's hindquarter. "Venom drift. Have we spoken of this before? Your Elderling garb will protect you if it's only a mist, but as soon as you possibly can, you should change clothing and discard the contaminated clothing. But it will protect only the parts of you that are covered, so if you see mist, cover your face and hands."

He looked around sternly. He had freed a deer haunch from the carcass and had severed the shank free from it. "If it's more than mist, if it's a spray, then nothing can save you." A look of knowing, of terrible weariness, came over his face, aging him far beyond his years. "If it's thick and coming your way, blow all your breath out, and breathe deep when it hits. Suck it in and you'll die fast. You won't even have time to scream."

"Sweet Sa," Reyn breathed out, horrified. Nortel's eyes were huge. Kase had gone so pale that the orange of his scales stood out on his face like errant flower petals.

"Does that happen?" Sylve asked. Her voice was steady but small.

"Sometimes," Rapskal replied. "I've seen it." His gaze was distant. He began to carve slabs of flesh off the haunch. Kase came with an armful of toasting sticks cut from a nearby bush. Without a word he passed them to keepers, who matter-of-factly began to claim shares of the meat. Reyn took his in turn and followed the group to the cook fire.

For a time, the conversation was of ordinary things. Who had salt? Did anyone want to eat the liver? Wondering what the ones who had remained in Kelsingra were doing and thinking. Reyn spoke of missing Malta and hoping that Phron did not grow too much while he was gone. Kase teased Sylve about being away from Harrikin. She blushed but freely admitted missing him. Sedric stared quietly at the fire.

Rapskal looked thoughtful. "Amarinda," he said at last, and smiled sadly.

Jerd folded her legs, dropping down to sit beside him. She sighed. "You've seen many things in the stone, haven't you, Tellator?"

He looked at her consideringly. "I lived many things," he replied. "And other things I know from the stone ancestors I chose for myself. If one is to be a warrior, then one chooses the accounts of warriors, to read them from the stone and to use their experience again. And so I am Tellator, but I am also the ones that Tellator incorporated into himself."

Jerd was nodding slowly. Her eyes were traveling over his face in a way that made Reyn uncomfortable. Sylve spoke sharply. "And Amarinda? Did she also choose a stone ancestry for herself?"

Rapskal's eyes shifted from Jerd to Sylve. He measured her and her reaction. Something in him went still before he replied diffidently, "She chose other talents for herself. Some things, as you know now, were not stored in the stone. Those she learned from her masters, and in time became a master herself. But some things she chose to learn from stone.

"Body skills are much easier to learn that way. Tumbling and juggling and sculpting, for example, are easier to master if one knows how the body feels as it performs those maneuvers. The flexibility and muscle, of course, must be gained from practice. They are much easier to achieve if one remembers the experience of having done it before. One feels confidence that it can be done. Swordsmanship, for instance."

"And other physical skills?" Jerd asked him with a knowing smile.

He grinned back at her. "There are some topics that a man can never know too much about. Or a woman."

Jerd shivered. She glanced at Sylve, and then asked him, "Could any woman be Amarinda? If I went to her memory stones, could not I learn her days with Tellator? And her nights?"

He looked at her consideringly. "You might," he admitted. He started to say something more, than paused as if he had forgotten it. A line divided his brows, and for a moment he looked tragically young to Reyn. As if he might next crumple forward and weep like a child.

Sylve spoke for him. "You might learn all of Amarinda there is to know, but you still would not be Thymara."

Jerd faced Sylve squarely, fists on her hips. She was a full head taller than Sylve, and for one horrified instant, Reyn thought she was going to hit her. Her voice was low and venomous. "I wouldn't want to be Thymara! Who would? She doesn't know what she wants. She just likes tormenting people." She swung her gaze to Rapskal. "She wants to keep both you and Tats for herself, with no regard for your feelings."

Rapskal dragged in a breath. His voice was a bit ragged. "Well. One thing Thymara does know is what she doesn't want. Or who."

Jerd leaned closer. Nortel, her bed partner of the night before, narrowed his eyes as she said quietly to Rapskal, "She isn't the only woman in the world. Choose another."

Sylve appeared to be choking as she tried to think of an appropriate insult for Jerd.

Rapskal stared at her, and for a moment his eyes were wide. He struggled with something. Then the instant passed, and a grim smile claimed his mouth. "I shall." He looked at Jerd and dismissed her. He did not have to add the cutting words, "Like Thymara, I know well who I do not want." He stood and stretched, his broad shoulders straining the Elderling fabric of his tunic. The captain grinned around at his men gathered around the campfire. "We should all get some sleep. Tomorrow we will reach Chalced. A city that is full of women, many of whom will doubtless be grateful to see the Duke fall. And willing to thank the victors."

"Oh, Rapskal!" Sylve cried in a low, stricken voice.

Reyn thought that perhaps only he heard her. He thought of his own father, drowned in memories in Trehaug, of a man who was never himself again, never recognized his children or wife again.

But Kase's loud exclamation overrode all else as he said, "A city full of women!" He grinned at Boxter and added, "Tellator, what can you tell us of grateful women?"

"SELDEN. SELDEN. IT'S time to be awake. You need to eat and drink."

He opened his eyes. Full daylight was streaming into the room. The potted roses on the balcony had leafed out, and the wind that wandered into the room was mild. As if in answer to spring, Chassim had discarded her pale shroud. He had never realized her hair was so long. She had left it loose, and it cascaded past her shoulders. The simple robe she wore was a pale pink, sashed with white. There were little rosebud slippers on her small feet. She was crouched by his couch, patting his hand to awaken him. A laden tray waited on the low table beside him.

"You look like Spring herself," he said sleepily, and she blushed as pink as her gown.

"You need to wake up and eat."

He lifted his head and the room spun. He set it down again. "Is it today? Already?"

"I'm afraid so. I want you to eat and then rest again before they come for you."

He lifted his arm and looked at it. Both his arms were swathed from wrist to elbow in neat white wrappings. But he knew what they looked like underneath. Black and blue bruising covered them. "One of the healers spoke of making a cut at my neck. The others argued, saying they might not be able to stem the flow of blood afterward."

She rose abruptly and went to the balcony to stare out of the window. "You should eat," she said hopelessly. In the distance, trumpets blared.

"Chassim. I fear I won't come back to you this time. Or that if I do, I may never awake again."

"I fear the same," she answered in a thick voice. "And as you see, I have prepared myself." She gestured at her garments and then at the open window. "I've made my little plan. After they take you, I will wait on the balcony. If they are angry when they come to my door, I will jump then, before they can seize me. If they bring you back to me, but I fear you cannot wake again—"

"Take me with you," he said quietly. "The worst fate I can imagine is to wake in this room and find you gone."

She nodded slowly. "As you wish," she said in a very small voice. She pulled herself up straighter and said, "But for now, you should eat."

"I don't want to feel that depraved old man's mouth on my throat."

She had started across the room toward him. At his words she shut her eyes tightly and turned her face from him, sickened. She drew a deep shuddering breath. "Just eat something," she suggested.

"There's no point. If I'm going to take my own life, I'd sooner do it before they cut my throat and he sucks my blood again."

"Selden—"

"Unless you'd like to dine with me. Shall we have a final meal together, Chassim?"

She came to his bedside, lifted the tray, and took it to a low table on the balcony. "Do you mind sitting on the floor?" she asked him. Her voice had become very calm. "If we are interrupted, if they chance to come early—"

"We can still escape. An excellent idea."

He lifted his head, and this time the world did not spin. She came back to help him stand, letting him take his time. They crossed the room slowly, his legs wobbling with every step. His arms and wrists ached abominably. He was grateful to sink down on the floor beside the food. Chassim hastened to bring him cushions to lean against, and a coverlet to wrap about him. Spring was in the air, but he still shivered. "It feels good to be alive," he told her.

She smiled and shook her head at him. "You make no sense. And yet you do. Selden Vestrit fostered by Khuprus, you are the first man I've ever talked with. Do you know that?"

With difficulty, he tugged a cushion closer. "That doesn't

seem possible. You had brothers, you told me. Your father. Three husbands. You must have known other men."

She shook her head. "My status meant that males were kept at a distance from the time I was a child. I sat at dinners; there were polite exchanges. My suitors courted my father, not me. And when I was given over to my husbands, they had no interest in conversing with me. I was not even an object for pleasure; they had much more skilled women at their disposal for that. I was for making a child that would mingle my lineage with theirs. That was all."

"And they all died."

She had mentioned some of her history to him, but he had never prodded at what she had told him. She met his gaze. "The first one died accidentally," she said. She poured wine for both of them and then lifted the lid off a fat bowl. The aroma of a rich beef soup rose from it. She ladled out servings for each of them. "Do you think I am hateful?" she asked him.

"You have not seemed so to me," he replied. "There were nights when I dreamed of killing my captors. Times when I lunged against my chains and would have done death on any of the gawkers that I could have reached. So what is the difference between us?"

She smiled at him. "That I was more efficient than you were?" she offered. She lifted a fold of cloth to reveal a warm loaf. When she uncovered the little dish next to it, she said, "Look how yellow the butter is! They must have put the cows out onto new pasture."

Trumpets sounded again, more urgently. They both turned to look out over the city. In the distance, other horns blared a response. Selden turned his head sharply. "What is that?" he asked her.

She shrugged. "A diplomatic visit, most likely. The guards at the city gate will blow an alarm that announces the arrival. Then the horns sound again as the visitors pass each checkpoint in the city." She sipped her wine. "It is nothing to do with us, my friend."

THE WINDS HAD favored them. Sintara knew that Tinta-

glia had not expected to arrive at the city before noon. They
had come from the direction of the dry lands, and as they
came to gentler territory, more than one herd had scattered
in terror as they overflew them. One shepherd had dared to
shout and shake his fist at them. The herdsmen they saw
spurred their horses and fled, leaving their cattle to fend for
themselves.

We will feast later! Icefyre promised them.

*For now, fly steady and strong. We want no warning of
our coming to precede us,* Mercor reminded them all.

That had all been settled back in Kelsingra. Icefyre had
battled humans before and had very definite ideas of how
they must proceed. There would be no trumpeting to one
another, and the path that they had followed to Chalced had
taken them over the deserted lands, away from eyes that
might send messengers ahead to the city. Men on horses,
dragons had learned long ago, could not outrun a dragon,
but they could and would continue to travel by night, with
no need to kill and eat and sleep. The old black dragon had
been very intent on surprising the Chalcedeans and attacking them with as little warning or challenge as they had
given him.

So now the dragons flew, swift and straight, making no
kills, regardless of how easy the prey that was offered. The
scattered huts and farmhouses grew more common, and
soon they were flying over the outskirts of the great city.
Ahead of them loomed the city walls, and high above it,
on a hill within the fortified city, stood the towers and ram-
parts of the Duke of Chalced's stronghold. It was more for-
tress than palace, and as they approached it, Sintara knew
a moment of unsettling doubt. This was a bad place, a very
bad place, and her inability to summon up the specific
memory that told her that only made it appear more ominous. Icefyre had been insistent that the entire city must be
completely annihilated. That was the only point on which
Mercor had directly opposed him.

"My memories may not be as extensive as yours, but this
I do recall. Stirring an entire city of humans is like lying
down to sleep on a hill of dagger ants. They are tiny, but

they will attack endlessly, summoning their fellows from other hills if they must. To be rid of them, you have only to kill the queen in the central mound. Tintaglia has spoken of being well treated by the folk that live in the Icy Islands, and along the Black Stone Coast. The Six Duchies, she called it, and said that whenever she visited there, she was offered gifts of fattened cattle and a safe place to sleep. Will destroying Chalced threaten that?"

Icefyre had been angry that the golden dragon directed his question to the blue queen, but Tintaglia had obviously been pleased. "The Six Duchies has long warred with Chalced. They will probably not care at all if we destroy that city. But as one who has fought a city alone, and far more recently than Icefyre, I will say that it was a task that was dangerous and yet became annoying. It takes a lot of venom to destroy ranked soldiers, and while one is smashing ships and towers, one is not hunting, eating, or sleeping."

Icefyre had drawn himself taller and taller as Tintaglia spoke. Beside the blue queen, Kalo rumbled ominously as the black dragon expressed his dominance. Now the old dragon broke in with, "And while humans are poisoning you or attacking you with nets and spears, are you eating or sleeping? Or dying?"

"Which is better, a quick kill by snapping a neck, or a long battle that inflicts wounds on both combatants?" she had retorted.

They flew over a fortified holding. It astonished her how quickly warning horns were sounded. They glanced back to see the walls bristling with armed men. The gates of the keep were open, and six men on horseback bearing banners raced out.

Messengers, Tintaglia confirmed. *But they will be too late.*

In response, all the dragons picked up speed. Sintara heard the keepers calling to one another, their thin voices snatched away on the wind. Mercor had been leading them. Now Icefyre suddenly left off his rivalry with Kalo and winged past them all to try to take the lead from Mercor. Was he startled to see that Heeby and Rapskal had beaten him to it? The red queen and her rider arrowed to the front. Rapskal was leaning forward on Heeby's neck, singing wild encouragement and praise to her. She had flushed a sparkling scarlet, and her wings opened and closed so swiftly she was like a hummingbird flying with crows. She looked almost comical as she sped ahead of the others. As Relpda, overshadowed by evil little Spit, suddenly moved forward past both Icefyre and Mercor, the old black dragon trumpeted angrily.

As if that were a signal, all the dragons suddenly roared, announcing their coming as they arrowed toward the fortified city on the hill.

"WEREN'T YOU ALL going to keep silent and take them by surprise?" Sedric objected.

"Don't like Heeby in front of me," Relpda responded sulkily.

Sedric was crouched in the abbreviated dragon saddle that Relpda had insisted they use, holding tight with both hands to a harness ornamented with silver bells. Carson had added a harness of rawhide straps to the saddle and Sedric trusted it, but he could not make himself loosen his grip on the harness. His eyes were squinted nearly shut and still tears streamed from them from the kiss of the wind. "We are in more danger here, my lovely one. Let us fall back and let the larger dragons lead the way."

Spit trumpeted derisively. "Yes, listen to that skinny little flea on your back. Fall back, and when they spit acid, you will fly through the cloud. Such fun for both of you."

Sedric clamped his jaws tight shut, wondering if Spit spoke true or was once more delighting in tormenting Relpda. They were flying so fast that the landscape beneath them raced by sickeningly. There went a village, bells ringing and horns sounding warnings, and on a streamer of yellow road, a man leaped from his laden cart and raced off into a grain field, to fling himself flat as if that could hide him from the dragons overhead. The dragons paid no mind to him. Farmsteads and hamlets surrounded Chalced the city. Sedric braced himself for the attack to begin. He did not want to be here, did not want to watch Relpda deal death to unsuspecting and helpless humans.

They would kill me if they could, she reminded him, and shame rose in him. Once he had been of that mind. *Forgiven,* she reminded him. *But I cannot forgive those who would still take my blood and scales.*

Below them, people ran about furiously, some taking shelter in houses, others racing out into the streets to see what was happening. Thin screams of terror rose into the cool morning air, and then the blaring of horns. The dragons trumpeted their own mocking response to the horns and then, so abruptly that Sedric gave a shout of surprise, the dragons tipped away from each other, dividing neatly into smaller groups and descending sharply. The screams of terrorized people reached him more clearly. For an instant, he shared that terror. Dragons were coming, to spit fiery acid that would melt the flesh from their bones. Their houses would fall, any man who lifted a hand against them would certainly die, and their orphaned young would whimper and snivel in the deserted and smoking streets. There was nothing, nothing they could do to oppose the dragons, the great and glorious and beautiful dragons that were deserving of their obeisance and obedience. They should flee, flee, leave their houses and run out of the city; it was their only chance . . .

Oh. Not you. Relpda suddenly interrupted the daunting stream of emotion. Sedric felt muffled suddenly, his thoughts closed off from a flood of dragon glamour directed at those they overflew.

They circled the city in an ever-tightening spiral, bombarding the humans below with glamour. Horses, dogs, and even yoked oxen seemed as vulnerable, for Sedric saw them go suddenly mad with terror, bolting down the streets headed out of the city regardless of obstacles, living or otherwise, in their paths. New screams rose, more trumpets, bells rang wildly, and he felt sick with horror to be a part of it. "I just want it to be over," he muttered to himself.

Soon, Relpda promised. *Soon.*

THE SOUP WAS nearly gone. Chassim refilled their wineglasses. "The condemned are eating heartily," she observed.

In the near distance, a woman shrieked. A chorus of screams rose. "What is it?" Selden endeavored to rise, but she waved him back. She rose a bit unsteadily and went to the balcony wall. "The streets are filling with people. They're running. They're pointing up, at us." She gazed down at them in consternation. Then she turned her head over her shoulder and gazed up. And gasped.

She turned, leaning so far back that Selden reached out and grasped her ankle. "Don't fall!" he commanded her. "Don't go without me!"

She lifted her hand and pointed. "Dragons. A sky full of dragons."

"Help me up," he begged her. Then, as she continued to stare at the sky, he demanded breathlessly, "A blue queen. Do you see a blue queen dragon among them?"

"I see a red dragon. And a silver and two orange ones. A queen?"

"A female. Gloriously blue, with silver and black markings as well. Graceful as a butterfly, powerful as a striking hawk. Shaming the sky with her blueness."

"I don't see any blue dragons."

He pushed himself away from the cushions and onto his hands and knees. Not strong enough to crawl to the edge of the balcony, he slid and lifted his body until he was able to sprawl on the floor and look up at the sky. She was right. His dragon wasn't there. "Not my dragon," he said, and hopelessness filled him.

The dragons swung in an arc past the Duke's grand palace. They were coming lower. A small silver one trumpeted wildly, spraying venom with the sound. "Sweet Sa, no," Selden prayed. He had seen Tintaglia rain venom down on Bingtown when she had repelled the Chalcedean invaders. He had seen droplets strike men and, an instant later, fall out the other sides of their bodies, followed by blood and guts. Nothing stopped it. He tried to find words to warn Chassim and could not form them.

The silver dragon's mist fell randomly, the droplets caught on the wind. Selden's horrified gaze followed the silvery mist as it was wafted down and onto a statue in a garden. He did not hear the hiss, but he imagined it as the newly sprouted plants withered suddenly, turning to sodden brown heaps on the soil. A moment later, the statue collapsed in a gush of powder.

"They're attacking the palace," Chassim said breathlessly. "They spit something and whoever it touches crumples. Quickly. Get back inside!"

"No." He felt numb. "Hiding inside will do us no good. Not unless you want to be under the rubble when it all collapses on us." His mouth had gone dry, his voice hoarse. "Chassim, we are going to die today. There's no help for it."

She stared at him, her eyes wide. Then she looked out over her city again. A ribbon of destruction, encircling the Duke's stronghold, was now clearly visible from the tower. It was growing wider, the swath of collapsed buildings and melted bodies growing closer. The dragons' plan was obvious. All within the circle would be drenched with acid venom. They stood in the center of oncoming death.

"My people," she said softly.

"They're fleeing. Look at the streets, the more distant ones." Selden sat up shakily. *Fear gives a man strength,* he thought to himself.

"The dragons aren't following them." Chassim spoke slowly as she looked down at the streets choked with people. It looked as if every inhabitant of the city was running away from them. "My father. The Duke. They've come for him, haven't they?"

Selden managed a nod. "I'm sorry. They will destroy everything to get at him, I think."

"I'm *not* sorry." She spoke the words without remorse. "I pity my people. I am saddened to see them terrified. But I do not pity my father or the end he has brought upon himself. Nor am I sad that he will not drain you dry and bring your body back to me. That, at least, I am spared."

Abruptly, she sat down on the floor beside him. He reached out blindly and took her hand into his. Tears were running down her cheeks, but a smile trembled on her lips. "We will still die together." With a shaking hand, she reached for the teapot. "Will you have a last cup of tea with me?"

He turned his gaze on her. An odd calmness was welling up in him. "I would rather have a kiss. My first and last, I think."

"Your first kiss?"

He laughed shakily. "My circumstances have not lent themselves to the giving or receiving of kisses."

She blinked and the tears spilled faster. "For me, also." She leaned a little closer to him and then stopped.

He looked at her. She had closed her eyes. Her hair was sleek, her skin like cream, her lips pink. Her first kiss would come from a scaled dragon man. He leaned in and found her mouth with his. He kissed her softly, unsure of how it was done, expecting her to pull away in revulsion. Instead, when he leaned back, she was smiling through her tears.

"To be touched by a man, with gentleness," she said, as if that wonder were so great it dispelled the circling dragons.

He put his bandaged arm around her, and she leaned close to him. Together they watched as the dragons swept out of sight. A moment later, they returned in another sweeping arc. For the first time he saw that two of them carried riders. Their scaled bodies gleamed in the sun as brightly as the dragons they bestrode. One of the dragons trumpeted, and suddenly the three of them swept in a wider, lower circle. As the dragons flew, they gave cry. Gleaming droplets of acid venom drifted from their wide-stretched mouths, and then they suddenly beat their wings more strongly, all three rising above the path of death they had spewed.

Chassim put her arms around him. She held him closer, and her face was white as she said quietly, "It looks a quick way to die. Perhaps faster than a fall." She helped him to stand. He clung to the stone railing of the balcony and they looked down on the city.

In the distance, the streets were full of fleeing people. Horns vied with screams to fill the air, but the trumpeting of the dragons triumphed over all. They fled away from the widening circle of scorched earth. A circle, a moat of death and crumbling masonry, was forming around the Duke's grand palace. Selden saw the dragons' plan clearly now. "They will seal the castle so there is no escape without running into the venom on the ground. And then they will slowly destroy it," he said quietly. The plan came so clearly into his mind. He could almost see it unfolding as if he were with the dragons above. He lifted his eyes to the sky.

"I wish we could live," Chassim said wistfully. "I wish I could live to see Chalced dragged out from under my father's foot." She turned her face and her soft lips brushed his scaled cheek. "I wish *we* could live," she whispered.

"Tintaglia!" He cried out his dragon's name with every ounce of strength he had, shouted it in desperation. "Tintaglia! If you live, then I do, also! Blue queen, gem of the skies, where are you?"

REYN FELT SICKENED, but not by the swaying flight of the dragon. Below him, buildings were slowly crumbling. Those too slow to flee had fallen beneath dragon spray. He had pulled his tunic up over his head and tugged the sleeves down over his hands, having seen what dragon venom could do. He viewed the world through a narrow fabric window and wished devoutly he did not have to see that much.

He could not fault the courage of the Chalcedean soldiers. He had watched them loose arrows that arced far beneath the dragons and then watched their ranks literally melt in a fall of acid. Some gave way to the dragons' glamour as they overflew them, breaking to run. But they ran the wrong way, away from the stronghold and into the acid-riddled streets that now ringed it. Poor bastards. He caught a stinging whiff of dragon venom and drew his shirt tighter over his face.

He tried to admire the dragons' strategy. No dragon flew behind or below any other. They had broken into groups, and in each group, each dragon flew alongside the others, all spewing their venom so that it fell below them, and then they turned back and retraced their arc, each time getting closer to the center of the Duke's castle. Their timing was perfect, so that the dragon groups never encountered one another. The outer walls of the castle had received several passes. They were old and very stout, but the dragons were intent on killing people, not crumbling stone. Within the arcs they had overflown, nothing moved.

Tintaglia shuddered suddenly and broke ranks. She rose so sharply that Reyn lunged from the shelter of his tunic, thrusting his hands clear of his sleeves to seize her harness. He thought she would loop over backward. "Are you hit? Have they hurt you, Tintaglia?"

"Hark!" she responded and shot higher in the air with a speed that left him gasping. Above all the other dragons, she banked in a tight circle over the Duke's stronghold. *Where? Where? Where?* she demanded, ignoring Reyn's cries of "What is it? What is wrong?"

And then she was diving, diving alone on the tallest tower of the keep, ignoring the angry trumpeting from Icefyre that she was ignoring their plans. Reyn could do nothing but hold tight to her harness and bellow his terror as she arrowed straight for the side of the tower.

"SHE COMES LIKE a blue star falling through the heavens. She is the Empress of Destruction, the Queen of Vengeance, and if I must die, let her deliver my death to me!"

"That is her? She is like the fire inside a blue opal!" Chassim stared, her eyes wide in terror and delight. Her body was behind his, holding him pressed against the stone balustrade so he could stand, watching the blue miracle streaking toward them.

Selden lifted his voice and found that not all music had fled from him.

"She is both wise and terrible. Clever beyond cleverness is hers, swift winged, sharp taloned, and keen of sight. Tintaglia!" His voice broke on the last word.

Tintaglia tipped back, giving them a view of her sparkling belly and the glittering claws on her feet.

Chassim held him tightly, but her entire body was quivering. "Like glittering blue steel is she! Bring my death then, lovely one. We await you."

But it was not her jaws that came at them, but her clasping front talons. Chassim staggered back from the brink as Tintaglia seized the stone balustrade of the balcony and clung, the wind of her battering wings a hurricane around them. The talons of her front feet scored and slipped on the stone balustrade; her hind feet were braced on the tower below, and the wind of her wings battered all. Cracks raced through the stone railing.

"Climb up, climb up now, now, NOW!" The man on her back was roaring the words, and then, *"Climb now, now!"* commanded the dragon, the words echoing through Selden's bones.

He tried hard to do as she commanded, but the weakness of his body betrayed him. He felt Chassim grip the back of his robe and push him forward. He caught at the strap on the dragon's chest. The man on the dragon clambered down the harness, clamped a grip on his bandaged wrist, and dragged him up. He screamed in pain and scrabbled feebly with his feet, then his hands found leather and iron rings to grip. Chunks of the balcony were falling away as the dragon tore them free in her desperate bid to cling to the side of the tower. The rider dragged him up and held him before him on the dragon's back. Selden sagged forward, and then gripped tight as the dragon pushed off from the tower face. She swooped away from the structure as he screamed, "Chassim! No, go back, Tintaglia, fair queen! Chassim!"

"I . . . am . . . here!" Her voice was weak with terror.

He looked down. Chassim clung grimly to the rings of Tintaglia's harness, her garments whipping in the wind as the dragon fell suddenly away from the tower. He more saw than heard her wild scream as they plummeted together.

Then, with a sickening lurch, the fall became a glide. With a beat, beat, beat of Tintaglia's powerful wings, they slowly began to rise. Chassim, her teeth bared in a determined snarl, her hair a wild stream of glory around her face, climbed doggedly, ring by ring, until his reaching hand closed over her wrist. Wisely, she did not trust his grip, but he could not let her go. Ring by ring, she came closer and then was hugging him as tightly as the man who held on to him. He twisted to see the rider and found himself looking upon an Elderling such as Selden had seen only in old tapestries.

"Sir, I thank you," he gasped. "Oh, Tintaglia, blue queen of the skies, most powerful and wisest of all dragons, I give you thanks."

"Little brother, I am always doomed to find you in the damnedest places," the rider said, and abruptly he knew that it was Reyn who clasped him so securely. "You look but two heartbeats this side of death," Reyn added.

"If only you knew," Selden replied. He was suddenly dizzy and faint with relief. "What do you here? Whence come all these dragons?"

"Don't you know them?" Tintaglia was ignoring her riders, carrying them higher and higher above the city, away from the death and destruction below them. "You saw them encased, you saw them hatched! We come from Kelsingra, Selden, and we come to kill the Duke of Chalced for daring to hunt dragons for their blood."

He felt Tintaglia's assent to those words course through him, strong with her anger.

"But what of you? You sent us no word! Your sister thinks you're dead, and your mother fears she is right. What happened to you? I do not think you were in that tower willingly, by the look of you. And who is this you have brought with you?" Reyn asked.

Selden drew breath, but before he could reply, Chassim spoke for herself. "My name is Chassim. And if this glorious queen and her dragons are able to fulfill their mission today, by nightfall I shall be the rightful Duchess of Chalced. And in your debt."

✧ ✧ ✧

Day the 10th of the Greening Moon

Year the 7th of the Independent Alliance of Traders
From Selden Vestrit, Singer to Tintaglia,
Kelsingra
To Keffria and Ronica Vestrit of the Bing-
town Traders, Bingtown

Dear Mother and Grandmother,

I write this tiny scroll to be carried by Tarman to Trehaug and from there dispatched by Dunwarrow to Bingtown. A much lengthier account of my misadventures will follow, in a scroll far too heavy for any pigeon to bear. I will ask Alise to pass it to Althea to bring home to you.

For now, the essentials. I was betrayed by my companions. I was held captive and eventually treated as a slave in Chalced. But I am alive, and once more in the incomparable company of the magnificent queen Tintaglia, to whom I owe my life and the restoration of my health. I do not wish to go into great detail about the trials I have endured, especially not on this tiny slip of paper. I will say only this now; I assure you, I am recovering and among good people.

You will doubtless hear many strange rumors about my role in the fall of Chalced and my friendship with Duchess Chassim. I will say only that the truth is undoubtedly stranger than any gossip you may hear, and the truth is what you shall have from me when the scroll arrives.

Mother, you ask me when I will come home to stay. Please do not take these words amiss. I am home. In

Kelsingra, among the other Elderlings and near the dragons, I feel more at peace and more safe than I have felt in many months. My sister, Malta, is here, and Reyn, like a brother to me for so many years, and so many other Elderlings! The beauty of the country here is healing by itself, and I have access to thousands of records of Elderling dragon poets who have gone before me. I am almost shamed to think I considered myself a singer, now that I have heard for myself the poets of old! And there are traditional songs that I must learn, songs for welcoming dragons, for celebrating the first flight of a hatchling, songs to thank dragons for sharing their presence with us. I think it will take me a score of years before I shall again claim I am a competent singer!

This does not mean I do not wish to see you. When my health permits, I will come for a visit. And I hope that in time you and Grandmother will be willing to undertake the journey to see me here. I would show you my city and introduce you to the keepers and the other dragons. Especially Tintaglia's mate, Kalo. Such a handsome fellow, and so strong! I am as pleased to see her with him as I am sure you were delighted to see Malta settle with Reyn.

For now I must let this missive be enough, for I am already weary with writing this. Please be patient. A more detailed account will soon be in your hands.

As ever,
Your Selden

✦ ✦ ✦

CHAPTER TWENTY-TWO

SUMMER

I t had begun rather formally as afternoon tea in the captain's stateroom on the *Paragon*. But by the end of the first hour, it had become mugs of coffee on the foredeck of the liveship, with the figurehead fully involved in the conversation. Tarman was moored alongside Paragon at the docks of Trehaug. Alise wondered if the two ships communicated on a level that excluded humans, but decided it would be rude to ask. It seemed decades since she had last been aboard Paragon. She looked back at her memory of the journey to the Rain Wilds and recalled her awkward conversation with the ship and with Althea and Brashen Trell. She laughed to herself, but no one remarked on it, for Paragon was in the middle of a lively tirade against the indignity of transporting chickens and sheep.

"And I wish Tarman well with the nasty creatures. Worse than seagulls for squawking and mess on the decks."

"Perhaps so, but our boy is going to miss them," Brashen observed.

"I think he'll miss the fresh eggs more than he'll miss the messes he's had to clean up," Althea countered, laughing. She stood up and leaned to see past the deckhouse. "He and Clef have just about finished transferring the stock to Tarman's deck. So we have perhaps ten more minutes of adult conversation before you are inundated with questions about the dragons and the One Day War."

"We'll be happy to answer them as best as we can," Alise said. "Not that we were there for any of it. And if we are to believe what every dragon told us of it, then each one was personally responsible for the fall of the city and the death of the Duke."

"And the rise of a Duchess," Althea added. "We've had bird messages from Selden, but they are not very satisfactory. We have only the bones of his tale, and each time he writes, we learn a bit more; but he also tells us that still he cannot come home just yet. That there are still things he must 'settle' there in Kelsingra." Her emphasis on the word *settle* made it clear that she thought there was more going on than her nephew had confided. She looked from Alise to Leftrin, perhaps seeking confirmation or gossip.

Leftrin spoke hastily. "Your youngster looks like he knows his way around a deck. When you think he's ready to try a term under a different captain, he'd be welcome aboard Tarman. Things are a bit more rustic and he'd be sleeping in the deckhouse with the crew, but I'd be glad to foster him for a trip or two."

Brashen and Althea exchanged a look, but it was not his mother who said, "Not quite old enough yet. But I'll take you up on that offer when he is. I know he'd like to see his aunt and uncle soon. Not to mention his cousin Ephron." Brashen smiled as he attempted to change the subject. "When do you think Malta and Reyn might be bringing the baby downriver for a visit?"

"You'd take Boy-o off my decks?" Paragon was appalled.

"Only for a short time, ship. I know he's yours as much

as ours," Brashen replied placatingly. "But a slightly wider circle of experience wouldn't hurt him."

"Hmph." The figurehead crossed his arms on his carved chest. His mouth went to a flat line. "Perhaps when Ephron is old enough to take his place here for a time. An exchange of hostages, as it were."

Brashen rolled his eyes at them. "He's in a mood today," he said in a low voice.

"I am *not* in a mood! Merely pointing out that you are a liveship family, and that you should think well before letting one of our own go off on another liveship, with no guarantees that he will be returned. Ideally, the exchange should be a member of Tarman's family." He turned his gaze to Leftrin and Alise. "Do you expect to breed soon?"

Leftrin choked on his tea.

"Not that I'm aware," Alise replied demurely.

"A pity. It might be productive for you just now." Paragon was politely enthused.

"Can we please just not?" Althea asked him, almost sharply. "It's bad enough to have you offering Brashen and me your helpful insights into productive breeding without you extending your wisdom to our guests."

Alise could not tell if Brashen were embarrassed or red from suppressing laughter.

"It was Tarman's suggestion that they might find such information helpful, as so far they have enjoyed breeding, but fruitlessly. That's all." Paragon was unflustered.

Brashen cleared his throat suddenly. "Well, speaking of hostages—"

"Were we?" his ship interjected curiously.

"We were. Speaking of hostages, how did all that work out? There were rumors in Bingtown, but we left to go south to pick up your stock, and then returned right up the river. So we haven't heard much of that."

"Sadly, if you ask me," Alise replied. "I'm sure you know that the Chalcedeans chose to drown themselves rather than face the Council or be ransomed to their duke. The Council did finally pay us, but only, I think, because I was present to speak for the keepers, and to testify that nothing nefarious had befallen any of us, except what some members of the Council itself had planned for us. Trader Candral went back on his word and denied everything, even when confronted with all the pages he had penned while in Kelsingra. He maintained that we had forced him to write such things, and one of the Jamaillian merchants vouched for him. Personally, I suspect that some sort of a private trade agreement was brokered during the voyage back to Trehaug, one that was very profitable to the Jamaillian merchant. I fear we will never see justice for what was done to us. We should, perhaps, have kept Candral sequestered from the others." She looked to Leftrin as she said this, and he shook his head.

"As loaded as Tarman was? Small chance of that. And I think there were others on the Cassarick Council that had more than an inkling of what was going on. He was protected." He shook his head. "Well, they'll pay a price for that. Tarman will never carry any cargo for them again. Nor will the *Warken* or the *White Serpent*." At Brashen's quirked eyebrow, Leftrin clarified, "The keepers and dragons have finally named their impervious ships. Come the end of summer, they plan to make their maiden voyages on them, but to Trehaug. They won't stop in Cassarick at all. No goods from Kelsingra will ever be traded there, until the Council investigates and punishes those who plotted against us."

"The most solid blow that a Trader can take is to his purse," Althea said approvingly. "You may yet rout out the rotten apples in the barrel. And the others?"

"The slaves who were working the ships stayed in Kelsingra. Some seem to be adapting. Others may want to leave. We've left that up to them. There were others, some from Bingtown, a few from Trehaug. None of them wanted to stand as a witness against Candral. So we can't actually prove that Candral or any others on the Council were either bribed or threatened by the Chalcedeans to sabotage us."

"So. Refusing to trade with them is as much as we can do to them," Leftrin concluded somberly.

"They tried to kill Tintaglia," Paragon reminded them all severely.

"The orders to attack her and Icefyre originated in Chalced," Alise pointed out gently. "And Sa knows they've paid for it a hundred times over."

Paragon made a skeptical sound, but all the humans fell silent for a time. The reports of the fall of Chalced had been dire. The Duke's palace had fallen to Icefyre's orchestrated attack. The old black dragon had been both ruthless and relentless. He had not been content with killing the occupants. By the time the dragons had finished, nothing but crumbled ruins remained. There had been a disorderly military response that Spit had enthusiastically retaliated. The populace had quickly learned that not even buildings offered any real protection against dragons newly infused with Silver. By evening, a cowed group of nobles offered a surrender, only to discover that the dragons had "captured" the Duchess of Chalced and already arranged terms with her.

"Rapskal and Heeby remained in Chalced. Nortel, Kase, and Boxter and their dragons stayed as well. Strange to think that four dragons are deemed an ample force to back the new duchess as she establishes her authority over Chalced."

"So Kelsingra favors her rise to power?" Althea asked.

Alise lifted one shoulder. "The dragons favor her rise to power. She set very favorable terms for an alliance. Chalced had always had harsher laws than Bingtown. She has imposed a death sentence on anyone who lifts a hand against a dragon. Shepherds and herdsmen are to pay a dragon tax that sets aside a certain number of beasts each year as prey for dragons. She had some opposition from some of the nobles at first, but she was ruthless with them. That the nobles must recognize her authority had been a key term of their negotiations and the end of hostilities. Only one defied her. She sent the dragons. That was the end of it."

"Harsh," Brashen said quietly.

"Chalcedean," Leftrin replied. He shrugged. "I don't think she could establish order there any other way. There is still restlessness in Chalced, especially in the outlying provinces, but I don't think it will reach civil war as some said. Duchess Chassim seems to be trying for other alliances as well."

Althea broke in with, "We heard an extraordinary rumor that the new duchess was actually negotiating a truce between the Chalced States and the Six Duchies region of Shoaks."

"Preposterous," Alise said. "No one remembers a time when those two countries weren't warring."

"So preposterous, it's probably true," Brashen offered. All of them fell silent for a moment, considering the changes.

"Selden," Althea abruptly said. She looked directly at Alise. "How is he? Really?"

Alise looked for a long moment at Leftrin, decided that they were owed honesty, and met Althea's gaze. "You are his family. You need to know. He is scarred, and not just physically. The Duke was literally devouring him. Sucking the blood right out of his veins. The marks on his arms were still visible weeks after Tintaglia brought him back to Kelsingra. When first I saw him, I could not believe he was standing upright by himself; he was so thin and his face so drawn."

Althea went pale. "We'd heard rumors. Sweet Sa. Little Selden. I think of him, and I see him always as a noisy little fellow of seven or eight. But we heard other rumors, ones that link him with the Duchess of Chalced? They made no sense to us!"

"They were prisoners together," Alise confirmed. "And they seem to have formed an attachment. More than that, I don't know, so I won't gossip. Except to say that I know some have been critical that the dragons and Kelsingra have backed the young Duchess of Chalced in taking over rule of her country. They say we should have made Chalced completely subservient. But if not for the efforts of the Duchess Chassim, Selden would have died there. From what he tells us, her imprisonment was worse than his and for years longer. Given all she did for him, as an Elderling and as Tintaglia's singer, those who negotiated the terms felt that putting her in power would be the swiftest path to peace in the region."

Brashen scratched his chin and then smiled at Althea. "Changing history seems to run in your family. First Wintrow and Malta, now Selden." He took a sip of his tea.

Paragon spoke up, his voice wry. "So fortunate for you that you married the sane, responsible female in the family."

Brashen choked. Althea slapped him on the back perhaps a trifle harder than she needed to. She spoke through his choking laughter. "But Selden is recovering?"

"Quite remarkably, given all he endured, and not just at the hands of the Duke of Chalced. Tintaglia has hinted that some of his illness was simply due to his unsupervised growth. He was young when she changed him, and away for quite a time, so not all was right inside his body . . ."

"That is dragons' business!" Paragon interrupted indignantly.

"That is *family* business. Selden is my nephew, Paragon, as well as Tintaglia's Elderling. I have a right to know how he progresses, and therefore so do you! And you should care as much as I do."

The rebuke from Althea subdued the ship. Paragon's face grew thoughtful. He lowered his voice. "Did not they think to treat him with Silver?"

Alise stared at him for a moment, shocked that he would speak such a secret aloud. Then she decided that if it was dragons' business, then he had the right to know the whole of it. "The knowledge of how to do that is lost to us," Alise told him. "But his dragon oversees him daily. His outer injuries have healed. He walks among us, and eats well, and sings to Tintaglia once more. And I suspect that you will see him again, down this way. He desires to visit not only the Khuprus family in Trehaug, but also his mother in Bingtown. And eventually to return to Chalced and the Duchess."

"I would not allow that, were I Tintaglia," Paragon offered.

"She was instrumental in keeping him alive when her father's treatment of him would have otherwise killed him. It's a very long story, Paragon. There is a great deal more than what I have told you."

"But tonight you will return to tell it to us?" the ship suggested.

Leftrin stood and walked to the side. Alise followed

him. He looked down on the deck of his own ship. Hennesey looked up at him unhappily and gestured at the animals penned on the aft deck of the barge. Clef was grinning and describing something to a horrified Skelly. Boy-o sat on Tarman's railings, swinging his heels and laughing. Leftrin glanced over at Alise. "We should get under way. But I think we can stay until morning."

"THERE HAS TO be a better way to house these birds," Sedric complained. He ducked as one of the message birds took sudden unreasonable fear and leaped from its perch to flap crazily past his head. It alighted on one of the nesting boxes fastened to the wall.

The structure was one of the smaller, more dilapidated buildings near the river's edge. Already in poor condition, the keepers had decided that housing pigeons in it could scarcely do it more harm. Carson scowled at the musty straw, thick with bird droppings that floored the small house where they had confined their small flock of pigeons. "Or a better way to send messages between here and the rest of the world," he countered. "I think we were too hasty in asking for messenger birds. Especially since none of us know much about them." He squinted at the birds. "Which one just came in?"

"They all look alike to me," Sedric replied. "But . . . this is the only one with a message tube tied to its leg. Come here, bird. I won't hurt you. Come here."

He moved slowly, his reaching hands framing the bird. It rocked from foot to foot on its perch, but before it could decide to take flight, Sedric gently closed his hands on it. "There. Not so bad, is it? Not so terrible. No one wants to eat you. We just want the message tube." He held the struggling bird's wings smooth to its body, offering it feet-first to Carson.

"Just a moment, just a moment . . . this string is so fine. It's hard to find, ah, there's the end. And here we have it. You can let him go."

Sedric held the bird a moment longer, soothing it and smoothing its feathers, before setting it back on its perch.

The animal recovered almost immediately and began greeting his mate with a cooing, bobbing dance. Sedric followed Carson outside into the sunlight.

"Who's it from? Leftrin? Are they delayed in Trehaug?"

"I'm still trying to get it open. Wait a moment. The cap's off, but the little paper won't come out. Here. You try." The hunter passed the small tube to the curious Sedric and smiled to watch him eagerly tap and shake the tube until the edge of the paper showed.

Sedric coaxed out the tiny roll and opened it. His brows went up in surprise as he read, and then a furrow formed between them. He let the paper coil in his hands.

"What is it? Bad news?"

Sedric rubbed his face. "No. Just a bit of surprise for me. I recognized the handwriting. It's a note from Wollom Courser. And it's actually addressed to me. He's an old friend from Bingtown. One of Hest's circle."

"Oh?" Carson's voice was slightly cooler.

"They've raised a substantial reward for anyone who can send them news of what's become of Hest. Wollom adds his own plea. Evidently he thinks that perhaps Hest is hiding here with me, avoiding his old life and his family's disgrace and living well in Kelsingra." His gaze met Carson's.

The big man turned up an empty hand. "No one saw him again after that day. I don't know, Sedric. I've wondered about it more than once, but I just don't know what became of him. We left him there in the tower. You've said he wasn't a hunter or a fisherman. No food has gone missing. No one, keeper or dragon, has seen him. We've told them that."

Sedric's hand closed on the paper, crumpling it. "You don't know what became of him. And I don't care." He tossed the message to the ground, and the wind off the river gave it a small push. Carson looked at it for a moment, and then put his arm across Sedric's shoulder.

"The pigeons are all right for now," he said. "But what we should give some thought to is where we want to house the chickens." The summer sunlight glinted on the two Elderlings as they turned away from the river and walked up into Kelsingra.

"WHAT DO YOU think is beyond the foothills?"

"More foothills." Tats panted. "Then mountains."

They had paused to catch their breath and drink from their water skin. The day was warm. Summer was growing strong. Thymara had freed her wings from her tunic and held them half open to cool herself. Tats and Thymara had been climbing steadily since morning. They both carried their bows, but Thymara was more interested in exploration than hunting today. She turned and looked down over the green-flanked hills to the city below them. Most of it remained still and uninhabited, but there was activity down near the docks. The crew of the *White Serpent* had taken her out on the river. The oars moved evenly as the ship moved against the current. The wind carried the faint shouts of Rachard as he called the stroke beat to them. The former slave was the teacher now, and he seemed to be adapting well to his new role.

"Look." Thymara pointed in a different direction. "Sedric's trees. The ones he and Carson dug up and moved to the big pots on the Square of the Serpents? You can actually see the leaves on them from here. They almost look like trees now instead of sticks."

A dragon trumpet, a taunting challenge, turned Thymara's eyes to the clear blue sky above. "Again?" she groaned aloud.

"Apparently," Tats said with vast approval. He swiveled his head. "Where is he?"

Tintaglia was overhead. As they watched, she spiraled upward, ever higher. She trumpeted again, and they heard it answered from the east. They both turned to watch Kalo coming. This was not the leisurely circling of a dragon seeking game, nor the diving fall of a dragon strike. His long powerful wings drove him forward and upward. He looked black against the blue of the sky, except that each downstroke briefly bared the silver tips of his wings. His long tail snaked and lashed behind him as he flew.

Tintaglia was a glittering blue set of wings in the sky. She hung, circling effortlessly. Her mocking call reached them clearly.

Tats scanned the rest of the sky. "I don't see Icefyre this time."

"That last battle was pretty savage. Alise told me that from what she learned when she first studied dragons from scrolls and records, the males seldom did serious injury to one another in mating battles."

"I don't think Kalo read the same scrolls she did. I think that after their last clash, Icefyre conceded. Probably went off to kill something big, eat it, and sleep it off." Tats nodded to himself. "The better dragon won. I'm glad Kalo got a mate."

Thymara corked the water skin. "Let's follow that cleft up to the cliffs. I want to look at them and see how hard they'd be to climb."

Tats stood staring upward. Kalo's deep frustrated roars were answering Tintaglia's clear trumpeting. "Don't you want to watch?" he teased her.

"Thank you, but half a dozen times was enough. Can't they be done with it for the day?"

"I think they're enjoying it. Wait. What's that?"

Something had caught his attention in a different quadrant of the sky. Thymara strained her eyes. "Sintara. But what's she doing?"

The younger blue queen was moving faster than Thymara had ever seen her fly. Arrow-straight she flew. Then as golden Mercor crested the ridge behind them, Thymara heard Sintara utter the same challenging trumpet that she had first heard from Tintaglia. Scarlet Baliper and orange Dortean suddenly rose from the forested hillside. "Oh, this should be good," Tats exclaimed and sat down. He flopped back in the meadow grass and stared at the rivals as they closed in on Sintara. "Baliper might have a chance against Mercor," he speculated. "They're about of a size, but I think Mercor is cleverer. Dortean? I don't think so."

As if the dragons had heard him, Mercor suddenly looped in his flight and turned on the hapless Dortean. The orange male fled but could not evade the golden. Mercor chased him as he fled, and as he neared the ground, he dived on him. Dortean no longer had the altitude for evasion. He crashed into the trees, sending a large flock of starlings into mad flight. Mercor narrowly avoided following his rival into arboreal disaster. Wings beating strongly, he pulled up just above the treetops and skimmed over them. The branches waved wildly in his wake.

Baliper had made good use of the distraction. The red dragon battered his way skyward, while Sintara continued to mock him. Mercor roared a challenge at him, but the scarlet dragon did not waste his breath in a response but continued to gain on Sintara. Her mockery changed to an angry cry. She flew at him, they clashed in midair, and Baliper fell away in a mad spiral. In a dozen wing beats, they had both recovered, but he had lost more altitude than she had. He was focused completely on his pursuit of her when Mercor struck him from behind.

Baliper writhed back, flipping to face the golden, and the males gripped, talons to talons. Roaring, with wings beating wildly and front talons clenched, they were falling through the sky as they tore at each other with their clawed hind feet. Sintara, silent now, circled above them, watching her suitors batter each other. Far above her, the silhouettes of Tintaglia and Kalo had merged.

"They're falling, falling . . . break it up, fellows, or you'll both die!" Tats cried out in awe.

But they did not break apart, not for another two breaths. Then with an infuriated scream, Mercor abruptly tore himself free of the scarlet dragon. Wings beating wildly, he careened off. Baliper managed to flip over, and then to veer away from the trees that had awaited him. He landed badly in a meadow, rolling and bending a wing before crashing to a halt. Thymara stared at him, sick with dread, until she saw him lift his head, stand, and then shake his wings back into position. As if aware of her gaze, he gave a final angry trumpet before stalking off into the shelter of the woods.

"He's nearly caught her!" Tats exclaimed admiringly.

Thymara turned her eyes skyward. Sintara seemed to

be making a very genuine attempt to escape Mercor. She looped back once, slashed at him with an angry scream, and then tried to resume her climb. It was useless. The tempo of Mercor's golden wings increased and his speed with it. Suddenly, the golden dragon overshadowed the blue. His head snaked in to seize the back of her neck in his teeth.

"He's got her." Tats sounded very satisfied. He rolled his head to grin at Thymara and then continued to watch the mating dragons.

Thymara made a disgusted exclamation and gave him a strong push. He turned to her, still grinning, and before she could draw his hand back, he seized her wrist. He tried to pull her to him, but she jerked free of him, turned and ran. Her heart was beating wildly. "Thymara!" Tats shouted and "No!" she called over her shoulder.

She ran, but the sudden thunder of his footfalls was close behind her. She felt him catch at the trailing edge of her wing. She snatched it from his grip, felt a sudden lift from her spread wings, and closed them on the downbeat. Behind her, Tats gave a wordless startled cry.

"The ravine!" he shouted, and she saw it wide before her. It gaped, a steep-sided crack in the hillside, possibly a scar of the same quake that had leveled parts of Kelsingra. She started to slow, to turn to elude him, but he was too close behind her. "Don't be stupid!" he shouted, but it wasn't, she decided; it wasn't stupid at all.

She snapped her wings open, managed two downbeats that nearly lifted her off her feet, and then she leaped. For a dizzying moment, there was nothing under her feet save the sudden drop-off. In the ravine far below her, she glimpsed a narrow rushing stream cutting its way toward the river. Three more beats of her wings lifted her and then, as she lost focus and altitude in amazement at what she had done, the meadow on the other side seemed to reach up for her. She landed running, caught herself, skidded to a halt on her knees, and then turned. "Tats! I flew! I really flew, it wasn't just a jump. I flew!"

Tats had halted on the other side of the cleft in the earth. He was staring at her, a very strange expression on his face.

Abruptly, he turned away. He walked off and then, putting his head down and pumping his arms, he ran from her.

She watched him go. Her heart that had been beating so wildly with joy and excitement now seemed to pump coldness through her body. Too strange. She was too strange for him. She glanced down at the black claws on her hands that had set her apart since the day she was born. She had always been too strange, too changed by the Rain Wilds. The wings and the flight had been too much even for loyal Tats. Tears stung her eyes as she watched him go.

A shrill keening turned her eyes upward. Yes. Mercor had caught Sintara. Joined, they circled high above her. She shook her head, tried to clear it of the dragon's heat that she had experienced so clearly. Time to be practical. Her bow. Had she dropped her bow in her wild flight from Tats? Where? On the other side?

She looked back the way she had come and saw Tats coming at her. He had gone up the hill slightly and now was running back down it in silence. His teeth were gritted in determination. "The gully!" She shrieked the warning at him, but it was too late. In two strides he reached it and flung himself forward in a wild leap.

He couldn't possibly make it.

But he did.

He hit on his feet, tucked his head down, rolled in a wild somersault, and came up on his feet again. His impetus carried him forward and he crashed into her. But as his arms wrapped around her and he carried her to the ground with him, she knew it was no accident. "Caught you," he said.

The impact had driven the breath from her body. She gasped in air and answered, "Yes. You have. At last." She saw his eyes widen. Then, as she took a deeper breath, his mouth covered hers. She closed her eyes, feeling his weight on her, smelling him, pulling him closer. The sun was above them, warming the whole world, and the only sound she heard was the joyous trumpeting of dragons.

Epilogue

GENERATION

Tintaglia awoke in midmorning. She lifted her head and looked at the sun. Then she rose and stretched and limbered her wings. The same restlessness that had afflicted her for the last ten days filled her again. It grew stronger as the sun rose higher.

She had chosen to sleep high on a rocky ridge on the cliffs behind Kelsingra after her morning kill. She had felt an urgency when she had first awakened, but dismissed it as only hunger. But now, fed, rested, and awake, heritage memories were stirring in her. She studied the sun's position in the sky. Yes.

She smelled him in the waft of his wings on the wind. She turned to watch Kalo circling slowly down to alight beside her. The blue-black drake had grown since she had first encountered him and would continue to grow for all the days of his life. He took two steps toward her and extended his neck, snuffing the air around her. *Today.* He offered the word and waited for her.

Today, she confirmed. It was time.

Icefyre swept past them. He knew better than to attempt to land near her. Kalo had established that with him in several bloody battles. But the old dragon was within his rights and knew it. "Today!" he trumpeted the word as he overshadowed them briefly.

Downhill of them she saw other dragons lift their heads from where they had been dozing on the rocky cliffs. Far below them, in the city, she knew that the keepers would be pausing in their coming and going, stopping their anthill lives to stare up in wonder.

Kalo stared at her, his eyes spinning possessively. *Who flies with you?* he demanded.

What sort of a drake asks that of a queen? Icefyre mocked him as he swept past again. *I am sire of this first generation. To me is what is mine. I travel with her, to the nesting beaches, to watch over the digging of the nest and keep the Others at bay. Have you no memories of this and the proper way of doing things?*

Tintaglia considered. She eyed the ragged black dragon as he swept past once more. Kalo had stretched himself tall and partly opened his wings. *I have memories,* he replied sullenly. *I have memories of a time when there would have been a dozen queens on the island, and drakes doing battle for the best nesting sites. Those days are gone. We begin a new time. Perhaps we begin with new ways.*

And Kalo will accompany us, she decided. *He is young and strong. I will have him fly with me as well.*

That is NOT how it is done! Icefyre was outraged. *You have no memories at all! Only the sire goes with the queen to the nesting beach to guard her. Other drakes are not to be trusted. He will destroy the nest and trample the eggs.*

Kalo stretched his neck and opened his wings wide. He was still not as large as Icefyre, but his wings were unrent, his muscles full and limber. The deep midnight blue of his scaling was now spangled with tiny silver stars. He snapped his wings once, and toxins welled to each clawed tip. *Do you challenge me for this, old dragon?* He swung his gaze to Tintaglia. *I will not destroy the nest. There are too few dragons in the world. What do I care if the first clutch you lay are his get? The clutches to follow will be mine, and my offspring will need mates.*

You think like humans! Icefyre issued his proclamation in disgust. *Were the clutch not mine, I would not care. But I warn you now, youngster. Disturb the nest, and the fight will be to the death.*

Tintaglia snorted disdainfully. *Any male that disturbs my nest will die! No queen needs a drake to make that so.*

"Today, then!" Icefyre trumpeted it loudly to all, dragons and Elderlings alike. *I leave now. You had best follow soon, for otherwise I doubt you will recall the way.*

I know the way, she responded angrily.

Go then. Kalo dismissed Icefyre. *You should probably fly swiftly, for soon we both will overtake you.*

Icefyre roared a wordless insult at Kalo, then banked his wings and swept away. She watched him go, saw him diminish in the distance. He was a dragon from another time, she decided. It was good that her first generation of young would inherit his memories. It would be even better if they were wise enough to adapt to a world in which there were less than twenty mature dragons. She wondered how many eggs she would lay, how many would hatch, how many would survive their time in the sea as serpents, and if those serpents would have to be guided home to the cocooning grounds as Maulkin's tangle had. Then she snorted the thought away. In one way, at least, Icefyre was right. She had acquired many human ways of thinking. Why worry about a tangle that was not even hatched yet, let alone serpents that must grow for years before returning to the Rain Wild River?

She looked down on Kelsingra. "Today!" She trumpeted the announcement loudly. And then she waited. Icefyre might be correct that she did not have all her memories, but she had some. Some traditions must be observed. What was the delay?

In the city below her, a slender form emerged onto the

tower parapet. He was robed in silver and deepest blue, and Selden lifted his voice to the sky, in praise of the day. The ancient words shivered in her blood, standing up her crest and the ruff on her neck.

"Today, today, the queen goes forth today. Her belly is rich with eggs, she carries inside her the generation to come. Today, today, the queen leaves us today! Sing, sing all, sing her praise, and wish her good fortune on her flight!"

He paused. She listened. Voices were lifted, humans, and then dragons joining in and drowning them out. "Today! Today! Tomorrow begins today!"

She and Kalo basked in the roar of sound. She lifted her wings wide to them, wove her head on her long neck to accept her adulation. The cacophony died away. It was over. Now she would fly.

But suddenly Selden's voice rose again, in praise of her alone. She set her eyes on him, listening in pleasure. "The queen rises, the blue empress, Tintaglia, she of the wide wings touched with silver, she who led the serpents to Cassarick, she who fed the first of the new generation! Eldest of our queens and wisest, bravest, always cleverest! Wide-winged Tintaglia goes to the nesting ground!"

As she watched, other Elderlings emerged onto the tower top. Reyn. Malta. She held aloft the child Tintaglia had saved and joined their voices to Selden's. "Today! Today! Today!" Malta lifted Ephron high on each word, and the baby's newly found laughter rose to her.

"Today!" she trumpeted out a blast in response, and she felt the good wishes of her Elderlings rise to her as she opened her wings and leaped into flight.

THE *RAIN WILDS* CHRONICLES BY *NEW YORK TIMES* BESTSELLING AUTHOR

ROBIN HOBB

DRAGON KEEPER
978-0-06-156165-8

DRAGON HAVEN
978-0-06193155-0

CITY OF DRAGONS
978-0-06-156169-6

BLOOD OF DRAGONS
978-0-06-211691-8